KU-299-339

Wise Child

Wise Child

Audrey Reimann

First published in Great Britain in 1997 by
Judy Piatkus (Publishers) Ltd of
5 Windmill Street, London W1

A catalogue record for this book is available from the British Library

ISBN 0-7499-0383-X

Set in 11/12pt Times by
Action Typesetting Ltd, Gloucester
Printed and bound in Great Britain by
Mackays of Chatham plc Ltd.

Part One

Chapter One

Macclesfield, May 1948

Everyone knows me as Isobel now. I have not used the name I was born with for years, yet within half an hour of arriving in Macclesfield I passed my old enemy in Chestergate and heard her say to the woman on her arm, 'My God! It's Lily Stanway!'

I jumped, hearing Doreen Grimshaw's flat tones, turned my head and caught the other girl's reply: 'Lily Stanway? What's she come back for?'

They glared after me and I knew it again – the nervous leap of the pulse, the metallic taste of fear. I have long since settled old scores with Doreen, so why does it come back to me now – the childish dread that Doreen will uncover my deepest, most shameful secrets and, jeering and mocking, hold me up to ridicule for them?

My old tormentor's face has set into hard lines. We're the same age – twenty-nine – but she looks older than I with her brown hair cut short, permed and set in a parody of the 'bubble cut'. I keep my dark hair at shoulder length and wear very little make-up but Doreen is plastered in Max Factor. She is wearing a New Look dress that swirls about her thin legs, six inches above clumsy white platform-sole shoes. I'm wearing a full-skirted tangerine suit with a nipped-in waist and flared peplum and black patent-leather high heels. My suit was made in Paris and Doreen's dress was clearly made here from a length of cotton print.

Oh, God forgive me! I sound spiteful and I know I'm not. Dressing well and fashion have played a big part in my life. I really don't care tuppence for Doreen's opinion. But I care about Macclesfield. I belong to this ancient town. All that I am, all I aspired to be, was fashioned here. My youthful ambition was to marry a good man who would be a kind father to the dozens of children I wanted. We'd live in a big house in the hills and I'd be looked up to for what I was, not pitied for being Mam's daughter.

I did it once. Can I do it again? Can I rise above my beginnings when I was little Lily Stanway, shunted back and forth between my grandparents' farm in the hills and Mam's shop on Jordangate?

Can I live here again? I am not homesick for Macclesfield, but an old unsatisfied curiosity might make me return. My new husband will join me here in two days' time. He will want an answer. It is ridiculous that at last I have a choice about my future and instead of being rational I'm shaking in my shoes because I passed Doreen in the street.

You'd imagine old fears and excitements were behind me, forgotten and buried as so much else ought to be. Yet I am here, reacting in the same way to Doreen and to Macclesfield, and knowing how much I've changed in the last three years I half expected Macclesfield to have changed in my absence.

Nothing has changed.

Absence should have made me see my home town objectively; from a distance as it were, for when you have your feet planted, rooted in a place you cannot see it all of a piece.

Now if you were a migrating bird you'd see it all of a piece. You could spot Macclesfield easily from the air. The medieval town is set on an escarpment in the foothills of the Pennines, to the west of the mountain range where the hills fall away to the plains of Lancashire and Cheshire. But you could live all your life here and not know this. You could live all your life here and only know that Macclesfield has scores of steep cobbled streets lined with red-brick cottages and that most of the streets slope down to the cotton and silk mills on the banks of the River Bollin. Over a hundred mills fill the air with their throat-catching fumes and fill the river, which in medieval times was called the River Jordan, with waste and stink.

Medieval Macclesfield had only the four streets which radiate from the Market Place. Chestergate, crowded with shops and taverns, joins the old coach roads to Manchester and Chester. Mill Street runs south and descends, cobbled and steep, to the mills and the river. Jordangate and Old Cockshutte Lane ran down to the River Jordan. Old Cockshutte Lane now is Hibel Road. The River Jordan is the River Bollin, but the street where Mam and I lived has retained its ancient name of Jordangate. Elsie Stanway's, Mam's dressmaker and haberdasher's shop, was at the poor end of Jordangate.

Doreen Grimshaw lived nearby. Like me she was an only child but she had one supreme advantage of me. Doreen had a dad. All I had was a photograph and a Mons Star medal. Tommy Stanway, Mam's first cousin, was killed at Ypres only weeks before I was born. I also had a memory. Mam later denied ever saying it, but I did not imagine it – my paternal grandmother's name was Lily. I was very young when I overheard Mam saying to one of her customers, 'We named her after both grandmothers – Lily and Isobel.'

It's a bright spring day, the sun is warm on my back and there is a soft, gorse-scented breeze blowing fresh from the hills, lifting my spirits, awakening memories of the golden years of childhood spent with my grandparents at Lindow hill farm. I'm standing in Sparrow Park – a small square of stone setts, grass and trees – looking down into the valley, over the Hundred and Eight Steps and the tortuously steep Churchwallgate which link the high Market Place to Waters Green below.

The Waters, as it is known, is on the poorer side of town, where the Bollin runs underground beneath the square. The Waters is always noisy with chatter, shrieks and the cobble-striking clatter of mill-workers' clogs. The mill girls, with arms linked, at the sounding of hooters and sirens stream in and out of Hammond's and Chancellor's factories.

Macclesfield is a woman's town; the women are the workers. Because of wars and a lack of man's work, women outnumber the men by almost two to one. There is competition for the available men for not every girl can realise her heart's desire for marriage, a home and a married woman's position. Macclesfield man recites, 'Cheshire born and Cheshire bred. Strong in th'arm and weak in th'head,' but if every Macclesfield man can count on the flattering attentions of at least two women, when he marries he will expect his wife to earn her living and think it his due that a woman will fall over herself to keep him.

I see very clearly now how it was for Mam.

Mam had to live here to earn our living. Mam had to put aside her repressed, religious childhood. Mam, who was indoctrinated from a baby with her parents' faith, had to survive as a widow with a child in the competitive women's marketplace that was Macclesfield.

The real Market Place is the centre of 'Macc' – which is the diminutive pet name for my town. At its centre, the Town Hall with its great sandstone columns, is flanked by the old parish church of St Michael and All Angels. The square is encircled with shops and banks and dotted about with inns, alehouses and wine vaults. Macclesfield has hundreds of taverns and public houses. Grandpa detested them.

Grandpa, my dear Grandpa Stanway, was sixty-eight when I was born. He had been a workhouse child, as had his old partner, Enoch Hammond, who was always referred to as Old Man Hammond. Charley Stanway and Enoch Hammond ran away from a Staffordshire workhouse when they were twelve years old to become silk weavers' apprentices in Macclesfield. They seized every chance that came their way and built up from nothing what has become one of Macclesfield's largest mills, Hammond Silks. No weaver could do that today. Today there are few hand-weavers of silk. But unlike the increase in profit and output of cotton manufacturing, the silk trade was volatile for silk has always been a luxury cloth and expensive to produce. Fortunes and factories came and went in the repeated ups and downs of silk-weaving in the 1860s.

The two young men were hard workers. Grandpa was also a good man who, even after he started to work, bought books and went on learning at the big Sunday School. He listened to the great preachers of his day, learned to speak well – he could quote long passages from the Bible and Shakespeare – and later became a lay preacher in the chapel. But Grandpa's ambition was not for riches but for land, a wife and a family.

Enoch, on the contrary was an angry man who wanted wealth and power. His ambition was for the small mill he and

Charley Stanway owned to be amalgamated with Pilkington Printers. With all their hard work it took Grandpa and Enoch Hammond twenty-five years to build up their mill. They were on the brink of prosperity when Old Man Hammond married an immensely rich widow and the men's partnership ended.

Old Man Hammond, with his wife's money, became a director of a bank which he renamed Hammond's Bank, and from there he bought the two-thousand acre Archerfield estate to build his house upon. His repeated offers for Pilkington Printers were turned down – but he bought Grandpa out. And instead of paying Grandpa his half-share, Old Man Hammond gave him an annuity and Lindow Farm – the hundred acres of unproductive hill grazing with fifteen acres of hay meadow and no arable land.

A few years after Old Man Hammond's marriage and the birth of John Hammond, their only son, the rich widow died. Enoch did not wed again. But his old partner married. Grandpa was forty-three when he fell in love with a girl twenty years younger than himself. Isobel Mary, my darling Nanna, was a farmer's daughter. Mam was their only child.

Mam used to say, 'Grandpa was done out of a fortune by Old Man Hammond.' But I think such things are said in every family to account for the lower social ranking that's bound to result from the unequal division of property. Whatever Mam might say, there was no ill-will between Grandpa and his former partner. They remained friends to the end of their lives and Grandpa was content, saying, 'I have everything a man needs. Nobody could ask for more.'

When Mam was a young girl she was in awe of her father but I knew Grandpa as a gentle man and a fine preacher.

Grandpa's was a fiery, nonconformist religion. He and Nanna did only essential work on the Lord's Day. Nanna's hens and Grandpa's horses were attended to and unless the roads were thick with mud or snow, when we used the trap, we walked morning and evening to chapel, me in the middle, holding a hand of each of them.

When Grandpa preached, the chapel congregation was still and enthralled as he told Bible stories and parables to illustrate commandments. One I particularly remember was told on a winter Sunday evening: the story of David's sin with

Bathsheba; the breaking of the seventh commandment. I can close my eyes and picture it now; it is impressed indelibly upon my mind. For it was the last time Mam went to chapel to hear her father.

The chapel which seated sixty, was full. Candles in wall niches above dark oak pews flickered in the draught from the high, vaulted windows. Grandpa climbed into the carved wooden pulpit, raised his arms, and after calling for the light of the Lord's countenance, began.

'"A good understanding have all they that do his commandments. Thou shalt not commit adultery." The seventh commandment.'

The congregation fell silent. Mam sat on one side of me, eyes fixed on her father. Nanna held my hand in case I was afraid but I had no fear. I had never heard of this adult sin, adultery.

'"And it came to pass, at the times when kings go forth to do battle, that David sent Joab, and his servants with him, and all Israel; and they destroyed the children of Ammon and besieged Rabbah. But David tarried still at Jerusalem.

'"And it came to pass in an eveningtide, that David walked upon the roof and from the roof saw a woman washing herself; and the woman was very beautiful to look upon. And David sent and enquired after the woman who was called Bathsheba, the wife of Uriah, the Hittite. And David sent messengers who took her and brought her unto David. And he lay with her."'

Mam started to fiddle in her handbag for a handkerchief, trying not to make a disturbance. Nanna passed her hankie to me and I slipped it into Mam's hand as quietly as I could.

'"And the woman returned to her house. And Bathsheba conceived and told David, 'I am with child.' And David sent to Joab saying: Send me Uriah, the Hittite. And when Uriah came to his call David made him drunk: and at evening Uriah went not down to his own house.

'"And it came to pass in the morning that David wrote a letter to Joab, and sent it by the hand of Uriah the Hittite. And he wrote in the letter saying: Set ye Uriah in the forefront of the hottest battle and retire ye from him, that he may be smitten and die. And in the battle there fell some of the servants of David; and Uriah the Hittite died also.

'"When the mourning was past David fetched Bathsheba to his house, and she became his wife, and bore him a son. But the thing that David had done displeased the Lord."'

I held fast to Nanna's hand. Mam seemed not to be breathing, she was so still. The congregation was silent, so I dared not whisper to ask why the Lord was displeased. Nanna gave my hand a gentle squeeze while Grandpa told of how the Lord caused David to be his own judge. The Lord sent Nathan to David to tell the parable of the rich man who took the poor man's own ewe lamb.

'"And David's anger was greatly kindled against the rich man who took the poor man's one ewe lamb. And David said to Nathan, 'As the Lord liveth, the man that hath done this thing shall surely die.' And Nathan said to David, 'Thou art the man. Wherefore hast thou despised the commandment of the Lord? Thou has killed Uriah the Hittite with the sword and taken his wife to be thy wife.'

'"Nathan departed and the Lord struck the child that Bathsheba bore unto David, and it was very sick. David therefore besought God for the child; and fasted and lay all night upon the earth and would not rise. And it came to pass on the seventh day, that the child died.

'"The seventh day. The seventh sin. Thou shalt not commit adultery.' Grandpa leaned out a little way and the candlelight flickered in his breath as he said in the deep, sonorous voice that he used for sermons, 'If we break the Lord's commandments the Lord will avenge and the sins of the fathers shall be upon the children . . .'

I knew how the quotation ended, '. . . unto the third and fourth generation', but I was crying and could not listen to the rest of the sermon because I didn't want to hear about God striking down a baby to punish King David. I cried louder and stuttered through my tears to Nanna, 'Why didn't God strike King David down?' I wanted to ask, 'Why did God strike down my Dad in battle?' but I knew I must not speak about my dead father. Nanna cuddled me and wiped my eyes.

'"And the scribes and Pharisees brought unto him a woman taken in adultery; in the very act. Jesus stoooped down, and with his finger wrote on the ground, and said unto them, He that is without sin among you, let him first cast a stone at her."'

Grandpa's sermon was done. The congregation rose to their feet. Grandpa lifted his hands and prayed, 'Brothers and sisters. Let us pray. Let us pray that the strength of God is with us as we renounce, in His name, lust and villainy, brazen behaviour, adultery, drunkenness and devilry!'

I looked up and, eyes shining with conquered tears, my infant heart swelled with pride as I gladly forswore these and all the other unnameable wickednesses that the breaking of commandments entailed.

Mam had tears in her eyes too. But she never went to chapel again.

Mam, twenty-six when I was born, was always dressed in the fashion of the day. She had a slender waist, a full-busted figure, bobbed dark hair that fell into waves, a wide mouth and sapphire-blue eyes. Mam had the loveliest face I have ever seen. She also had a way of attracting attention to herself. Mam liked 'a bit of life'.

When Man came home with her bottles of sherry or port wine hidden deep in her cloth bag she would wave a slender arm in the direction of our shabby living kitchen and say, 'One day we'll rise above all this, our Lil. We'll get out of it one day.' Then she'd laugh, open the sherry, fetch a glass and say, 'All I want is a little drop of sherry. A little bit of life. Don't tell Grandpa.'

But that was later. Until the age of five I lived with my wonderful grandparents at Lindow, their farm in the hills. I loved it as much as a grand palace but Lindow was a small house. Unlike Mam's house in Macclesfield, where the unused rooms were dusty and neglected everything here was spotless for Nanna was tireless and happily houseproud. In the kitchen the shelves had paper linings, the range gleamed and on a hook halfway down the cellar steps hung a burnished zinc bath which Mam used after me every Saturday evening, cleanliness being next to godliness, according to Nanna; and Saturday being next to Sunday made the Saturday-night baths right and fitting in my young mind. We were clean and godly, Mam and I.

One Sunday afternoon, I remember sitting in the garden at Lindow on Mam's knee and looking into her eyes, while Nanna and Grandpa sat side by side on the garden seat. Mam was seated on a kitchen chair. She said, 'I have to go soon, Lil. I'll be back on Wednesday and take you for a picnic at White Nancy.' White Nancy was the whited stone monument on Kerridge Hill; a windowless picnic house with an iron door.

'Don't go away, Mam. Stay with me. Please.' I had on my Sunday best dress, and my dark hair, brushed and shiny, fell in ringlets about my shoulders. 'Why do you have to go?'

Mam said patiently, 'I have to earn our living.'

Grandpa grunted a protest. 'Your place is here, with our Lil. Why lower yourself trading in Macclesfield? Anyway, it's Barnaby. All the shops are closed.' Barnaby, feast of St Barnabas, the patron saint of Macclesfield, was the June holiday, when the mills and most of the shops closed down.

Mam said, 'I'm staying open. I need the money.'

'I know!' I had a marvellous idea. 'We can both live here. We haven't got a dad in Macclesfield. Grandpa's our dad, here.'

Mam unfastened my hands and stood me down. 'You have got to get used to it, Lil. In September you'll be with me in Macclesfield for good. You have to go to school.' At this point Grandpa stumped off into the house.

I idolised Mam. She was my beautiful butterfly with dark hair gleaming, blue eyes clever and knowing. She was full of talk, gossip and laughter with Nanna. In Grandpa's presence she was more subdued. But she never changed her mind. 'I am learning,' I said. 'With Sylvia and Magnus.'

Sylvia and Magnus were the grandchildren of Old Man Hammond. And because of the unusual circumstances – our grandfathers having started out in life together – I was their daytime companion and friend. Most mornings I sat with them at lessons, getting things right more often than Magnus did.

'Why don't they go to school?'I asked Mam last week. 'Sylvia's eight and Magnus is six and a half.'

Mam said, 'It's because of Magnus's illness.'

'What's he got now?' I asked. Magnus often spent weeks in bed with what his nurse called 'a little knock'.

Mam was quiet for a few seconds, then, 'Don't say. They keep from Magnus how bad things are.'

'I won't say.'

'It was a terrible shock to Mr Hammond. When Magnus

was born he was at death's door. It was a week before he stopped bleeding where he'd been joined to his mother.'

'Is it a secret?' I had the sinking feeling – excitement mixed with fright – which came when Mam gossiped for it was a sin, Grandpa said, to talk with a wanton tongue.

Mam said, 'They called in specialists. Magnus has haemophilia. It runs in families but only affects the boys.'

'Has Sylvia got haemo . . . haemo – that thing, Mam?'

'They don't know. Three out of four of their children will inherit it. One in four will be normal. Sylvia might be the normal one. Or she might be a transmitter, like her mother.'

But Sylvia, upon whom I tried to model myself, had roses in her cheeks and abundant blonde curls. 'Is that why Magnus can't play rough games?' I asked, knowing Magnus was afraid of hurting himself. His mother bossed and interfered, giving the nurse and governess orders never to oppose Magnus, not to let him fall or do anything dangerous.

Mam nodded. 'They think he'll grow out of it and become a normal boy. He won't. Don't tell them I've told you.'

'No, Mam.' I would not tell. But I'd worry in case I banged the dominoes too hard and caught Magnus's fingers and made him bleed for Mam said if he bled they'd never be able to stop it. Magnus was so pale I could believe he had already lost most of his blood. And here in the garden, only a week after she had told me all this, Mam was acting as if she didn't know that I went every day to Archerfield to be with Magnus and Sylvia.

'Does our Lil go round there for lessons as well?' Mam said to Nanna. 'I didn't think their mother would . . .'

Nanna, on the defensive, said, 'It's not all one-way. Mrs Hammond asked me to have Sylvia here when she and Lily caught measles. She was afraid poor Magnus might go down with it an'all.'

'More fool you,' said Mam.

'Eeh! I loved doing it,' Nanna protested. 'Sylvia and our Lil are best friends. You'd never think there's three years between 'em.'

I'd enjoyed it. I'd had Sylvia all to myself. We'd sworn never to break friends, and to share all our secrets – not in those words, of course. Sylvia's own words were beautiful: 'Best friends never part. Never, never fail us.' Mine were,

‘Cross my heart. Hope to die. If I ever tell a lie’ Then we each spat on our right hand and clasped the other’s, tight. Sylvia said this was the way to seal a bargain and our friendship was like a marriage. She said, ‘We must share everything. For ever. First, we’ll share Nanna.’

We did not take the disease badly but Nanna made us stay indoors in the parlour that housed her pride – a walnut piano resplendent with fretwork and brass candle holders. Nanna drew the summer chintz curtains in case we went blind, and she played the piano, cuddled us, made cool herb and honey drinks, nature’s cures, and told us wonderful stories about the olden days when she was a girl. Nanna must have been recalling this too for she smiled as she said to Mam, ‘Our Lil and Sylvia are happiest together.’

Grandpa came back into the garden, wearing his Sunday suit and gold watch and chain. I ran across the grass to stand by him and read the time out loud for soon Mam must go down to Bollington station. Mam hadn’t seen Grandpa but said to Nanna, ‘I thought Mrs Hammond wanted to break all connections between us.’

‘Mr Hammond likes to keep connection. He’s a fine man, is Mr Hammond,’ Nanna said. She pronounced it ‘Mistrammond’ and never used the word ‘the’ if she could leave it out.

Mam would not drop the subject. ‘His wife’s a jumped-up nobody with a pretty face. She set her cap for him all right. Came down from Edinburgh on a visit and swept the board clean! Scooped up the most eligible bachelor in Macc. The jealous Scotch—’

‘No!’ Grandpa ordered in his chapel voice, catching Mam out in a gossip, which to Grandpa was almost as bad as telling lies. ‘The ninth commandment. Thou shalt not bear false witness. I’ll have no scandal-mongering. No wanton, idle talk in my house.’

Nanna, trying to bring the talk round to something we would all agree on, got to her feet and said, ‘Shall I fetch our Lil’s copy-book? She can show her Mam what she’s done . . .’

Grandpa said, ‘Not on a Sunday, Isobel!’ and Nanna sat down quickly.

In a couple of hours I’d be in chapel again, clean and starched, holding Nanna’s hand. I never wearied, even when the sermons were long, for Grandpa had taught me a funny trick of the mind: mesmerising. Nanna called it 'The Iron in Our Lil', but Grandpa had taught me how to split my mind in two, so that one part of my brain told the other what to do. I could make myself do things like sums, or force myself to remember exactly what I'd done or read. I'd sit in the pew, an open hymn book on my lap, concentrating, repeating, memorising – all the time wearing an attentive expression so nobody would know I was not listening but was practising this magical 'mesmerising'.

'Why don't you come to chapel with us?' I asked Mam now.

There was a painful silence before Nanna came to the rescue again. 'She'll come back to it,' she assured us, as if Mam were not there. 'Sometimes I think we pester poor old God to death with all this praying. Everyone has a time in life when they lose a bit o' faith. What I say is, "If you take it to our Lord Jesus Christ, in prayer ..."'

'Don't talk daft, Mother!' Mam got to her feet. 'I have to go soon, because I'm not walking to Bollington station.' Macclesfield is six miles from Bollington and there were few trains on Sundays.

Grandpa said, 'Why not?'

'I'm getting a ride back.' Mam did not meet his eye. Instead she said to Nanna, 'You said you'd give me a bottle of elderberry ...' She hesitated, then rephrased it. 'I said I'd help with the wine ...'

'It's Sunday,' said Grandpa. 'Your mother does no work on Sunday.'

'Goodness!' Nanna leaped to her feet. 'I have to do t'wine this afternoon, Dad. It's waiting. It's an essential task. Not work.' She said to Mam, 'I'll give you a bottle of elderberry – and what about rhubarb?'

'Thanks. I'll put them in my bag. I've been "bound" lately ...' Mam gave a relieved smile.

Grandpa said, 'What do you mean? Getting a ride back? Who's giving you a ride back? Where to?'

'Don't get alarmed,' Mam said. 'It's only Frank Chancellor. He goes to see his mother on Sundays. He passes the end of our lane at four o'clock. If I'm there he'll drive me back to

Macc in his motorcar.'

'He's a married man,' Grandpa said.

Mam laughed. 'Frank's a country man. I've known Frank all my life.'

'Is Mrs Chancellor still in that little cottage at Pott Shrigley?' said Nanna, incredulous. 'Well I never. Her son's got a big house in Park Lane. And all that money.'

'It's Frank's wife and his father-in-law who have all the money. They keep a tight hold on it . . .'

'I said no scandal-mongering!' Grandpa boomed out.

'I am not scandal-mongering. It's common knowledge,' Mam said.

Mam knew everything about everybody in Macc. 'And nobody knows a thing about me,' she boasted, for she was full of secrets. Mam knew which women said, 'My drink is water bright', but got drunk in secret; who their fathers were, what they had done, where they'd come from and where they'd finish up if they didn't watch out. She knew which woman got her blonde hair and her navy-blue parting out of a bottle. She knew whose wife had run off with the tallyman, leaving her mother-in-law and husband behind.

I dogged Mam's footsteps, saying nothing, hoping to follow her down the lane and watch her drive away in the motor car.

Nanna brought the two bottles and put them in Mam's shopping bag. 'Do you want to hear our Lil play piano?'

Grandpa had taught me to speak well and to read and write a little, but Nanna had taught me to play the piano. Nanna had 'the gift', which she had passed on to me. She taught me how to hear a tune and pick out the melody. Within a few minutes I'd be adding the chords with the left hand and arpeggios that Grandpa called the twiddly bits with the right. My hand could not stretch the octaves but it was easy, picking out tunes.

What I wanted to play was what I thought of as Show Pan – the Chopin waltzes Mr Hammond played. Nanna could not play Show Pan. There was very little money spent at Lindow. A trip to Macclesfield was a once-a-month event yet only last week my lovely Nanna had put on a round straw hat and her fawn coat with a velvet collar and taken me to the music shop on Churchwallgate to buy a Smallwood's tutor book and *The Chopin Waltzer*. And I'd seen at once that if I were to play even the exercises in the tutor book I'd need fingering and theory lessons like Sylvia had every week. But that day, I wanted to show off. I'd mastered 'Bluebells of Scotland' and 'Merry Peasant'.

Mam glanced at the big clock on the kitchen wall. It said it was a quarter past four. 'No time. You should have said. Earlier.'

Tears of disappointment came prickling behind my eyes but I said, 'It doesn't matter.'

'Good. Then I'm off.' Mam took the shopping bag from Nanna and without stopping to wave, much less kiss me goodbye, she was gone, out of the kitchen door, her Louis heels catching on the gravel path as she hastened away on to the lane and her ride home.

When she had gone my tears fell. 'I won't see her till Wednesday,' I wailed. Wenesday was Mam's half-closing day.

'No. Come here, love ...' Nanna's blue eyes clouded with unhappiness as she knelt down and held out her arms.

I fell into the comfort of them, crying on her shoulder, 'W...w...will you teach me to play "Blaze Away"? W...w...when it's not Sunday?'

'Course I will.' Then gently she asked, 'What makes you think we can't play a march on a Sunday?'

I pressed my teeth into my bottom lip, to stall the tears. 'Isn't blaze a bad word? Like brazen?'

'Eeh! Our Lil! You are a comical little soul. Blaze isn't a bad word!'Nanna laughed and after a second or so the corners of my mouth were fighting to join in. 'Not unless you say, "Go to blazes!"' Nanna stopped laughing and clapped her hand to her mouth, in case Grandpa heard, making me laugh, turning away tears with that infectious good humour.

I loved my warm, demonstrative grandmother. Nanna and I were never apart. At Nanna's knee I was learning to knit and stitch; at her side I learned to knead and shape and prove and bake the crackle-crusty loaves and floury barm cakes that were our daily bread. With Nanna I walked for miles, picking hedgerow berries and gathering beech and hazel and chestnuts in autumn. In the spring we found meadow flowers and pressed them between the pages of a heavy book. We pressed the little common heartsease and the rare and glorious Felwort gentian.

And we plucked by the bucketful cowslips and oxlips for Nanna's country wine.

A little while after Mam had gone. Nanna took me to sit outside the wooden shed. I had recovered my good spirits and was happily munching on a consolation – a crust plastered with butter and honey.

Nanna, rosy-cheeked and happy, stood in the doorway of the shed, sliding pieces of toasted bread spread with brewer's yeast into a barrel of mash – the yellow cowslip heads crushed into sugar and lemons and water. It was a shady corner of the garden where the sky was filled with flighty tortoiseshell butterflies and the heady scents of the woodbine flowers and pinks were all about us. But instead of watching the flight of the insects I was puzzling over the difference between the drink Grandpa railed against and the wine Nanna availed herself of whenever she felt a cold coming on.

'Nanna?'

'Well?'

'Doesn't cowslip wine bring men to brazen behaviour, drunkenness and evil?'

Nanna's blue eyes twinkled. 'Good heavens, no, child!' she said, before once again dipping her fingers into the barrel. Scooping and sucking vigorously, she added, 'This isn't going to be a drunkard's brew! This is medicinal wine. To keep winter cold out. Jesus himself drank wine.'

It must be right if Nanna said so. All the same, I wondered why Mam should be so keen to take home the bottles of wine every Sunday – and why she invariably hurried away before Grandpa could offer to walk with her to the station. Did Mam get a ride home with Mr Chancellor every Sunday?

Chapter Two

Frank Chancellor drove downhill from his mother's cottage – the cottage she refused to leave – until he reached the cross-roads where he pulled the bright red Alvis in close to a high drystone wall. He switched the engine off then climbed down and drew the canvas hood up to screw it on to the chrome pegs of the windscreen frame. It would be hot with the roof up but Elsie was afraid of being seen in the back of his motor car.

The thought amused him. It was Barnaby Sunday, for heaven's sake! The mills were closed. Thousands had queued yesterday, for the trains taking them to Blackpool and Rhyl, but Elsie was afraid someone might see her in his car and put two and two together. Where on earth was she? He glanced at himself in the wing mirror and ran a sun-browned hand through the thick mass of dark curly hair, to straighten it. He walked downhill a few yards to the spot where he would be able to see all over the lower end of Bollington. He could make out the elementary school that he and Elsie had attended, and there was the railway station where, from the age of twelve, he had caught the train every school day. He had won a scholarship at twelve; won a place at the King's School, Macclesfield – where he had excelled.

He was a country man at heart. He had been born in these hills – a mile or so up the hill from Lindow. His father, a tenant farmer on the Archerfield estate, had been a hard-drinking, hard-hitting man who hated Old Man Hammond, the new owner of the land that generations of Chancellors had farmed. Whenever his father had to doff his cap to Old Man Hammond, he would come home in a filthy temper. 'Get out of me road!' he'd yell, or, 'I'll thrash you to within an inch of your bloody lives!' He used to beat the daylight out of his four eldest sons.

Frank, ten years younger than his nearest brother, escaped the worst of his father's foul temper. Frank was clever – and an opportunist. He learned early on how to avoid his father's wrath. He'd drop to the ground before his father could touch him, and he'd call out for Ma who came to his side to intervene for the apple of her eye. Ma was forty when Frank was born and when Frank was four, Jimmy, the last of his brothers, left home and Ma stood up to his father. When he won the scholarship she said, 'Frank's going to accept it. Learning is what Frank needs. Chancellors have farmed this land for centuries. It's a proud old family but none of them had any learning.'

Frank's only carefree hours in his boyhood, though, had been spent with Elsie and her parents at Lindow Farm. And Ma used to warn Frank, when he was only a sixteen-year-old schoolboy with years of study ahead of him, 'Don't go giving Elsie ideas. Never steal a girl's affections unless you mean to marry her.' Frank smiled now at his thoughts. If Ma knew half of what went on between himself and Elsie – and all that had gone on when they were nothing but children – she would have taken a strap to him today.

There was only a year between him and Elsie. As children they wandered the hills on summer nights and bathed naked in ponds and streams. In adolescence, on winter evenings they bedded down under the barn's rafters on the straw bales, high above the cattle, kissing and petting and fondling. My God! Thinking about her was exciting him. Where was she? He looked behind. No sign of her.

Ma could not protect him from everything, though. Ma was not there when the rich King's School lads got their laughs from the sight of him in second-hand school uniforms that were either too big or too small, for Ma's purse didn't stretch to outfitting him with new clothes.

On his first day at King's School he saw the gulf that lay between him and his new school friends – town boys from the middle classes; the new rich – and the greater gulf between their families and his own. He couldn't ask any of these boys to his home, where his father spoke in oaths and his sweet, tired mother cried in secret. His new school companions grew impatient with what they saw as his standoffish behaviour.

Frank had nothing outside school – no interests but his studies and Elsie. He soon became a loner who would never have a close man friend. But he observed the other boys and adopted their mannerisms and speech. He'd say, 'How's things, old boy?' and sound choosy when anything was offered to him, with an, 'I will give it a bit of thought, eh?' or 'Not for me, I'm afraid.'

He took a lift of an eyebrow from one, a careless shrug from another, a lazy but confident gesture from yet another boy. He copied the ways of the leisured classes so that he could use them at will. They never became an unconscious part of him but he learned how to lead a double life. He put aside his act only when he was with Ma or Elsie.

And because there were no distractions, he passed his School Certificate at fifteen and the Higher School Certificate at sixteen and a half. He was good at most subjects; so good it was difficult for him to decide what to do. He was too clever for the hard grind of tenant-farming and too poor for the simple indulgence of his tastes in poetry and literature. There was always the possibility of studying classics and earning a small living teaching. Or should he study commerce and chartered accountancy at Manchester? Become rich and independent and after some years, buy the farm and more land and set the Chancellor name up high like a landed family? He worked harder and again his efforts were rewarded. He was offered a place at Oxford – the only lad in his year to be offered a place and a bursary. There was nothing he could not do now. Anything might be his for the taking.

So he thought. Except it was not his for the taking. Not after his drunken father died in an alehouse brawl.

After the funeral they held a family conference. Ma said, 'I can't manage the farm. Our only income is from the sale of the young cattle. There's never anything over when the Michaelmas rent's been paid.' Frank's married brothers couldn't help. Ma and Frank could have a home with them but there was no money to spare. It was Jimmy – who was 'promised' to a dairymaid – who said, 'I'll tell me fiancée we'll wait a few years. I'll come back home, Ma. As long as our Frank gets his education.'

'And I'll work,' Frank promised. 'I'll do two hours on the land before breakfast. I'll work Saturdays and Sundays. Till I go to Oxford. Then I'll work on the land when I'm home.'

'First things first,' Jimmy said. 'Let our Frank get his learning.'

'I'm used to hard work,' Ma said. 'It won't be any different.'

Frank had been humbled and grateful. Ma could have an easier life if she went to live with one of his married brothers. 'I won't forget it,' he told them all. 'I'll help you all when I'm earning good money.' He'd be a chartered accountant. 'I'll buy the farm for you, Ma. I'll make the name of Chancellor respected again.'

Ma smiled for the first time in months. 'As long as you get on, son. We'll tell Old Man Hammond.'

By September that year the hay was safely in the barn, ten young steers had been sold and there was money in the cash box under Ma's bed. Another year's living was assured and on the appointed Michaelmas day when agricultural rents are paid, Frank dressed smartly in a shirt and tie, flannels and his good jacket. Ma put aside her mourning and put on her Sunday costume of navy blue, with Michaelmas daisies as a buttonhole. Frank put the money into a chamois bag and escorted Ma to Archerfield.

They were shown into the hall. It was the first time Frank had been over the threshold of Archerfield House and he was knocked out by the sight of it – paintings on the walls of the reception hall where a log fire burned. The butler took them down a long corridor and into a small, wood-panelled room where Old Man Hammond sat behind a great mahogany desk.

Ma stood, twisting the black-edged handkerchief, nervous about facing the master, then all at once, to Frank's alarm, his Ma bobbed down to curtsey to Old Man Hammond. Frank felt his gorge rise, and he felt angry, hot, suffocating shame, for Old Man Hammond remained seated at his desk. The owner of their farm did not even ask them to sit. He merely nodded at Ma then coldly said, 'I'm not renewing the tenancy. Plenty wants it.'

Frank felt as if he had been struck. He looked at Ma and saw the colour drain from her face, saw tears come rolling down her cheeks. It was a few seconds before she whispered, 'We can pay! I've got money. Sir . . . ?'

Frank couldn't bear it; his mother crying and pleading with this ugly, weasel-faced old man. He came forward quickly and dumped the money bag on the desk, untied it and let the gold pieces tinkle on to the mahogany. 'Will this change your mind, Mr Hammond?'

Old Man Hammond ignored him. 'I am giving you a cottage at Pott Shrigley, Mrs Chancellor. One and sixpence a week. Paid in advance. Have your stuff in the yard ready. Move out next Monday.' He did not even glance at Frank as he said, 'Pick your money up. You'll need it.'

Blood rushed to Frank's head. His knuckles were white as he clenched his hands to stop himself from hitting the old man. He had never in his short life known fury like this; never thought he was capable of violence. If Ma were not beside him he'd . . . Frank's face was white with anger as he took the gold and put it back in the bag. Behind him Ma went on crying while the old weasel watched her without a flicker of interest or feeling. Frank put the bag in his pocket. 'Come on, Ma,' he said. 'Keep your pride. Let's get out of here.' He thought Ma was going to follow him out of the room but to his horror Frank saw her take a step towards the chair and drop to her knees at the old man's side crying, 'Mr Hammond, sir. Frank's won a place at Oxford! Didn't you know? You wanted your son to go to Oxford, sir . . .'

John, Old Man Hammond's son, was four years older than Frank. John was a young gentleman – but not a bright one. He had never passed an exam in his life. At twenty years old, he had been refused a place at just about every university in the land. He was running Hammond Silks with his father. John himself was content, as would be any rich, good-looking young man. But Old Man Hammond's ambition had long since been diverted from himself to his son. The last thing he wanted was to hear that his tenant's son had gained something that, for all the tutoring and expensive schooling, his own son had not.

Ma twisted the damp handkerchief and jabbed at her eyes. 'We can manage, sir,' she wept. 'Our Jimmy's coming home.

Frank's worked hard for a free place. He has been given a bursary, sir . . . Please . . .'

Frank could take no more. 'Get up, Ma.' He helped her to her feet and put a protective arm round her. 'Come on. Don't ever let me see you begging anything of anyone again. Especially a Hammond.'

Old Man Hammond's back was bent. He couldn't move fast but he wouldn't allow a whipper snapper to get away with disrespect. 'It's a son's duty. Your responsibility, lad. Get to work! Earn some money and support your mother.' He was red in the face. 'Get out or I'll have you thrown out. If I catch a Chancellor on my land after this I'll get the police to you.'

Ma was shaking and weeping and leaning on Frank but all the same he managed to hurl back at the old man, 'Don't you tell me where I can't go! Chancellors have been here longer than you.'

Then they were at the front entrance. Frank opened the inner glass door and gently led Ma outside and down the drive. It was not until minutes later, as they went through the gates, that Ma recovered. 'You go to Oxford, son. I'll take the cottage. I'll manage.'

'I am putting it behind me,' Frank said. 'I'll get a job. We'll not be beholden to anyone.' And when he looked into her dear old face, expecting tears and protests, he saw only relief. That clinched it. 'We'll never bend the knee or doff our caps again, Ma. I'll make sure of that. Oxford's not for me. I'll earn our living and set the name of Chancellor above the Hammonds one day. I won't be brow-beaten, turned out of my home again. Plenty of successful men never went to university.'

There would be opportunities. As long as he could take care of Ma, keep a roof over her head, he was free to do what he wanted. And as he realised this he gave a laugh. It had been good, telling that miserable old devil what he thought. Instead of spending half his evenings studying he'd spend his time with Elsie who was becoming increasingly attractive to him as she grew ever prettier and lavished her passionate nature on him. Though she went to chapel and had a high moral conscience, Elsie had none of the false modesty or prudery of the times. She was proud of her body and felt no shame in taking her clothes off for him. She had beautiful breasts. They were milky white and heavy and, naked in the straw, she let him lie on top of her as they fondled one another to the point of release. He told her, in those days of sorely tried innocence, that what they indulged in was not 'the sinful lusts of the flesh' but in his opinion, 'as near to being wed as dammit is to swearing'.

God. Where was she? Thinking about her like this, on a hot summer afternoon, his brow was breaking out in a sweat.

He climbed back into the car, put it into gear, switched on and let the Alvis roll down the hill a little way, until the revolutions were fast enough for him to engage the clutch and let the engine burst into life. If he turned right at the foot of the hill, right again, then first right, in fifteen minutes he would be back here. If Elsie was not here by then, he'd give up. And as he went he remembered more about that time – the time when he rolled up his school certificates and went to Macclesfield empty-handed.

To obtain clerical work a lad's family usually paid a premium, for articles or indentures. He did not see how he could get round this – but the years of copying the manners of King's School boys had paid off. He borrowed three guineas from Ma for a suit, overcoat and bowler hat. He knew how to put his shoulders back and look a man straight in the eye and he struck lucky on his first day, finding work as a wages clerk at Pilkington Printers.

The chief clerk, Mr Grimshaw, interviewed him. 'Twelve and sixpence a week until you reach twenty-one,' he said. 'A tidy wage for a young man.'

It was not a tidy wage at all. Pilkington Printers were known for paying the worst wages in town. But it was a job. 'Thank you, sir,' he said. 'I will not disappoint you. What are my prospects?'

The stolid Mr Grimshaw said, 'Mr Pilkington is a fair boss. If you work hard you are assured of a good salaried position for life.'

'Very well,' said Frank. 'I'm sure I'll be an asset to Pilkington's.'

He found cheap lodgings in a respectable working men's house in Macclesfield, gave Ma half his wages when he went home at weekends, tried to enjoy office work and waited for his opportunity.

But he was young and keen and impatient for success. He hated his lowly position and the people such as the chief clerk, Mr Grimshaw, who liked a quiet office and warned, 'Know your place. Be thankful you have a job at all in these hard times. Stop larking!' when Frank teased the women of the counting house and the girls in the design room – the pretty, artistic young women who painted flowers and repeat patterns for the silk-screen printers. The girls were good for designing cotton prints – and good for a laugh – and life was not all gloom.

At a time of deep unemployment, Frank was lucky to have work. Though he knew this, he could not settle for conformity and a subservient role in life. But for three long years he stayed put, learning the business of printing on cloth, which interested him, and learning to pennypinch on workers' wages which disgusted him. He also knew that he could do any job in the mill, except designing, better than anyone else. He could run the place more efficiently and still pay good wages and it came hard, taking orders from pompous old men. So though he longed for escape he had no choice. There was no way out.

Then – and it came out of the blue, on a glorious June day in 1914 – an assassin shot dead the heir to the Austrian Empire, Archduke Franz Ferdinand, and his wife. They were on a state visit to Serbia. The Vienna government made a series of demands that Serbia could not accept without humiliation, and the world sat up and took notice.

In the office at Pilkington's, Mr Grimshaw said, 'The territorials have been called up. But if war comes it will be sport for some!'

In the public houses of Macclesfield the older men said that war would be a gentlemen's show, like the South African campaign had been, when officers and gentlemen of the regiments reduced their rank in order to be allowed to go out to join the fight. From the end of July young officers were strutting about the town. The narrow pavements of Mill Street and Chestergate were only wide enough for two officers abreast, swinging their swagger sticks. At the sight of the smart uniforms, pedestrians stepped into the gutters to let them pass. Soldiers were in training at the barracks and Drill Hall, and they marched through the town, an officer at their head, horses and carts and motors pulling aside to wait their passing.

Abroad, the Kaiser took offence at the British attempt to mediate. The Austrians were encouraged by the Kaiser and war between Austria and Russia was declared at the end of July. Soon treaties and pacts with foreign countries had to be honoured, boundaries and borders had to be defended.

Frank envied the young officers. He compared their lives with his. All he had was the dull routine of clerical work and his Saturday nights with Elsie, who would not give in to his requests for total lovemaking. He was more easily aroused now he was older. He believed himself to be suffering physically – believed, in common with most men that sexual arousal followed by denial was weakening him. Elsie said, 'I am saving myself for marriage, Frank. It's all I ever wanted. A home in the country. Marriage and children.' He was twenty-one. Too young, too poor for marriage, and afraid of being tied down before he had made his fortune.

It was demoralising, seeing the young officers – men with rank, position and a purpose. He had to listen to the design-shop chatter, the girls' cries of 'Oh! Look at him!' when they saw the young blades' riding boots and flashing buttons.

Then on 4 August, because the Kaiser would not respect the neutrality of Belgium, Britain declared war on Germany. Cheering crowds gathered in all the cities. In Macc, young men, filled with national pride, waved their hats in the air on their way to the recruiting office. Frank went in his dinner hour and asked the recruiting sergeant, 'Will you take me?'

'Are you fit? Can you ride?' they asked him.

'Of course I can ride. I am a farmer's son.'

'Have you a horse of your own?'

He put on his confident, educated and easy air. He said, 'Not at present. I'm in reduced circumstances. When my dear old dad died we gave up the farm.' They questioned him further then told him that, because he had School Certificate and Higher School Certificate, he was 'officer material'. He went back to Pilkington Printers, collected a week's wages, shook hands with Mr Grimshaw, slung his overcoat over his arm and walked out, convinced that this was his opportunity to change his life.

Ma wept. 'It's not even our country's argument, son. It's

Austria and Serbia's fight. Change your mind. Marry little Elsie. Settle down and raise a family like your brothers.'

'How can I afford marriage? I'd need a house. Money.'

Ma wiped her eyes on her overall. 'Elsie's a pretty girl, Frank. And a good girl. She'll make someone a nice little wife. She's been to sewing lessons. Her mother's taught her to keep house. She'll inherit a farm. You'd be a landed Chancellor. A man of property.'

'Hang on, Ma!'

She would not be stopped. 'If you go away someone else will get her.' He was amused at her attempt to persuade him of Elsie's charms. She said, 'John Hammond's smitten with Elsie. So her mother says. You don't want to lose your girl to John Hammond, do you?'

He was out of touch with country living and though he knew Elsie was a bit secretive, what they called 'a close 'un', he didn't think she would keep anything like that from him. Elsie knew very well that he had no time for the Hammonds. So he laughed. 'John Hammond? After Elsie? Get away!'

He laughed again and hugged her. 'I am not going to marry. I want to go to war. I want to teach the Kaiser a lesson.' He lifted her off her feet and swung her round the tiny cottage room. 'It's the gentlemen's regiment, Ma! They don't take riff-raff into the cavalry. The Cheshire Yeomanry's the finest in England. I am going to Eaton Hall – home of the Duke of Westminster. Your son's going to be an officer and a gentleman!'

Less than six months later, at the end of January 1915, to a background of war fever – for Britain had suffered heavy losses at Mons and in the line of trenches that stretched from the North Sea to the Swiss border – Frank Chancellor passed out as a lieutenant with the Cheshire Yeomanry. He had three days of freedom before he would report back to Eaton, where he would be given a troop to command and drill for a month. Then he would be posted to the Western Front, or – and rumour and counter-rumour was ever changing – he and his men would be sent to the Balkans, where Anglo-French forces were pitted against the Turks who guarded the fortified entrance to the Dardanelles. He hoped to God he would put up a good fight when the time came, but he was in a high state of nervous anticipation when he came home for his first leave, determined not to dwell on what lay ahead.

He clipped into the office of Pilkington Printers in his uniform, the cavalry twill breeches, worsted jacket with lighter braiding and pips on his cuffs proclaiming his rank, his riding boots polished until they shone like old mahogany, back ramrod straight, slimmer, fitter and commanding – on his once-boyish face – the supercilious expression that he had been practising.

The designers – the girls who had demanded that he come in and show himself in uniform – were struck down with shyness. The other clerks were envious and respectful – something they had never been before. Mr Grimshaw, impressed, lumbered off upstairs to tell Mr Pilkington about the credit being done to Pilkington Printers by their young clerk. Then Mr Grimshaw came down and said in his pompous way, 'You are required in the office, in five minutes' time. They want to see you in your splendour. Mr Pilkington and his daughter, Sarah.'

Upstairs in the office, Sarah, dressed in drab grey, stared out of the window at the dull sky. Everything was grey and cold. The slate grey of the sky was reflected in the waters of the Bollin where dirty grey snow clung to the clumps of dead grass on the river's bank. Downstream of the other mills and their own wastepipe, which gushed dye all day long, the Bollin was a dirty river – and not even deep enough to jump into and drown oneself. Then, drowning would be a slow death and a great sin. The gates of heaven were closed to sinners. Dizzy waves of sickness washed over her as she put her hand on to the sill to steady herself.

She had walked here from Park Lane to talk to Father and tell him everything – here at the mill where he would have to listen to her. What would he do? Would he send her away in disgrace? Would he have her committed to an institution for those of unsound mind? If only there were some way to avoid telling him. If only she could spare him. If only all she needed to say was that she had let her last chance of marriage slip through her fingers.

She stretched out those long and graceful fingers. Her mother's hands. She kept them white and soft, rubbing them daily with cut lemons before working lanolin cream into them. She had the pale thin skin of girls of her colouring. Her deep coppery hair, thick and wavy, would have been any other girl's crowning glory. Any girl other than she would have worn it swept up and back in wide wings to frame her features, make her face appear round and appealing. Sarah wore it scraped back, plaited and coiled.

She was plain. She was old – thirty-five years old – and a terrible fear was gnawing at her. She had fallen in love with John Hammond when he was a dashing twenty-three-year-old catch and she a thirty-three-year-old spinster who had only experienced the spiritual, sanctifying love of God. Her father accused her being the self-appointed linchpin of St Michael's, the parish church. She taught at Sunday school, embroidered altar cloths and went three times a week to Holy Communion.

Until she met John Hammond she had been content to give herself to God. She had no need of living men, those coarse, impure creatures. Then, two years ago John Hammond broke away from the rigid chapel and joined their church. Sarah set eyes on him. She set eyes on him and fell into that enchanted state of romance, 'such stuff as dreams are made on . . .'

At last she understood the passion behind poetry and works of art. Her heart raced at the sight of him. She knew that everyone saw her as eccentric – deep, intense and obsessive. To make John love her she had to change, become soft and sweet, pliable and frivolous.

She did everything she could think of to make John Hammond love her. For two years she never missed a chance to show herself in an attractive light. She contrived to be invited to the places he might be. That part had been easy. Old Man Hammond was ambitious for an alliance of Pilkington and Hammond and he invited her to all the Archerfield social events. Mutual friends did the rest. She spent long weekends at country houses all over Cheshire, bored if he did not come, in seventh heaven in this presence. She infested his environment. He could not turn his head but she was there, devouring him with her eyes. And for all that time he, her only love, never noticed her love for him. He never saw what all their friends saw – that when she gazed at him she was not the touchy, intense woman whom men avoided. She was pretty. Love shone in her watery blue eyes and her heart melted. And he? He saw her as a friend – a friend he could confide in. He confided in her his hopeless passion for a farmer's daughter.

Once and only once did he need her. Once, he weakened and made love to her in his own home where she was a weekend guest. He came into her bed in the dead of night. He came into her room, begging, 'Sarah! Comfort me, will you?'

The act was shocking and painful but she sacrificed herself to his need. Her dear, dead mother had told her that married women must put up with it to please their husbands, because for men it was the necessary foundation of marriage. Sarah suffered it because John needed the comfort of her body.

Afterwards she had not been able to stop crying. It was a mixture of relief that he had stopped doing it to her and happiness that it had come to pass. And he, her love, her John – mistook her tears of joy for those of regret.

It was then, to stop her from crying, that he held her close and said, over her weeping form, 'I am sorry, Sarah! Oh, so sorry, Sarah!' She could not stop crying and he continued to apologise. 'I've used you, Sarah. Please forgive me. I proposed to Elsie. She turned me down. My heart is breaking...'

Her crying became louder. He, perhaps afraid that she might wake the household, held her tighter and said, 'I can't believe I have behaved like this. I'm disgusted with myself. Forgive me, Sarah! I regret it with all my heart.' He was apologising for making love to her! He was disgusted. He asked her forgiveness and said he regretted it. He repeated it all, in his letter. She trembled when she thought of his letter. She had read it so many times, his words were imprinted in her mind.

Archerfield House
5 January 1915

My dear Sarah,
Where have you been hiding these last weeks? My letters have gone unanswered. I have missed you. I wanted to talk to you and I have not seen you since the night last November when I came, undeserving, to your bed and you gave yourself so generously. Your love gave me such comfort.

I am glad there have been no repercussions. My one

regret is that on that memorable night it was clear to both us, from my ineptitude as a lover and the storms of tears that overcame you, that I was not the man for you.

I want you to be the first to hear, before the announcement in the papers, that Miss Catriona Mackenzie and I are to be married in Edinburgh next week. We met at Christmas and immediately lost our hearts to one another. I know you will wish us well and I hope that you, my dearest and best friend, will become as beloved a friend to Catriona as you are to me. Yours for ever in friendship.

John

Now what could she do? Kill herself? Death was preferable to disgrace. Who could save her?

Her father's voice broke in on her thoughts. 'Sarah!'

Sarah turned away from the window to face him. Their office boy was standing in the open doorway – in uniform.

'Look who has come to see us, Sarah,' Father said. 'Our junior clerk. He's in the Cheshires. My old regiment.'

She remembered him, the lad who'd been the life and soul of the counting-house. She studied him. He was holding his head back, chin tucked in, his peaked hat shading his eyes. Shouldn't a man take his hat off in the presence of a lady?

'Well,' she said slowly. 'Little Frankie.' He was only an inch shorter than herself – and she was tall, five feet ten inches tall. 'Who ever would have thought it?'

He gave her a supercilious look as if he were mocking her. he snapped to attention, whisked his hat off, tucked it under his arm and made a little bow. 'Lieutenant Chancellor. At your service, ma'am.'

Was he making fun of her? Sarah blushed for her rudeness. There was boldness in his eyes as he held her gaze. Sarah's blush deepened.

Father said, 'Now then, Sarah! Mind your manners. Invite the lieutenant to dinner tonight. It will be good to have a bit of company. What with all your friends engaged to be married or off to war —'

'And my last hopes gone, do you mean, Father?' she snapped as she swung round on her heel, picked up her coat and hat and went past both of them to the door, hearing her father, behind her, explaining her rudeness to the office boy.

'Don't mind Sarah,' he said. 'She is a very sensitive girl. Too sensitive for her own good. Now then, about dinner tonight.'

If Frank thought Archerfield a splendid house, then Pilkington house came a close second. It was set back from the road in Park Lane, the dignified residential area of Macc where the professional classes lived. Inside it was a palace: fine maple floors, Portland stone fireplaces. Chinese carpets, modern tapestries, art nouveau lamps and figures – all periods and styles jumbled together to exquisite effect.

They dined, seated at one end of the long table. First they served him River Dee salmon with Chablis white wine. Frank had never eaten such food. They served a red claret with entrecôte steak that ran with pink juices. There were no other guests. Just Frank, who quickly became merry from the wine, a sober Mr Pilkington and a very different Sarah from the clever girl he knew from her visits to the office.

Sarah was wearing a green velvet dress with a deep pointed neckline. He had only ever seen her in severe tailored costumes in dark colours. The dress suited her, drawing attention from the thick waist to her big bosom that was plump and white and swelled over the top of her dress as if there were not enough room for it all to fit inside her camisole. Looking at her across the table you could forget the keen, avid eyes – they said in the office that she had 'bats in her belfry' – and try to imagine what the rest of her body was like; wonder how it would feel to bury your face in that deep, soft cleavage.

He must stop thinking such thoughts and concentrate on the food and Mr Pilkington's conversation. Mr Pilkington gave him port to drink with the Stilton cheese. Sarah excused herself at this point, saying – rather rudely, Frank thought, for he had only ever dined with men in the mess – that it was late and she was going to tell the servants they could have the rest of the evening off. Mr Pilkington evidently was used to her ways and without the distraction of Sarah's full bosom across the table from him, Frank gave his host all his attention. His former employer was talking to him as an equal, reminiscing about his young days when he had been an officer with the Cheshires.

Before the table was cleared, Mr Pilkington said, 'Come to my study, Frank. We must have a serious talk over coffee. I have a proposition for you. Afterwards we'll join Sarah.'

In the study Frank relaxed over coffee, cognac and cigars, and the conversation turned naturally to Pilkington Printers and the new orders that were flooding in for the camouflage print.

Mr Pilkington said, 'We will have to take on more hands. We are employing women now. Women workers – not just designers.' He refilled Frank's brandy glass as he spoke, dismissing with a wave of his hand Frank's half-hearted protests. 'The girls are coming out of their homes, making shells and casings in the small factories that have gone over to armaments. The churches have lent their halls to the town council for use as Christian hostels for working girls from the villages.'

Frank was mellow and relaxed. The cognac made him feel wise and confident so it startled him when Mr Pilkington abruptly changed the subject from war to his worries. 'You know that Sarah is my heir?'

'Yes.'

'She has had a disappointment.'

Mr Pilkington as a boss was distant and watchful and Frank was surprised by his lack of reserve. he said, 'In what way, sir?'

'Sarah has gone into a decline since John Hammond married. She used to come into the office, interest herself in the mill. Now she goes nowhere but to church. She won't accept invitations. Women are highly strung, irrational creatures, Frank. My late wife was the same.'

'John Hammond?' Ma had told him about Hammond's whirlwind romance and his engagement to the Scottish girl. Sarah Pilkington was about ten years older than John Hammond. And Sarah was clever. She could never have wanted to marry a dim fellow like Hammond. He said, 'Sarah is a very intelligent girl, sir. A lesser man would be afraid to marry a woman who is cleverer than he . . .'

'Or richer!' Mr Pilkington gave a harsh laugh. Then he stood, refilled their brandy glasses and placed a hand on Frank's shoulder. His voice went low, confiding, deliberate.

There was no mistaking that what he was about to say was well thought out. 'Old Man Hammond wanted to buy me out. His son was not tempted by the property settlement and a directorship at Pilkington Printers, which will go to the man my Sarah marries.' He watched Frank's face.

Frank jabbed his fingernails into the palm of his hand to prove to himself that he was awake and not dreaming this extraordinary interview. He *was* awake. He said, 'Is this the proposition, Mr Pilkington?' Mr Pilkington, with an expression of immense sadness, said quietly, 'I want to see my daughter married. She is shy, oversensitive, and has not much youth left.'

Frank said, 'I can't be bought, Mr Pilkington.'

There was a brightness in the old man's eyes. 'I am not trying to sell my daughter. Sarah knows nothing of this. Let us go and join her.'

And it was there, in the drawing room, when her father had gone to bed and the servants had been sent away and told not to disturb them, that Sarah enticed him. She invited him to remove his jacket because, she said, 'The fire's blazing. You're hot, Frank.' The fire *was* blazing. He *was* hot. He discarded the jacket. Then Sarah, with her long, slender fingers played with the buttons on his shirt. She came closer, so that the scent that rose from the deep valley between her breasts intoxicated him, urged him to bury his face in her.

She leaned back, inserted her slender fingers between the buttonholes of his shirt, playfully, loosening them. This was not the behaviour of a girl who was pining for somebody else. His very breath was heated. He was growing hot and hard. But he was not sure what she would allow him to do – or what she expected him to do.

And it was there, on a gilded *chaise-longue* in Pilkington House, that Frank discovered how easily he could be seduced. For soon there was no doubt in his mind – Sarah was excited by him. She found him attractive – and she was intent on seduction. Before he even kissed her she became coy, provocative. 'Loosen the hooks on my dress, Frank. Please? The bones in my bodice are cutting into me.'

He waited for a few moments, watching her, to be sure that this was what she wanted. And she glanced down at her hands, bit her lip and said, 'Please. Kiss me. Don't make me ask ...'

He pulled her close, roughly, because she had made him feel unequal to her. He pressed his fingers down on her chin, to make her open her tight-pressed lips. He would show her he could do what she wanted. He knew how to kiss a woman. He held her fast. His tongue explored her mouth while his fingers expertly unfastened the hooks on her velvet dress and tugged it down to her waist. Then he stopped and held her away from him. The seams were tight. They had made marks all over her pure white flesh that was every bit as soft as Elsie's. He suspected that she had drunk a little too much, for she whispered, 'Careful! I have never done this ... Don't hurt me ...'

He did not tell her that he had never done this before either, never completed the act. He made her stand up while he took off her clothes, so that she could call a halt at any moment if she chose to. She did not utter a word but her strange, wary eyes were misty and her beautiful hands were helping him undo laces and suspenders. Those slender white hands were guiding his head down on to her heavy bosom that was pendulous but full and so ripe it inflamed him beyond reason.

Quickly he unfastened his clothes and pulled her down on to the rug. He had done more than this with Elsie and been able to stop himself. But this time the woman was as heated as he. She was shaking with nerves and excitement and her breath was coming quick and shallow on his neck when he caressed and kissed and held the big swollen breast she was offering to him, like a mother to her infant. Her trembling fingers were moving all over his shoulders as he pressed her long, slender legs apart. And he stroked his finger inside her until she became slippery so that he could go into her slowly, not to hurt her. She gasped and made a little stifled cry of pain and he held back a little until she said, 'Now. Do it now. Quickly!' and went soft and weak under him. She clung on to him as he thrust himself deep into her generous enveloping body, experiencing astonishing sensations and excitement like no other, at the same time discovering his appetite for, his delight in and his great talent for indulging in what Ma and Elsie called 'the sinful lusts of the flesh'.

And when it was over Sarah wept like a woman demented; like a woman who had lost her virginity against her will. He held her close, tenderly. He kissed her tear-stained face and told her that it was his first time. Making love to her was the most marvellous thing that had ever happened to him. He did not think he could survive their being parted, for already he was thinking of next time. And please would she stop crying and kiss him because he wanted her again.

She stopped crying at once. She loved him, of course. But did he love her? Was she not a foolish virgin? Had she not made a cheap, silly fool of herself? He kissed her passionately. There was nothing cheap or silly about her. Nor – and he smiled as he said this – was she a virgin any longer. If not here, now, again, could he see her the following night? And the next?

It was no surprise when her father demanded of his commanding officer that Lieutenant Chancellor be given leave to wed. They were married by special licence three weeks later, the week before he embarked for Gallipoli. He would be away for almost two years. It would be 1916 before he set eyes on their son.

And here, in the hills above Bollington, almost ten years later, all this reminiscing about Sarah and his first sexual experience was making him hot and hard and impatient for Elsie. Where the hell was she?

Chapter Three

The drystone wall was high where the lane dropped. Elsie could not see over it, and red-faced and breathless, she ran the last yards to the lane end. The bright-red Alvis was there, facing downhill towards Bollington with the engine running.

He leaned over to open the door. 'You're hot and bothered! Hop in the back,' he said. The cleft in his chin went deeper and his hazel eyes were blazing with love for her. He was rugged and virile and as she hauled herself up, Elsie's heart was hammering.

She lifted her skirt above her knees and clambered in. 'Sorry I kept you waiting. Our Lil didn't want me to leave.' She had to cock one leg over the long front seat to get into the back and when she was straddled with one toe on the narrow back seat she heard him chuckle, felt his hand sliding inside her thigh until his fingers touched the soft skin above her stocking tops. Shuddering pleasure took hold of her as her insides went weak with need of him. 'Stop! Don't you get enough?' she teased as she dragged her leg over the top and dropped lightly on to the seat.

'I can't. I can't get enough of you.' He roared with laughter, pushed the long gear lever and released the handbrake. The great lumbering vehicle rolled down the hill. 'Where to, love?'

'Anywhere. I've brought a picnic. Have you a corkscrew?'

He laughed. 'Don't ask such questions. You'll get a rude answer.'

'Never mind the rude answer,' she said, as if it were some clever quip. 'You know what I meant.' But his humour lifted her out of herself, cheered her as much as a bottle of sherry. 'Where are we?'

'Palmerston Street. I'll stop in Flash Lane.'

She saw his capable hands on the wheel, those hands that fired and mastered her body as no other man could. She had tried to feel for others what she felt for Frank. She attracted suitors easily, and when Frank had cut the ground from under her feet ten years ago – when he had shocked everyone by marrying Sarah – she had gone a bit wild. She could not bear to think about the time Frank had deserted her. Even when she drank too much to deaden the pain, it flooded back.

Yet it was not desertion – she had simply taken it for granted that the years and years of being first friends, then sweethearts would naturally lead to marriage. She turned down John Hammond because she expected Frank's proposal. At that time John Hammond followed her everywhere – invited her to look over his mill – as if to say 'This could be yours if you marry me.' John Hammond used to call at Lindow, to ask her parents, 'Would you and Elsie like to go out for an afternoon's motoring?' She was twenty then, ingenuous, and she never suspected his intentions, though John asked her to Archerfield on any pretext. 'Will you help me look at the silk pattern swatches and choose the curtains for the music room?' he'd ask one day; 'Would you like to see the new bathrooms we've had installed?' he'd say the next. He was a photographer. Would she pose? She did those things. She was not shocked at John's suggestion that she pose nude. She had no self-consciousness about her body but she refused to take all her clothes off in front of a camera. However, she giggled a lot and at last went halfway – stripped to the waist, she allowed him drape her in a diaphanous silk, and stood for ages while he posed her this way and that and studied her until he got the light, the angles and the focus right. How naive she'd been not to have expected John's proposal, that came when Frank was away in training at Eaton. She refused him. She turned down the richest, most handsome man for miles around – the 'catch' of Cheshire. She was saving herself for Frank.

Now she studied the back of Frank's head where his strong black hair, all curly and untamed, met in a point at his neck.

'Are you too hot in there?' He glanced quickly at her. His eyes went swiftly over her and he made a great indrawing of breath as he faced the road again. 'Phew, Elsie. I'm hot under the collar. Where do you want to go?' He bounced his hands impatiently on the wheel.

'Jordangate?' she suggested.

'It's all right by me, love, but nobody would believe I came for the rent on Barnaby Sunday. How about that riverman's hut by the Bollin? There's nobody left in town. We can walk down separately.'

'It's a bit dirty.'

'I'll take my coat off. Play Walter Raleigh.' he laughed at his own joke. 'There's a rug in the back.' He stopped at Flash Lane and helped her into the front. 'Come on. Quick,' he said. He left one hand on her thigh and placed the other about her shoulder. 'Give us a kiss.'

Desire came burning through her, blinding her to sense, to virtue, to everything she'd been brought up to be – blinding her to everything but this unquenchable thirst. Elsie put her hands about his strong neck, smelled his rough male smell, and the flame burned faster as his mouth came down hard, bruising on hers. Then she drew back and playfully pushed him away. 'Hurry, Frank. We don't want to be all afternoon.'

'I do.' He grinned. 'I'll drop you off. You take the picnic and walk down the footpath. I'll follow in five minutes with the rug.'

She did not speak until he stopped the Alvis. Then she hopped down to the pavement and said, loud enough for a bystander to hear, had there been one, 'Thanks for the lift, Mr Chancellor!' and down the shady sloping path she went, through the ferns, her heels slipping on the rough stones. In five minutes' time they would be together and she would possess him completely. He was the most virile, sensuous man God had ever created and he was hers. Had it not been for his one mistake, he'd be her husband today.

There was nobody about on the way down to the river, but she picked some late bluebells and mayflowers in case anyone saw her. The hut was dark and cool when she reached it, and she waited, heart beating faster, for his footstep until he came crashing down the path, whistling like a man without a care in the world. Then he closed the door behind him and threw the rug on to the floor for her while he wedged a piece of wood under the catch so they'd not be distrubed.

Elsie laid out the rug and unfastened her blouse. She shrugged it off her shoulders and removed her camisole, aware of his eyes on her, pleased that the sight of her exposed breasts excited him. He loved her breasts. He often said, to make her laugh, that her breasts were his fixation – because he had never recovered from the shock of being weaned. Elsie now looked at him through narrowed, vivid blue eyes and put her hands out, inviting him.

He knelt before her and lifted her skirt until the pleats were folding all about his strong arms, and his hands were deft as he undid her suspenders and the button at the waist of her French knickers and let them fall. And his hands were sweeping round her thighs under the skirt and his face was nuzzling into the livid, gathered hysterectomy weal that he called her 'battle scar' as she swiftly unfastened the petersham band of her skirt and let everything go tumbling down until she wore only stockings.

She was trembling from head to foot as she rolled down the stockings and slipped them off, while Frank stood up and took off his own clothes. The scent of the bluebells, discarded and loose on the rug, was heavy in the dusty hut. He was ready for her; a fine, big man, powerfully built, with a smooth tanned chest, strong arms that could hold her shaking body, control, pleasure and eventually still her.

'Come here,' he said and reached out for her. Then they were lying on the rug, and his hands were on her hips and his lips on her breast, gently, wet and tugging as he stroked and teased until she moaned and felt herself running inside like liquid fire.

Easily he rolled her on to her back and pushed her legs apart, and in a voice that sounded rough said, 'Hold me, Elsie. Hold me . . .'

She held him gently as he pushed into her, and his face was damp with sweat, rubbing into her neck, going from her mouth to her breast again until she was crying out softly, guiding him in as he slid inside her and filled all the narrow tube of her. Then she wound her legs about him and felt him moving deep inside her as her muscles contracted, pulling him higher and deeper. He made a hoarse sound and clamped his hands about her waist and held her fast, his head up a little, holding himself back, watching her lovely face with the silky eyebrows drawing together; heard her cries of pleasure as he went harder into her; grunted a litle with the effort to control himself until he felt her tightening on him, grasping him inside; felt her involuntary movements and heard her breath speeding up until she was calling, 'Oh, Frank ...' and softly whimpering. She was almost there.

And then he let his weight down on her and covered her mouth with his own and went faster, spending himself, taking her with him as he gave a loud cry of delight in her and in himself and the oneness that he made of their bodies. At the height of her pleasure she called out, 'Oh God! Oh my God!' as they went flowing together, he running hard and deep into her and down ... down ... until it was over.

And he lay, heavy on her, for a little time before he eased out of her, looked into her face and laughed softly. 'That was the best one yet, Elsie.' He waited for her reply, and when none came, 'That was for you. We'll do it my way after our picnic. Put your clothes on. Let us go down to the river.'

She got up, put on her skirt and blouse and picked up the picnic bag, and hand in hand they went down to the little patch of grass where they could dangle bare feet or wade out, knee deep where watercress waved under the surface of the fast-flowing River Bollin. Today, with the mills closed, the river was crystal clear. Frank put down the rug and they sat watching the river swirling around the stones that had mossy caps where they stood proud of the water, until suddenly he said, 'Elsie! Look! Over there. Dragonflies.'

He pointed to the far bank and she saw dozens of them; long metallic-blue bodies with double transparent moonstone wings beating as they hovered and swooped over the water. She said, 'I've never seen them before. Are they only out in June?' Frank loved the natural world as she did. But he was clever. There was nothing he didn't know.

'They have just come out of the beetle stage and are feeding on insects,' he said. 'You won't see them go into the water but they lay their eggs on the surface in the little still pools by the bank.'

'They were beetles?' Impulsively she kissed his face.

'An hour ago.' He took her hand. His expression was boyish,

eager to impress and teach. 'It's an amazing natural change,' he said. 'You only see them when the sun shines, but they last for weeks, months in their aerial stage.' He smiled and quoted Tennyson to her:

Today I saw the dragon-fly
Come from the wells where he did lie.
An inner impulse rent the veil
Of his old husk; from head to tail
Came out clear plates of sapphire mail.
He dried his wings: like gauze they grew;
Through crofts and pastures wet with dew
A living flash of light he flew . . .

He was a complicated man. She would never know him completely. He'd hold her, look deep into her eyes and sing or recite Shakespeare or poetry after they made love. Elsie wished she knew what he expected from her in response. She knew so little, he so much. She said, 'You'll overtax your brain. Learning all that stuff by heart.'

He was surprised. 'Don't you like poetry?'

'I love to hear you recite,' she said. 'I like poetry. I write poems.'

'Show them to me?'

'No.'

'Why not?'

There was a catch in her voice. 'They are about you. That's why!'

'Oh, hell!' He was silent for a few moments and his expression was thoughtful, troubled. He said, 'Don't set too much store by me, Elsie. I'm weak. Not a good man.'

'To me you are.' She couldn't pretend to flippancy any longer. 'I wish we were married.'

She had annoyed him. His face went dark and there was a hardness in his voice. 'I'm married to Sarah.'

Elsie said in a soft voice, 'If you were not married to Sarah . . . you'd have married me?'

'I can never get divorced.'

'People do,' she said.

'Not if they want to live here, succeed. I want to make things happen.'

War had changed him. He had come back angry – about the war, and the fighting men who returned to find untilled fields and empty factories and the money men who had taken over in their absence. The money men were giving the orders now, offering low wages, saying, 'Take it or leave it.' Frank came back from the war wanting to change the world.

Elsie said, 'What can you do?'

'A lot. I won't have my name brought low, paying low wages, getting a bad reputation. I want to make the name of Chancellor respected.'

'And associating with me would ruin your chances?'

'Not you. Anyone. I've a lot to do. I'm treasurer of two charities.'

'Why do you do all this charity work?' she said.

He went quiet for a few moments, then, 'I have done wrong by you, Elsie. I can't marry you. The charity work is my way of making up.'

She said, 'Charity begins at home, Frank.'

They were both silent. Then he said seriously, 'It was wrong, but you knew what you were doing when you got into this. I said I don't love Sarah. But I never lied. I never pretended I'd be free to marry you.'

It was true. She had gone into this love affair with her eyes wide open when he was twenty-three and had been fighting a war for two years. Her father found her a place in a church hostel in Macclesfield and she left Lindow with her parents' blessing to do war work, making soldiers' shirts. She'd shared a room with Minnie Cox, who went on to marry Bert Grimshaw. It was exciting, being a single girl, away from her strict father's watchful eyes. Her father did not approve of display – dancing and painted women – but Elsie had painted her lips, bobbed her hair and danced with the few young men who were left and the many convalescent or on leave. Men were drawn to the girl who helped them get through the dark days. She had countless proposals from young boys who went back to the Front carrying her picture. Howard Willey-Leigh, a Manchester factory owner much older than herself wanted to marry her too.

But Elsie could not feel for any man the passion she had for Frank; try as she did to hate Frank for his treachery in making love to Sarah. And he came to her, 1916, on his first leave. He came to her in need, not in deceit, saying, 'Sarah nearly died giving birth to Ray. Another pregnancy would kill her. All she wants from me now is conversation and companionship. She wants me to accompany her everywhere, be her friend but not her lover. I can't be with a woman day and night and only want to talk! I want to be a good father. I know which side my bread is buttered. My marriage is over.'

Elsie said, 'It never was a marriage.'

'I don't know. I wasn't brought up like you. All I want to know is – do you still love me? Love me enough to...?'

She knew what he was asking. Adultery. he wanted her to break the seventh commandment. She said, 'I can't do it, Frank. It's the way I've been brought up. God will punish me. I'd be struck down if I committed adultery.'

Then he said, seriously and quietly, 'I love you, Elsie. I wouldn't ask you to go against your beliefs. But I'm the one who will be breaking commandments, not you. You can't commit adultery unless you are married. You are not.'

'Then what will I be doing...?' she whispered, for she was already in his arms, being held close to his heart.

He was hard and muscular, and she felt the power in his hands as he lifted her until their faces were close. 'You'll be my mistress ... my love ... my wife in all but name. A wanton, not an adulteress.'

Then she had gone to him; gone willingly, and discovered a depth of passion in herself and in him that she had never dreamed was possible. And he was careful so she should not find herself with child.

When he went to France, to the trenches, there was war work and other suitors – if only she could get comfort from them. But she had given herself wholly and completely to Frank. Frank was the only man she would ever love. She was being courted by Howard Willey-Leigh, a rich, older businessman, when Frank was given leave for the second time, before the last battle of that dreadful war. It was Barnaby then too – a midsummer heatwave – when he asked her to come to him. He told her that Sarah had no room in her life for him. Sarah's letters were brief and he gathered that she spent all her time at church or with their baby, Ray, and her close friends John and

Catriona Hammond. John Hammond was in hospital recovering from a leg injury. Sarah had to visit him every day because Catriona had a haemophiliac boy who could die without his mother's close attention.

Frank did not go home on that leave. He did not see Ray. He had four days' leave only and he believed that when he went back to France he would not survive another 'push'. He telephoned Elsie at the hostel, from the dock. 'I love you, Elsie,' he said. 'I can't go on without you. Will you. . . ?'

He loved her. He could not go on without her. Would she come to him? Elsie, frantic now with love for him, went down on her knees to thank God for his life before she caught the next train to London. They spent four days of bliss in a small hotel overlooking the Weald of Kent where, in midsummer, before sunrise and under the rising dog star, Lily was conceived.

Elsie wanted to conceive. If Frank were killed she'd have something of him. If he came back and found himself with two 'wives' then he would have to make a choice between herself and Sarah.

Now, with Lily five years old, Elsie was caught in the oldest trap. She loved a man who would not leave his wife. Many a marriage fell apart after the war. They could have run away when Frank came home, had he agreed. It would have been a scandal but with Frank at her side she could have borne it. Frank could not. he set his love for her and Lily, whom he called his 'precious lass', below duty to a loveless marriage.

Elsie now looked into his beloved face. 'You haven't deceived me but I can't help it. I wish you were mine.'

'I take care of you. Give you the shop rent-free. The rent book's a farce. I pay your bills, buy food and everything for you and our Lil.' He was deadly serious. 'There is nobody else. I love you and Lily. But I have nothing but love and money to offer. I need your love but I won't stand in your way if you find someone else. You've known from the start that I can never give you the name of Chancellor.'

She said nothing. She brought from her bag the packet of sandwiches and laid them on the rug. Then she took out two tin mugs and the bottle of elderberry wine. 'Open it.' She smiled, to show him he was forgiven.

She'd go on hoping for marriage though Frank might never be free. You could not choose to be divorced. Frank would have to be sued by the innocent party. Divorce was only granted on the grounds of adultery on the part of the errant husband or sometimes the wife. Neither Frank nor Sarah would go for 'Restitution of Conjugal Rights', which was the only other way out of a sham of a marriage – the only way to divorce without the charge of adultery. In Macclesfield divorced women were looked down upon, their children pitied. Sarah would not want that any more than Frank would. Elsie had to hold her head up.

She had done it so far. She went to Manchester when she was expecting Frank's child, telling everyone, even Minnie Grimshaw, that she had married her cousin. She often wondered if the Grimshaws suspected that she had never married. Elsie kept Minnie as a close friend, in case. When she came back from Manchester in widows' weeds with a babe-in-arms, everyone, including the vicious-tongued Minnie, was sorry for her. She was offered a shop and house in Jordangate by the man they called 'good old Frank Chancellor', who had recently returned from the army.

Nobody knew that she and Frank were lovers today. They had kept their secret and must go on in secret. If it should become public knowledge, she'd be known as Frank's fancy woman and Frank's ambitions for power in the town would never be realised – nor would respectability ever be hers. But one day in the future, if ever Frank were free, she knew he would marry her.

Frank gritted his teeth, making a face as he pulled out the cork. 'Your mother must have a strong arm, getting these in,' he said as it came free. 'Pass your mug!'

'She has a special tool for hammering in,' Elsie held out her mug for her mother's ruby wine that was smooth and rich as old port.

Frank threw back his head and roared with laughter. 'So have I, love. Got a special tool for hammering...! Hurry. Drink the wine. I'll show you mine in the hut, after.'

She laughed with him as she drank. They were prudish times, but to her he appeared natural and open. She had been brought up strictly, and it was a kind of small rebellion – being natural, revelling in your body. 'Wait till I'm ready, Frank. You can't have everything your own way.'

But he did. He always did – and half an hour later she was in his arms on the floor of the hut. His arm was under her head, and she lay back, eyes closed, peaceful and languid. After they had made love in 'his way', she could say anything she liked; ask him anything. 'We won't be able to do anything at weekends soon. I'll have our Lil with me.'

'Our Lil. My precious.' He had the most possessive attitude to his daughter. He smiled broadly. 'I haven't seen her this week. How is she?'

'I'm bringing her home in September. When school starts. I'd have liked a holiday this year, but . . .' She opened her eyes.

His face was inches from hers, and he said eagerly, 'I'm going to Southport next week. Come with me. We'll stay in a big hotel.'

'Don't talk daft. If anyone saw us . . .'

He laughed. 'How could they? We'd spend the week in bed!'

She pushed him away, leaned on one elbow and said, 'It's Barnaby. Take Sarah. You could be together again . . .'

He sat up and looked away. Elsie had been wanting to ask him this for a long time. She said, 'You've never told Sarah about us?'

'Of course not.'

'I couldn't bear it. . .' She was going to say 'I could never share you', but instead she added, 'I'd never be able to face her . . .'

He said, 'The fact that she comes to you for her dresses proves it. Sarah doesn't know.'

'She might have suspicions . . .'

'She would have to hear it from someone. Nobody knows.'

'You have never – in a weak moment? When you are in bed . . .?'

He did not answer at once. Then, 'You know very well that Sarah and I have separate rooms.' He spoke the truth. Why did she torment herself, thinking he lied? After another few moments he said, 'We could go to Torquay for a week if you're afraid of bumping into anyone from Macclesfield.'

She sat up and reached for her camisole. 'Take your family, Frank. I want to be with our Lil.'

'I'll only be away a week. I'll try to find a new designer if I've nothing better to do. The Macclesfield girls are all turning out the same old stuff. Paisley or little roses.'

'Pass my blouse, will you,' Elsie said, 'And now you mention it, will you let me have some of that paisley print before you go to Southport?' He gave her cloth, at cost. 'I'll order from Howard Willey-Leigh as well.' Howard would bring her buttons and belts this week.

'All right.' As he picked up her blouse, he suddenly laughed. 'You don't buy from Willey-Leigh, do you? That poor, silly old bugger?'

She'd wanted to make him jealous by mentioning Howard, and he'd seen through it. She became snippy. 'He is not a silly bugger. He is not poor. He has a huge factory in Manchester. And a big house in Southport.' She was cross with herself for rising to the bait. She never put herself into a position where Frank – or Howard, or anyone – could question her. Doing the questioning and no answering was the way to learn other's secrets and keep yours.

He had no interest in Howard Willey-Leigh. 'Sarah's taking Ray to Archerfield for a few days,' he said. 'The Hammonds can't go away from home, with little Magnus so weak.' He stared into space for a moment before saying, 'I'd take Ray on holiday, but Sarah and her father don't let him out of their sight. I've told them he'll grow up thinking the world's waiting for him.' Then he brightened. 'Still, we all want the best for him. He is a lad in a million. No man has a finer son.'

Elsie had to bite her tongue, because she did not want him to sing Ray's praises when he had barely mentioned Lily. She put her clothes on while he watched. She dared not show jealousy but could not resist saying, 'How old is he? I always forget.' She never forgot.

'Nine in August.'

'That's right. he was conceived just before Christmas the year war broke out, wasn't he?'

'Just after. I was in training that Christmas.'

'You must have it wrong, Frank. It takes nine months and a week, sometimes a bit longer . . .'

'You know very well that we had to get married.' He would soon be angry with her. 'I told you about it. Sarah and I did it in January. It was Sarah's first time. And mine. Ray was premature.'

Elsie sighed. 'He was a beautiful baby,' she said as she handed Frank his shirt, 'I saw him before you. I used to see the nurse pushing him round the park in his pram when he was only a week old.'

Elsie had made it her business to see Frank's baby and talk to the nurse – the very nurse who had been engaged for Sarah's confinement. When Frank was in Gallipoli, fighting a war, Sarah Chancellor gave birth to a lusty ten-pound baby with long fingernails you could trim down to size; the sort of baby who arrived late, not prematurely. Frank was supposedly a clever man, but men didn't know much about childbearing, and no doubt had ever crossed Frank's mind, Elsie was certain. But it did not tax the brains of a half-baked sheep to draw a conclusion from the size and weight and fingernails of Sarah's baby.

One of them was lying: Sarah to Frank, or Frank to Elsie. For herself, Elsie did not believe that Ray was Frank's child. Sarah was crazy enough to give herself as a religious favour to a man of God – and clever enough and rich enough to buy her way out of trouble. Frank had been bought by the Pilkington family, in Elsie's opinion – bought for a row of houses and shops – and he'd be sold when they had no more use for him. But she knew better than to suggest to Frank that Ray was not his own flesh and blood.

He took the shirt from her and knelt on the rug while he put his arms in. 'How will we manage? When our Lil comes to live with you?'

'Come round late at night,' she said. Frank spent three evenings a week with her. He had keys to her gate and back door. He'd go to the Swan, and when there was nobody about he'd take a short cut through an alley or an entryway. 'Come after our Lil's in bed.'

It would be better when Lily came to live with her. Frank did not see enough of the child. And it was Elsie's belief that Lily was Frank's only child. It would be better for all of them when Lily lived with her in Jordangate.

Lily was five and could not bear to think that her time at

Lindow was running out. Macclesfield was not home to her. She was taken to Mam's house at least once a week and she hated it. Mam's shop had a window on to Jordangate, filled with cards of buttons, hooks and eyes, lace and reels of cotton. Inside, on a long, polished counter, cloth samples and pattern books were heaped. There was no place for childhood's things. A thin partition separated the windowless storeroom from the shop. The living kitchen lay behind and this was the only part of the house Lily liked.

At the back of the kitchen was a damp scullery with a stone-flagged floor and a slopstone sink with a rank, sour smell where Mam and she must wash themselves as well as the pots and pans. The only big room was above the shop, full of the paraphernalia of Mam's trade; a treadle Singer, tailor's dummy, pressing table with gas ring and flat iron, long cutting table and cloth everywhere; cloth bits on the floor, stiff cloth patterns, cloth lengths on the shelf and windowsill. There was nothing in the house for her, for Lily. The promise of a friend, Doreen Grimshaw, was the only prospect that beckoned. Mam talked about Doreen a lot, saying to Nanna, 'Doreen will have green eyes in September. I've made a big fuss of Doreen over the years because I didn't have our Lil.'

And in Jordangate there was no garden, just a yard with a high, whitewashed brick wall, and behind it an alley, another wall and a ten-foot drop on to the wasteground behind Crown Street. Mam's home had dark, echoing hallways with terrible shadows that leaped up the walls as you went by with your candle. There was no cosiness, no warm clippy mats, no feather mattresses – just lumpy flock beds – at Mam's.

'Where will I sleep?' she asked Mam on her last visit to Lindow.

'Top floor.' There were two bedrooms above Mam's work-room. 'In a room of your own next to mine.'

'I want to sleep with Nanna,' she wailed. It was comforting, knowing Nanna was only a whispered call away from her feather-bed nest in the low cot under the window. Lily was always awake when Nanna came huffing and puffing up the stairs. She peeped when Nanna took off the layers of clothing; the woolly, the frock, the big white petticoat and huge cream-coloured knickers that came down to her knees, the stiff pink corset and, winter and summer, two pairs of stockings and the long knitted vests she wore night and day. Lily would watch Nanna fold her clothes carefully, put up her lovely fat arms and pull the voluminous winceyette nightdress over her head; watch her kneel at the bedside and say her prayers. When she finished praying, Lily would let out a long sigh, 'Ah-ah-ah!'

Nanna understood. She would stop before she blew out her candle and whisper, 'Are you waken, our Lil?' and Lily would slide out of bed to clamber in and snuggle down beside her warm, soft grandmother.

She'd miss those loving arms wrapped round her in the night, and she cried again, 'I want to sleep with Nanna...'

'You are too old for that,' Mam said.

She stopped crying for a second, seeing a chance to have a little of her own way. 'Can I take the piano?'

Nanna and Grandpa smiled. Mam said, 'I have no room for a piano. And you'll be here at weekends. You can play it then.'

A lump came into the back of Lily's throat. She could not bear to have no more sing-songs with Nanna. She clung on to Nanna's arm. 'Who'll sing with you when I've gone?' she cried.

Nanna had taught her all the chapel hymns, and they would sing them as loud as they could – Nanna's feet pedalling, her fingers flying and dropping so fast the little cottage piano rocked back and to.

Shall we gather at the River?
The Beau-oo-ti-ful, the Beau-oo-ti-ful, the Ri-ver.
Shall we gather at the Ri-ver,
That flows by the Throne of God.

In a powerful, piercing soprano voice, and jerking her head to help her keep time, Nanna sang the first verse, while Lily stood beside the piano and piped back,

Yes! We'll gather at the Ri-ver.
The Beau-oo-ti-ful, the Beau-oo-ti-ful, the Ri-ver.
Yes! We'll gather at the Ri-ver,
That flows by the Throne of God.

She was sobbing, and this time she could not stop. 'Who will you sing the hymns for, Nanna?'

'I'll sing for Jesus, till you come home again,' Nanna said, with tears running down her face.

Chapter Four

Before she went to Macclesfield for good, Lily wanted to say goodbye to the Hammond family. It was a cloudless day and she dressed in her best – a sprigged organdie frock, white pinafore and straw bonnet with silk rosebuds on the brim – to walk the half-mile to Archerfield House. To get there she had to pass along the driveway that ran by a brook, a tributary of the Bollin, one side overhung with rhododendrons. On the other side a low wall and grassy slope separated the carriageway from the water.

She was afraid of Magnus's mother, but she loved Mr Hammond, who had a beautiful voice and an aristocratic manner, though he was not cold or standoffish. He made every lady or girl feel unique and fascinating, and Lily adored him. She always put Mr Hammond's patrician face on God when she imagined Him.

Mr Hammond went every day to Macclesfield to attend to his mill and his bank but he was also a keen photographer, often to be seen in one of the local beauty spots on Saturday afternoons with his camera. He was a pianist as well. When he was at home Archerfield rang with his playing of popular classical pieces – the corridors alive with the music of Schubert, Chopin and Beethoven.

But what Lily admired most was that Mr Hammond was a devoted father. Once she said to Grandpa, 'I think Mr Hammond loves Sylvia and Magnus better than anyone in the world. Did my dad love me, Grandpa?' She was desperate to hear about her father. But nobody told her anything about the fair-haired young boy in the uniform of a private soldier of the

West Lancashire Regiment, whose photo and medal were the only proof she had of his ever having lived.

'If he's dead, where's his grave? Was he kind like Mr Hammond? Would he love me, do you think?'

'If he could see you, he'd love you as much as your Grandpa does.' Grandpa's eyes were bright, and it wasn't fair, asking for comparisons and making Grandpa's eyes fill with tears, so Lily did not pursue her questioning.

Sylvia and Magnus must have told everyone she was coming because before she could go round to the back entrance where the maids usually let her in, the front door was opened by the butler who led her into the drawing room, a big room filled with glowering portraits and chairs and *chaises-longues*. They were all there, Sylvia and Magnus; Mr Hammond, tall and dignified; Mrs Hammond, tall and imperious, terrifying to Lily, with a high feathered hat on her head as if she'd just come in from Doing Good.

Mrs Hammond had a fair, classical beauty but to Lily she appeared high and mighty, tall and thin, with high cheekbones in a long face and china-blue eyes like Sylvia's. Her mouth was set firm and she spoke in the strange voice which Mam said came from Edinburgh. She made her intentions known, starting her sentences with 'I insist ...' and 'I cannot allow you to ...' And Lily sensed that it was only because of Grandpa that she was allowed to play with Sylvia and Magnus. Grandpa went to see his old partner once a week, to play chess.

Lily was never asked round when the Scottish cousins came to visit or when Mrs Hammond invited other children; rich mill-owners' children. She would catch Lily as she left the house, saying, 'It's not good for Magnus to have no other friend but you, Lily. Don't come tomorrow when the Ryles boys and Ray Chancellor are here.'

Lily was proud and would not have gone to Archerfield if Mrs Hammond didn't want her but Nanna said that Mrs Hammond was not being horrible. It was just that being foreign – Scottish – she knew nothing of English snobbery. She did not know what embarrassment was, nor did she mince words or gush. Mrs Hammond devoted her life to her children.

But Lily saw that Mrs Hammond treated Nanna like an old

retainer. A maid would come running down to Lindow at breakfast, saying, 'Please, Mrs Stanway, Madam says will you please come as soon as you can?' for Nanna was wise and good-hearted and full of nature lore and country remedies. 'Magnus is not at all well. Bring the girl with you.'

Lily hated seeing Nanna spoken down to by Mrs Hammond. Mrs Hammond was a workhouse guardian and she Did Good. Perhaps that was why Nanna got flustered when Mrs Hammond asked the driver of her Daimler to stop at Lindow gates if she saw Nanna in the garden. Lily noticed it every time, heard the note of apology in Nanna's voice as Mrs Hammond questioned her. Mrs Hammond took exception to Lily's presence and would look down on her as if she were a great burden to be borne, and ask when Nanna was going to have a bit of time for herself. At other times, as now, here in their drawing room, Mrs Hammond looked right through her.

Turning away from Lily, she smiled at Magnus, 'Your little playmate is going to live in Macclesfield?'

Magnus's blue eyes were alight with happiness. 'Lily's going to school, Mama,' he said. Then, to her, 'I love you, Lily. Come back soon.'

Lily smiled in relief and took his cold, thin hand in hers.

Mr Hammond said, 'Which school, Lily?'

'Beech Lane,' she said. 'The one near Mam's shop.'

Mrs Hammond's eyebrows went high. 'Let's hope you don't turn out like the little savages who go there, then.'

Sylvia said, 'Lilies are not savage. Lilies are pure and beautiful, Mama.'

'Lily's coming back. She's coming to see me again,' said Magnus, who was becoming upset.

Lily pressed his hand gently. Mam had told Nanna not to be afraid when Mrs Hammond wore her high hat. Mrs Hammond was a 'jumped-up nobody' with a pretty face who'd set her cap for Mr Hammond. If Mam said not to be afraid, Lily was not.

At Magnus's words Mrs Hammond's expression softened. She glanced at Lily before she let her eyes go to the clock, and said, 'Is there anything else? Anything I can do for you, Lily?'

A rush of colour came to Lily's cheeks. Mrs Hammond was asking if she could do anything for her. Maybe she'd been wrong ... Lily could scarcely believe her ears. She hesitated, and Mrs Hammond repeated, 'is there anything I can do for you?'

Lily took a deep breath, let go of Magnus's hand and said in her best voice, 'Will you jump over your hat?'

'Jump?' Mrs Hammond said. Mr Hammond smiled, then tried to hide it.

Lily wanted to see Mrs Hammond go heels-over-cap. 'Mam says you can set your cap and jump up.'

There was a shocked silence. Mr Hammond began to cough and Lily saw at once, with a sick, sinking feeling in the pit of her stomach, that she'd said the wrong thing. Blushing hotly, she tried to make matters right. 'It doesn't really matter, if you are too old.'

Mrs Hammond's face was red. Furious, she rounded on poor Mr Hammond and said, 'I cannot allow this brat to play with our children, John. Don't think I am not sorry for her. I pity her. I would pity any child who had that woman for a mother ...' She drew breath again. 'There is not a chance in Hades that this girl will make a decent life for herself. She'll be just as brazen a little hussy as Elsie Stanway was.'

There were cries of, 'No, Mama!' from Magnus and Sylvia, and 'Oh, dear!' from Mr Hammond, but Lily hung her head. Her mouth was dry. She couldn't utter a word. She only half understood the significance, but Mrs Hammond said that she'd never be decent and that was a lie. She had a bath every Saturday night. Mrs Hammond pitied her. She did not want pity. But what she had said about Mam hurt most. 'Brazen', she'd said. Brazen was a bad word. Mrs Hammond had used it of Mam.

The injustice, without Mam here to speak for herself, was more than Lily could bear. She trembled with confusion and panic. She wanted to shout 'Go to blazes!' but instead she ran from the room, tripped over the carpet at the door, righted herself clumsily and looked over her shoulder to see them all staring after her. Sylvia and Magnus's faces pale and fearful.

She would not let them see her cry. Choking back tears, she fled down the long hall, shrugged off the butler's restraining hand and flung herself against the front door. He opened it and she was out – tearing down the driveway as if devils were snapping at her flying feet. Then, out of sight of the house and over the stone wall, she flung herself on to the bank beside the tumbling brook, and pressed her face into the sweet, cool grasses.

Nobody followed. It was quiet and she lay for minutes in her misery hearing nothing but the burbling water, until after a little while the feeling that she'd been unfairly treated grew very keen in her. Slowly at first, then with more conviction, there came to life a new emotion - anger - and with the anger came a need for retaliation that in future would spring up at every bad turn she endured.

Magnus started to scream when Lily left. 'Why do you hate Lily? I hate *you*, Mama!' He flung himself at his Mama in a rage.

'Darling. Magnus. Don't cry!' His Mama took hold of his arms in a panic. 'What is the matter?' she said to Sylvia, while she held Magnus as firmly as she could. 'Run upstairs for Nurse. I'm afraid he'll throw himself on to the floor and bruise.'

Sylvia gave Magnus one of her bossy looks, and at the top of her voice said, 'Stop that noise, Magnus! Stupid boy. If you bruise, you will be in bed for weeks. You will not see Lily. Or Rowena and Ian.'

'I will.' Magnus tried to pull away from Mama and throw himself on to the floor to make Mama cry. He screamed, 'Lily's going to school.'

His Mama was weeping and pleading with him. 'Cousin Ian and Rowena will be here tomorrow. Ray Chancellor's coming today. Please ... darling ... Please ...!'

John Hammond raised his voice to be heard over the din. He could not stand this screeching. Exhibitions of temper ought to be kept for the nursery. It was intolerable in the drawing room. 'Catriona!' He was horrified to find that he too was shouting. 'Let Magnus go! He's old enough to know what he's doing. You are ruining the boy. You have spoilt the day for poor Lily.'

Cationa ignored him. She crouched, hat discarded, cradling Magnus, murmuring, 'Sh ... sh ... darling. There ... there!' rocking him and stroking the blond head. 'You want to go to school, don't you?'

'I want to be with Lily.'

John's annoyance was dissolving. Catriona was calming the

child, crooning to him. 'You cannot go to school, my darling. Not until you are a much bigger boy.'

A wave of tenderness came over John, making him regret his outburst. His wife's long arms were wrapped firmly and protectively about Magnus, her head angled so that she could see her son's expression. She was an incredible woman. A tigress when her baby was in danger, and her temper belied by her looks for she had the cool beauty of Greta Garbo, their favourite actress. He was so lucky that Catriona had come into and taken charge of his life. His wife was his treasured delight.

She calmed Magnus, saying, 'You will grow out of it, my darling. The least knock and you injure yourself.'

Magnus would never grow out of haemophilia; both he and Catriona knew that. And for all his forbearing, loving nature, John would speak firmly to Catriona later. He would not tolerate histrionics.

The nurse and Sylvia came into the drawing room and the nurse put her hand out for Magnus. 'Come along, Magnus. Rest time. After that you can go upstairs and visit your grandfather. You too, Sylvia.'

When they left John said, in a reasonable voice, 'That was a dreadful thing to say to little Lily, Catriona.'

She was dry-eyed. She only cried over Magnus, and surprised that her husband had made any criticism of her, she said, 'I spoke the truth, John. That woman's child will grow up to be exactly like her mother.'

'Catriona!'

'I know! You find it impossible to break the connection because your father and Elsie Stanway's were partners.'

Her eyes were sparking. She was magnificent, strong, outspoken – and utterly lacking in tact. The only person she bowed to was Sarah Chancellor. She merely conceded to her husband. But John would not let her have the last word. Nor would he allow Elsie or her child to be denigrated. So he said, very sternly, 'That's enough. I will not witness another display of temper in my presence. Not from you, or Magnus – or anyone else.' He tried to keep displeasure on his face as he left.

'John?' Her voice was soft. 'Where are you going? I apologise, dear.'

He stopped at the door, his hand on the knob. She was irresistible. With her strong personality, she understood exactly when to appeal, when to ride roughshod over him, but their marriage was a delicate balancing act of power. He would not accept her apology. She could coax him into a better humour later. All the same, a smile softened the fine chiselled lines of his face. 'I'm going to see Dad. Afterwards, I will be in my study, if any matter arises.' he paused. 'And you, Catriona? What are your plans?'

'Sarah Chancellor,' she said. 'Sarah and Ray are coming to stay for a few days. Had you forgotten?'

He did not like to admit to her that he had indeed forgotten that Sarah was coming to stay. Again. When he thought about the one time in his life that he had behaved like a cad, and remembered that it was Sarah with whom he had behaved so badly, it was to her credit that Sarah had any time for him. Yet hardly a week went by but Sarah visited them, acting as if she had a part to play in their lives, behaving like some kind of senior wife ... Quickly he dismissed such disloyal thoughts and said, 'Sarah? Good.' Then, 'I will see them at tea. Here or in the dining room?'

'Here, John. Half past four.'

He went slowly, thoughtfully up the fine oak staircase of the house his father had built, ready to found a dynasty. Dad had expected to have more than one son. The corridors were carpeted in red Turkey-pattern Axminster, as were the three wide staircases. The eight main bedrooms, painted and papered in different floral themes, had separate dressing rooms. Dad's suite of two rooms and a newly installed bathroom were at the front of the house, over the entrance hall, far from the room he and Catriona occupied.

He tapped and heard his father's assertive voice. 'Come in.'

Dad's sitting room was sparsely furnished to make easy the passage of the great wheeled Bath chair which he was now seated in, by the window. He could walk only with the help of sticks but he was as shrewd in old age as he had been in his youth. He said in a quick, sharp voice. 'Not at work, John?'

'It's Saturday.'

'Can we afford to close on Saturdays?'

John gave the disarming look that would soothe ruffled

feathers and remove the querulous expression that he saw upon Dad's clever face. 'All the mills close at twelve on Saturdays. It's overtime after that.'

'Overtime? Never heard of it!'

'Yes, you have.'

'We should have kept to hand-loom weaving on the putting-out system. Nobody told those old weavers when they could work. There was no talk of "overtime" in the old days.' He paused, frowned and shook his head slowly as he pretended a sigh of bafflement. 'When Charlie Stanway and I started, a hand-loom weaver – working in his own home, mind – could earn three pounds a week. That would be a fortune today. He paid and housed his apprentice out of it, mind.'

John was in for an hour at least of his father's reminiscing.

' … We started employing hand-loom weavers, putting-out, Charlie and I. Went on to get our own premises. Variety! Variety of woven goods. That's why we were successful. Handkerchiefs, ties, silk twill, chenille and crêpe de Chine. Never took out more money than we needed. Unstable and hazardous, is silk. We took a big chance when we went in for buying the raw silk, spinning and weaving.' Here the old man had to stop for breath. He coughed before wheezing on, 'We kept track of every penny. You must keep the weavers working to be a success.'

'We are a success. Hammond Silks is very much in business. Many of the old mills aren't.' But John lied. The mill was barely ticking over. In 1889 Hammond Silks had had a turnover of forty thousand pounds and showed a profit of three thousand. This year, with twice the turnover, they would make a loss. It would improve. In the meantime he'd ride out the downturn, and dip into his own money rather than sack workers. he said, 'It's my birthday on Monday.'

'How old?'

'Thirty-five. Catriona is giving a little dinner for me. Her brother, Kenneth, and his children are arriving tomorrow.'

'The doctor? Will he have a look at Magnus?' Dad said.

'No. It's the usual family gathering. Magnus has been all right for months. He's looking forward to playing with his cousins.' Catriona's brother was an Edinburgh doctor who had brought up his two children alone since their mother died, and had made a spectacular job of it. Ian and Rowena were intelligent, outgoing children. It was always a treat for Sylvia and Magnus, having their cousins to stay.

Dad said, 'Where *is* Magnus?'

'Resting. He'll be along.' The old man liked to see Magnus every day.

'Is the doctor going to see to the lad's legs?'

John shook his head. 'There is nothing to be done, Dad. We hope that one day they will find a cure.' The great shadow hung over their lives, his and Catriona's. Magnus would never be a fit, healthy boy. They had asked a dozen medical opinions and the diagnosis was always haemophilia. And the outlook? 'No cure. Wait and see. He may get to adulthood without being crippled from bleeding into joints and body cavities. Nobody knows. Keep him safe. A scratch or minor injury could prove fatal.'

A black Singer motor car came rumbling up the gravel drive and both men leaned forward to watch. 'Who is it?' the old man asked.

'Sarah Chancellor. And her son.'

'Used to be Pilkington? Drives her own motor car?' Dad was offended at the idea. 'How's the printworks doing then?'

John could barely keep his face straight. 'Very well, I believe.'

'You know the man she married?'

'Yes, of course I know Frank Chancellor,' John said. 'So do you. His father was a tenant farmer at Archerfield. The Chancellor brothers have their own holdings now.'

'I remember Frank Chancellor. Cocky fellow. Struck me as a feckless sort. Has he ever done a day's work?' Dad had a crafty look.

Dad was talking this way just to provoke. John said, 'He's an exceptional man. He practically runs the printworks. Must have saved the company a fortune.'

Dad sighed. 'I once made an offer to Pilkington. Wanted to buy him out. Offered a partnership. Hammond and Pilkington! We would have been the biggest employer in Macclesfield. We could have done anything.' He gave John a sharp, knowing look. 'She was after you, son. You could have married her. Had a printworks and half a dozen healthy sons.'

'Dad! You brought Catriona and me together. I was very lucky she took me on,' John said.

Dad had been match-making when he invited Catriona and the Mackenzies to Archerfield just before John was called into the army. Catriona was a distant relative of his late mother. She had been invited to Archerfield only a week after Elsie turned him down.

'She wanted you badly enough.' Dad was reminiscing. John listened fondly as the old man went on, 'She begged me to ask her to Archerfield, to all the parties and balls.'

John smiled and said, teasing, 'Who? Catriona?'

'No. Sarah Pilkington. The religious one. Mind, she always struck me as a fanatic – a desperate girl, capable of anything. Always asking to come here. I told you.'

'Your memory is going, Dad.' He remembered the parties and balls – the evenings when he'd have given the earth to have Elsie at his side instead of the simpering girls Dad invited. Sarah was always there. They moved in the same circles and he saw Sarah everywhere he went; the tense, wet-eyed Sarah who was so plain and always ready to listen to his tales of woe. She used to say she would pray for him. Thinking this way, he shuddered again, remembering his behaviour when, tipsy, despairing, sleepless and at his lowest ebb, he had climbed into Sarah's bed and almost raped her. Thank God she'd behaved well. She could have accused him of rape. She could have found herself with child. She'd been engaged to Frank Chancellor all along.

He remembered, with a blush, how he had once, a few years ago, said to Sarah, 'Ray's a fine boy. I feel so drawn to him. You must be very proud … ' She'd had that intense, strange look on her face – and seeing it, all at once he had had a treacherous thought. He'd said, 'He's … he's not mine, is he, Sarah?' Then he'd wished he could have cut out his tongue, for she'd flushed a deep, blood red and, almost exploding with outrage at the suggestion, replied in a fierce, hissing voice, 'No. How dare you ask me …' And he'd known that she, too, wanted to forget that anything had ever happened between them.

Downstairs, Sarah and Ray were shown into the drawing room

where Catriona waited. She kissed Sarah on the cheek and ignored Ray.

Sarah said to Ray, 'Run upstairs, darling. Sylvia and Magnus will be waiting for you.' She looked, enquiring, at Catriona. 'I take it they are in the nursery?'

'Yes. Off you go, Ray,' Catriona dismissed him.

Ray was a much more advanced child than either Sylvia or Magnus, and Sarah recognised the obstinate look. His bottom lip was jutting out. He said, 'I want to play at the pond. Not in the nursery.'

Sarah glanced from Ray to Catriona. 'Why not? Is that all right?'

'Unaccompanied children are forbidden to play by the pond,' Catriona said.

'Oh! Mother!' Ray's voice rose petulantly.

Sarah put a hand on his shoulder. 'He's perfectly safe.'

'Yes. I'm sure he is. But the fish won't be.' Catriona pointed imperiously towards the door. 'Off you go. Ray. Up to the nursery.'

To Sarah's relief, for her darling adventurous boy could be just the tiniest bit difficult, Ray obeyed. Catriona closed the door behind him and said, 'So glad to have you to confide in, Sarah. John and I have had words.'

'Oh, dear!' Sarah was happy to be Catriona's confidante. 'You have upset John. How?

'I spoke the truth, Sarah.'

'You always do, dear. What did you say?' Sarah gave Catriona a look of encouragement. She was Catriona's indispensable friend.

'I said that Elsie Stanway's child will grow up to be a brazen hussy like her mother,' Catriona told her.

'Elsie Stanway?' Sarah really did not have any sympathy with Catriona on this. She said, 'What on earth made you say that?'

Catriona went to the window and looked out over the lawn for a few moments. Then, quietly, 'John wanted to marry her. He proposed to her, before he met me.'

Sarah tried to sound as if this were news to her. She walked over to the window and took Catriona's arm. 'But he changed his mind when he set eyes on you, Catriona. Don't forget that

I met John long before you ... He took one look at you, my dear – and proposed to you.'

Catriona did not at first reply, then, as if she were confessing, said, 'It was I who proposed.'

'You proposed? To a man you had only known for a week? I cannot believe my ears.'

Catriona said, 'I knew I'd been asked to Archerfield so that John could look me over. The old man had given John an ultimatum. John wanted to volunteer for the army. An heir was wanted. John was told to marry or the mill would be sold.'

Sarah said, 'Did John tell you this?'

'No. He did nothing but talk about the girl who had turned him down. It was crass and impolite. I told him so.' Catriona was working herself up into high old dudgeon. 'John introduced me to Elsie Stanway. I saw how it was.'

This brought a quick laugh from Sarah. 'For shame, Catriona. I thought better of you. You're jealous.'

'I am! That woman has never lost her hold over John. He has feelings for her. I have tried to sever connections with the Stanways but John will not hear of it. Elsie Stanway need only crook her finger to get him back.'

'I never heard such nonsense!' Sarah replied. 'Mrs Stanway is quite blameless. John had a schoolboy pash on her. It was never serious. Not at all. You are talking like a Twopenny Blue heroine.'

'John married me on the rebound,' said Catriona. 'I said, "John Hammond! Pull yourself together. Stop groaning like a lovesick calf over that cheap, brazen hussy! Unless you do I shall take the next train to Edinburgh." I said, "It's Elsie Stanway – or me. Take your pick!"'

'"Cheap, brazen hussy"?' Sarah said. 'You dared? I'm amazed ...'

'You'd have said it if you'd seen what I saw.'

'What was that?'

'You know that John is a keen photographer?'

'Yes.'

'He had a collection of disgusting photographs. Of Elsie Stanway. Naked. Well, half-naked. Disgusting.'

'Well, I never ...' Sarah could barely keep the smile off her face. 'What did you do with them?'

'I destroyed them, of course.'

So Catriona might not have married John. But – Elsie Stanway! Sarah saw Mrs Stanway as no threat at all. When John had told her he was in love with Elsie, almost nine years ago, she had dismissed the notion. The idea of John – her true spiritual love – falling for, lusting after that skinny little farmer's daughter was ridiculous. As for Catriona's jealousy, Catriona only need ask herself, could a man like John respect or want to marry a girl who would pose for photographs in the nude? Nothing Sarah had seen or heard since had altered her mind. John had never been *in love* with Elsie Stanway. He had clearly succumbed to a base desire when he'd taken the photographs. And so had Elsie. Love did not die just like that, with a snap of the fingers and a new pretty face to replace the old. What nonsense. Could Catriona not see for herself that John had fallen instantly in love with her?

Sarah could bear to think that Catriona had fulfilled John's animal needs – the base, disgusting part of marriage – and left the loftier realms of human understanding to her, to Sarah. She said, 'You are exciting yourself unnecessarily, Catriona dear. I am certain you have nothing to fear from Elsie Stanway. Nor ever had. And she is quite the best dressmaker in Macclesfield.'

Doreen Grimshaw came to the shop with her mother on a Wednesday half-closing day in early September, and Lily was on her best behaviour, keen for Doreen to like her. Doreen was taller than Lily. She had round brown eyes, not green as Mam said they were. She had thick brown hair cut in a neat, pudding-basin style.

Mrs Grimshaw said, 'I'm killing two birds with one stone, Elsie. I'll have a fitting for the mauve two-piece you're making for the Harvest Festival.' Her husband was a sidesman at the church. Mrs Grimshaw was a proud member of the Mothers' Union.

Mam led the way upstairs and the children followed her into the workroom until Mrs Grimshaw said sharply, 'Doreen and Lily! Off you go while I get undressed.'

Lily took Doreen to her top-floor bedroom where Doreen threw herself on to the bed, leaned against the slatted wood headboard and said, 'What a horrible room.'

'What's the matter?' Lily asked.

'I've been told not to tell you anything.' Doreen gave a swift glance about the shabby room. 'I've got a dressing table and a silver hairbrush. I've been christened.'

Lily said, 'Do you want to play house?' Under the window overlooking Jordangate her doll and a doll's tea service were set out for Doreen on the deep windowsill. House was Lily's favourite game, where she pretended she was Mam, pretended that Dad would be home any minute and she was making tea in their big house in the hills.

'Babies play dolls.' Doreen came to stand by the window. 'Open the window and shout out.'

'I'm not allowed.'

'Don't tell anyone.' Doreen stared hard. 'I dare you.'

Lily hesitated. 'What do I shout?'

Doreen said, 'If it's a man, shout, "How's your belly for spots?" If it's a woman, "Pull yer knickers up!"'

A shiver of fear ran through Lily. 'S'pose they tell Mam?'

'They won't know who said it. It makes me laugh when they look round.' Doreen gave a wild laugh.

'No.' Lily stood stock still. 'You do it.'

Doreen lifted her eyebrows to heaven, opened her pouting mouth wide and gave another of the staccato, mirthless laughs Lily would come to know and fear. 'You're scared. What a baby!'

'I'm not.'

'Take your clothes off, then.'

Taking your clothes off in front of strangers was brazen. Everyone knew that but Lily saw that she would have to do it, having refused Doreen's first demand. 'All right,' she said, hurriedly ripping off her best blue dress and underwear until she was stripped bare.

'My mum said you haven't any dad. She said you're different,' Doreen said. 'Turn round.'

Lily was cold, going pale blue and bumpy all over but she turned right round, only to see that Doreen was laughing.

'Fat bottom,' she said. 'Thin arms. I don't like you.' Then, before Lily could think of a reply, Doreen ran to the door, opened it and shouted, Mrs Stanway! See what Lily's doing. It's rude.'

Lily went sick to the pit of her stomach. She tried to cover herself with her hands but she was shivering with fright when Mam and Doreen's mother came dashing upstairs.

'Lily Stanway! I'm surprised at you,' Mrs Grimshaw said viciously. She said to Mam, 'What can you expect? All the same, if she were mine she'd get her bottom smacked. I'd take the strap to Doreen if she behaved like that!'

Mam stood back while Mrs Grimshaw took Doreen by the arm and dragged her down the stairs. Lily couldn't cry or speak, for terror. Mam waited until they had gone before heaving a sigh as if she had expected brazenness and without even asking 'Why?' put Lily over her knee, took off a slipper and gave her a sound whipping before leaving her to cry herself out on the bed.

Most children were beaten. They were accustomed to it and thought little of it, but Lily knew she would never get used to being struck. And on that day she cried bitter tears. If she had a dad he'd have championed her. A dad would have understood that she was not brazen, that it was all the fault of her enemy, Doreen Grimshaw.

Chapter Five

The golden years were behind her. Lily had been sheltered until she came to Macclesfield, which was noisy with roaring klaxon horns, iron-rimmed cartwheels, hooves on horse-mucked cobbles and the cries of street traders. And here, Mam had no time to amuse her.

Mam was 'fully occupied' with the succession of people who came to the stop to talk and to buy. At first it was hard, after Nanna's loving, even-tempered nature, to adjust to this vivacious Mam – and her quick changes of mood. In the mornings, before she had 'a drop', Mam would be at her best, sparkling but listening mostly, not stooping to gossip, drawing people to her like a magnet, and her customers came from far and wide. Later, when she had taken her first drink, she'd lower her standards and say things she shouldn't; gossip and tittle-tattle. She'd miss out words so Lily wouldn't understand, 'haw-hawing' and 'hem-hemming' and Lily's heart would beat fast and anxiously. Then, when the drink gave her courage, Mam would be on her high horse.

'Nobody gets the better of me,' she'd say, all hoity-toity as she set off to put someone in place – a shopkeeper or stall-holder who had given short weight, or the men in the Town Hall who sent out the rates bills to her instead of to the landlord, Mr Chancellor.

There was also a woman she crossed swords with, an unmarried woman a few years younger than herself. Nellie Plant, brought to Macclesfield in 1924 to work in the design shop at Pilkington Printers, lived in High Street, one of the good streets of Macc, whose houses had tiny gardens and iron railings in front. Nellie Plant said she had an invalid mother in Southport whom she supported. Mam did not believe this. 'Why would anyone come to Macclesfield from Southport?' she asked, in spite of its being a time when family men walked ten miles a day to seek work. But Southport, a wealthy coastal resort, was sixty miles distant so something else had brought Nellie to Pilkington's and Macclesfield, in Mam's opinion. 'Nellie Plant must have grabbed her chance of work at Pilkington's. She's probably in debt. Her creditors can't catch up with her in Macc.'

Mam went twice a week to whist drives; one in the Conservative Club, the other in the Liberal Club. Politics had nothing to do with her preferences for the whist drives. Mam was strictly Conservative, but they had a snowball and a bigger jackpot at the Liberal Club. In both places children played in a side room or stood quietly behind their parents at the card tables, and Lily saw at once that Mam and Nellie Plant were rivals. Nellie Plant was heard to say that Mam gave herself airs and was no better than anyone else. Mam would order Nellie Plant to stop 'passing comments'.

These comments, made at Pilkington's were overheard by Doreen's father and relayed back to Mam by Mrs Grimshaw. Mam had taken to the Coco Chanel fashion and looked like a rich, aloof lady, but on one occasion, after one of Nellie Plant's comments had riled her, Mam tightened her pretty mouth into a firm set not at all like a lady and went down to High Street with Lily trailing behind, to 'see to Nellie Plant, once and for all'.

Mam rattled on the brass knocker, and when Nellie Plant appeared said, 'I want a word with you.'

Nellie Plant, a pretty, fair-haired woman, plump and blowsy, had an accent that to Lily sounded exotic. To Mam it was broad Liverpool. 'Come inside, Elsie,' said Nellie. 'I don't want the neighbours to hear.'

'Certainly not!' Mam put her shoulders back and with the same set look on her face said, 'You've been telling everyone at the mill that I have men round at my house. Why wouldn't a man come to my shop, may I ask?'

Nellie put her hands on her hips and opened wide her big blue eyes. 'I said you're not short of men. They go into your house as well as your shop. Everyone says you're hot stuff!'

It was a wicked thing to say. You could not be too careful. If a woman on her own invited a man into her house, everyone talked about her. She would never hold her head up again. Women who did not mind their reputations were 'asking for it'.

Mam lowered her voice. 'How dare you! Gossiping at the mill about what I do in my own house. That's rich, coming from you.' She stepped forward. 'I'll have you summonsed, Nellie Plant. You won't get away with spreading libels and lies about me.'

Nellie gave a world-weary sigh. 'I know for a fact that Mr Hammond calls on you. Howard Willey-Leigh from Southport – that toffee-nosed twerp with a woman in every town. And Frank Chancellor comes round on half-day closing!'

This was too much. Mam went closer. Her face was now only inches from Nellie Plant's. 'He comes for his rent. He owns my shop. Same as he owns your house!'

Lily hung back, sick to the stomach in case they came to blows, hoping not to be noticed, trying to please Mam with an expression of innocent trust. Mam grabbed her hand and pulled her forward, saying, 'Isn't that right, our Lil?' then, issuing more threats of summonses, said that if she heard another comment, Nellie Plant could repeat them in court. Then Mam grabbed Lily's hand and marched out of the gate and off up High Street, with Lily running to keep up.

To Lily's surprise, once they were round the corner and into Park Lane, Mam was warm and loving, stroking her hand as they walked home, saying, 'I'm glad I've got you. You have to feel sorry for Nellie.'

Lily held tight on to Mam, 'Are you really sorry for her?'

'Yes. She won't last long. She's a rotten designer – all those clashing colours, bright reds with orange and purple – ugh! You have to be good at your job to get on at Pilkington's.' Then she was generous towards Nellie Plant, in thought if nothing else. 'She's a poor thing! Just a poor, poor woman!'

'We're poor. Aren't we, Mam?'

Lily was eight and not so afraid of Mam's moods, but she minded very much about their poverty. Mam hadn't a penny piece saved and what was worse, she didn't care. It was sinful to set store by riches, Grandpa said, but since leaving his care Lily had become a mercenary child. When anyone said they would not do a thing for love or money, she did not understand. They were the most important things in her life. Fear of debt made Lily feel ill.

She would never know the hopeless poverty Grandpa had lived with as a child, but his tales of the workhouse, the evil-tasting skilly they were given and the shame of destitution had burned deep. She'd heard Mrs Hammond telling the governess that the inmates of the workhouse loved her visits. They were delighted by the handshakes they received. Mrs Hammond only need remember a few of their names, need only ask about their health to see the delight her personal enquiries brought. Perhaps that was why Lily knew a cold dread whenever Mam said, 'People think we're well off because of the shop. I can put a good front on. We just don't have any money.'

'Nanna has,' Lily said. 'Can't she give us some?'

Mam looked at her as if she were a worm who had come out of the cracks in the flagstones. 'I'd never ask Nanna for money.'

Lily was ashamed of thinking of it, but she hated going down to Leadbetter's, the greengrocer's in Hibel Road and having to say in her most polite voice, 'Can we pay you later, Mrs Leadbetter? Will you put it on the slate till the end of the month?' It was always she who asked for credit. And as if credit were not enough, she had to ask for an orange or tomato box, so Mam could chop them with an axe in the back yard for kindling. Mam would not lower herself to ask.

It was Lily, not Mam, who ran up to Wragg's butcher stall in the Market Place when it was dark and the stalls, lit by paraffin flares, were about to close, to scramble with the poorest for something cheap – neck end of mutton or a bit of beef skirt for a stew. And she had to hide, to stay silent when the order boy from Seymour Mead's was heard coming up the entry. If Mam was in they were expected to pay, but if nobody was there he would plonk the box by the back door and then they avoided the shop until the end of the month, which was when Mam said she settled up.

And though Seymour Mead's delivered that box of groceries which they paid for at the start of the month, and the box they couldn't pay for a fortnight later, they ate badly in Jordangate and Lily learned what it was to go to bed hungry, to lie awake, feet cold, stomach rumbling. To Mam, cooking a hot meal was an effort. If she had a few coppers to spare she would send Lily running to the chip shop in Crown Street, or along Coare Street for a hot meat-and-potato pie at noon, there being no food in the house.

Lily was given a thick crust and margarine with a mug of tea for breakfast, before Mam handed her either a halfpenny or a penny to take to school – depending on how much she had – for a Ha'penny Milk or a Penny Milk and Biscuit.

There must have been some money coming in, Lily reasoned. They paid rent and sent the sheets, pillowcases and towels to the steam laundry. Mam worked hard. She was energetic. Lily never saw her sitting about in the daytime. She was constantly working, so there must have been money from her trade to buy material and stock for the shop, and to pay for sherry and port, which cost five shillings a bottle. Lily had no money box, no savings, and she saw it as a disgrace to have nothing – to be broke. Children boasted about their savings at school. Doreen Grimshaw especially. Doreen brought her Penny Bank book to show to everyone at playtime at Beech lane School, where she was the boss of the playground.

The school was a low brick building, flanked on three sides by cobbled streets and backing on to the muddy Spring Gardens, an unmade street that sloped downhill through a 'gennel' to the River Bollin and Lower Heyes Mill. The classrooms' windows had frosted glass below and plain above so they could not see out, and there was a high brick wall topped with broken glass surrounding the school. The playground was divided into two, one side for boys, one for girls, but there were other divisions, social divisions between the children. The social walls were just as difficult to breach.

At the bottom of the heap were a handful of very poor children who came from the crowded slums; frightening places of danger and foul smells where women fought and screamed abuse across courtyards shared by as many as ten two-room cottages. The children were often absent, but when they came they were hungry and would gather round a better-placed child in the playground, begging, 'Save us the core' if the child had an apple, or 'Give us a bit!' of the biscuit or the butty. They thought nothing of swearing or striking out at the children who, like Lily, had nothing to give. Some had fathers; others had none. Either they had never had them or, like her own dad, theirs had been killed in the war.

Doreen questioned them. 'Did you have a father once?'

If they said no she would tell Lily they were bastards, which meant that they were born in sin and would never go to heaven – nor would their mothers. Doreen said that bastard was swearing and she never swore. The real word was 'illy-jittie-mate'. She called all the bastards 'Illy-Jitties' behind their backs. If she said it to their faces they would have set their big brothers on to her, since they didn't have fathers.

Lily hated herself for not standing up to Doreen. Instead she said, 'I had a dad, once. Before I was born. He was a hero.' Tommy Stanway's photograph stood in the middle of their mantelshelf at Lily's request. She could prove that she'd had a dad – a hero dad.

Then Doreen demanded to see her baptismal certificate. Lily asked Mam for it and discovered that she had not been done, because in Grandpa's nonconformist chapel, baptism was carried out in adulthood.

On Tuesdays and Thursdays they were tested on the catechism by the curate, who stood in front of the assembled school and asked, 'What is your name?' All of them called out their names. 'Who gave you this name?' The answering singsong chant was 'My godfathers and godmothers in my baptism; wherein I was made a member of Christ, the child of God, and an inheritor of the Kingdom of Heaven.'

Doreen was an authority on God. She said, 'Your Mam's name was Stanway before she got married. How can you be called Lily Stanway?'

Lily explained. 'My dad, Tommy Stanway, was Mam's first cousin. That's why. I'm Lily after my dad's mother.'

On a higher plane than the rest were three children from the big houses in Tytherington, about a mile from Beech Lane. They were spoken of at school as the Posh Girls and were brought to school and collected and never played in the school yard before the bell went but stood with their mothers or grandmothers outside the high gate, speaking in soft voices.

Lily saw their expensive clothes – little coats of Harris tweed, soft kid boots and tailored dresses – and wondered why they were there at all. They could have gone to St Bride's, the paying school.

Mam said that they came to Beech Lane because the standard of teaching at their little Church of England school was second to none. She said that the girls' parents were middle-class intellectuals. Mam said over and over that she and Lily belonged to the mill-owning class and the people they met in Macclesfield were their inferiors; even the jumped-up nobodies from the big houses. But that did not stop her putting on her best voice when she spoke to these nobodies, Lily noticed. And to the delight of Mam and the fury of Doreen, Lily was the only girl from school who was ever invited to tea at the Posh Girls' houses. But though she was desperate for a friend of her own, Lily wanted one she could tuck arms and play with, all easy after school, and she was sure it was not for friendship she'd been invited.

She wanted to run free and play wild climbing and running games in their gardens, but their mothers insisted on brain-teasing games like the 'problems' they had at school. Lily wondered if they did it to try to catch her out so their girls would win. The mothers did not get angry when their daughters lost, but they would say, 'Ask Lily to tell you how she got the answer so quickly, darling.' It was condescending, the way their mothers spoke to her through their daughters. 'Thank dear Lily for the lovely flowers her mummy sent, will you, darling?' they'd say. Or, 'Shall we thank Lily for coming? Ask her to come again?'

Lily was jealous; jealous of their warm, comfortable homes, big strong toys, plentiful good food and doting mothers who didn't drink port wine or sherry every day. But worst of all, she knew an empty aching inside when she saw those girls with their daddies. These daddies read to them at night and sat on the side of their beds, telling them what was good and right and fair. Lily wanted a dad of her own; a dad who would comfort her and tell her all was well and what was good and right and fair.

When they asked, and they always did, about her parents, Lily said, 'Mother is a tailoress,' as Mam had told her to. But

Mam, Nanna and Grandpa would be shocked to know that she told lies. She had promoted her father from private Stanway to Colonel. Colonel was high up, because that was what Mr Hammond had been in the Great War.

'My daddy was a colonel,' she'd say. 'Colonel Tommy Stanway.' but it was not such a whopper, because if her father had lived, that was what he'd have been – a handsome, kindly, doting colonel who loved her and Mam.

Mam was secretive and refused to talk about her dad. She would talk about 'the memory of my dear departed husband' when she needed to freeze somebody off, but Lily knew better than to pester her. All Mam would say was that if she were married to him now they would not be living in Jordangate, worrying about who said what to whom and where, wondering where the next halfpenny would come from. They would have a bungalow. They would be middle class, and Mam would be in the Mothers' Union.

Mam knew about class – who'd come down in the world and who'd gone up – for never was there a town with so much moving up and down a place or two. You could have a foot on the slippery slope – and a reputation to match. Mam knew where they all came from. She knew where everyone stood. Standing and place depended on keeping your good name, making sure you were not the subject of gossip. Your place might change, but class was obvious and unchanging in Mam's eyes and was not demonstrated by money or morals or where you lived. 'You can always tell a lady by her clothes and her voice,' she said.

If clothes were the criterion then Mam fitted the part of a lady and Lily that of a lady's daughter. Mam made their clothes from the best materials. She put fur collars on her winter coats, wore expensive shoes to match her outfits and bought the smartest and best of the deep cloche hats that so suited her.

If voice were the deciding factor in placing your class, then Mam was not on such safe ground. Mam had two voices. One was the good English she had learned to speak at Grandpa's knee. This voice was used for the high-class clients she called real ladies, who came from far away for their dresses. The other voice, strong with the Macclesfield dialect, was used for chatting with local customers to put them at their ease and loosen their tongues. Mam alternated the accents easily. She also had a third way of speaking, overlaying the accents with a tone that was husky yet girlish, and this special voice was used when any of the three men she was on first-name terms with came to the house.

Mr Hammond called to see Mam every week. He was a director of the bank his father had built and, though he went daily to Hammond Silks, on Fridays he spent a half-day at the bank before calling in at Elsie Stanway's at three o'clock. Mam did not have a bank account but she would give cash to Mr Hammond when she had a large bill or suppliers to pay. Mr Hammond made the cheques out for her.

'It's common practice,' she told Lily. 'That's why John comes on Fridays. To see if I need a cheque making out.'

Lily never saw money changing hands but every Friday afternoon when she came in from school, Mr Hammond, in his morning suit, was sitting in the front shop on a Bentwood chair, leaning an elbow on the counter, gazing into Mam's sherry-flushed face as if she were an angel.

Lily loved Mr Hammond, who always touched her arm and patted her gently on the head and asked what she'd been doing since last time. He asked if she were top of the class and spoke in a sad voice about Magnus whose haemophilia was getting worse. Lily knew this. She saw Magnus and Sylvia every Saturday when she stayed at Nanna's. She and Magnus played house when he was well. When he was in bed Lily read books, recited and sang to him to take his mind off his pain. Magnus spent months on end in bed after some minor injury caused bleeding into his hips, knees and ankles.

For Mr Hammond Mam used her best voice. She encouraged Lily to copy her because it was only through 'talking nice' and keeping well-in with a better-off class of person that she'd be ready for the day they would 'get out of it'. Lily believed that this was why they never had the walls papered or the house painted. They would be getting out of it any day.

The second man who called on them, Lily hated. His name was Howard Willey-Leigh. He had a factory in Manchester and Mam bought fancy goods, ribbons, trimmings and cravats from him. He was tall and thin and, at forty-four, very old. He acted like a lord, boasting of his big house in Southport, the seaside town where rich Manchester mill-owners lived. He lamented that he'd been done out of an inheritance and should have been a sir. His mother's maiden name was Willey and he had added the hyphen himself to join her name to his own. Lily once said, 'I wouldn't boast about that! He's showing off! Fancy pretending to be someone! Fancy giving yourself a double-barrelled name, specially with a middle name like Willey!'

Mam flared. 'You must never be rude to my friends! Do you understand?'

'Yes,' Lily said meekly, but she would only call him Mr Leigh.

Mam, putting it on like mad, made his name sound like 'Hah-d', and this affectation annoyed Lily so much that she'd deliberately drop her aitches to deter him from coming or cause him to refuse Mam's invitation to 'Have a seat and take a cup of tea with me, Hah'd.'

She couldn't abide the way Mam behaved for Mr Leigh, looking out for the black Lanchester, painting her mouth like a fast woman, pursing her lips, primping in the glass, leaning over the counter until you could peer down the V of her blouse into the shadows. Mam would gaze up at him, licking her lips, laughing softly like a young girl at his every word.

Mam said he was handsome, but Lily thought he was ugly. His eyes drooped at the corners. He had crowded teeth – and one of his side teeth was gold that glinted and flashed. His dyed black hair was plastered slick with brilliantine that smelled sickly sweet and left comb marks like channels across his head.

Mam did not order much from him, but he spoke in an over-familiar way about 'my best customer', saying things like, 'Good little business, this. You must be rolling in money.' What Lily hated most was when, behind Mam's back, he'd catch her eye, lift his eyebrows, wink and bare his teeth in a flashing smile. It was a little thing, but she did not know what to do. She couldn't tell Mam.

Mr Leigh was ten years older than Mam and unhappily married to a very old invalid lady. He was childless, and Lily was afraid of being left alone with him because of what happened when she was nine.

She was recovering from mumps and longing for an orange once the swelling went down on her neck. She had not been able to swallow proper food for a week and Mam, worried that she might get thinner, said. 'Will you be all right if I run down to Leadbetter's for some oranges?'

'I'll sit in the shop and watch through the window,' Lily said.

Mam wrapped her in a blanket and sat her in the wooden armchair placed near the shop window, where, with the sun streaming through the lace curtain, Lily could watch the activity of Jordangate. Mam went to the door, saying, 'If Hah'd comes you'd best let him in. Nobody else, mind.'

She had been gone seconds when the Lanchester drew up. Mr Leigh tried the door. Lily got up and unfastened the catch.

'You are looking better,' he said, and his artificial manner made her flesh creep. 'Where's your mother?'

Lily never meant to encourage him. 'She's out. Shopping.' She spoke in a rare loud voice, then threw herself back into the chair.

He put down his cases, went to the door, opened it and peered up and down the street, looking for Mam. When he came back Lily spoke up again – why, she would never know. She was not bold. What made her say 'Hurry up and shut the door, will you? My body's shivering all over, waiting here.' She never said the word 'body' out loud. It was thought coarse.

He shut the door and slid the bolt. Then he drew the brown chenille curtain, hiding the sun, making the shop gloomy. Next he dragged the Bentwood forward. His face was near. She clutched the chair arms and froze.

'I'll warm you up, my Jordangate Lily.' He reached over and lifted her blanket and all, on to his knee.

She should have bitten him, fought or screamed instead of sitting there frozen with fear as he held her tight with one hand and let the other slide about, under the flannelette nightdress, feeling her bottom. then he put cold thin fingers between her legs, stroking, trying to move her thighs apart, hurting her with his knuckles and fingernails.

Why didn't she kick or bite him? Why did she start crying instead of fighting back?

At the sound of her cries he took his hands away, dumped her back on the chair and stood up. 'Stop that noise! We don't want your mother to find out what you asked me to do, do we?'

'No,' she cried. Why did he say she'd asked him to do it? She had not asked.

'We don't want your mother to know that you are an impudent little tease who asks men to do naughty things,' he said. 'We'll keep this to ourselves. Shall we, Lily?'

'Yes.' She wouldn't tell a soul, she could assure him of that. She dared not tell Mam. She wanted him to go away, leave the house and never come back. And she wanted to do the trick of the mind, force herself to forget what had happened. It worked when she wanted to remember, so it would surely help her forget. Afterwards she flinched if he came near, but she pushed it to the back of her mind and later the memory became bound up with oranges, fevers and lack of assurance with men; so different from Mam.

Lily liked Mr Hammond and hated Mr Leigh, but she was full of admiration for Mam's third man friend – Mr Chancellor. And it was clearly important to Mam that she shone for him, for Mr Chancellor owned their house and shop, the office next door and any number in Jordangate and Hibel Road. All his properties backed on to the yard and waste-ground behind Pilkington Printers. He was a good landlord, always on hand, checking his properties, keeping his buildings in good order, having running water put in and real WCs in place of the earth closets that had to be shovelled on to muck carts by the night-soil men.

Mr Chancellor was clever, quick and restless, with hazel eyes that were full of laughter. Mam said he was unhappily married but he and his wife stayed together because of their son Ray, whom the sun shone out of. Once, Lily said, 'Is that why you call him Ray?'

'What?' said Mr Chancellor.

'Your son. Ray? For the sun that shines out of him?'

He roared with laughter. 'No,' he said.

Mam said afterwards that she had been cheeky and she must never speak that way again to Mr Chancellor who was an important man in Macclesfield. He was well respected because he hated injustice and helped people. Mam also said that he was not only good-hearted and generous, he was astute. He bought and sold property. He had recently registered anonymously a trading company under which he could deal, buy property and lend money; as Mam put it, 'without all the nosy parkers in Macc knowing who's behind it'.

Mr Chancellor's brothers and his mother lived in his properties. He owned the Swan Hotel next door to the shop, for he had started to buy public houses in good positions in the town. He put managers into them and when they were closed down by the licensing justices in Crewe – and this happened regularly to Macclesfield pubs – he got as much as nine hundred pounds in compensation. And he still owned the buildings, which he could rent out.

Lily promised never to be cheeky to him again, so the next time he came for the rent and asked, 'How's our Lil?' she replied in a prim, well-mannered way, 'Very well, thank you.' Then he came back with one of his working-man sayings, 'Good lad, little 'un! and biffed her affectionately on the cheek. He always spoke to her first, she noticed, before he went on to pass a private little joke with Mam who always laughed merrily, forgetting her airs in his presence.

Lily wanted Mr Chancellor to like her and she thought he did because sometimes, when she was alone in the school holidays, he would drop by on half-closing Wednesday and ask why she was playing inside. Didn't she have a friend? 'No,' Lily answered. 'Only an enemy.'

'An enemy? At your age?' he said. 'Who is it?'

'Doreen Grimshaw.'

'Our chief clerk's daughter?' and he roared with laughter again when she nodded. 'Can't have little girls with enemies!' Every holiday Wednesday after that he gave her a silver sixpence for a bar of chocolate, a bag of toffee and an afternoon at the Picturedrome. Lily always sat in the front row and kept threepence change.

Lily also noticed that Mam was quieter than normal when Mr Chancellor brought his wife to the shop, and that Mr Chencellor was not so funny when he escorted her. Perhaps that was because in Mam's eyes Mrs Chancellor was a religious fanatic; Mam never went either to chapel or to church.

But Lily knew that secretly she'd like to be one of the select few who were in the Mothers' Union.

Sarah Chancellor looked at her husband over breakfast and gave a little cough to get his attention. They sat far apart, one at each end of the oval dining table. Bessie, the maid, was at the sideboard, putting out the dish of scrambled eggs Frank liked every morning. The girl was loitering, listening. Sarah did not want her to go rushing down to the kitchen, telling the staff that madam and the Master had had 'words' again. The servants speculated on the state of their employers' marriage, implying that the Master must have lady friends because he had no need of his religious old wife. There was no other woman in Frank's life, of course. He was not, like those in the lower classes, a demanding man. In a town like Macclesfield it would be impossible to keep infidelity, a natural source of gossip, a secret. There were no rumours, no scandals about the good name of Chancellor.

But here, in the house, the servants would see that he never came to her bed. A good man would have shared her bed without expecting favours, if only for appearances' sake. And for the sake of their son who tried to make a joke of it, saying, 'Why do you keep Dad out of your bed, Mother? I'm beginning to think you don't love him!' She never refused Frank the right to share her bed. It was he who decided they should sleep apart. Frank had done well out of marriage.

He looked over the pink pages of the *Financial Times*. 'Well?'

Sarah waited until the girl had gone before she spoke. 'I hope you've remembered,' she said. 'It's my birthday.'

'Fifty.' He smiled, then went serious again. 'Many happy returns. I have sent you a card. The post hasn't arrived.'

'A card? Is that all?' He had never bought her a present. He said she had everything she wanted, when in fact it was he who had all he wanted. He had built up quite a little empire of property. The printworks had a factory manager. Frank's work there only took up two full days of his week. And though he enjoyed his house and his way of life, he seldom spent an evening in her company. Sarah said, 'Where are you off to tonight?'

'Council meeting,' he said. 'Why?'

Frank was an alderman – a council legislator – and if he continued the way he was going, one day he'd be mayor and a justice of the peace. She said, 'I want you here tonight. I am having a dinner party.'

'Who's coming? Let me guess. John Hammond. Catriona Hammond. The Bible Society. And half the town's mill-owners.'

'And Ray.'

Frank put the paper down and went to the sideboard, dark and angry. He said, 'He's only been back at school for four weeks.'

'He won't mind.'

'I bet he won't. And it costs an arm and a leg.'

'It's not you who pays!' At great personal sacrifice, for she hated being parted from the son she had moulded to her ways, Sarah had sent her darling boy to Edinburgh, to the school John Hammond recommended; the school John wished to send Magnus to as soon as he was well.

Frank carried his plate back to the table and cast a cold eye on her. 'True.' He sat down. 'If I were paying he would be at my old school and I'd be able to keep an eye on him.'

'He's fourteen. He's had my guiding hand up to now. He doesn't need your example any longer,' she answered quickly. John Hammond said that Ray was a son to be proud of; a fine boy. Frank was hard on Ray, too demanding. Ray and Frank did not have an easy relationship though Ray admired Frank and treated him with respect. But it was not Frank's capacity for work that Ray admired. It was his free spirit. She said, 'Ray knows you don't practise what you preach. You tell him to buckle down to school work. You tell him to have respect for his mother. You don't show any.'

'My God!' Frank's face darkened. He pushed his breakfast plate away. 'You do it deliberately. Why do you want to come between me and my son?'

'Why don't you spend an evening in our company?' she said. Then, suddenly, she changed tack. 'It's Ray's half-term. I'm too busy to collect him from the station.'

'I'll meet him.' He got up from the table, leaving his food untouched. 'What are you doing that's so important?'

'How can you ask? Father's sinking.' The doctors said that Father had three months to live, at the most.

He raised his eyebrows. 'Love for your father wouldn't keep you away from Ray,' he said. 'What else are you doing?'

'I'm going to be shown round Hammond Silks.'

'I see.'

'No, you don't,' she said. 'You see nothing of my worries. You spend your time and money looking after your own. Your mother. Your brothers. Your tenants. Your property. Your – Macclesfield!'

There was cynical amusement in his eyes. 'Airing your grievances, Sarah? Let's talk about what you are up to. You were saying...? Your father wants to make sure there are no death duties to be paid, and—'

'All right!' she said harshly. 'I agree with Father. We've changed the name to Chancellor printers. Everything is in Ray's name so he comes into it when he's twenty-one, without death duties and liabilities.'

'You should be glad to pay your taxes.' His voice was rough now. 'You are not using your father's weakness to try to persuade him into a merger with Hammond Silks, are you? Your father never gave in to Old Man Hammond. He wouldn't sell. Nor would I give that old weasel the satisfaction... Anyway, silk manufacturing has been in the doldrums for a good few years. Things can't improve.'

'I'm no fool.'

He lifted his eyebrows as if he did not believe her. She would not jeopardise Ray's inheritance. It would be an act of madness, to join forces with Hammond's. Even Frank said that the printworks needed to expand to cope with all the work they had. They needed money to increase the size of the premises. They had never been so busy, printing cottons and the new cellulose fibres, as well as silk.

But she had to think of everything. She was ageing. She might die young, like her mother. What if, with her dead and her father gone, Frank then took another wife? Had more children? The printworks and all they had worked for must not be lost to Ray. Still, she was going to be with John Hammond all morning.

*

'Hello, Sarah my dear!' In his office, John greeted her with a peck on the cheek. 'So glad to see you.'

Sarah's pulse quickened. It always did. She felt like a young girl again when she was near him. 'Thank you, John dear. I am looking forward to it. I have never been inside the Hammond Silks mill.'

He put his hand out to take her overcoat and hat and place them on a chair then looked, smiling, at her for a full five seconds before saying, 'You look different. What have you done?'

She'd had her iron-grey hair hennaed and bobbed. It had taken twenty years off her, the hairdresser said. She patted her head. 'I had my hair done . . .'

He was smiling. 'Catriona will be here in half an hour. We'll wait for her. We can all go round the mill together.'

He had not remembered that it was her birthday – and he was coming to dinner tonight. She supposed all men were the same. He led her towards a seat by a small table in the window. An open book was set upon it. 'I thought you might like to have a look at this book of drawings,' he said. 'Made by the Chinese two hundred years ago.'

Then he pointed to a print on the wall; an old print of cocoon-reeling in Europe, from four hundred years back. 'Much the same methods are used today, Sarah,' he said.

He went to sit at his desk, to wait for Catriona's arrival, and she had no choice but to examine the book in which was depicted to the tiniest detail every process, from the rearing of silkworms to the woven material. This was not what she wanted. 'I had hoped to have a private talk, John,' she said. 'I need advice – about Ray.'

He looked up from his papers, surprised. 'Ray? What can I . . .'

'Nothing!' Her cheeks burned. 'It doesn't matter.' Why did she allow herself to react like this whenever he mentioned Ray? He had asked her, years ago, if he were Ray's father. She remembered how the question had affected her then; how she'd seen in a flash that unless she denied the truth she would be betraying Ray. She had tried to put the truth from her mind there and then. She'd prayed for forgiveness and after giving herself a lengthy and arduous penance had received God's pardon, in private, as a sign. God had told her, in the sign, that Ray must never be told the truth. All the same, she could not help her enormous pride in seeing Ray standing so high in John's eyes. For a reason she would never understand, she liked to think that John envied her her flawless son. And it was only right that his natural father should see that Ray was one of God's finest creations.

Ray was what the Bible called 'whole'. When Jesus cured the woman with the issue of blood, she who touched the hem of his garment, he said, 'Thy faith hath made thee whole'. Ray had not inherited the sickness that had affected John's son. Nor would he. Sarah had bought books on the inheritance of haemophilia when John's children were born. She made an amateur study of the disease. Haemophilia was never passed from father to son, it said in the books. Ray was healthy and clever and good. He was perfect.

John said. 'He has not done anything wrong, has he? Ray?'

'No,' Sarah replied. 'It's Father. He hasn't long to go . . .'

'I am sorry.'

'Don't be. He is being well cared for. He's not in pain. Father wants to secure Ray's inheritance. We need to spend what we hold on deposit. We must raise money if we can. We will expand the printworks. We don't want it all going in death duties.'

'What does your husband think?'

'We haven't asked Frank's opinion.'

'Frank runs the printworks. Is he not to benefit from all his work?'

'It sounds underhanded. Put that way.'

He was silent for a second then, lowering his voice, 'Your marriage did not turn out well?'

She found herself defending her marriage. 'Frank and I have an understanding. Frank has all he wants. He holds ten per cent of the shares. He is a director of the printworks. He has property. Frank and I are both devoted to our son and determined to see him provided for.'

'He's a grand young fellow, Sarah. Catriona and I have often said how we admire the boy. How very lucky you are to have . . .'

'It's Ray I want to talk about,' Sarah interrupted. She did not want to hear him say 'Catriona and I' again. He used to have a mind of his own. 'I want to ensure that everything possible goes to Ray. He will be the majority shareholder in the print-works. Pilkington House belongs to him.' She made light of it, saying, 'Father put the deeds of the house in his name when he was born. We are living with Ray. Not he with us.'

John said, 'I'll make an appointment for you to meet the head of the bank's stocks and securities. You could raise funds by issuing bearer bonds.'

'Thank you.'

He said sadly, 'You are a lucky woman, Sarah. Magnus may not live to twenty-one. It is Sylvia who will inherit Hammond Silks. And Sylvia has no interest whatever in the mill.'

The door to the office flew open. Catriona, in a blue woollen costume and wearing one of the new dipped-brim hats, sailed into the office. Magnus, looking frail and thin followed her with his tall, older cousin behind him. Soon the room was filled with laughter and light-hearted chatter.

'Sarah,' Catriona said as she presented the tall boy to her. 'Do you remember Ian?'

'Of course I do.' She looked at the dark-haired young man who was taller by far than anyone else in the room. 'You were a little boy the last time I saw you. We sent Ray to your school, on your Uncle John's recommendation. Have you come down on the train with Ray? Has he arrived safely?'

Ian shook her hand. 'We were met at the station by Mr Chancellor. Ray is safe,' he said.

Magnus gave a loud snorting laugh. 'I expect Ray kept them all on their toes, did he, Ian? He is a rogue – isn't he?'

Sarah was pleased that Ray was the centre of attraction outside the home as well as in. She did not like to hear Ray being referred to as a 'rogue' – but Magnus liked to be one of the boys – so she took their ragging in good part. 'Your turn will come, Magnus. When are you going to school?'

Catriona answered for him. 'Soon. We have applied for a place. Magnus has to get the go-ahead from the specialist first. Magnus and I are going to Edinburgh next week. We have found a good doctor.'

'Can't wait,' said Magnus confidently.

John said, 'Right then. Are we all going to look over the

mill?' There was a chorus of agreement and he said, 'First, to the Throwsters.'

They followed him out, into the passageway and down a flight of steps to a big damp cellar room where skips of raw silk, which Chinese and Japanese women had wound from the cocoons by hand, had been packed, lumpy and jumbled in huge brown hanks of wiry thread.

'Magnus can tell you all about it,' John said. 'He's terribly keen on the mill. He knows more than I do.'

Magnus, flushed with pleasure at being asked to do the honours, indicated the hanks with an enthusiastic sweep of his arm and explained the processes. 'It's covered in a gummy substance. And it has to be softened in vats of oil for a long time, before it goes to the girls for winding. Shall we watch the winders?'

Obediently, Sarah and everyone followed Magnus's awkward tread up more steps to machines that had revolving winding arms, like umbrella frames over which the hanks were stretched. Girls were feeding fine silk that had had the gum removed, from the hanks onto bobbins. Magnus spoke to one of the girls – she could have been no older than Magnus – saying something in her ear that brought a shy look as she said, 'This is the best stuff. It's one continuous thread, see. It goes for men's ties and ladies' scarves, for underwear, knitted stockings and fine filters.'

The tall boy, Ian, who was Magnus's cousin asked her, 'How long did it take you to learn all this?'

The girl looked up at him, blushed and said, shyly, 'Not long. Wait till you see the skilled work.'

Sarah watched Magnus and Ian closely. Ray had a much easier way with the hands at the printworks – a little casual, like Frank, she sometimes thought. But her boy was young, and eager and fine and ... She tried to concentrate on what she was seeing and not think about Ray and how he would be looking for her. She would drive him to Chester Cathedral, to the service there on Sunday. It would be a lovely treat for him. he was deeply religious, like herself.

They were at the huge whirring machines that doubled and twisted the yarn. Magnus was shouting, 'Ringspinning!' They moved on to the high speed machines that spun two or more bobbins together to put a twist on the thread. 'Uptwisting!' Magnus called. Then, 'I want to show you what we do with the rest of the silk.'

Sarah went from one great shed to another with Magnus instructing, like a teacher, at every stage. 'You wouldn't recognise this as silk, would you?' He pointed to the hard bales of gummy silk that had come from the cocoons in such short lengths that they could not be reeled by hand. Sarah saw men, in a room as hot as the tropics with air that caught at the throat, boiling this silk waste in smelly soap vats until nearly all the impurities were gone and the men took from the vats a lustrous, tangled mass of silk which they wheeled on carts to the drying ovens. Then she followed Magnus on to where this silk was passed over spiked cylinders and rollers. 'Filling Machines!' he called as they watched the fibres being combed and straightened and sent to the 'Dressing Machines!'

It was an eye-opener to Sarah. All these processes and they had not reached the weaving stage yet. Small wonder silk manufacturing had its ups and downs. So many hands had to be paid. Dad was wise not wanting to merge with this expensive business. It would not do to saddle Ray with such a big responsibility when her father died. Now, where were they going...?

Men and girl operators were leaning over an iron guard as they spread masses of fibres over huge rollers. Magnus said, 'They are taking out the first Drafts. They will go for spinning. First drafts go for the finest silk yarns. Second drafts from shorter fibres will be blended or used for cheaper yarns.'

Sarah wanted to handle the lovely soft and shining hanks. She watched women spreading the drafts through another machine and then watched girls with sharp eyesight laying the silk hanks on an underlighted glass table, picking off every tiny hair or thread that had got into the silk.

'Are you enjoying it all?' Magnus beamed with pride. 'Now, to the Spinning Sheds ...'

It was too much for Sarah. 'I think I've seen enough,' she said. 'My brain is spinning. I will have to leave. Ray will wonder where I am.'

Chapter Six

Lily had not found what she wanted: a best friend. Girls offered friendship but Doreen always ridiculed them for wanting 'Silly Lily' when they could have Doreen herself. A girl Lily particularly liked, Shirley Anderson – Shandy – had no best friend either. Doreen tried to grab Shandy for herself, so Shandy kept her distance.

And Doreen, off-hand with Lily, would suck up to Mam, flattering her, asking how she got the finger-waves into her hair, admiring Mam's clothes, Mam's ways. Mam thought Lily was being difficult, being rude to Doreen, whom she saw as a well-brought-up girl.

But Mam, under the influence of sherry, let herself go a little and now it was getting worse for she had started telling risqué stories in front of Doreen. Seeing Mam's pleasure in Doreen's flattery made Lily jealous – and knowing how Mam was about Nellie Plant, she did not dare tell her that Doreen Grimshaw passed comments about Mam behind her back, saying, 'Elsie Stanway's a case. What a scream!' A clutch of girls gathered about Doreen at school, but outside she associated with much older girls, girls of thirteen and fourteen.

Occasionally Doreen would ask Lily to play at her house, but she never did so without inviting one of the older, more interesting girls as well. Doreen looked and acted much older than her ten years and had started making up to Mollie Leadbetter, who was fourteen, very pretty and what people called 'vacant'. Mollie could not even write her name. The Leadbetters were quiet, respectable people and Mollie was the only one out of the six children born to them who had survived. Even with Mollie there – and Mollie Leadbetter hadn't a wicked thought in her simple mind – Doreen would set up one of those awful threesome games, the ones where two ganged up against the odd girl out, changing the rules until Lily would be reduced to tears and a shameful retreat home with Doreen's taunting ringing in her ears.

Soon she had worse to fear. She was afraid that Doreen would find out about Mam's weakness for the bottle. Mam's drinking was getting worse. She could not stand upright after she'd been at the sherry, and Lily hated helping her to her feet when she fell flat on her face. It worried her more and more, because Mam said she was old enough to be left in the house alone when she went to the Angel every second Friday to a meeting of the Chamber of Trade, she said. Mam came home as drunk as a sailor.

Lily was always sent early to bed; a chamber pot under the bed in case she needed to 'go' and under Mam's strict orders never to come down at night. Mam said the bogeymen would jump out at her if she tried to get downstairs, and at first this was enough to keep her in her room. But she was more afraid of being left alone in the dark than she was of bogeymen, so if she couldn't sleep she forced herself on to the landing, strained to hear Mam in the kitchen.

Sometimes she was wakened by the sound of the back gate clicking to. It had to be their gate because they had no domestic neighbours, only shops and the Swan and Mr Chancellor's property office next door. Lily would tiptoe down to the landing and hear voices, a man's voice murmuring and Mam's muffled, tipsy laughter as if someone had covered her mouth. Once or twice Mam said, loud enough for Lily to hear, 'No! Down here! I don't want to wake our Lil.'

She felt guilty. She was spying. But she stayed there or crept nearer to the bottom flight to try to find out who was with Mam. She never heard the other person speak, but after a few minutes she'd hear the fire being poked and what sounded like the table being dragged back against the wall.

Then came a rustling and Mam going, 'M-m-m... Oh! M-m-m...' before the other sounds came: the bump ... bump ... bump ... bumping, steady and rhythmic, of the fender being pushed repeatedly into the fireplace wall. This was followed after ages of thumping and bumping by a speeding-up of the sounds, faster and faster, until all at once Mam would cry out, 'Oh, love! Oh, love!' and a rapid 'Oh! Oh! Oh!' before an abandoned wailing sound that subsided slowly into her last cries of 'My God! My God!'

When it went quiet Lily would leap back up the stairs fast, because Doreen had told her about people who got in touch with heavenly spirits who banged on the table, bringing messages from beyond the grave.

When she reached the top of the stairs she'd wait on the landing until she heard the back gate close, then she'd go back to bed and say her prayers, just as she did when Mam went out to the Angel and Lily lay awake in bed in the dark, empty house.

'Oh God,' she prayed. 'Don't let anyone see her. Please God. She won't be in the public bar. She has to mind her reputation. She will be in that private room at the Angel. It's that big old pub in the Market Place, God. I will never tell another lie. I will never think bad things if you look after Mam. She has to have a bit of life. Send her home safe, God. Don't let her fall over in the street like a common drunk, will you?'

A common drunk, a woman, had been fined five pounds and her name put in the paper – for being caught drunk in the street. There were terrible goings-on in Macclesfield; the real scandals almost as bad as the rumour and gossip everyone indulged in. Cases were reported about well-known men – some owned small factories – picking up women in alehouses or out on the street in broad daylight. They gave them drink and took them to the fields and lanes in motor cars and there, in the fields, intimacy took place.

When Lily asked Mam what intimacy was, she said. 'Have you been listening to common street gossip?'

'No, Mam. Honestly,' Lily said. 'I just want to know what it means.'

'Some women will do anything for a shilling or two,' Mam said. So Lily read the paper assiduously. There had been a long-running case in the *Courier* of a girl who claimed that the owner of one of the small mills was the father of her baby. He had picked her up in his motor car two Saturday evenings running and had taken her to the bluebell woods for intimacy.

She was suing him for fifteen shillings a week for the baby's keep. The man denied it, saying that the girl had done this intimacy before, with other men. The judge said he hoped the day would soon come when paternity could be established by testing the blood, instead of having all this wrangling and waiting to see who the child looked like.

The girl got her fifteen shillings. The baby was his spitting image.

After all this reading Lily discovered that intimacy had something to do with babies, but she did not know what it was. She knew very well what 'drunk' was, though. For Mam drunk was a different person from Mam sober.

When Mam came home from the Angel she always stood at the foot of the stairs yelling, 'Our Lil. Come down here!' Lily would go downstairs to see to her and help her to bed, relieved that she was home safely but shamed at Mam's ramblings and grumblings as they struggled upstairs. Then, not content to sleep it off, Mam would stagger about her bedroom, dropping things in the darkness. She then slept for an hour before stumbling noisily downstairs to find something to eat.

Once, she came into Lily's bedroom and swayed against the door jamb. Lily started to cry. 'Don't get drunk, Mam. Don't die.'

'Die?' Mam slurred. 'Die? Who said die?'

'I have no dad,' Lily cried. 'I would have nobody if you died, Mam.'

'If I did . . .' Mam lurched nearer. 'If ever anything happens to . . .'

Lily was afraid Mam was going to fall. She jumped out of bed and slid an arm round Mam's waist. Mam leaned her weight against it and they both toppled on to the rug at the side of the bed. Mam gave her a skenny-eyed look and muttered, 'If ever . . . If anything happened to me . . . don't tell anyone. Except . . . except Mr Chancellor!'

'I will, Mam,' Lily said. 'I promise I won't tell Grandpa or Nanna.' She heaved Mam to her feet and took her back to bed. She would never tell a soul about the state Mam got into. Least of all Mr Chancellor.

The next day Mam was pale and ill. Before Lily left to catch the motor bus up to Lindow Mam said, 'About last night. I am sorry. I'll make it up to you. Do you love your Mam?'

'You know I do. I'll always love you. No matter what you do.' And Lily went off with a heavy heart that was not stilled until she had spent a few hours with Sylvia and Magnus.

Sylvia was a pupil at the Macclesfield Girls' High School but Magnus had a tutor for lessons and spent all his spare time at the mill with his father. He had not had any injuries for two years, none of the bleeding into his joints that came at the least knock and kept him confined to bed, the lower half of his body under a protective cage so that not even the sheets should touch the great purple areas of haemorrhage under his skin. It was believed that he had outgrown his haemophilia since going twice a year to Edinburgh, to receive treatment from a specialist there.

Lily told him that he was growing tall and slim and handsome, like his father. She loved to be with Sylvia and Magnus at Archerfield, but her life in Macclesfield had become one long round of fears. Doreen Grimshaw had begun to follow her about after school, spoiling every move she made towards friendship with anybody else, enticing the new friends away, making a big, showy fuss, giving them things, making Lily appear foolish when she let them see how upset she was.

Lily waited until she got home before crying, to Mam, 'Why does Doreen hate me?'

Mam said, 'She's jealous.'

'She's not!'

'Listen, Lil,' Mam said. 'Doreen's a nice girl but she wants everything you have. When I make a new coat for you, within hours Minnie Grimshaw's round here asking me to make one the same for Doreen.' She took a handkerchief and wiped Lily's eyes but she had a faint smile on her face, so Lily recoiled, cried harder and pushed Mam's hand away. Mam shrugged and stood back. 'I can only tell you, our Lil,' she said. 'She's jealous.'

'Why? What have I got? She has more than I have.'

'Like what?' Mam's voice went high with impatience.

'Like a dad!' Lily cried. 'Dads watch over their girls. All the girls say, "I'm telling my dad. He'll fix you." If I had a dad, he'd fix Doreen Grimshaw. And friends. Everyone likes her best. You do!'

Mam said, 'I don't like her better than you, you silly!'

'Don't call me silly! That's what she calls me.' Mam said nothing, and Lily asked again, 'Why does she hate me? Why is she jealous?'

Mam said, 'Because you're prettier ... because you'll go a lot farther.'

She was not all those things. She wished Mam didn't see them as better than everyone else. Lily had no dad, no best friend, they had no savings and Mam 'went in for drink' like the lowest of the low. Lily pleaded, 'Tell her not to call me Silly Lily.'

'Say, "Sticks and stones may break my bones but names will never hurt me!"'

'It's not true! Names hurt. You don't like it if Nellie Plant says things about you! Tell Doreen to stop.'

Then Mam, trying to put some iron into Lily's soul, sighed and said, 'If you don't stand up to a bully your life will be misery. Fight your own battles. Take the battle to her! Beard the lion in his den!'

Finally she understood what Mam meant.

It was December, frosty underfoot, and just as it was coming light at about half past eight – she had gone early to school to avoid Doreen – Lily had to run the gauntlet. Doreen and eight of her gang were waiting in Fowler Street, the narrow cobbled lane near school.

Doreen left the others grouped together, leaning against the wall of one of the cottages. She came forward. 'What did you say to my mother about me, Lily Stanway?'

Lily was shaking but she stood her ground. 'I said nowt!' Then she was mad with herself for saying 'nowt' just to be like the others.

Doreen curled her lip up at one side. She was taller than Lily, broader, and her thick brown pigtails hung heavy down her back. Her eyes narrowed. 'Say you're sorry!'

'Aye. Say yer sorry,' chorused her troop. They tried to be threatening, but Lily was not in the least afraid of them.

There were a few seconds of silence, and she knew, in those few moments, that if Doreen killed her she wouldn't say sorry. And knowing she would not apologise gave her soul the iron it needed. Her face was burning; she was dragging freezing foggy air into her lungs with loud rasping noises, and at the same time she was filling with a powerful energy and the knowledge that it was now or never. It was time she stood up for herself. Lily straightened her shoulders as Mam did, then went forward until her face was right up against Doreen's.

'Bugger off!' she yelled, exactly like the carter's lads. 'Bugger off, Doreen Grimshaw. Great fat bully!' There was a shocked silence as her words rang out on the still air. The onlookers drew breath as one, and then quickly let it out with long sighs of pleasure. Lily's eyes never left Doreen's face.

She was trembling with rage when Doreen slapped her hard across the face. Lily staggered backwards and fell heavily, landing winded in a pile of horse muck in the middle of the street. Her best coat was covered in it. Mam had only finished it yesterday. Now she had nothing to lose but her life. Screeching with fury, she leaped up and grabbed Doreen Grimshaw's pigtails, dragging her down to the cobbles. They were rolling, punching, kicking, screaming for what seemed like hours. Doreen was the stronger, and every blow sent Lily reeling backwards until she got her wind and charged Doreen again. Again and again she went for the girl.

She used her chapel trick to concentrate on what she had to do. 'Keep hitting her. Hold her down,' she ordered herself. 'Don't stop. Don't cry.' And she thought, right to the end, that she was losing, because she could hear Doreen's supporters shouting, 'Give it to 'er, Doreen. Go on!'

There were sharp stabbing pains in her knees, in her ribs, in her stomach. Her ankles were wrenched and her stockings torn and filthy. Her hands were grazed, stinging, smarting, but Lily fought on, holding Doreen's head, trying to bash Doreen's face into the spread-out dung on the cobbles.

Then she heard first one, then a few more urging her on – the poor boys who wore mission jerseys and police charity clogs. They had not gone into the boys' playground but were stamping and cheering for her. 'Come on, Lily!' they yelled. 'You're winning!' They must be wrong. Doreen had not begged for mercy. Doreen covered her head with her arms as Lily tried to pull her to her feet so she could hit her again, until, with blessed relief, they heard the clanging of the school bell. The fight was over. The shouting stopped. The boys' clogs went ringing on the cobbles, clattering towards the school gate. Doreen's friends ran ahead into the playground, and with grazed hands Lily bashed her clothes before slinking in after them.

Lily and Doreen were seized by their head teacher who stood over them while they washed. 'I'm ashamed of you,' she said. 'I never thought I'd see the day my two cleverest girls would behave like street urchins.'

'It wasn't me, miss,' Doreen whined. 'Lily Stanway started it. I'm telling my mother when I get home.'

'That's enough!' Miss Kirk was sharp. 'I'm going to speak to your mother – and Lily's. I will not have my pupils brawling in the street.'

Lily was in awe, like everyone else, of this terrifying authority but in spite of the fact that every bone in her body was protesting in pain, though Mam would be angry about the fight and the coat she knew, as Miss Kirk spoke, that nothing in her life would ever seem so important as having fought Doreen Grimshaw and not lost.

She'd done it. She had shown them all. When pushed too far she could prove that she was a soldier's daughter. She felt as if she'd won her dad's medal. Nobody would beat her now.

Miss Kirk said, 'I won't cane you. I'll speak to your mothers. Shake hands. Promise never to fight again.'

Doreen closed her eyes as she took Lily's hand. From now on she would be wary. She would never challenge Lily again. What Lily had not expected was that Doreen would make a pretence of friendship for her. She would say nasty things but with the 'You know me – I speak my mind' sort of preamble of one who is entitled, through closeness, to be critical.

The other surprise outcome was that Lily made a friend. Shandy – Shirley Anderson – was the nicest girl in the school. She had never belonged to anyone's gang, and now she became Lily's bosom pal.

Lily felt as if she had won not just a battle but a campaign. She would meet challenges head on now. She began to assert herself, to shout. 'Mind your own business!' and 'See if I care!' in public – on the streets – at every intrusion and insult that came her way.

*

Frank and Elsie's first quarrel came on a blustery March morning, a Wednesday half-closing day. Elsie was doing the shop window, first thing, because Frank took her to bed on Wednesday afternoons. It was risky. The three nights a week were safe because he was always round this end of town and had keys to her back door. Wednesday afternoons were different. Last week he missed bumping into Howard Willey-Leigh by a whisker. There was nothing between them, but Frank didn't like Howard.

Tackling the window would take her mind off the niggling doubts she had. Frank didn't try to teach her those highbrow things or recite poetry to her any more. She could not remember when it had stopped, but sometimes it seemed as if he wanted to provoke a quarrel, to justify a waning interest. Last night they had had a tiff – about Nellie Plant, who was still at Chancellor's though her designs were hideous. Elsie took a pail of water and a soapy cloth through to the shop and set to, trying not to dwell on last night. But it kept coming back ...

Last night, when he came in, he gave her a beery peck on the cheek and immediately pushed the table out of the way and wedged the armchair against the stair door, in case Lily came downstairs. Lily never came down at night. 'What's the hurry?' she whispered.

'Come on. Get your clothes off.' He was smiling, but he meant it. He was not patient as he used to be.

'I can't just turn it on like a tap,' she said. 'It takes a woman longer to get in the mood ...' But he pulled her towards him and kissed her roughly. He needed her. Now. She'd tell him later ...

His mouth was on hers and her body was leaping in response, as it always did. He unfastened her blouse, her skirt... His tongue was moving about hers and she was trembling as she tried to slow him down, taking her time as she took off his shirt and slid her hands round his hard, muscled back.

He did the rest, threw their clothes across the room and, holding her, sank down on to the rug. Desire was leaping, burning through both of them as he pleasured her body, making her ready until she was whimpering for him.

'My way?' he whispered.

'Yes. Oh, yes...' she said. 'Hurry...'

Sometimes 'his way' was when he made love to her sitting on a chair, she straddled across him, his hands firm on her waist, holding her where he wanted her. This time he rolled her over, pushed her legs apart and slid his hands under her to raise her hips so that, kneeling...

He gripped her hips and slowly went sliding deep and high into her, filling her, moving inside her. Then he was holding her tight, driving into her, and she could do nothing but let go ... let go... 'Oh God! Oh God!' she called out as she felt her thighs going weak and her insides moving in perfect time with him and the muffled noise of his last plundering.

Then when it was over and they lay, limp and relaxed, he propped himself up and held her against him, her back to him while he held her breasts and tenderly kissed the back of her neck – trying to rouse her again. Elsie loved it when they lay like this; relaxed after their first loving, with hours and a longer, slow-burning lovemaking ahead of them. She said, on an impulse, because lately he had been casual, 'Do you ever want to do it with anyone else, Frank?'

He gave her a playful little tweak, then he held her fast and said softly, 'What makes you think I don't?'

And there was something in the way he said it – there was challenge in him. She pulled away, sat up and faced him, and said, 'I think I would get to know if you did.'

He laughed, and she had to tell him to hush in case Lily heard them. He said, 'There'a woman of forty-five – a rich, well-kept widow-woman. And then there is that young lass who works in our design—'

'Stop!' Her peace was shattered. 'Nellie Plant! I knew all along!' He did that – made her mad. It amused him to see her rise to the bait. He put his hands over his face and she saw his shoulders shaking with laughter as he said, between bouts of stifled laughter, 'I knew it. You're jealous!'

'Of Nellie Plant? You must be mad. You'd want someone with a bit more class than Nellie Plant!'

He threw his head back. 'You're right! Nellie Plant's not my sort.'

She was getting angry. 'What is your sort?'

He put his hands on her shoulders as if they were acquaintances. 'One of my women – a hot piece – likes a bit of rough stuff . . . the common touch. . .'

One of his women? Was he trying to upset her? She was utterly faithful to him. She would be devastated if she thought he had anyone else. But he told her time and again that she was his only love. Jealousy flared, consumed her. 'Don't! How dare you say that?'

He took his hands off, and, in a swift change of mood regarded her angry face. 'Don't get possessive, Elsie. I'm not answerable to you.'

She stood up. He'd never said that she was possessive. 'You've been happy to be possessed.' She grabbed her clothes then kicked his things across the floor. 'Get dressed. Go to Nellie Plant! Go wherever you want. I'm not answerable to you, either!'

To her astonishment, for lesser tiffs had ended in endearments, loving caresses and assurances that she had nothing to fear, he dressed quickly and left without a word. That was last night. He'd be back this afternoon. He couldn't stay away – he needed what only she could give him. He had told her so. He always told the truth, and not only in the heat of passion.

She cleared the window, laid everything on the counter and was washing inside the glass when he came into the shop. 'You're early,' she said breezily, as if nothing had happened yesterday. She backed out of the window. 'It's only just gone eleven.'

He carried a long box, some kind of peace offering, and was dressed in his best suit, a navy-blue pinstripe with a white shirt and striped silk tie. He had gone to all this trouble to make up with her. 'Here,' he said. He put the box on the counter with the sheepish, apologetic look of a schoolboy.

Elsie rinsed her hands in the bucket and dried them. 'What is it?'

'A china doll. For our Lil's birthday.'

'She's a bit old for dolls. . .'

'It's an old-fashioned one. I thought she'd like it.'

She pulled the lace curtain so nobody would be able to see through to the shop. Frank edged towards the door. 'Don't stand there,' she said. 'If anyone comes in. . .'

'I can't stop, love,' he said. 'I've a lot of work to do.'

He had not dressed to please her. 'This afternoon as well?'

'Yes. I'm going down to the PA.'

'The where?'

'Public Assistance. There's a man in charge who's going power-crazy, refusing genuine claims. You'd think it was his money.'

Elsie hadn't much time for others' hard-luck stories. She said, 'Friday then. It's our Lil's birthday.' Lily had drawn and coloured a few invitation cards. She had given one to Frank and asked him to come to tea on her eleventh birthday which fell on the Friday after Easter, rent-collecting day. Frank liked to take Ray rent-collecting with him, when the boy was at home. Lily had written on his card, 'You can bring Ray.' Lily had never met Ray but she had seen him, out with his mother or father.

Frank said, 'I've told you before. We can't let them grow up together as we did. They might fall in love.'

'That's a poor excuse,' Elsie said. Sometimes she wanted to shake him and tell him that there was not a drop of Chancellor blood in Ray, but she would not. She was hurt. And so would Lily be. Frank was doing well – an important man now in the town. The way he was going on he'd soon be mayor and then he'd have even less time to himself. He was leaving her behind. She said, 'Isn't our Lil good enough? Is your Ray so grand he can't take a bite on Lily's birthday?'

His expression hardened. He said, 'Bolt the door. Come in the back. We have to talk.'

He went ahead and, nervous because she had never seen him so determined, she pulled the bolt on the door and followed him to the kitchen where he stood with his back to the fire. She would try to take control. 'Well?' she said. 'You haven't answered my question.'

'You don't know what it's like for me,' he said quietly. 'The big sorrow in my life is that I can't tell our Lil that I'm her father. I want to tell her but I know you're right when you say we can't burden my precious lass with our secrets. But I don't have the same feelings for Ray. You have to let a boy go. I have to protect Lily and yet I have to stand back and have no say...'

'Ha!' she interrupted. So that was what he wanted. He wanted to tell Lily he was her father. They had made a pact right at the start, that neither of them would tell Lily unless the other agreed. Now he wanted to tell so he and Lily could have a cosy little secret. Where would that leave her, Elsie? On the losing side, that was where. She gave a bitter laugh and her eyes flashed. 'I am sorry! It must be dreadful for you. Free to come and go – all the nice bits. "Here's sixpence. Spend it! Eeh! What a clever girl you are..." Let me tell you something now. Lily's better off believing she has a dead father than thinking she's our shameful secret. Why would she want to be the daughter of an adulterer?'

'Stop!' He was furious. 'I have no shame about my precious ... I love that child. I'm proud of her.'

'You are not! When I told you she was going wild – shouting across the street in a loud, common way – what did you say?'

'When was this?'

'Last week she had a street fight. With fists. And swearing. Minnie Grimshaw said Lily attacked Doreen. The head teacher came here.'

He was shocked. 'I can't have that.'

'Exactly. You are ashamed of her! You say, "Send her to elocution. Send her for music lessons, dancing lessons! Take her away from Beech lane. Send her to St Bride's!"'

He snapped. 'Well! Do it.'

'And how d'you think I feel when your precious lass calls the daughters of jumped-up nobodies, the Posh Girls? Eh? Your precious lass feels like their inferior. She didn't give the Posh Girls invitations to her birthday party. She never asks them back here for tea. *You* don't know what it's like for *me*.'

He dropped into a chair, his face pale, anger gone. 'I know what it's like for *her*, poor child. I know how it feels to be the odd one out.'

She said, 'She's envious of them. And I don't know why.'

He said, 'Take her away from there. Please. Send her to St Bride's. I don't want her to feel as I did.'

'I can't. She knows I don't have enough money.'

'I'll pay. You know that.'

'And who do I say is paying? What do I tell my mother? My father?'

'What more can I do?'

'You can come to tea on her birthday. You and your Ray. It's only an hour of your valuable time.'

He stood up. His face was set, determined. 'No. No. No.'

This was an impasse. He would not change his mind. Elsie said, 'Why?'

'How can I explain to Ray? And what's Ray going to say to his mother? "Dad took me to a child's tea party?"'

'What do you tell Sarah? How d'you explain three nights a week and Wednesday afternoons?'

'I tell Sarah nothing. She thinks I spend every night on my properties or at council meetings.'

'Then it's high time she woke up! Learned the truth!'

Her face was red. His was white as they faced one another. She wanted to apologise but she would not. The seconds ticked by. Then he relaxed, 'You aren't going to come clean. Nor am I,' he said. 'Come upstairs.'

She could not resist. He put out a hand to her and she took it and followed him to the top floor where, on her rumpled, unmade bed, he made love to her so tenderly, so sweetly, with such protestations of undying love that all her doubts were dismissed from her mind as unworthy jealousy.

Afterwards he stroked her hair and, smiling, sang to her 'Only a Bird in a Gilded Cage' until she told him to stop teasing her. He said, 'You didn't mean it, did you – that our Lil's better off not knowing I'm her father?'

Elsie had him back, though she could not explain how it had come about. So she leaned over and kissed him on the ear and tried to sound deep and mysterious. 'She can't be told,' she said. 'But it's a wise child that knows its own father.' Then, because he often quoted him, she smiled at Frank and said, 'Shakespeare.'

'Robert Greene.' Frank smiled at her. 'Fifteen eighty-nine. *Menaphon*.' There was a boyish, eager look in his eye. 'Greene lived at the same time as Shakespeare. But it was Will who paraphrased Greene when he wrote, in *The Merchant of Venice*, "It's a wise father that knows his own child."' Frank got up from the bed and fished for pencil and notebook in his jacket pocket. Then he came back and said, as he wrote it for her, '"Wise are the Children in these dayes that know their owne fathers, especially if they be begotten in Dogge daies when their mothers are frantick with love."' He tore out the page and handed it to her.

Elsie took it, read, looked up and said, 'What are dog days?'

He put an arm about her bare shoulders and brushed his mouth against her cheek. 'They are the long, hot days of summer. When the dog-star rises before the July dawn.'

Elsie turned her head so that he could kiss her mouth. 'That's how it was when our Lil...'

'And you were frantic with love,' he said, as she pulled him down on to the bed again.

Chapter Seven

Mam said, 'You're going to elocution lessons.'

'Why?' Lily suspected it was because she now spoke with two voices. Her school voice was loud, and heavily accented.

'I want you to talk nicely. So you'll marry well.'

'Is that all it's for? So I can marry someone posh?' Lily was horrified at the thought. 'I can speak properly when I want to.'

'Nobody will marry a girl who yells and shouts in the street, Lil.'

'When I marry, I'll marry a good dad. I'm going to live in a big house in the hills, and have dozens of children. And I'm going to eat delicious food. Bacon and bananas every day.'

'Then you will need to marry a rich man,' said Mam.

'No, Mam.'

But she had to go – and she hated elocution; the teacher standing at one end of her parlour listening as the other girl and Lily recited by turns, 'Be goo-ood, swee-eet ma-id. And le-et who wi-ll be clairvah!' Every inflection was false and rehearsed and made a mockery of the poem. She did want to be a good, sweet maid but she did not want to speak that way.

'Enunciate! Enunciate!' the old spinster called out as Lily tried to speak deliberately and roundly. But at the end of the one term she vowed she would not go back. She discovered that Mam was at it again – paying for her lessons by sewing for the teacher. She had recently been shamed at the dancing class. The highlight of her week was Miss Sidebottom's Saturday-morning Ballroom, Ballet and Tap for Girls class. It cost sixpence for an hour of sheer delight, practising ballet positions and partnering one another in the waltz and two-step.

They had half an hour of clattering tap-dancing, and before going home the session ended with the modern dances like the Charleston and the Black Bottom that churchmen were calling 'a return to the jungle'.

On Saturday mornings all the little girls queued in the entryway of the big house on Roe Street where the class was held. Lily never spoke to anyone because she only knew the others by sight and they were all paired off. Once inside the hallway she would be in a lather of excitement; the very sight and smell of the dancing shoes in the changing room made her heart beat faster. Gold and silver kid pumps, satin ballet slippers and red leather tap shoes with red ribbon ties were set out in rows for the children, of whom she was one, who did not bring a shoe bag with their own dance shoes.

But first she had a palm-sweating charade to go through. The girls in front of her slapped down on the hall table their sixpenny pieces or their six heavy pennies, and the lady pianist let them through. And Lily was not to put anything down because Mam 'did a bit of sewing' for Miss Sidebottom in place of payment. She would slide past the table with her head high, bright red with embarrassment, hoping nobody would see that she had no money. Then one day it was not the lady pianist at the table. When Lily reached her, the new woman demanded her name before shouting over her shoulder, so everyone could hear, 'Is it Lily Stanway who doesn't pay?'

After that, Mam said she would never embarrass her again, yet here she was making her go to elocution, up to her old tricks. Lily determined to tackle her. When she did, Mam turned the tables on her, saying, 'You are always on the want. You want to learn everything that's going. I want! I want! That's all I hear.'

'Like what? What do I ask for?' She seldom asked for anything, knowing she wouldn't get it.

'Music lessons. Swimming lessons,' Mam said. 'Only last summer, all at once walking was not good enough. You wanted a bicycle. You begged me to buy you one.'

'I was hoping. But I didn't get one.' In fact Lily prayed for one every night. Every morning she ran outside, first thing, looking down the entryway to see if God had left her bike.

Mam was sharp. 'You'll have to earn money then, for a bike.'

'I wish I could.' There was nothing she wanted more than to have enough money. 'How can I?'

It was like a red rag to a bull, arguing with Mam. Anyone would think something else was wrong with Mam and she was taking it out on Lily. Mam said, 'How? You've a cheek, our Lil! There are girls younger than you going out cleaning to fetch a bit of money into the house.'

Lily did not answer, and Mam went on, 'The world's going to the dogs. American money's worthless. A stock-market crash on Wall Street. Mills closing. People with no work!' She was red with shouting. 'We'll never get out of it at this rate! I work my fingers to the bone and you expect me to spend hard-earned money on bicycles – and dancing lessons!'

At any second Lily expected to feel the weight of Mam's hand across her legs, but she did not flinch. 'Why don't you pay me for all the sewing I do?' She spent hours at night, treadling the machine and threading needles for Mam, since the gas light was bad for Mam's eyes.

Mam's hand came up. She was going to hit her. 'I had to sew for your lessons! I am not made of money. Don't look like that!'

The coldness left Lily at once. Love for Mam flew out of her mind and, just as she had been when she fought Doreen, she burned to get her own back. She thought of a clever, sarcastic answer, put her shoulders back and stared Mam out. Then, with a sneer on her face, in a loud, flat Macclesfield accent she said, 'No money? How do you pay for yer booze at the Angel, then?' She saw the shock in Mam's eyes, but she did not stop. 'If you don't sew for booze, what do you do for it?'

There was a moment's silence before Mam smacked her over the head, harder than she had ever done. Lily overbalanced and fell to the floor. 'Don't ever question your mother,' Mam shouted. 'If it was not for you, I'd have finished up a lady.'

Lily would not put up with another minute of bullying. Not from Doreen and not from Mam. A flaring, reckless urge, a 'to hell with the consequences' impulse would come again and again to plague her, but this was only the second time in her life it had happened and she had not yet learned to recognise the loss of self-control that could make her insides boil with fury. As she scrambled to her feet, she saw the shock in Mam's eyes and heard the stinging slap as she delivered it, right across Mam's face. She loved her Mam more than anyone in the world – her own lovely, beautiful Mam. And she hit her hard and heard herself crying, 'Don't blame me for the way you've finished up! If you are a drunken fool it's not my fault! I'll never, never, never pick you up off the floor again! Next time you fall down drunk, you can stop where you lie!'

Mam's blue eyes filled with tears but she made no sound, no retaliation. She went back into the shop, in silence.

Afterwards Lily was ashamed but could not say sorry. But she could pray that Mam had not turned against her for ever, and that Mam wouldn't tell Nanna and Grandpa about it. She tried to make amends, cleaning the house from top to bottom, opening the windows to air the rooms, closing the doors when the rooms were done, then scrubbing the stairs until the varnish was all but gone.

And Mam told Nanna and Grandpa. She must have said not to say anything, but Lil saw disappointment on Grandpa's face when he took her aside and in a voice deep with disappointment said, 'It's come to something, Lil. It's come to something when a girl lifts her hand against her mother.'

Not until then had it occurred to Lily that Mam was Grandpa's first concern. He was Mam's father. Mam came first with him and always would. Lily hung her head, knowing in her heart that it was right that Grandpa was chiding her. He loved Mam best and Lily knew the awful emptiness of having no father to champion her.

A few days later Mam said, 'If you want to earn a bit of money, why don't you make up a few pairs of camiknickers? You can keep your profit once you have paid for the material.'

Lily thought for a minute. 'What should I make them in? Celanese or silk?' Celanese, a rayon material that was said to be doing the silk mills out of business, was all the rage. They printed it at Chancellor's, tiny rosebuds on peach and pink and pale green. 'Will you teach me?'

'Yes, I'll teach you to be a dressmaker, if you like.'

'Will Mr Chancellor let me have a few yards of celanese?'

Mam thought for a minute, then she laughed. 'His father-in-law is dead. Frank's in charge now. Yes. I'll ask him. I am sure he'll do it.'

He did. After he had marked up the rent book he gave Lily one of his affectionate taps on the face and said, 'Well, our Lil! You are a resourceful young lass.' Then he laughed and said, 'Good lad, little 'un! Pay me when you've sold everything.'

Lily did not want him to say 'Good lad, little 'un' any longer. She kept her face straight. 'I have two shillings,' she said. Mam's jaw dropped. Lily had been saving her milk halfpennies – hiding them behind a loose brick in the lavvy.

'I'll consider what you have.' She might have been offering to buy one of his alehouses. 'I can put down two shillings. For good faith.'

The camisole sets, in flimsier styles and materials than Mam's, were gone within two weeks and Lily paid for the material and bought, for two guineas, a lovely bicycle – shiny black all over, with a carrier on the back and a deep basket in front. And not content with one success now that she could make a little money, from that day on she always had something for sale in the shop – a pair of camiknickers with matching shift, or a nightdress and peignoir. She would put them in the window when they were done – there were hours of hand-sewn shell-edging in those sets – and within a week or two Mam would sell them. Mam kept a bit of money back, suggesting that they save it towards the day they could send her to St Bride's. Lily snorted in derision. 'I'm not going there! I love Beech Lane.'

Mr Hammond opened a savings account for her at his bank, and she gloated over the little red passbook. She was earning her own money at the age of eleven. It would be she who would save Mam and herself, get them 'out of it'. And at last she could pay for piano lessons, which she took at Lindow on a Saturday morning.

It was late November. Country men were predicting that 1930 would be the coldest winter ever, and it was bitterly cold at the back end of the year. Doreen's mother came for a fitting, and

Doreen and Lily were sent outside to the back yard.

Lily was pleased with herself because Mr Chancellor had sent an invitation. She said, 'I've been asked to Chancellor's party.'

'You're going?' Doreen said, incredulous. 'It's only for the workers' children. Why have they asked you?'

The party was an annual affair. Every year there were photographs in the paper of a line of smiling, happy children clutching gifts.

'Why shouldn't they?' Lily said with a cocky air. It was the first time she had been invited.

Doreen said, 'My dad's the chief clerk. I go every year.'

'Well?' Lily tipped her head back and looked down her nose.

Doreen's mouth was working itself into a twist, then holding. 'You'll have to sit with the orphans,' she said. 'On the bottom table.'

Lily pulled her coat tight. 'I'm not an orphan. I have a Mam.'

'But you haven't got a dad. Never did have one.'

'I did. He was a hero.'

Doreen sniffed loudly and then flung over, in the taunting way she had, 'I bet you're no good at games. Postman's knock and that.'

Lily was good at playground games. She always won at hopscotch and tenzie against a wall with a tennis ball, where you had to do twisters and bouncers and under-the-legs. She hated team games and relieve-oh. But she had not heard of this one. 'What's postman's knock?'

Doreen looked pleased by this extra proof of her ignorance. Tomorrow she would jeer, 'Silly Lily can't play postman's knock.'

'I've never played postman's knock,' Lily said. 'How d'you play?'

Doreen gave one of her sly smiles. 'They give you a number, and if a boy calls it, you have to go outside with him and kiss him on the lips.'

Lily felt heat come into her face, spreading up from her neck, bathing it a shameful red. Doreen was making it up. There would be horrible boys at the party; boys who fought with girls and pulled their hair. She had to think up a clever answer. 'I won't tell anyone my number.'

'Ha! Ha!' Doreen jeered. 'They pin the number on you when you go in. You're blushing. You great baby!'

Lily tried to appear nonchalant but – it could not be true. Could it? They couldn't make you kiss a boy – could they? 'I don't like kissing. I don't want to kiss a boy...'

'You would like it if you practised,' Doreen said, full of experience.

'I would not.' She would die of fright if a boy kissed her.

Doreen was looking far away into the distance. 'If Ray Chancellor kisses you, you'll like it.' She leaned against the wall. 'I wish he'd kiss me. I saw him kissing Mollie Leadbetter up our alley. She liked it.'

Mollie Leadbetter was only fifteen. Girls who went about with boys had to watch out or they'd get a bad name. Lily said, 'I would not like it. And I don't think Ray Chancellor *would* kiss Mollie Leadbetter.'

'He'd kiss anyone,' Doreen said. 'He says I'm pretty. I went to the mill with my dad, and when my dad wasn't looking Ray tickled me round the waist and said I was the prettiest girl in Macc.'

'I am *not* kissing anyone at the party,' Lily said.

'You'll have to. If you don't want to kiss the boys you have to tell Mr Chancellor. You can't refuse to go.'

The thought of telling Mr Chancellor that she did not want to be kissed was worse than suffering a kiss from a boy. But she was saved. Mrs Grimshaw came to the back door, calling out for Doreen.

'Isn't that right, Mam?' Doreen looked back at Lily as she sauntered towards her mother. 'You have to kiss the boys at the mill party?'

Mrs Grimshaw gave her clucking laugh, like Nanna's hens after an egg was laid. 'It's only a bit of fun. Silly girl.'

Lily had to say something before Doreen spread it all over school that she was a baby. 'I'm particular!' she shouted across to them both. 'I am particular who I kiss!'

'Well, you don't get that from your mam!' Doreen called back. 'My mam says that your mam's been kissed by every man in Macc.' She turned her head then, and began to say,

'Isn't that right...?' but Mrs Grimshaw was setting about Doreen's head and face, slapping and shouting, 'You are a wicked girl, our Doreen! I don't know who teaches you such things!' She took Doreen roughly by the shoulder and dragged her, protesting, into the house.

But Lily was spared the ordeal of the Christmas party. Mr and Mrs Hammond were giving a children's party on the very afternoon of the mill party, the Saturday before Christmas. The invitation had arrived and been accepted for her by Nanna, though neither Nanna nor Lily could have foreseen that the three young men she would fall in love with would all be at the wonderful Christmas party at Archerfield.

The day of the party was bright and sparkling with sun and frost. When it was light Lily dressed and ran down the stairs, past the kitchen door where Nanna was raking cinders from the range. The garden wall was high so, putting the toe of her boot into a crack in the wall, she heaved up, looking along the lane. The sky was pale blue, the grass at the edges of the roadway was stiff and starchy white, and through the open gateway she saw the rhododendron bushes, dark and rimed with silvery frost. The only sound was the water of the brook tumbling over its stony bed, until slowly this sound became overlaid with a growing mechanical noise. In a noisy gear a taxi cab was climbing the hill.

It reached the top and with a crashing of gears picked up speed. Lily was only a foot or two from them but none of them saw her: a man wearing a tweed cape and huge checked cap, a dark-haired young man, and a girl a little older than herself who was wearing a coat and beret of rich red tartan. On the flat luggage place sat two great trunks, fastened about with address labels and pasted-on stickers.

She ran into the kitchen. 'Nanna! I've just seen a taxi. Going to Archerfield. Full of Scotch people.'

Nanna laughed. 'Scotch is name o't'whisky. People are Scottish.'

'Are they Magnus's cousins? The ones I've never met?'

'Yes. They are here for Christmas this year. Hammonds are going to Scotland for New Year.'

Today she was going to her very first party. And she was

going to meet Rowena and Ian Mackenzie. Magnus and Sylvia had talked about their cousins for years. Lily's stomach was churning with excitement.

At two o'clock on the day of his thirteenth birthday party, Magnus stood before the washbasin in the bathroom and carefully placed a dollop of Father's brilliantine into the palm of his left hand. This was how it was done.

He glanced into the big mahogany-framed glass over the basin and, pleased with what he saw, rubbed his palms together quickly and ran sticky hands over his bland, flyaway hair. Next he rinsed his hands and took from the shelf Father's two silver-backed hairbrushes and wielded them about his head, trying to get the action right, the way he'd seen Father do it.

'OK ... OK ... OK...' he said as he laid the brushes down and carefully made a very straight parting with the tortoiseshell comb he kept in his breast pocket. Then he gave a little frown into the glass, practising his expressions. He was a man. Well, from the neck up he was. There was the misshapen ankle that the last of the knocks had left him with. But his shoes were specially made to correct the slight shortening of his left leg and the in-turned foot. He stared at his reflection and tried the sardonic smile of the hero in that romance he had read. He had asked the kitchen maid to lend him her book. The hero was blond – and he had a limp and a sardonic smile. He whistled 'Happy Days are Here Again' through his teeth as he replaced Father's brushes in exactly the same position. Then he nearly jumped out of his skin when his cousin Ian opened the door.

'Sorry!' Ian said. 'Thought it was free.'

Magnus, relieved it was not Father, said, 'Come in. I've finished.'

Ian was sixteen, taller and heavier than himself; dark-haired and, Magnus suspected, very handsome. Ian would sweep the girls off their feet, no doubt. Magnus glanced at himself again before asking, 'Has Mother told you about the parties?' There was to be one for the young ones at three thirty until half past seven, followed by an adults' dinner party with dancing.

'Yes. Great idea – a party.' Ian's voice was deep and humorous. 'Your mother says that Sylvia, Rowena and I are to go to both – the children's party and the grown-up do.'

'Not me?' Magnus felt his face redden. 'I am thirteen, dammit! Am I the only one to be left out? I am not an invalid!'

'Your mother thinks so,' Ian said. 'Seriously, you *do* have to watch it.'

Magnus gritted his teeth, determined to go downstairs and confront her. This infernal patronising of a chap! 'She knows I'm all right. I've seen the specialist in Edinburgh. Soon I'll be out of her reach. Mother won't have any say once I'm at school.'

Ian grinned and put his soap bag, shaving tackle and towels on the wicker chair. He went to the iron bath and dropped the plug plunger into the hole. The bath took ages to fill. He would need the bathroom to himself for an hour. He said, 'I agree. If you are fit enough to live with us in Edinburgh. . .'

'Exactly!' said Magnus. 'I have been pushed around by Mother.'

'Will you stand up to her?' Ian said. 'I wouldn't dare.'

'Wouldn't you? My mother? Why not?'

'I don't have your confidence,' Ian said. 'I don't remember my mother. Apart from Rowena – sisters don't count – I never know what women are thinking.' He held open the door for Magnus. 'Off you go.'

Magnus found his mother in the drawing room, supervising the placing of chairs around the cleared floor, ordering the gardeners about in an imperious voice. 'Here with the Hepplewhites, Jackson! Don't put the love seat in the alcove, Watts. Keep the far end clear for the band. Oh! Really!'

'Mother!' he shouted and saw surprise on her face as she came over. He liked surprising her. He had stopped calling her Mama, for starters. Men of his age never called their mothers Mama.

'What is it, darling?' She placed a hand gently on his shoulder. 'You *are* handsome, my pet!'

He could not remain cross with her, but he steeled himself. How could she show him up before his cousins? 'I insist,' he said, echoing her dogmatic manner, 'I am going to both parties. I am not a child.'

Mother climbed on to her high horse. 'I cannot allow—'

He interrupted her. 'I'm going. To both.'

She walked away, up the hallway to her little study. 'The servants will hear us,' she said over her shoulder. We'll talk about this in private. Follow me.'

There was muffled laughter from the staff as Magnus went, angry, to her room. He closed the door and faced her. 'Father expects me to have a social life. If I can go to Edinburgh to school...'

'It's your father's decision to send you. I wanted you to go to King's, in Macclesfield, where I can supervise...' She broke off, and concern came over her face. 'Have you *been* today? I don't think you went yesterday. Take your opening medicine if there is the slightest risk of...'

He could explode. Father never said a cross word either to Mother or to Sylvia, but it really was time he spoke up. 'I have told you, Mother. I will not have you nagging, pestering me. I am better. Don't ask, "Have you been? Done anything?"'

She made a sharp intake of breath. 'It's only because of my constant devotion that you are standing here – daring to challenge my decisions!'

'Today is my birthday. Tonight my farewell party!'

'I invited your friends to the children's party. Tonight is for adults.'

'Sylvia's one year older than me. Ray is fifteen. Ian and Rowena are fifteen and sixteen. Not much older than me.'

She hesitated, then, in a pleading voice, 'You have to rest, darling. Build your strength slowly, Magnus.'

Her tone of voice told him he had won. He filled out his chest, pulled his narrow shoulders back and stuck out his chin. 'You must accept that your son is a man. He is leaving home. And may never come back!'

He was no longer her little pet, her little invalid. He would always have to come back because he was besotted with Lily. His love for her was growing whilst that for his mother was diminishing. He had loved Lily from the first moment of his life. Bolder now, he said. 'Soon I will take over the mill. In a few years' time I will marry. Have children.'

He had gone too far. Mother said, 'I have told you, Magnus, as tactfully as possible, but very plainly. You can never be a normal man. Your last haemorrhage was into your—'

'That's enough!' He would not allow her to talk about the most personal details of his manhood. Not even to him. 'I am normal.'

She'd expect him to have his own way. He always did. She softened. 'Very well. You can go to the party.'

'Can Lily stay for the dinner and dance?'

Mother flared. 'Don't be ridiculous, Magnus.'

'You hate her, don't you?'

'I hate nobody. It's too close, that's all...'

'You don't think she is good enough for me and Sylvia?'

'I did not say that. There's nothing wrong with Lily. It's her mother I object to. Putting herself and her child beyond the pale, letting her good parents down by bringing the child up in the slums of Macclesfield!'

'Jordangate is nowhere near the slums,' he said.

'I don't want you to make so much of a childhood friendship.'

Magnus only had to listen while Mother let off steam, which she did whenever he or Sylvia mentioned Lily's Mam. 'All right, Mother,' he said. 'I'll ask for your approval of my girlfriends in future.' Then he left her study, whistling, as he went to his room to put on his whitest shirt and the new school blazer in readiness for Lily's arrival.

By three o'clock Lily was ready. Nanna had brushed her dark hair until the springy curls were softened into long, loose ringlets tied with satin ribbon and fastened with a mother-of-pearl clasp. Mam had let her buy, from her savings, a pair of Cuban-heeled dancing slippers; silvery kid with crossover straps on her high, dancer's instep. White rayon stockings, shiny and opaque, were held up by six long elastic suspenders attached to a Liberty bodice; cotton drawers lay flat, not bunched up like fleecy school knickers; a fine white petticoat over them, and on top, the most beautiful party frock.

Mam had excelled herself. The dress had gold-embroidered sleeves on a bodice of sea green foulard silk that dropped low over her narrow, childish hips before the skirt sprang out in froths of net frills upon silk flounces beneath a wide dark-green sash of satin. Over all this she would wear a white cape that had belonged to Nanna's grandmother. It was in heavy, dense velvet and both cape and deep hood were edged with white angora.

'I feel like Cinderella,' Lily said as Nanna fastened the cape ties. 'As if a fairy had waved a magic wand...'

Nanna said fondly, 'I hope you have as many parties as a young girl could wish for.' She pulled Lily close. 'It's been like old days, getting you ready. Eeh! I remember your Mam getting dressed up to go gallivanting!'

'That's enough!' Grandpa said. 'Our Lil's only young.'

Grandpa drove her to Archerfield in the trap. He was acting the gallant, saying she was his little princess and should arrive in style. 'We'll walk back,' he said. 'I will bring your overcoat and boots.' He looked splendid in the blue striped suit and black bowler he usually kept for Sundays. He wore his tweed overcoat and leather gauntlets. Though he was seventy-eight, he looked like a young man with his white hair hidden under the hat.

There were two motor cars ahead of the trap and two behind in the slow procession down the drive that curved away from the brook towards the house. There were lanterns, more than two dozen of them, strung across the semicircular stone balustrade at the front of the house. There was light enough not to need them, yet they burned and flickered in the slight breeze. Beyond them the front doors were thrown open to reveal the firelit entrance and Mr and Mrs Hammond framed in the doorway, receiving the guests.

Grandpa halted and Lily sprang down from the trap. She heard the harness jingling and hoped that everyone had seen Grandpa's shining brass on the gleaming trap. Then she was on the top step and it was her turn. Edwards, the butler, was leading Clive and Bertie Ryle, a mill-owner's sons the same age as herself, towards the drawing room. Lily put out her hand to Mrs Hammond. Mrs Hammond ignored it and called out, 'Come back, Edwards. It's only Lily Stanway. Take her as well.'

Colour burned in Lily's cheeks. Behind her, a girl giggled. Then Mr Hammond waved Edwards away and took her hand. 'All right, Lily?'

'Yes. Yes, thank you...'

'Magnus asked me to send you up to the schoolroom. He

wants you to wait with him there until everyone has arrived.'

She ran swiftly along the hallway and sped up the wide, carpeted staircase to the schoolroom that had once been a nursery. Magnus and his Scottish cousin were standing by the fireplace. Magnus, tall, gangling and with the same cool good looks as his father, towered over her. He held out both his hands. 'You look spiffing!'

Lily unfastened the neck ties and dropped the cape into his arms. 'Thanks.' She laughed to see him standing there, not knowing what to do with the thing. 'Where's Sylvia?'

He put the cape over a chair and took her hand in a proprietorial grip before turning to the other boy. 'Let me introduce my best friend – my best *girl* friend, Lily Stanway,' he said. Then, 'My cousin, Ian Mackenzie.'

She gazed into blue eyes that were level and steady. Sylvia's cousin was taller than Magnus. He had a long, aquiline nose, sleek black eyebrows and a lock of wavy black hair that fell forwards over a fine high forehead. He put out his hand, Magnus let hers go, and as Ian's firm hand enclosed hers Lily felt the strangest sensation, as if warm water were rippling up her arm.

She had learned how to behave from watching Sylvia and trying to copy her charm – not unfeeling like Mrs Hammond or bold like Mam. 'Hello,' she said without letting on that there was anything out of the ordinary in meeting him, in holding his hand. 'I saw you arriving this morning.'

He let go of her hand and the smile that transformed his serious features sent another shock through her. His teeth were strong and straight and very white against his tanned outdoor skin. His eyes crinkled, and at the sides of his mouth, deep lines creased. 'We travelled overnight,' he said in a rich, warm voice. He made an attractive curly sound when he pronounced 'travelled', as if the consonants were rolling off his tongue. 'Arrived in Manchester at six this morning and were in Macclesfield for seven.'

Magnus's voice was beginning to break. It would drop very low and gruff and he would cough to get it back. He said, 'Ian's sixteen. I'm going to his school so I expect I'll have to kow-tow to him.'

Ian said, 'We'll hardly see one another in school. At home

you will just be my cousin, as ever.'

Lily asked, 'Where's Sylvia?'

'In the drawing room,' Ian said. 'We thought it best to leave her and my sister to make the introductions.' He smiled. 'Rowena might pick up a few hints. `Fraid we are a bit plain-spoken. No English social graces.'

Magnus said, 'We'll go down in a few minutes.'

'How many are here?' she asked, looking at Ian.

'About two dozen.' Magnus tugged her arm to get her attention, to make her take notice of him.

'Anyone I know?'

Magnus recited a string of names. Lily recognised only one or two until he said, 'And Ray Chancellor.' He said it like a boast – as if one of the gods from Mount Olympus had come down and accepted his invitation.

'Won't Ray Chancellor be at the mill party?'

'Heavens, no. Wild horses wouldn't get Ray to a mill party,' Magnus said. 'He's too – too grown-up.'

'Too clever by half,' Ian said.

'Have you met Ray Chancellor?' she asked.

'He's in my house at George Watson's College,' he said coldly.

Lily was full of bubbling happiness. 'I heard he went to a famous school. Like Eton.'

Magnus took hold of her arm, talking quickly and eagerly. 'George Watson's is a much better school than Eton, Lily. And Ray...! You know Ray! Nothing but the best.'

She laughed. 'I've never even spoken to Ray Chancellor.'

Magnus took a very firm grip on her arm. 'Then you are in for a treat. All the girls fall for him.'

All except me, Lily thought. I've fallen for Ian Mackenzie.

Ian straightened his face, tightened the knot in his tie and tugged his jacket into line. 'Let's go down.' He sounded a bit nervous as he went towards the door.

Magnus whispered, 'Ian's afraid that Sylvia will catch Ray's eye.'

Suddenly Lily felt small and foolish. It was silly to think she was in love. Why were they talking of flirting and eye-catching and falling for boys and girls? Would she be as far out of her depth here as if she'd been playing postman's knock at the mill party?

Chapter Eight

Chairs were placed round the walls of the drawing room and dozens of young people – Sylvia's new friends from the high school, their brothers and sisters – were laughing and chatting easily, as if they did this every day. Lily knew a momentary panic. Did these young people all live in grand houses like Archerfield? Were there other families who provided as the Hammonds did for their children? Were the others used to this? Then Ian's tall, dark-haired sister Rowena was at her side, smiling as she took Lily round the room to meet the other girls. Lily was not the youngest. Her shyness melted away.

Opposite the fireplace, on a raised wooden platform, was a three-piece band of piano, violin and bass. There was a master of ceremonies, in tails, exactly like the one at the Majestic Picture House. Bubbles of excitement exploded in Lily when the MC held up his hand for silence and asked, 'Has everyone been given a programme?'

To a chorus of 'Yes, yes!' and 'Rather!' Magnus pushed a folded, deckle-edged, ribbon-slotted card into her hand.

'Before the magician, you will see that we are going to commence with dancing. Please form two circles for the Paul Jones.' The master of ceremonies signalled to the band and they were off.

The programme promised dancing, a magician, a dance, supper, a dance, a game of hide and seek and a last dance. Lily looped the programme's ribbon over her wrist, as the older girls did. Her knees were weak with excitement when the music stopped and Magnus stood in front of her, beaming with pleasure.

'It's a waltz,' she said.

He put his arm about her skinny waist. 'That's a-one-two-three and a-one-two-three, isn't it?'

'Yes.' She was about to explain waltz time in music but they were twirling about the floor, she going very carefully so as not to knock Magnus's legs, he looking proud and grown-up.

Sylvia, in pink chiffon with silver embroidery, was dancing with a tall, red-haired boy: Ray Chancellor. He had grown up so much since he'd gone away to school, Lily barely recognised him.

They circled again, and in the next dance, the veleta, she partnered Ray Chancellor. Lily looked at Ray. He was taller and slimmer than his father. He looked like his mother, but he gave the same impression his father did, of tremendous energy and strength. He said, 'What's your name?'

He brought out in Lily the very feeling his father did, that she wanted him to notice and like her. She wondered if he would look down on her if he knew she was Elsie Stanway's daughter – that they were poor, that his father owned their house and gave them cloth at cost. She was ashamed at herself for her thoughts, but all the same she just answered, 'Lily.'

'I'm Ray Chancellor.' He cast his eyes about the room. He would hardly want to get into conversation with her, but seeing Magnus looking over, he asked, 'Are you the girl – the Lily – Magnus talks about?'

'Probably.' It was like Magnus to talk about her.

He said, smiling down at her from his great height, 'Magnus says that you are going to be another "it" girl when you grow up.' Everyone was saying, 'She's Got It' about Clara Bow.

'Is that a compliment?' she said. Fancy Magnus saying that. Magnus had never been to the cinema. His mama was afraid he'd be bitten by fleas.

Afterwards Sylvia and she demonstrated the Black Bottom while the others stood round, watching. After that a magician came on to the floor. The lights were dimmed and they sat on mats and tried to see through the tricks – but they were all convinced of his magical powers when finally he produced Magnus's wrist watch from Ian's pocket. Then everyone came back on to the floor for the progressive barn dance, and Lily danced with Ian four times. It was a marvellous party. They were served a delicious supper of three courses, waited on by maids, sitting around the big oval dining table where candles in silver holders flickered.

After the meal there was more dancing, a game of charades and then, it being dark outside and all the curtains having been pulled, the master of ceremonies announced, 'The last game of the evening, before the last dance. Hide and seek.'

It was to be played in an exciting way. They were to leave the room one at a time every two minutes and could hide anywhere. 'Hide yourselves singly, anywhere a light is burning,' was the rule. Magnus and Sylvia were to remain until everyone had gone, and then they were to search, each trying to find more players than the other. A box of stationery was the prize for the last person to be found. Lily determined to win it.

She was the fifth to leave the drawing room. Nobody was about and she went fast along the lighted hallway, past the dining room, butler's pantry and flower room until she came to Mr Hammond's study. A light was burning, and in she went.

She'd never been in the study before. It was spoken of by Suylvia as Father's holy of holies, since nobody – staff, cleaners or even Mrs Hammond – was allowed in. He must have relented this evening, for there was a lamp upon a huge mahogany desk. Around three walls were bookshelves. A small fire burned in the grate on the wall where a door, slightly ajar, led into a second room. The second room was dimly lit but she had to go in; there was no hiding place in the study.

It was a tiny, windowless box room, where the facing wall was lined with shelves above a long working ledge. From the shelves, hanging by metal clips, were photographs and negatives, all of Sylvia and Magnus. It was Mr Hammond's darkroom. There was a high stool in a wide space under the ledge and in that space a deep shelf where a stack of photographs lay. Lily pulled the stool forward and ducked under the ledge, crouching, facing the shelf. No one would find her.

Once she had settled, she found that she could hear a murmur of voices through the wall. Lily worked out the plan of the house and realised that only the panelling separated the box room from the place where Mrs Hammond spoke to the housekeeper and the governess.

Her eyes alighted on the photographs and, lifting them carefully so as not to leave any trace, she began to look through them.

There were views of Archerfield taken from White Nancy, and views of the pretty little hill villages of Rainow and Pott Shrigley; photographs of Hammond Silks with the date and name inked in a fine, spidery copperplate handwriting that had elaborately inscribed flourishes on the capital letters and the tails of the g's and the y's.

Feet were running in the corridor. The study door was flung wide. 'Don't go in there!' Magnus called. 'Father's study is out of bounds. Nobody will go in.' She heard his footsteps – she could not mistake Magnus's tread – crossing the floor to extinguish the lamp.

Only then did she realise she should not be here, and now she was afraid that Magnus would see the band of light under the door. But his footsteps faded. The door closed. She would go once it was quiet. Her heart thumped. She felt like a criminal. She wanted to run from the darkroom but could hear the others, in the corridor and up and down the stairs, running and laughing. She must wait for five minutes.

She put the photographs back and in doing so saw another dusty envelope, hidden in the darkest corner of the shelf. She pulled it out, opened the flap and drew out two photographs about twelve inches square. They were covered in semi-transparent paper such as were placed over illustrations in expensive books. She peeled back the top one, and her mouth opened in astonishment. It was Mam.

Just the head and shoulders. Mam with her hair down, tumbling about her bare neck and arms, holding a piece of chiffon which went about the tops of her arms and dipped in front, out of sight. Mam was beautiful. Her expression had an alluring quality. That was the only way to describe the set of her head, the heavy-lidded eyes, the parted lips that were inviting but not smiling.She had been even more beautiful then than now. Under her picture was the date: 1914.

Lily replaced the transparent paper cover on the photograph and peeled back the one over the second picture. Then her stomach turned over. It was Mam again. Mam, wearing only a skirt, naked from the waist up. Lily closed her eyes. Fright and shock made the blood drain from her face. Her mouth was numb as she forced herself to look again. It was sickening, seeing Mam posed like that, leaning backwards against a table, thrusting forward the heavy breasts that were the focal point of the picture. Mam's head was back, mouth open to show her teeth, eyes half closed; ecstatic. It was bold and it was brazen. Shame and sick fear swept over Lily.

No wonder Mrs Hammond hated Mam. There came back to Lily all the little half-forgotten remarks Mam had made – that Mrs Hammond had scooped up the prizes, swept Mr Hammond off his feet. Had Mrs Hammond seen these disgusting photographs?

She could not stay there for another second. There was no sound in the corridor, no servants about so she went, softly, to open the door and creep on tiptoe from the study and into the lighted hallway, all the time telling herself not to think about the photographs; telling herself to put them from her mind for ever. When she reached the drawing room door she let her shoes clatter as she ran in, forcing a smile. 'You couldn't find me!'

'Where were you?'

'Never mind. Where's my prize?'

There was laughter. Magnus handed over the box of stationery, urging her to write to him when he went to Edinburgh. She made a supreme effort, using the chapel trick, the mesmerising trick to split her mind so that one half told the other to blot out the memory of all she'd seen and heard.

'It should have been the last dance, Lily.' Magnus was saying. 'But the band has gone to the kitchens for supper, before the grown-ups' party.'

'Are we to go home, then?'

'No. Ian's going to play the piano.'

Everyone gathered about the grand piano where Ian was seated and being plied with requests to play this and that. Without responding, without another look at anyone, he stared at the far wall, half smiling as he played the popular ballads, the old folk songs they could join in and sing. He played part-songs and modern romantic tunes, and as he played Lily felt her worries dispersing, melting away. Music could change her mood. Piano-playing was her way of expressing feelings. It must be the same for Ian.

Ian led the singing in a fine tenor voice. Lily was calming down, refusing to let her thoughts dwell on anything but what she was doing at that moment; joining in with the singing and chorusing. Then Ian stopped. There was a shocked moment's silence before, with a faraway expression on his face he went back to the keys and began to play the cleverest, fastest jazz she had ever heard.

He was possessed. It was magic. Everyone held their breath. Nobody clapped. Nobody hummed, tapped their feet or made any sound. Ian's right hand was skimming the keys, his touch fast and light, the runs crisp and sharp, and all the time the boogie-woogie beat of the left hand kept the music afloat. It never seemed to touch the ground. The notes were jumping, rippling and cascading all about the room. The very air was throbbing, dancing and singing for joy.

It was jazz such as Lily had heard once or twice on a gramophone. She had seen the first talkie last year. Ragtime was nothing like this. She had tried to play 'The Charleston', practising syncopation. Never in her wildest dreams had she imagined that jazz could sound this way – inspired, inventive.

Ian's hair had fallen across his face. His brow was glowing with beads of perspiration. A crowd of adults had gathered around the piano as well, and at the open door a group of maids stood, with the butler. Then, just as everyone was being carried away with it all, Ian crashed down his hands in four final emphatic chords, got to his feet and gave a quick bow.

They went crazy, applauding and begging for more, but Ian caught Rowena's eye and nodded to her before acknowledging the acclaim. Rowena went from the room quickly and returned with a piano-accordion, which she handed to him. Ian put up his right hand for a moment's silence. 'Scottish dancing,' he announced as he strapped the bulky instrument about his body and slipped his arms through the straps, before wheezing the great instrument in and out.

When he had it set he called, 'Can anyone play the piano?'

'Father!' Magnus shouted.

Mr Hammond, who had been standing at the back, shook his head. 'Afraid not. I don't play by ear. Have to practise everything.'

Magnus said, 'What about you, Lily?'

Ian grinned. 'Can you vamp a bit? If I give you the melody?'

'I can try,' she answered shyly. She had no idea if she could do it, but she was going to have a go. She went to the piano and sat down, as Ian began a reel and called across. 'Key of G.'

It was bewitching. It was all she had been taught, all she knew and more. The music and the excitement struck the pit of her stomach, but her mind was sharp and receptive. Ian nodded after a few bars, to bring her in – and she was doing it – playing as if they'd played duets for years. Ian, head thrown back, laughed in enjoyment, gave her a few bars to take the melody, then grabbed it back.

Everyone was clapping. Rowena was in her element, calling out the steps, ordering everyone to form two lines for Strip the Willow. Her voice carried over the heads of the whole room. 'It's danced with total abandon at every children's party and every eight-to-eighty gathering in Scotland!' she called. 'Form two lines. Boys one side. Girls the other.'

She nodded over her shoulder for them to play, then, 'Top couple, swing your partner. One, two, three, four. Girl swing the first boy. Right arms linked ... then your partner. Left arms linked ... then the next boy. Down the line ...'

All the time Lily's fingers flew up and down the keys and she bit her lip in concentration. Ian's face was wreathed in smiles as Rowena banged her feet and yelled. Everyone on the floor was red in the face with laughter and the effort of not putting a foot wrong.

Rowena called them out into eights for the eightsome reel, and sixes for Dashing White Sergeant. Then she let them slow down to a gentler pace for the last three dances, until the very last, when the whole party, adults and all, joined hands for 'Auld Lang Syne'. Lily knew this one. They said, 'Should auld acquaintance be forgot, And never brought to mind...' She could span the octaves easily. Both she and Ian did a little improvising on the tune while everyone swung their arms and moved into the centre of the circle. Then Ian's father, in a rich baritone, sang the second verse: 'And here's a hand, My trusty friend, And here's a hand o'mine...' and

Ian and Lily played it better than most of them could ever have heard it before.

The party was over. The young ones went to the door, chattering and laughing, as Lily reluctantly put the lid down over the keys. Ian unfastened the accordion and put it on the piano stool. 'You play very well,' he said. 'It's the hardest thing of all, accompanying a piano-accordion.'

She beamed with pleasure. 'Thank you.'

'Next time I come to Archerfield we must have an hour together,' he said. 'Making music.' Magnus was holding out her cape and Ian, laughing, said, 'Magnus! I refuse to play here again without my wee accompanist.'

Then everyone was going to the big front door, saying goodbye, climbing into motor cars, waving and disappearing down the drive. Lily walked back to the Lodge, holding Grandpa's hand, under a half-melon moon that hung low in the sky ahead of them, as happy as if she'd been crowned Queen. She had no cares, no worries. It was the best day of her life. She could put from her mind the awful things she had learned about Mam. Tonight her head was ringing with happiness and music and song – and the knowledge that she had made a friend of the boy she loved, Ian Mackenzie.

Two years had passed since Magnus left home for Edinburgh. He was fitter, healthier, stronger here from all the exercise he took, for exercise was a requirement in the Mackenzie family. Magnus had learned to swim, and now his shoulders were broader with his developed biceps and deltoid muscles. He had hopes of swimming for his house. He was very fast over two lengths.

Every day he walked, first from school to the tram at the crossroads, where churches stood on the four corners, or else to the station at Craiglockhart. Then again from the tram stop on Princes Street to Uncle Mack's house in Charlotte Square.

Today his legs ached from battling against the icy east wind. The heavy oak front door, painted lacquer black, was closed. He hesitated with his hand on the brass lion's head, decided against lifting it and went out of the iron-railed area round to the side door and in at the surgery entrance. Evening surgery was for the panel patients, and always busy. He could hear the hum of voices in the waiting room, half an hour before surgery.

He reached the dispensary door as the elderly Miss Pettigrew opened it and in that confidential whisper said, 'Your results were all right, Magnus. Dr Mackenzie asked me to tell you.'

He smiled in relief and loitered there for a moment, glad to stop before he entered the tiled hall and climbed the stairs to the living rooms. The whole ground floor was taken up with the surgery; consulting room, waiting room and dispensary. Uncle Mack treated patients from the wealthy New Town area of the city as well as the panel patients from the Old Town on the other side of Princes Street. He said to Miss Pettigrew, who tested his urine for blood once a week, 'No traces?'

'None,' she answered. Then, 'Come inside. I will make up your powders. You should have three left...?'

'I have.' Magnus followed her into the dispensary and sat down. He loved it in here: the banks of wooden drawers with Latin abbreviations in gold and black lettering, the tall, clear bottles in elegant shapes, the deep-blue ones whose contents were poisonous, the long white-enamelled bench, the drachm weights and tiny scales, and the smell, the carbolic cleanliness of it all. He lived with the hope, as his father did, that one day, by some alchemic magic, the formula that would put an end to his haemophilia would appear. It was good to know that the treatment was working. He said, 'Is Ian home?'

'He's upstairs. He came in half an hour ago,' she replied.

He sat and watched, enjoying seeing Miss Pettigrew at the pill-rolling, mixture-bottling, powder-weighing, paper-folding and ointment-boxing that filled six hours of her every day. When he had his powders in his hand he climbed the stairs to the drawing room overlooking the square.

Ian said, 'You're late. You look whacked! Been swimming?'

'I walked to Holy Corner and caught the tram. Strengthen my legs.' Magnus laughed. 'All I've developed is a strong list to port from battling against the wind.'

Ian said, 'It'll serve you well if you're coming down to North Berwick with me next Saturday.'

'Are you taking the boat out?' Magnus enjoyed the odd Saturday morning at North Berwick, working on Ian's boat, varnishing and oiling and mending sails, but he wouldn't be here next weekend.

Ian said, 'Are you coming?'

'I can't.' Then he added hastily, 'I've been given leave and I have to see the dentist. What a fuss that is!' It was a nuisance, having every tooth examined for the tiniest cavity. But he could not risk extractions. And going home meant he could see Lily. He said cheerfully, 'No match on Saturday?' Ian was eighteen, captain of rugby and deputy head boy.

'We're not playing.' Ian's smile vanished. The good-natured bantering tone he used with Magnus and Rowena was a reflection of his enormous sense of humour. Under it lay a forceful nature. 'Where does Chancellor go at night? What's he up to?'

Magnus shook his head. 'What's the matter?'

'He's missed rugby practice for the last three weeks. We've had to cancel Saturday's match.' Ian organised but did not join the second fifteen at the twice-weekly training sessions which were run by a coach and referee. With a face like thunder he said, 'Chancellor's been forging my signature. Getting out of the boarding house two nights a week, supposedly for rugby practice. God knows where he goes.'

Magnus whistled through his teeth. The week after next, Ray's father was going to be inaugurated as Mayor of Macclesfield. They were going to ask leave from the school to bring Ray home for the ceremony. 'What's going to happen? Will he be expelled?'

'Severely disciplined,' Ian said. 'Unless he has a plausible excuse. It had better be good.'

Magnus said, 'What does "severely disciplined" entail?'

'He will be given a week, maybe two,' Ian said, 'to mend his ways, or he will be out of the boarding house. His parents will have to find somewhere else for him. As it is, I'm chucking him off the team. I'm going to his boarding house tonight to tell him.'

'I'm going upstairs,' Magnus said. His attic study was on the top floor. 'I have a lot of work to do tonight.'

'Right. See you at supper. Unless Dad is called out we'll have an easy night,' Ian said.

'For once!'

Magnus heard Ian's shout of laughter following him up the

stairs. Magnus's idea of an easy night was one in which he sat by the fire in his attic study, reading or working, watching the sun set over the slate roofs, spires, leafy green places and Adam crescents of the city.

To his cousins an easy night was one where they gathered in the drawing room after supper, as they would this evening. Uncle Mack would talk to the three of them – Magnus was included with Ian and Rowena – about the need to work hard, to apply themselves. They were to see their hobbies – painting for Rowena, music and sailing for Ian, reading for Magnus – for what they were: enjoyment. The main purpose of their young lives was to prepare to be useful members of society, to direct themselves to learning, making careers, though money-making was not to be their aim. 'It will disappoint! Don't do anything for money alone!' Uncle Mack said. 'There is reward in doing something well.' These were Uncle Mack's maxims. Another was 'Effort in equals results out. A simple equation.' It was a purposeful household.

Everybody worked hard. They had no time for slackers. Uncle Mack was a strict man of the old school. Like Father, Uncle Mack was a good man. Magnus wanted to be like them: a good man who did good things.

In his attic room Magnus placed his school satchel on the chair. A fire had been lit and his study was warm and inviting. He loved having this room, this attic floor of the house, to himself. It had been like shedding a skin, like emerging from a chrysalis, having a life for himself, here in Edinburgh. He missed nothing from Macclesfield, missed no one but Lily. He went to the window and gazed at the distant view of the wide blue Firth of Forth and the hills of the Kingdom of Fire. Then he crossed the room to the opposite window and his eyes dropped to Ian's figure, striding across the square, on his way to tick off Ray Chancellor.

Ian walked fast. There were queues for the trams at teatime and a twenty-minute walk would give him exercise and a chance to think about what he'd say to Chancellor. He could not stand the fellow. What on earth would make anyone behave as Chancellor had? The fellow was seventeen. He had done well in his School Certificate – so it could not be worry about the Highers that were coming up next.

He crossed Princes Street and quickened his pace on the downslope of Lothian Road. It would take him a quarter of an hour to reach Holy Corner, but he was glad of it, for his ligaments needed stretching. He was having to spend hours in his room, working for the entrance exam for medical school.

He was never confident that he had it in him. Dad said he had, and so did his chemistry master, but Ian could think of a dozen areas he might be questioned upon and flounder. There was the big area of chemical reactions, molecular chemistry, aldehydes and metallurgy, a field of study of which he had scant knowledge. He could be questioned on anything. The solution was to work. If he had the facility to soak up knowledge, which Chancellor evidently had, he would make better use of his talents. What was the fellow playing at? He looked at his wristwatch. Twenty-five minutes. Not bad.

Mr McDowell, the boarding housemaster, was waiting for him in the hall. 'Come into the study,' he said. 'I think we should have a talk before you see Chancellor.' Inside the study he said, 'I think the boy is in some kind of trouble. He may confide in you. I can't get anything from him. I have to put his case to the head. It will not be overlooked.'

'Where is he?'

'I'll send for him. You can talk in here.'

Ian went to stand with his back to the fire, and was still there when Chancellor came in. He said, 'Sit down!'

'I'd rather stand.' Ray was pale but his hands were curled tight and there was an aggressive edge to his voice.

'Anything troubling you? Want to tell me anything?'

'No. Not particularly,' Ray said.

The insolence in Chancellor told Ian that the kid gloves were a waste of time. He'd go straight to the point. 'You forged my signature.' He was no good at soft-soaping. Perhaps others would handle it differently. He had no patience with cheats and liars. 'Your excuse?'

Chancellor hesitated, then evidently made a decision to come clean. 'Listen,' he said, 'I'm having a rough time in my personal—'

'Your personal problems are of no concern to me,' Ian said. 'Individuals are of smaller account than the team they are members of. You are a member of the rugby team and a representative of the school.'

'Don't give me all that,' Chancellor said in his former, fighting way. Then he changed again and in a whining tone said, 'It's about this trouble...'

Ian could not deal with it. He felt only contempt for the fellow. He said, 'It's not! It's all about honour. Integrity. Doing the right thing.'

'You have no idea what I'm going through...'

No. I have not. I don't want to. But you are going to tell them. You have to face the team. Give them your excuses. See what they make of you. They are waiting for you down at the field. Be gone!'

Chancellor's hands closed into fists. He gave Ian a murderous look, then quickly left the study. Ian heard the outer door bang.

Mr McDowell came back. 'Well? Did he tell you?'

'No.'

'Pity. He'll not last long here, I'm afraid. He sits his Highers next month, then I think he will have to go.'

'Good.'

The housemaster shrugged in a helpless little gesture. 'Maybe we could have helped, shown some understanding. If only he would tell.'

'I don't pretend to understand,' Ian said coldly. 'He has money, health, brains, and has had everything handed to him on a plate.'

'I think it's a girl. I think he's seeing a girl, in Edinburgh.'

Ian snorted. 'He would. He's the type!'

On his way home he tried to work up some sympathy for Chancellor but it was difficult. When he was with them in Macclesfield he tried not to let his dislike show, but he couldn't share his cousins' liking for the fellow. But ... if Chancellor had got himself somehow involved with a girl, then he was in real trouble. It was one of those rules, a code you had to learn, that until you had something to offer a lady you made no attachments.

He was prepared to wait. If he were to meet her tomorrow – and he would know if she were the girl for him – he would wait. There were ways of dealing with perfectly natural urges.

The way of dealing with them was to work hard, involve yourself in sport, sailing, playing team games. Chancellor was of a lower order altogether.

Chapter Nine

Mam had taken up smoking to help her digestion, which was troubling her a bit, and recently had handed over to Lily the money and duty of buying the food and cooking the dinner.

Lily enjoyed the responsibility. Mam was not much of a cook, wasting money on fish and chips and hot pies. Lily managed to have a little bit over every week from this housekeeping money. She put it in a tin box, against emergencies and took pride in the fact that since she had been in charge there was always enough to eat. But it was a struggle. She cycled home from the Central School at midday, because she did not want to pay for school dinners – and she wanted to make sure that Mam ate.

It was a long cycle ride. She would walk to school this afternoon. There was an uphill drag in each direction and today she pushed her bike up the steep Mill Street. It was windy and wet; an icy-cold March day. Her face was stinging and she was out of breath when she reached home and put her bike in the entryway.

Calling out, 'It's snowing, Mam! All the daffodils have keeled over. You wouldn't believe it!' she went through the shop to the kitchen, where Mam was taking from the range the dish of hotpot Lily had made yesterday.

Mam carried it carefully, for she was dressed in her navy-blue two-piece; unusual for a Monday. She placed the dish on a thick raffia mat and said, 'You had best put your winter coat on this afternoon. Have you seen the letter from Magnus? It came this morning.'

Lily took off her wet mackintosh, put it over a chair to dry and saw the letter propped against the mantel clock. It stood next to the photograph of her father and the invitation to the mayoral inauguration. She gave her father a wink, as if they were great pals, then caught sight of herself in the big mirror.

'I'll read Magnus's letter later.' She pushed the long dark hair back from her forehead and pulled down the bow at the nape of her neck. She used to wish she had straight hair, envying girls who could make smooth, silky plaits or have it cut in a fashionable bob and fringe. The more damp hers was, the more it curled.

Her face was wide at the temples, with high cheekbones that were bright red from the ride down Jordangate in the wind and sleet. Her grey eyes had little gold flecks in them. Her chin was pointed like Mam's, but her mouth was different. Mam's mouth was wide for her face, with long, strong teeth; hers was smaller and fuller, with square teeth in a very straight line. She was proud of her teeth and scrubbed them with salt and Kolynos every night. She thought her teeth were her best feature. Mam said it was her eyes.

'Sit down!' Mam said. 'Stop admiring yourself.'

'I wasn't. I was thinking of the medicals this afternoon. At least Doreen Grimshaw goes before me because it's alphabetical order.'

'Scared of Doreen?' Mam said. 'I thought you'd got over it.'

'I'm not scared. I don't trust her.'

'Soon you'll be able to avoid her,' Mam said. 'Her mother says Doreen isn't going to sit her RSAs. She wants to leave when she's fourteen.'

'I avoid her now. She's boy-daft. After school she runs off to town, hanging about the station in Waters Green. A lot of the lads from the King's School go on that line.'

'The advanced little monkey!'

'She likes people older than herself.' Lily loaded a dollop of hot pot on to her place. 'She hangs round the Andersons' bakehouse as well, dropping by to have a chat with Shandy, she says. She's taken a fancy to Shandy's brother, Cyril. Shandy and I are too young for Doreen.'

'She'll get herself a bad name,' Mam said, but she was smiling. Then she said, 'Howard's coming this afternoon. He sent a telegram.'

That would account for Mam's being dressed so smartly. 'Again?' Lily curled her lip. 'He was here last week.' Mam never took her dislike of Mr Leigh seriously. Mam brought him into Lily's clean, shining kitchen these days and let him sit at the table, drinking from the china cups they had borrowed from Nanna, as if he, not Mr Chancellor, owned the house.

Lily said, 'Are you going to Mr Chancellor's inauguration with Mr Leigh?'

Mam's bantering mood changed swiftly. 'I'm not going with anyone,' she snapped.

No sooner had Lily finished her meal than Mam began siding the table, in a hurry for her to go. Normally she liked to gossip for a bit, over a cup of tea. 'Take your letter. Get a move on.'

'Are you dressed up for Mr Leigh?' Lily took down her winter coat from behind the door. The wind was whistling round the back yard. She pulled the warm scarf about her head and tied it. 'You think he's keen on you, but Nellie Plant says that he has a woman in every town.'

'Nellie Plant will find herself in court answering a summons one of these days,' Mam said. 'Spreading lies...'

Lily held the scarf to her throat as she left the shop. The wind that yesterday had blown mild and soft was icy. It took the hem of her navy-blue Melton cloth coat and whipped it to and fro against her thick black stockings. Her leather boots were slipping all over the narrow pavement as she slithered down Jordangate towards Shandy's house on Brock Street. Shandy was watching out for her and ran down the entry between the bakehouse and their house. Freckle-faced and bubbly, Shandy was the only daughter in a family of four older brothers, who all worked at the bakery.

'Come on. We'll have to run all the way!' Shandy grabbed her arm and they went, laughing, helter-skelter down Hibel Road on their short cut.

One of the classrooms had been made ready as a medical room and Lily saw, through a small plain glass panel in the door, that the nit-nurse had set up two tables: one for herself and the other for the doctor.

It appeared that no classwork was to be done, for one of the prefects – the bossiest in the school – was in charge, and on each desk was a copy of *The Pilgrim's Progress*, the book for the RSA exam.

'One at a time,' the prefect said. 'Go into the cloakroom when your name's called. No talking.' A window overlooked the cloakroom, behind the desk on the platform. 'I'll hand you your medical cards when you go in to get undressed.' There was a long wooden box on the platform, containing big brown envelopes Lily had never seen before. 'Keep your knickers on and leave your bootlaces loose,' the prefect was saying. 'If you are cold, put your cardigans over your shoulders. It won't take long. When you've been examined come back quietly and sit at your desks.'

Lily hated taking off her clothes, hated anyone seeing the pale skin that was as white as milk and the little swollen bumps on her chest that were growing bigger and pinker every day but were nowhere near as big as some of the girls'. Thank heaven they were to be given some privacy. The prefect had said 'one at a time'. Lily lifted the book to read Magnus's letter.

Dear Lily,
I am coming home next weekend as I have a dental appointment. I hope you can find a little time to spare for me.

Magnus wrote in a textbook style that made him sound old-fashioned and pompous. She tried to picture him in Edinburgh in the house he had described for her, the high, elaborate ceilings, tall windows with tapestry curtains and thick tasselled swags to hold them back. Only yards from Magnus's room, Edinburgh Castle loomed over the city, impregnable on top of an old volcanic rock.

I am under the care of Mr Meiklejohn, a famous Scottish physician, and am recieiving a course of treatments and tests. They are not painful. They upset my digestion but I have spent no time confined to bed here.
You ask how we amuse ourselves at weekends. I am afraid it is not very adventurous of me but I spend hours in my room, catching up with schoolwork. It is expected of me. My uncle expects Ian to follow him into medicine and

Rowena wants to be a nurse. Ian does everything well. He is captain of rugby – and deputy head boy. I shall miss him when he goes to medical school.

Lily looked round the room. Half an hour had passed and they were well into the swing of things. The prefect sat at the desk, from where she could see the cloakroom and, over the top of the frosted glass between the classrooms, into the medical room itself. Every so often she'd look up and call out a name, and as the girl went up to her she'd hand her a brown envelope and watch her go into the cloakroom to undress. Then, at a signal from next door, when that girl had been examined, she'd call to the next one on her list.

I am being strongly influenced by my uncle, who says that we are not on this earth simply for our own pleasure and insists, 'You have to put something back in, for all the advantages life has given to you.' One day I shall run the mill alongside Father, but I believe that God has a purpose for us all. I am afraid my contribution to His work is not going to come from deeds of valour – I have not been granted the stamina – but I shall try always to do what is right and true. I want to be a good man and do good things.

Another half-hour passed. Doreen went in and came back looking pleased with herself.

'Lily Stanway,' the prefect called out at last, and she went to the front and was handed an envelope. In the cloakroom she put it down on the lift-up long box under the coat rack. But before she could take her clothes off, the prefect put her head in at the door and said, 'Wait a minute. They aren't ready. I'll tell you when to get undressed.'

Lily sat down, her back to the classroom, and waited. She picked up the envelope and turned it over, wondering what kind of records a school might keep. Did they say if you were stupid or clever? Did they say if you had ever had nits or impetigo?

There was no sign of her being called. It was not allowed, but Lily slipped the contents of the envelope out a little way. Inside was a big pink-coloured card, and attached to it, three long white sheets of paper. She took it right out. On the white sheets were listed all her marks, from every little test taken from the age of five, when she had gone to Beech Lane School.

Lily lifted the white sheets over the pink card; the medical record card. There were columns down it, and in the columns, in different handwriting, were the records of all the medicals she had ever had. There were hieroglyphics, numbers over other numbers like fractions, and several single capital letters and words in Latin abbreviations.

At the top of the card it said 'Lily Isobel Stanway'. Then, 'Jordangate, Macclesfield. Born 21 March 1919'.

Under that, 'Mother: Miss Elsie Stanway'.

Underneath ... She stared. She froze. Underneath it said: 'Father unknown'.

What could it mean? She had a father. Tommy Stanway, Mam's first cousin from Stockport was her father. There was a photograph of him on the kitchen mantel shelf, to prove it. Lily stared again, hoping to find something else, something to explain it. There was nothing else, except that Mam was named as Miss, not Mrs Elsie Stanway. *Miss* Elsie Stanway! Father unknown!

She shoved the cards back into the envelope. Horror had become disbelief, and slowly that disbelief was sickeningly turning into the terrible realisation of her state. Everything fell into place, the evasions and Mam's refusal to talk about her father.

She went through the medical in a state of shock. The doctor merely glanced at the card. He would come across them every day. She was just another little Illy-Jitty. He added a few more marks, patted her on the head and sent her over to the nurse. And forever afterwards the smell of carbolic lotion would bring that afternoon back to her with shocking clarity. The nurse took a comb from the carbolic solution and slowly lifted and parted her hair, inspecting every strand. Lily wanted to scream. She was a bastard! Mam had never been married. They had lied: Mam, Grandpa and her trusted Nanna, who had taught her the need for truth. Her arms and legs shook.

'Are you cold?'

'Yes.'

'All right. Return and get dressed. Clean head.' The nit-nurse wrote on the vile pink card that told of her shame and, unsmiling, dismissed her.

Lily went back to the cloakroom. It was all very well for Mam to say nobody knew anything about her secrets. Lily had discovered the truth, as had at least two more people: the doctor and the nit-nurse. That was as well as Mam, Nanna and Grandpa. And as she sat at the desk there came the realisation that there was at least one other. A child must have a father. She knew how it came about. She'd seen Nanna's cats mate and give birth, seen the scarlet-combed cockerel crowing pride in his hens. Nanna had told her everything – and said that it was the same with people, only better, because God had made people better than animals. It was because of human love that people mated and babies were conceived and born.

She could not concentrate on the book. She wanted to cry. She couldn't sit here. She had to get out into clean fresh air. All at once, she jumped up and barged to the front.

'I don't feel well,' she said to the prefect. 'I'm going...' Then, before anyone could stop her, she dashed into the cloakroom, grabbed her coat and went out into the freezing street, away from the hateful official records.

She ran like the wind down Byroms Lane, over the main road and rounded a corner into Pitt Street. Then she leaned against a house and faced the wall. Lily Stanway! You took the name of your father, not your mother. Her father was not Tommy Stanway. If she were brave she would demand the truth from Mam. But how could she ask if Mam had been a bad lot when she was young? It was always the girls who did wrong – the man was never to blame. Girls who let men do it to them were called trollops by respectable women. Suppose Mam said she had never wanted her? Nobody wanted a child born out of wedlock. There were girls who were whispered about – 'easy meat', girls who disappeared from Macclesfield in disgrace, to have their babies given away or put into homes. The girls returned, pitied by some and talked about by all, an encumbrance to their parents, with no hope of marriage, their lives ruined. But Mam had gone to great pains to give Lily a respectable background.

Round and round the questions went, and always they came

back to the central mystery – who was her father? And as she went through the windy, ice-cold streets, holding her coat tight against herself, she tried to imagine who he might be. Did she have any of his features? No, she was like Mam. Was he clever? Was he alive?

A shiver ran through her when she thought of it. She had to stop again and pretend to look in a shop window, but she could barely see for the blurring tears that blinded her. What if he were alive? What if she passed him in the street every day? What sort of a father would be able to see her – and not let on? He could not be the sort of man she'd want as a father – a good man who protected his child. No, she could not bear to think that he was alive and must know how she had always longed for a father. He must be dead – killed perhaps in the war, before they had time to marry.

She reached the house. Mr Leigh's motor car was outside, and for once she was glad. She could not call herself a coward for not demanding the truth in front of Mr Leigh.

They were in the kitchen. Mam's face was flushed with drink. Lily sat down on a hard chair at the table, with shivers running from the back of her neck down her spine.

Mr Leigh stood up, put out his hand and in his light, insincere voice said, 'Lily dear. I haven't seen you for weeks.'

She pretended not to see his hand. 'Hello,' she said coldly.

Mam had not noticed anything amiss. 'I think we'll tell Lily the sad news, Hah'd.' She said quickly, 'Poor Mr Leigh has lost his wife. Mrs Leigh died in a Southport nursing home after a long illness.'

She made it sound like a newspaper announcement. 'Oh,' Lily said. Then since they were both silent, waiting for more, 'I am sorry.'

Neither of them seemed the least bit sorry, and the whole scene and their excited manner was making her agitation worse. She wished she dared tell Mam to come to the bedroom and give her the facts. She couldn't. They were talking about where might be the best place for Mr Leigh to settle – Southport, Macclesfield or Manchester. His poor wife was not cold in her grave. She wanted to remind him of that, but what she heard herself saying was, 'I don't feel well. I'm going upstairs for a lie-down.'

She ran upstairs and threw herself on to the bed, wallowing

in self-pity. On Friday she'd go to Lindow and make Nanna tell her the truth.

The following day they were sent home from school because of the bad weather. The boiler had gone out overnight and pipes had frozen and burst when the furnace was lit again.

Lily kept out of Mam's way, cleaning the kitchen, tidying the workroom and her bedroom, her brain whirling with all the questions, wanting to cry for herself and the horror of it all, wishing she could rise above the feelings of shame that kept coming over her.

In the afternoon, when she could not stand her thoughts any longer, Doreen came to the house. Mam showed her into the kitchen but Lily couldn't pretend. 'What have you come round for?' she said, with such resentment that Mam rebuked her, 'Now then, our Lil.'

Doreen threw a sweet, respectful glance at Mam. 'You are a Silly Lily!' She gave that mirthless and explosive laugh. Mam was trying to keep her face straight. Doreen said, 'Your Mam's going to make my summer frocks.' She opened her coat, put her hands on her hips and admired her well-developed bust. 'I'm getting bigger in all the right places.' She made a taunting face, as if her figure were something to be proud of.

Lily raised her eyebrows and said, 'Huh!' hoping it meant something.

Mam said, 'You are much too young to be talking this way, Doreen.' She frowned and without saying more went into the shop.

There was more to Doreen's visit. Lily said, 'You haven't only come for that. What else do you want?'

Doreen took off her coat and put it over a chair. 'Are you going to ask me to sit down? Offer me a cup of tea?'

They had an enormous kettle, always at the ready on its hinged trivet over the fire. There were clean cups on the table, and seeing nothing else for it, Lily took down the tea caddy and earthenware pot from the fireside shelf. Doreen had come to stand by her elbow, looking to the door and back to her. She tapped Lily's arm and whispered, 'You'll never guess who's got a girl into trouble. Who's put Mollie Leadbetter up the spout.'

'Put her where?' Was she being stupid? 'Who?'

'Ray Chancellor!'

'Trouble? What sort of trouble?'

Doreen's horrible laugh never spread to her eyes, but the eyebrows were lifted to heaven. 'You don't know?'

Lily filled the teapot, resigned to having to listen. 'No, I don't.'

Doreen jeered, 'No wonder everyone calls you Silly Lily.'

'Everyone doesn't,' Lily said. 'You do.'

'Never mind.' Doreen was all-knowing. 'Getting a girl into trouble means giving her a baby.'

The metallic taste of fear was in Lily's mouth. She tried to conceal the trembling in her hands by pouring the tea, while Doreen repeated, 'You know about babies? What men and women do? Sectional intercourse?'

'Course I know. Course I do!' Lily did not know it by its proper name of sectional intercourse, but she knew all about having babies. 'What has it to do with Ray Chancellor?'

Doreen was exasperated. 'He's been a naughty boy!' Then, seeing Lily had not grasped it all, 'A dirty lad! He's done what he shouldn't. He's done it to Mollie Leadbetter. Mollie Leadbetter's going to have a baby.'

'No!' Lily's insides tightened. Her hands shook as she pushed a cup across the table to Doreen.

Doreen's lips tightened. 'Yes! Albert Leadbetter went to see Frank Chancellor.'

Lily took exception to Doreen's speaking about adults as if she were on familiar terms with them; calling Mr Leadbetter, that fierce little man who clumped about on a surgical boot, Albert. Doreen's familiarity was nowhere near as shocking as what she was saying, but Lily could not help but ask, 'Why do you call grown men and women by their Christian names behind their backs? You call Mam Elsie. She never said you could. You call Mr Chancellor Frank. Now Mr Leadbetter is Albert to you. Why?'

Doreen gave a long sigh and carried on with her story. 'Mr Leadbetter told Mr Chancellor that Ray has to marry their Mollie.'

Lily tried to sound casual. She dared not let Doreen see the turmoil she was in. 'Are they going to marry, then?'

Doreen was filled with importance. 'Frank... Mr

Chancellor said, "It can't be my son. Ray wouldn't bring our name down. Ray's a schoolboy. Seventeen. The baby could be anyone's." '

Lily's voice had gone down to a whisper as her stomach knotted again. 'What's going to happen?'

'Mollie Leadbetter's going to have to get rid of it.'

'How d'you get rid of it?' Lily was terrified Mam might come in.

'No wonder you're Silly Lily.' Doreen took a sip of her tea. She was sitting, smiling as she imparted it all. 'They are going to tie her legs up in the air so she can't move and then they push a long steel thing up her – inside her – until it comes loose – until she loses the baby.'

Lily wanted to be sick. 'Who told you all this?'

'I'm pally with Nellie Plant.'

Lily had heard about the friendship. 'What's that to do with it?'

'Nellie told me all about it. She tells me anything if I'll go to the back door of the Shakespeare for her – for a jug of ale.' She laughed at the thought. 'She can't hold her tongue when she's drunk.'

'Does your mam let you go round to Nellie Plant's?' was all Lily could think of to say.

'Don't talk daft!' Doreen said in a scornful voice. 'I tell them I'm at your house. Stopping in with you. Nellie told me how they do it. It's called a bortion. She's had two done but she won't say who she's had sectional intercourse with.' Doreen was relishing every minute. 'Albert Leadbetter's blaming Ray Chancellor and saying it will be all over the papers and then what? Frank Chancellor says it wasn't Ray. Ray Chancellor says it wasn't him. Now Mollie Leadbetter's mother and father have to find twenty-five pounds to send their Mollie to a doctor in Manchester for a bortion.'

Doreen drank her tea with genteel sipping noises.Lily held her cup between ice-cold palms, trying to believe this was not happening to poor Mollie Leadbetter, trying not to think about this other terrible end to an unwanted child. 'How did you hear about it?'

'I heard my dad telling my mam.'

'When is it going to happen? The bortion?'

'Today,' Doreen said. 'Mollie's gone to Manchester.'

Doreen had to be lying, but ... 'You saw Mollie and Ray Chancellor kissing, didn't you?' Lily said.

Doreen's expression was one of sheer pleasure. 'I saw them doing it. Last November.'

She had to be lying. Lily said, 'You couldn't have. You've never been to their houses at night ...'

Doreen exploded, splattering tea all over the table. 'They don't do it in the house at night, you great...!'

'Shut up!' Lily did not want to listen. She couldn't bear any more of it. 'Please, shut up.'

Doreen stood and glared, but her eyes were eager and her words came fast and scornful. 'I'm telling you, Lily Stanway. They were doing it standing up. They were by the Bollin, beyond the gennel in Spring Gardens. Under the railway bridge. Mollie's stockings and knickers were down round her ankles. Ray had one hand under her skirt. Mollie's jumper was up round her neck and he was sucking her titties – like a baby does. Mollie liked it. She was laughing and wriggling.'

'Don't, Doreen! I don't want to hear!'

But Doreen would not be stopped. 'Then he pushed her legs apart! Like this!' Here Doreen stood with her toes turned out, knees wide to demonstrate. 'And he stopped sucking her and dropped his trousers down. His behind was bare and he took his thing in his hand and pushed it hard up inside her.'

Lily felt the blood drain from her face. 'Don't tell me any more!'

Doreen's eyes were glittering and her cheeks were pink with excitement. 'He was hurting her. Making her cry out, "Don't do that! No! Ray. No!" That's what she said, "No, Ray! No." She was crying and making a big long wailing noise and calling out for her mammie. "Oh, Mammie!" He took no notice and went on faster, making horrible grunting noises, pinning her against the wall so she couldn't get away. And he said, "Shut up!" He put his hand over her mouth to stop her crying until he'd done with her.'

And Lily was crying; crying and trying to control herself in case Mam came in and asked why.

Doreen wiped her mouth with her sleeve. 'They never saw me.'

She picked up her coat and went out of the kitchen, high and mighty in her knowledge, and then Lily heard her in the shop, being sweet and respectful to Mam before she went home with the pattern books.

She hated Doreen then. Doreen must be making it up. Doreen and she were not allowed out on to the streets at night, so how could she have followed anyone in the dark? She couldn't have seen anyone doing those things. There was one single gas lamp on the other side of the Bollin. It would be pitch black under the railway bridge. Nobody could see anything. Ray Chancellor would have been at school in Edinburgh last November. And even if Doreen *had* followed a couple of lovers on a December night, what kind of girl was she to make up wicked lies about Ray Chancellor?

What kind of a girl would spy on poor, half-witted little Mollie?

Between Monday and Friday her mind turned it all repeatedly – Mollie Leadbetter's getting into trouble and the shame of her own birth. They sewed in the evenings, working quietly, Mam smoking and sipping her port, listening to the BBC on the beautiful wireless with a loudspeaker horn that sat on a little table in the corner of the room. Hidden underneath the table were two accumulator batteries. Mr Chancellor had set it up for them and taught them how to connect the wires to the batteries.

On Thursday night there was a talk by an old doctor, who said that young women were risking wrinkles and consumption with their abnormal lives: nights of frivolity and days of excitement, coupled with poisons like tobacco and alcohol. Across the table Mam was smoking and drinking and unwrinkled, and as Lily watched she thought how little she knew about her mother; how unpredictable Mam was. She had not been drinking hard or gossiping this week.

Lily wanted to unburden herself of guilt for having read the medical record, but she could not bear to hurt Mam or discover that she, Lily, was the result of any dirty business under the railway bridge.

Then, on Friday, she came home at midday to find Mam already seated at the table, silent and preoccupied. Lily said,

'You haven't forgotten? I go to Nanna's after school. I won't be home till Sunday.'

'I've remembered.'

'You are quiet.'

Mam leaned back slowly in her chair and pushed her plate from her. It was fried fish, and normally she ate most of it. Today she was pale, with washed-out eyes. 'What's the matter?' Lily asked.

'Mollie Leadbetter's dead.' Mam spoke in a whisper. 'They rushed her into the Infirmary last night.'

A cold trickle of horror ran down Lily's spine. 'What happened?'

'Septicaemia, Lil.'

'Oh, Mam.' The knife and fork slid from her fingers. 'Was it true? Nellie Plant told Doreen about taking a baby out of Mollie.'

There was a little silence before she heard Mam's shuddering breath. Then, 'Yes,' Mam said in a dead voice. 'Poor child. Sixteen, that's all she was.'

Lily wanted to cry but no tears came, only numbing coldness.

'There'll be an inquiry,' Mam said, in the same quiet voice. 'It's an illegal act, doing away with a pregnancy. I don't think Mollie can have a Christian burial. You can't if it's suicide – that's an illegal act.'

'Doreen said it was Ray Chancellor's baby. She said he would have to marry Mollie to make it legal and right. Is that true?'

Mam slammed her hand down on the table. 'It won't bring Mollie Leadbetter back, knowing who's responsible. But since you and Doreen... No! I believe Frank. Chancellor is the best-respected name in Macclesfield. Ray would never bring disgrace on his mother. And under all his importance and bluff, Frank is a man of principle. Frank would have taken care of Mollie if he thought his son...'

But it was bluff with Mam, too. She put her hands about her face and began to sob, great gulping sobs that shook the table. 'Oh!' she cried. 'Oh! I can't bear to think about it.'

Nor could Lily. If she were hard she might have said, 'Suppose it had happened to you, Mam?' She would have learned the truth there and then, Mam was in such a state. Lily was ashamed of her thoughts. Mam had kept her secret – perhaps with good reason. Lily ought not to feel sorry for herself. She was alive and lucky to have been born; lucky Mam had not done away with her and risked dying from the operation, like Mollie Leadbetter.

Chapter Ten

'Poor little Mollie. There'll be another death. See if I'm right.'

Nanna prophesied another death on Saturday, at Lindow. Lily sat with her head leaning against the back of the settle, waiting her moment to ask Nanna for the truth. Nanna was sitting close to the fire, her crochet hook twisting slowly in and out of the piece of work she was doing. Normally she did not sit in the afternoon, yet here she was, at only three o'clock, crocheting by the fire like an old woman. Grandpa had gone to the bottom field to fetch the horses in and bed them into loose boxes, out of the icy-cold easterly wind that had been blowing sleet and rain before it all week.

'Grandpa's taking a long time,' Lily said.

'It's too much for him now. He can't keep them much longer. Four horses to fetch in,' Nanna said. 'They should be out all day in March. And Grandpa's slowing.' Nanna gave one of her perceptive looks. 'What is it, Lily? You've been waiting till Grandpa's gone to get me to yourself. What's matter?'

'I hope you don't mean Grandpa.' Lily stared into the flames. 'Talking about dying.' Nanna was nearly always right in her prophecies.

'I don't mean Grandpa. I wish I had never said it.' Nanna put down her crochet. 'I asked, what's up?'

'Everything...' Lily hesitated, wanting to ask, dreading it and saying. 'I don't like seeing Mam upset.'

'Poor Mollie Leadbetter...'

'And Mr Leigh's wife,' she reminded Nanna.

Nanna's fingers stopped. 'Who?'

'Howard Willey-Leigh. His wife died.'

Nanna looked puzzled. 'I thought she must a' died long since.'

'She had been in a nursing home for years.' Lily tried to say it carelessly, and then, in a shaky voice. 'Do you like him, Nanna?'

'Don't you?' Nanna's brows came together in two deep lines over her nose. 'What would you think of Mr Leigh for a father?'

'I hate him!' Lily leaped to her feet. 'I don't want Mam married to anyone except my own true father.'

'I am sorry, Lil.' Nanna struggled to her feet and held out her arms. 'I was mistaken. I shouldn't a' said it.'

Lily shrugged out of Nanna's embrace and went to the window, pretending to look up the lane for Grandpa. She heard Nanna behind her, poking the fire. She had upset Nanna. It was the first awkward silence ever between them, and she heard Nanna saying softly, 'Two deaths. There will be another.' Then, 'Don't tell Grandpa, Lil. He says superstition is devil's work.'

She had upset her darling Nanna. Lily tried to do the trick of the mind, concentrate on something, think about the RSA exams, but it didn't work. She stared through the little leaded squares of glass into the fading white light of the late afternoon that made the lane and the drystone walls, the bare trees and the distant hills appear soft and smoky, the edges blurred. She tried to concentrate on the view. That didn't work either, but her anger had gone and her courage had come.

She turned and looked straight at Nanna. 'I saw my medical record. It said, "Miss Elsie Stanway". Miss not Mrs. It said, "Father unknown".'

The colour drained from Nanna's face. 'You know...'

'Why did you lie, Nanna? You taught me that hiding the truth was as bad as lying.' Nanna's lying to her had hurt almost more than anything.

Nanna was deathly pale. 'It wasn't my secret to tell.'

Lily drew in a long breath to steady herself. 'Who was my father?'

'I don't know.'

Lily could not believe that Mam had kept her secret from everyone. Nanna was pale, but Lily said in a voice that belied her tight, aching throat, 'You must know. You're Mam's mother.'

'This is dreadful. I never expected this.' Nanna's voice was weak. 'Your Mam refused to name him.'

'Why?' Lily's throat went tighter. 'Wouldn't she tell Grandpa?'

Nanna went to stand in front of the fire. Then, in a great effort at self-possession, she drew a deep, steadying breath. 'Grandpa demanded but I wouldn't have given tuppence for his life if our Elsie had told him who was responsible.' She added softly, 'Your grandpa asked, "Is he alive?" and Elsie said yes.'

Lily's control was going. 'But if he was alive, then...'

Nanna's eyes were full of sadness. 'I said to Elsie, "You will have to tell the child, one day." And she said, "It happens all the time. It's nobody's business but the mother's." '

'But if it happens all the time, children could grow up not knowing their own brothers and sisters. Marrying them...' Lily whispered.

Nanna said, 'I said same thing. Elsie said, "There's no chance of that happening. None at all." '

So the man who was her father had no children of his own? Then why didn't they marry? Lily's knees went weak. 'Was Mam speaking the truth? Saying he had no children.'

Nanna said, 'I'd stake my life. Your mam's not a liar.'

'Not much!' Lily's throat was tight and painful. 'She's lived a lie with me all these years.'

'Don't, lass.'

Lily tried to drive back the pain that was a heavy weight in her chest. 'Mam made you lie too. And Grandpa, who won't break commandments. It's bearing false witness telling lies!'

Nanna looked old and wretched now, but Lily couldn't stop. She had to find out. 'Did you stop asking?'

Nanna said, 'No. I said, "If nothing else, a father should pay." '

'What did she say to that?'

Nanna said, 'It was hurtful to your Mam, saying that. She said, "I'll support my own child. I'll not ask you and Dad for a penny." I felt so small. I felt as if I'd let her down.'

'You didn't. Mam let you down when she had me.' Then, realising that this at least was true, Lily dropped on to

Grandpa's chair, covered her face with her hands and, choking on the tears she'd held back so long, said, 'I don't want to live like this – afraid in case anyone finds out. What can I do?'

Nanna, seeing her crumple, gathered herself. She would never be crushed by anything, no matter how deep their troubles might be. She said, 'You can do nothing. It won't help, upsetting yourself.'

The old fear – the afraid-of-being-found-out fear – was back. Lily's voice had almost gone. 'That record... Will it follow me for the rest of my life?'

'Only doctors will see it,' Nanna said with absolute certainty. 'They'll have asked for your birth certificate when you were enrolled.'

'You can't hide the truth for ever, from everybody...'

Nanna said, 'No. There is no father's name on your birth certificate.'

Hopeless tears were rolling down Lily's face. She said, 'The only clue I have is that once I heard Mam say that I was called Lily Isobel after my two grandmothers.'

'She never said that to me...'

Lily said, 'Mam says now that I'm imagining. But I'm not.' She looked up at Nanna.

'I don't know anyone of my age called Lily. It's a common enough name. But no – I don't.' Nanna put her hand out to touch Lily's arm, but she flinched away.

'Your generation never use Christian names, except for children and close family, do you?' Lily's eyes were blinded with tears as she said, 'When will I find out? I have to, one day. Anyone would. Anyone would be curious.'

Nanna went to the settle, sat down and said quietly, 'No crying, our Lil.' She spoke with a calm authority. 'I want to tell you something. It may be hurtful, but ... but sooner you stop dwelling on it, faster you'll get over it.'

Lily went to sit beside her. 'I can't...'

'I prayed that one day you would understand. What I have to say has to be said for your own good.' Nanna took hold of her hands.

'Say what?'

'You have to do some good in this life. You are not here just to please yourself – or to please other people. You are here, on earth, to do your bit. God will tell you what. You can only ask God for thanks.'

'I don't want to be thanked. I'm crying because—'

Nanna would not listen. 'Don't expect anyone to feel sorry for you. Especially if you have a little bit more of anything they want for themselves - money, or good looks...'

'Or a dad?' Lily whispered.

'You have to be strong, Lily.'

'But I have to know...'

'You mean, you want to.' Nanna stood. 'There is nothing more certain. If she won't tell me, Elsie won't tell you. In this life we all have our loads, our crosses to bear. What's for you, what's coming to you won't pass you by. It's how you bear your cross that matters. Only you can fettle it. We have to shift for ourselves. Sooner you learn that, better.'

Nanna's strength was helping. Lily held fast and tried to ask, without tears, 'If I were to be baptised, could I get a new birth certificate? Would it make it right? Would I still be illegitimate?'

'Oh, Lil! You were born out of wedlock. You can't have a new birth certificate unless someone adopts you and you change your name. It has nothing to do with being baptised. You have to make something of your life, love. God's given you talents. Don't dwell on what can't be helped.'

She would have to summon her will, put this to the back of her mind until the time came to shift for herself. Before she could bury it deep she had to ask for as much as Nanna would tell. 'Will you tell me all you know?' she said. 'I'll never mention it again.'

Nanna smiled at last and patted her cheek tenderly. 'Come on. Put your coat on. We'll walk down lane. Meet Grandpa. I'll tell you.'

The lane was frozen hard. Here in the hills the snow had lain. Little drifts had been blown against the grassy sides of the drive, narrowing the way, and Lily clung on to Nanna's arm as they went slowly along, listening intently as Nanna recalled in a low voice the years before Lily was born.

'Before the war, when Elsie lived at home with us, she was as happy as a lark. Eeh! She was beautiful! Frank Chancellor and John Hammond were sweet on her.'

With a sick feeling Lily remembered the photographs. 'You don't think Mr Hammond or Mr Chancellor...?'

'No,' Nanna said firmly. Then, 'You were born in nineteen twenty. By then Frank Chancellor and John Hammond were well and truly married, both with young families. And away in France, fighting a war. You mam couldn't have ... and she wouldn't. Not with a married man...' Nanna held faster on to Lily's arm and pulled her close. 'It would be a terrible sin – breaking seventh commandment, Lil. And your mam had proposals galore from single men. She'd met Howard Willey-Leigh and brought him to meet us. He was single and he never went in army. But he was condescending, I thought. He acted as if he was too good for Elsie. He was going to inherit a title and a manor at Didsbury, but before we knew what, his old uncle married and had two sons – and that was end of Howard's big talk. Then Elsie fell out with Howard Willey-Leigh. Only she was expecting.'

'So Howard Leigh might be my father?' Lily had to say it – had to put it into words, although everything in her revolted at the thought of being the result of anything between Mam and Howard Leigh.

'I don't know,' Nanna said, then, feeling the stiffening in Lily's arm, she added, 'I always thought Howard was smitten with Elsie but against his better judgement. I didn't believe he had all that money. He was putting it on.'

'I think you are right.' Lily was sure Nanna was right. Howard Leigh was not the wealthy, well-bred gentleman Mam thought him.

'Elsie dropped him and Howard Willey-Leigh went off and married the rich widow-woman. I had a feeling Elsie just let him go, never told him she was expecting. I never heard his name mentioned again until today.'

'I can't understand it.' Howard Willey-Leigh could not be her father. A father would not do those things – touch a girl's bare bottom, wink and ogle his own flesh and blood – would he? 'What about Tommy Stanway?'

'He was real. A cousin who had gone to war. Elsie couldn't brazen it out in Macclesfield. We sent her to Manchester. When Tommy Stanway was killed at Ypres, we put it about that

Elsie was his widow.'

'But anyone could have worked out that I was born soon after they were married.'

'That's nothing, love. Many a proud woman in Macc had to get married quick. 'Specially in wartime.'

'Is that true?' Lily could hardly believe it.

'Oh, yes! There's plenty of shotgun weddings. No long dresses and bouquets; no photos. A quick trip to church or registry office and no questions asked. There's never been enough men to go round, see? Young men go off adventuring or fighting wars. Good girls had to make most of their chances. Precious few married women can talk about anyone else.'

'People do talk. You and Mam talk about people. Mr and Mrs Chancellor had to marry, you said. Because she was having a baby when Mr Chancellor went off to war. You said the baby was not premature because it had fingernails.'

'I know. I feel right ashamed of meself after.' Nanna sighed a little. 'There has always been hypocrisy and plenty of talk inside families, plenty of speculation. Nobody can afford to spread it about for fear of skeletons coming a-popping out of their closets.'

Lily's feet were freezing but her face was burning at the thought of all this gossip, this bearing of false witness. 'I think it's disgraceful!'

'It is. But it's life, lass and it's what people are like in Macc. I daresay people are same all over.' Nanna patted Lily's arm. 'You're not. Grandpa and I are proud of you. You've had a good religious background.'

'So had Mam,' she replied quickly.

'Don't be harsh, Lil,' Nanna said. 'It's good Lord's place to judge,' and seeing Lily's hurt expression, 'No matter what you do, people will talk.'

The injustice, the hypocrisy was hateful. 'So what will people say about Mollie Leadbetter? Will they say she asked for trouble?'

'They will not speak ill of dead. Nobody will do that.'

Lily quietened down as they went slowly through the fast-darkening afternoon, then she asked, 'Did Mam ever think about a bortion, Nanna?'

Nanna stopped in her tracks. 'No, lass! She wanted you. I admired her for it. We know that God punishes wrong, sending dead babies or babies with club feet and such as a punishment. But after I'd recovered from shock I said, "Our Elsie, it might be only one you ever have. Some of us can't have babies to order. Good Lord intends that you have a baby. It's God's will. I'll stand by you." And your mam would not have had any more. She had to have everything taken away after you were born. Good Lord must a' wanted you to do his work. You were a perfect child.'

Lily had a lump in her throat again. They went forward a few paces before Nanna added, 'Anyway, I had a feeling as she loved this man, your father. Had a feeling she was still seeing him.'

Lily drew in the cold air with a quick breath. 'I think she still does.' She could not tell Nanna about the night visitor to the house. Instead she said, 'The shop doesn't take a lot but we pay our bills. I used to think we were always in debt. We are not. Mam gives me money every week to buy food and pay the coalman.'

'And you think someone else is paying for it?'

Lily felt the shiver again. 'I'm sure we're being kept.'

'Your mam's busy, doing all that sewing. You could be wrong.'

'Nanna! There are twelve dressmakers and tailoresses in Macclesfield. None of them's rich. Mam is not trying to get by on what she earns. Or on fifteen shillings a week. That's what a man has to pay. Fifteen shillings for every bast—' She couldn't finish. But she made up her mind there and then that it must stop. When she could, she would take over all the household expenses: pay the rent, buy the coal, pay Seymour Mead's. If her suspicions were right – if her father was keeping Mam and herself, and not making himself known – Lily could not bear it. If he was alive and he had no children he must not want her. She and Mam wouldn't be kept any longer.

They slithered along the lane. It was growing darker and Nanna peered into the distance every few steps, anxious for Grandpa's safety. She said, 'There he is!'

Lily could just make out Grandpa's shape, walking and leaning on his stick, under the trees ahead. The road was slippery and he was slow.

'Don't say anything more,' Nanna said urgently. 'No more. I will tell your mam.'

'No, Nanna!' Nanna must not say anything. 'I'll tell her myself. When I'm ready. I don't want her to know that I know.' When the time was right she'd tell Mam. She was not afraid. She'd wait for the right moment.

'All right. Let me get to Grandpa.' Nanna went ahead, her sturdy feet crunching firmly in spite of her rheumatics into the frosty grass verge. Lily stood for a few minutes watching and waiting before she heard a motor car rounding the corner: the Hammonds' Daimler, with Mr Hammond at the wheel. Lily stepped back to give him room to pass, but he drew up alongside. Sylvia and Magnus were in the back, Sylvia wearing her school uniform of navy-blue coat and hat, her blonde hair tied back. Magnus had his elbows on his knees, face in his hands.

Sylvia wound down the window. 'Lily, we called at Lindow to ask you to come to Archerfield with us. Will you come?'

Magnus glanced at her. His face was chalk white. He didn't speak a word. Lily hesitated, peering ahead to where Nanna and Grandpa were approaching. Sylvia whispered, 'Please, Lily...'

'Yes...' Nanna and Grandpa had come to stand beside her.

Sylvia opened the door and held it wide. Lily said to Nanna. 'Sylvia wants me to go to Archerfield...' But Mr Hammond had left the engine running and got out of the car.

'How will I get back?' she asked Sylvia. 'It will be dark soon and I can hardly keep on my feet as it is.'

'I'll bring you back, Lily.' Mr Hammond put a hand beneath her elbow. 'Sylvia needs your company this evening.'

Nanna nodded. Mr Hammond started to speak to Grandpa and Nanna as Lily climbed in to sit next to Sylvia. She turned and stuck her head out of the open window only to see Nanna's hands fly to her mouth, as they did when she heard something dreadful. Grandpa put his hand to his ear to cut out the sound of the running engine. 'What was that?'

Mr Hammond was repeating what he had just said, louder this time. 'There has been an accident in Macclesfield. Mrs Chancellor. She must have slipped. Fell on to the line, under the London train.'

'God save us!' Grandpa said. 'Is she...?'

'Died instantly,' Mr Hammond said. 'Mrs Hammond's doing what she can. Magnus and I have to go back. Sylvia didn't want to be left in the house alone.'

Nanna said, 'If there is anything you want me to do...'

Mr Hammond returned to the driver's seat, and with a nod in Grandpa's direction, let in the gear. The Daimler headed for Archerfield, and Lily felt an icy hand of fear clutch her heart. Nanna's prophecy had come to pass. Three deaths: Mollie, Mrs Willey-Leigh, Mrs Chancellor.

Later Lily would come to see this day as a turning point in their lives, but now she sat in silence, waiting for Sylvia or Magnus to speak, waiting to hear from her friends' lips what had happened in Macclesfield.

Sylvia told a maid to bring food up to the old schoolroom. Padded armchairs replaced the old wooden ones. There was a fire, the lamps were lit, the maid brought in the wheeled trolley, and when the girl had gone Sylvia thumped down into a chair and stared at the flames. 'Serve it, Lily. I can't...'

Spread before them was the most tempting feast Lily had seen since her last visit to Archerfield. There were sandwiches and bread and thick slices cut from a roast rib of beef, with mustard, pickled cucumbers and cheeses on a huge platter. There was a pile of pikelets and oatcakes - Macclesfield's crumpets and oat pancakes - with toasting forks and a slab of butter beside them. There was honey and raspberry jam, scones and fruit cake. Lily could not wait a minute longer. 'May I start?' she asked. 'Will you pour the tea?' Not until she'd eaten a sandwich, loaded a toasting fork and held it up before the glowing coals did she ask Sylvia, 'What happened?'

Sylvia poured for them and leaned back in her chair, gazing into the fire. 'They were going to be Mayor and Mayoress,' she said. 'They were so proud. But Lily ... I can't believe it was an accident. She was out of her mind.'

'Mrs Chancellor?'

'Mama and she have been friends for years.' Sylvia's face had a faraway expression. 'Mrs Chancellor was madly in love with Father, you know. Mama never guessed but I could tell by the way she looked at him.'

Shen fell silent again, and Lily prompted, 'What happened?'

She passed Sylvia's cup. 'Drink this. You'll feel better.'

Sylvia drank a little, placed the saucer on the arm of the chair and leaned forward, talking in a fast, nervous little voice. 'Last week Mama and I went to Park Lane. Mrs Chancellor looked awful. She said Mr Leadbetter was telling dreadful lies – claiming that Ray had raped Mollie.' Sylvia paused, then, 'A boy has to marry the girl if she's expecting his baby. Mr Leadbetter said, "Ray has to marry our Mollie."'

'What did Mrs Chancellor say?' Lily sat at the table as Sylvia talked, eating her way through the vast meal, barely tasting a thing, remembering Mollie, thinking how it must have been for Mam – and trying to fill the aching hole inside herself with the warm comfort of food.

'She was in tears, but she said, "Ray has never heard of the girl. How could he have?"'

But Lily had a logical brain and could not help but think how they could have met. 'Mr Chancellor owns Mr Leadbetter's shop,' she said. 'Ray could have collected the rents.'

Sylvia couldn't bear Lily to have doubts. Tears sprang to her eyes, making Lily say quickly, 'I don't mean to say that he has done anything wrong, Sylvia. Only that he could have met Mollie...'

'Ray's not capable of low behaviour. He's religious, like his mother. And a bit snobbish. A simpleton like Mollie Leadbetter would have had no interest for him. Couldn't have!' She sipped the tea. 'According to Mrs Chancellor there was a terrible row. Mrs Chancellor demanded that Mr Leadbetter make a public apology, beg hers and Ray's pardon. She said Ray would not do a wicked, sinful thing. Mr Chancellor stopped her and said, "No matter who it was, Mollie will have to be seen to." Then Mr Leadbetter said he had no money, so Mr Chancellor gave him twenty-five pounds and said it was out of concern for the Leadbetters. Mrs Chancellor told us that then she turned on him – on Mr Chancellor. She lost her head and started to scream, "Don't give him a penny! I can't have Ray's name associated with this evil thing." But Mr Chancellor insisted that they give Mr Leadbetter the money. It did not mean they were covering up for Ray. Then Mrs Chancellor flew out of the room, shouting, "Ray has done nothing wrong. Call in the lawyers! I want to see my lawyer."'

Sylvia's words were tumbling faster. 'Mollie died... Operation in Manchester... Came home... Something went wrong.' She leaned back in her chair, her face white, her china-blue eyes staring into the distance.

Cold shivers trickled down Lily's spine. She reached over to touch Sylvia. 'Just tell me slowly, Sylvia. Tell me what happened today.'

Sylvia held on to the chair's arm, sitting bolt upright.

'Mama, Father and I were going to the station to meet Magnus. Father said he'd drop Mama and me in Park Lane. We were to tell Mrs Chancellor that none of us believed the terrible rumours that are flying round town. Father said to tell her that if he heard anyone repeating the vile things he would take very strong action. Father would meet us at the station.

'When we arrived, Mrs Chancellor was distraught, pacing the Chinese carpet, back and forth, crying out, "My darling boy is coming home. He's coming home to face them." Then she stopped walking. "There'll be an inquest. Ray will be blamed."

'Mama tried to calm her, saying, "Nobody will blame Ray. Please, Sarah! Don't get into such a state over a little hussy who dies through her own cheap, brazen behaviour." It had no effect. Mama tried to be stern. "Pull yourself together!" Mrs Chancellor paced up and down again, saying, "Leadbetter has written to Ray's headmaster. He's been to the police, accusing us of forcing his daughter to have an abortion..." She threw herself on to a chair and dashed a handkerchief to her eyes, then said to me, "I'm sorry, Sylvia. Sorry you are hearing such things at your age."

'Mama said, "The sooner Sylvia learns about such things, the better." Mama is so very practical, you know, Lily.'

Lily could well imagine Mrs Hammond saying that Mollie had brought it on herself with her brazen behaviour. Thank God Mrs Hammond did not know the truth about Lily's illegitimacy. Her stomach churned. 'Then what?'

'Mrs Chancellor was tearing her handkerchief to shreds, but she stopped the awful crying and said, "Come to the station with me to meet Ray. My husband"' – she never refers to him by name – "my husband phoned the school yesterday, demanding that they send Ray home early. For the mayoral inauguration, we said, but they'd have received Leadbetter's wicked letter..." Then she was in tears again, and Mama nodded to me. Mrs Chancellor threw her arms about my neck. "Come to the station. Ray will be frantic in case anyone thinks..."

'"We're going to the station, Sarah. To meet Magnus." Mama said. "They will be on the same train."

'We went in Mr Chancellor's car. Mrs Chancellor wrung her hands and every now and again took half a dozen quick breaths. Father was waiting but Mrs Chancellor wouldn't speak a word. She stared at us all with a strange expression on her face that I had seen before. She kept looking at Father with the look of love in her eyes that I recognised. It was freezing. The wind tore down the platform where the mothers were holding on to their coats and hats. I was silent, my coat collar about my ears, hat elastic clamped tight under my chin, asking myself how they could go on to be Mayor and Mayoress after this. The train was late. Magnus was on it. There was no sign of Ray. Magnus said they had travelled together as far as Manchester but Ray wanted to walk across to London Road station for the Macclesfield train. The Edinburgh train comes in at Exchange and Magnus has to go by taxi because of his ankles. Father was so kind and gentle to Mrs Chancellor. But whatever he said seemed to make her worse. She didn't speak. We all waited for the next train. And Ray wasn't on it. People were staring at us all – we are all so well known – and asking why we were there.

'Mr Chancellor was furious by this time. He kept going to the station master's office, enquiring and all the time getting increasingly angry, and ignoring his poor wife, who was shaking with cold and looking ill. "He can't have missed the blasted train!" he was saying, louder every time he repeated it. "Ray knows why he's been sent for. What's he playing at?"

'It was an hour before the next train came. This one was crowded but Ray wasn't on it, and again we had to wait. Mrs Chancellor's whole body was shaking by this time and Mama and I were standing close to her in case she fainted. She still would not speak and Father was making it worse, I thought. He kept holding Mrs Chancellor's shoulder to comfort her, saying, "Oh, Sarah dear. Oh my poor, dear Sarah!" But we waited, and waited, and all the while it grew darker and the far end of the platform could hardly be seen. At last we heard it coming.

'And, Lily...!' Sylvia put her handkerchief to her eyes.

Lily put a hand on Sylvia's arm. 'Don't tell me if it makes you cry.'

'I must.' Sylvia took a great gulping breath and after only a few seconds told the rest, very fast.

'Ray was not on that train. We were freezing, sick with cold. And we daren't leave. You don't know how awful it was. We could not leave Mrs Chancellor. We couldn't say, "Sorry, we have to go!" so we waited until the last person had gone. Then Mrs Chancellor went wild. She ran the length of the train, crying, "He's not here! I can't find my boy!" Mama grabbed her arm and held her back. "Wait for the next one, Sarah." But she pulled free and set off again towards the front of the train. Mr Chancellor stamped about saying, "It's going to cost more than money. We'll be ruined. Wait till I get my hands on Ray. I'll..."

'Mama gave her attention to him in case he thought Ray was afraid of facing the music. While all this was going on the station master blew his whistle, the guard waved his green flag, the engine pulled away and the guard's van disappeared into the tunnel.

'My eyes searched frantically for Mrs Chancellor, but I realised she'd gone. She had not come back up the platform once she had reached the engine – and the engine stops a few yards from the tunnel entrance. I broke out in a cold sweat, grabbed Mr Chancellor's arm and shouted, "Find your wife! Hurry! Please! I think she's in the tunnel."

'"What? Where is she?"

'"She went down the platform. Into the tunnel!" I could hear myself screaming. He didn't hear what I was saying until Mama came and shook me by the arm. I pushed her away, took Mr Chancellor's and yelled, "Your wife! Your wife's in the tunnel!"

'He looked startled. Angry. Then fear came flickering into his eyes and he said her name, "Sarah?" Then louder, "Sarah!" He drew away and ran to the station master, shouting. "My wife's in the tunnel."

'The station master blew his whistle hard and porters came rushing from everywhere, grabbing lanterns, leaping down on to the line to cross over. They pushed us – Mama and me – into the ladies' waiting room, and everywhere people were shouting and running. As soon as Mama was seated and had put her head back and closed her eyes I went out and followed the men. And then I heard, from a long way down the tunnel, a man's voice: "Don't let her husband see this, for God's sake!" But Mr Chancellor was there. I heard him saying, "She must have fallen on to the line. It was an accident."

'Two porters came out of the tunnel on to the platform. One leaned over the line, clutching his stomach before he was violently sick, whilst the other man held him back from toppling over. The second porter said, "That were nay accident, mate. Nay accident..." '

Magnus, sitting in the Daimler, noticed Father's hands tight on the wheel. His face was grey. Magnus had never seen his father look like this, even when Grandfather died. He loved being with Father, whom he admired above all men. He said, 'There is not a lot we can do. Do you think we should offer to stay at Park Lane overnight?'

'I expect he'd rather be left on his own,' Father said. 'If anything like that ever happened to me...' There were tears in his eyes. 'I don't think I could go on without your mother.' He caught his breath. They drove in silence for another couple of miles. Then, 'You OK? Had some food?'

'I'm all right. Cook gave me soup and cold stuff.'

Father was quiet for a few minutes, then, 'Did Ray say anything on the journey? Did he know why he'd been sent for? Did he give any indication?' He glanced at Magnus here. 'We can't be sure the poor boy knew what he was being accused of.'

Magnus, remembering the trouble Ray was in at school – and one never kicked a chap who was down – said, 'It was as much a shock to him, Father, as it was to...' He saw the relief on his Father's face.

Father put a hand up. 'I don't want to hear any more. I'm sorry if, by asking, I have given you the idea I had any doubt.'

Magnus stared into the darkness ahead and said nothing. He

had lied to his father, but he was tired after the long, terrible day.

At seven o'clock in the morning Magnus, carrying an overnight bag, had arrived at Edinburgh's Waverley station to catch the train to Manchester, It was cold, there were few people about and he did not see Ray until he came out of the booking hall.

'Over here, Magnus!' Looking along the platform Magnus spotted Ray sitting surrounded by luggage. On the telephone to Mother and Father last night Magnus had been told about this dreadful business with the Leadbetter lass.

Ray called to him, 'Find a porter. Give him half a crown, will you? See if he can find first-class seats for us.'

'I'm travelling second,' Magnus said.

'Second? Don't be a fool. Give the porter half a crown.'

'Not strictly fair...' Magnus protested.

Ray butted in with, 'Come on! If you never take a chance...'

'Four bob? How's that?' Magnus said, and chided himself for being a two-faced coward even as he hailed a porter. He did not want to travel with Ray because he couldn't think how to act.

Ten minutes later, in a plush first-class compartment, Magnus leaned against the upholstery in relief. Since he had done all the dirty work, he felt he had the right to question Ray, though it was best to pretend he knew nothing. 'What have you been up to? You're in trouble at school.'

'Fuck the school!' Ray said.

Magnus was not shocked by Ray's language. In a way he admired Ray's nerve. He kept a composed expression but, seeing scorn on Ray's face, said, 'Swearing's no help. You are in trouble at school.'

'Nothing to what's waiting for me at home.'

Magnus said, 'What's that?'

Ray had a defiant expression. 'The parents of some girl – a girl I've never seen – are claiming that I gave her one.'

Magnus had not heard the expression. 'One? One of what?'

'Gave her a baby. She died. The girl.'

The little hairs on Magnus's arms were rising. He was

shocked by Ray's heartless talk and now could not hide it. Ray was being accused of a callous crime. If it had been he, Magnus, who had to face them, he would have been a wreck. 'But she's dead! And the baby.'

'It could be anyone's baby. Bloody girl asks for it. Every man in Macclesfield's had his shilling's-worth of Mollie Leadbetter. She was a whore. The Leadbetters were on to a good thing, naming me.'

'Hell's bells!' said Magnus.

Ray continued, 'I've denied all knowledge, of course.'

Ray was in trouble in both Edinburgh and Macclesfield. He deserved to be in trouble at school, no question about that. But he had not done anything despicable. Could not have – Magnus and Sylvia had known him all their lives. Ray must be going through absolute hell. It took guts to stand up for yourself when you were being done a gross injustice. Magnus said, 'Is that why you're going home? To tell them to their faces?'

'I wouldn't give them the satisfaction! If anyone wants to think...' Ray said no more but turned his face to the window.

Magnus watched him. Ray was worn out, despite the bravado. He was unshaven and dishevelled, as if he had not slept for a week with worry. Magnus was sorry for him. He would not be able to face his own dear father if he were in Ray's shoes.

Ray glanced back, shrugged and held out his hands, palms upward. 'I hope to God my folks don't think I am responsible,' he said. 'Father's going to be Mayor. I'd never let Mother down.'

'They're on your side,' Magnus said. 'My family says you've been maligned.'

'How do you know?'

'I spoke to Mother and Father on the telephone,' Magnus said. 'They told me. Last night.'

'What did they say?'

'Father said, "It's scandalous. The good name of Chancellor is being besmirched. This vilifying gossip must stop. Ray will come back and put an end to it." Mother said, "It's preposterous, blaming Ray for this girl's death." '

Ray was clearly relieved, and Magnus went on, 'Mother said, "Tell Ray to come home. We are all behind him. Nobody in Macclesfield blames Ray. We'll defend him to the end..." ' Magnus was getting carried away. What his mother had actually said was, 'No one thinks he's to blame. Tell him not to be afraid to face his accusers.'

Ray said, 'How about Sylvia?'

'Sylvia thinks the same as Mother.' Magnus had not spoken to Sylvia. Sylvia always thought the same as Mother.

Ray smiled, and Magnus now came straight to the point. 'When you didn't go to rugby practice, where were you?' he said. 'We should have the same story when we get home.'

Ray said, 'I have a friend in Edinburgh. My friend was taken ill. So I went to see . . . Good Samaritan!' Then he threw back his head and roared with laughter.

'Why didn't you tell the school?' Magnus said.

'Fuck the school!' were Ray's last words.

Chapter Eleven

Shandy met Lily at the Central Station when she arrived back on Sunday afternoon. Since they became friends they had hardly ever been apart.

'Have you heard?' Shandy came running and shouting along the platform, one hand on the door to open it.

Lily was the only passenger. She jumped down and slammed the carriage door. 'Mrs Chancellor?' She had a sinking feeling in her stomach.

Shandy said, 'Everyone's talking about it. Mrs Chancellor wandering down the platform in the dark, falling on to the line.'

At the thought of all the talk, a wave of disgust washed over Lily. What sort of town was it where rumour and fact circulated faster than the wind? It must be nigh on impossible to keep a secret here. But Mam had kept hers. And she herself had told Nanna that gossiping was disgraceful, but she always repeated to Shandy everything Doreen said. They were in the cobbled area of Waters Green. 'Which way? Hundred and Eight steps? Brunswick Hill? Or the long way, up Churchwallgate?'

'The long way.' Shandy tugged at Lily's arm, pulling her through the deserted bottom market to the hill that wound steeply to the Market Place.

Lily gazed up at the sheer high wall and the tower of St Michael's, and made up her mind to go to church tonight. It was Palm Sunday and they would sing 'When I survey the Wondrous Cross' – one of her favourite hymns. She would sit at the side, under the Burne Jones window of the steely, kneeling knight in armour, and pray for Mrs Chancellor who would not get to heaven if she had meant to kill herself. God could read thoughts.

The church clock said five past five. Evensong was at half past six. The square was quiet and they made their way round the back of the church to Sparrow Park. Tragedy had no place here, for spring had returned and the daffodils were tumbled, muddy and higgledy-piggledy, but still in bloom about the patch of grass and the steep grassy hill under the wall they leaned upon. There was a soft, heather-scented breeze blowing from the hills, warming the earth again, drying the cobbles and flagstones in the Waters below. Lily said, 'What do you think? Do you think Mrs Chancellor killed herself because Ray didn't come?' She waited a moment, then, 'Doreen said Ray Chancellor was under the bridge with Mollie. She said she saw them.'

Shandy said, 'Don't believe a word Doreen Grimshaw says. Ray was on the next train. He came in an hour after his mother had fallen. He was heartbroken. The station lads told our Cyril that Ray was in a terrible state.' She said. 'Doreen's got a wicked tongue. Mollie had to name somebody to her mam and dad, didn't she?'

Impulsively Lily hugged Shandy and kissed her cheek. Of course! Mollie couldn't say it was any old lad. She wouldn't want her parents to think she was a trollop, doing it all over the place. She said, 'I am glad you're my friend, Shandy. You always think the best of everyone.'

'I don't. Not of Doreen Grimshaw.'

'What are you doing later?' Lily asked. 'I'm going to church.'

'You're very religious, Lily. That's what everyone says.'

Lily said, 'It's not only God and praying that I go for. It's the beautiful words and music. I love the boy choristers' singing and chanting and the organ playing.' It was only part of the reason she was going tonight. There was a bit in the Bible that kept coming to mind: 'Ask, and it shall be given you: seek, and ye shall find; knock, and it shall be opened unto you. For everyone that asketh receiveth; and he that seeketh findeth; and to him that knocketh it shall be opened.'

When she reached home Lily saw that Mam was excited, wrought up, standing by the range in the kitchen, one hand on the mantel shelf above the fire. Mam never had a good word to say about Mrs Chancellor, and Lily had been worried that she might be stricken with remorse. She said, 'Oh, Mam! What a terrible thing!'

Mam stamped her cigarette out into the glass ashtray, said nothing but reached for another Craven 'A' and held a paper spill out to the flames.

'Sylvia told me. She thought that Mrs Chancellor had lost her mind because Ray didn't come.'

'Did she?' Mam sent a stream of smoke upwards towards the clothes rack. 'I expect everyone has their own ideas.' Mam took a quick, nervous draw on the cigarette. 'It's the finish for Frank. He'll never be Mayor now.'

'Because people think Mrs Chancellor took her own life?' Lily was shocked by Mam's hardness. 'She didn't know what she was doing.'

'Sarah Chancellor always knew what she was doing. And why. It's going to make a big difference. Not just to the Leadbetters. John Hammond was here an hour ago,' she said. 'He's an executor of her will. Sarah Chancellor has left a lot of money.'

'I suppose she has...' Lily said.

'She's left money to over a hundred people, John said.' Mam threw this second cigarette into the fire. 'She'll have spread money about so Frank gets as little as possible. She was a clever woman.'

'Mam! Don't speak ill of the dead.'

Mam wasn't listening. 'We are mentioned. She's left something.'

'Who to?'

'To you and me.' Mam ran her fingers through her hair, making it go straggly. 'It's the will-reading after the funeral on Wednesday afternoon. John says that all the beneficiaries have to be there. Frank will have to close the mill for the day so the workers can go.'

'I'm too young, aren't I?' she said.

'John says everyone mentioned must go, even infants and minors.'

'I am not an infant...'

'In the eyes of the law you are. Until you're twenty-one.'

Mam did not sound sure. Lately, Mam asked what Lily thought about people and why they said or did things; she looked to Lily for a lead. Lily wanted Mam to rely on her, so she squared her shoulders and said firmly, 'We'll go to the funeral and will-reading.'

Mam shifted things about on the mantel shelf and Lily held her breath in case she noticed that Tommy Stanway's picture had gone. When she did it she'd wanted Mam to ask why. This was not the time to speak. But Mam had not noticed. She said, 'If you're going to church you'd best get off.'

Mollie Leadbetter was buried in consecrated ground on the Tuesday. It was a quiet family affair which few attended. But the following day hundreds of people packed into St Michael's for Mrs Chancellor's funeral service. Ushers guided people to their seats until there was standing room only in the side aisles. People crowded round the font in the baptistry and packed into the little side chapel inside the church.

Mam and Lily arrived early. Mam was pale but she cut a smart figure in her black velvet hat and velour coat. Lily wore navy blue. They were shown to seats a couple of rows from the carved pulpit. The Chancellor family, Mr Chancellor's brothers and their wives and old Mrs Chancellor, were seated at the front.

Lily was quaking. Mam's serves were all a-jangle; a little pulse was beating fast in her throat and the tiny lines at the corner of her mouth tightened as the church filled with so many well-known people. The air was filled with that familiar, dusty, candlewax-and-old-paper scent of ancient churches that charged Lily up like a wireless battery, making her aware of her own heartbeat and every movement around her.

Lily dropped to her knees on the hassock and tried to pray, but for the first time in her life she could not concentrate, so, kneeling, she took the Book of Common Prayer from the little wooden box holder on the seat in front. It was the first funeral she had been to and she searched through until she came to the order of service for the Burial of the Dead. Then the colour drained from her face. The first words, in italics, were notes for the clergy: *Here is to be noted that the office ensuing is not to be used for any that die unbaptized, or excommunicate or have laid violent hands upon themselves.*

Lily clutched the back of the rush-seated chair in front.

'Sh! Don't make a noise!' Mam whispered, elbowing and frowning. 'Stand up. They are coming in.'

Everyone fell silent as the vicar, at the back of the church, said in loud singsong intonation, 'I am the resurrection and the life, saith the Lord...'

Mam nudged Lily so she'd keep her eyes straight ahead, but Lily could not. White as death herself, she watched the clergy walking slowly ahead of the brass-bound oak coffin. Behind, pale with grief, walked Mr Chancellor, leaning on the arm of his taller son. Ray was ashen-faced and tight-lipped, staring straight ahead, expressionless as the men put his mother's coffin down on the trestles that stood before the chancel steps.

Mr Chancellor's eyes were shiny with tears all through the chanting of the words of the thirty-ninth psalm, and Lily was overcome with pity, seeing the solemn faces about her. She couldn't chant the psalm but could only whisper, '... For man walketh in a vain shadow. He heapeth up riches and cannot tell who shall gather them...' Such beautiful words, whose rhythms were music and whose meaning was hidden.

When the psalm was over, Mr Birchenough had collected himself. He stood without support, eyes closed.

'Oh God Our Help in Ages Past' was next, a simple tune but a powerful hymn for raising a lump in the throat. The organist drew out the male voices, filling the church to the high vaulted roof with resounding song: '...A thousand ages in Thy sight are like an evening gone. Short as the watch that ends the night before the rising sun.'

Those very same words were repeated in the ninetieth psalm they chanted after: '... Seeing that is past as a watch in the night...' and a few verses on, 'Thou hast set out misdeeds before Thee, and our secret sins in the light of Thy countenance. The days of our age are threescore years and ten. So soon it passeth away and we are gone...'

But, under the influence of the ritual power of words, Lily was asking God all the questions that the service was putting into her mind, knowing that if she prayed hard enough God would give her the answers. She prayed, and the words came to her as if from another place: 'Are our lives, which are all we have, to you, Heavenly Father, as short as a watch in the night?

And if we are sinners and born in sin. Oh, please let me see the face of my own true father, dear Lord. And if I have no earthly father. . . ?'

Perhaps she had part of her answer, for wave upon wave of relief flooded through her when the service was over and she walked down Chestergate with Mam. They processed in sunshine up Prestbury Road to the cemetery among the other mourners, who spoke in whispers. Mam said not a word. The cortège passed and all the people stopped at the kerbside. First came the hearse, pulled by four black horses, black-plumed. Then followed a carriage carrying Mr Chancellor with Ray at his side. Behind came seven motor cars carrying the chief mourners and the Hammonds.

Lily said, 'It was a moving service, wasn't it, Mam?' as the cortège passed and they moved on again, 'What does it mean – at the end of the lesson – when St Paul says, "Oh death, where is thy sting? Oh grave, where is thy victory? The sting of death is sin, and the strength of sin is the law." What does that mean, Mam – about the strength of sin being the law?'

Mam looked at her, aghast. 'Where did you learn all that?'

'Out of the prayer book. I just read it.'

'And you memorised it? Just by reading it over?'

'Yes.'

Mam held her hand tighter and quickened her pace. 'You are a funny girl, Our Lil. Learning things off by heart. You'll have to watch out. Watch you don't overtax your brain.'

'What does it mean?' Lily persisted.

'I don't know. Ask Grandpa.'

Mr Chancellor broke down at the graveside. He slumped against Ray, who stood ramrod straight, staring into space as if he couldn't take it all in. Lily took it all in. She took in Mam's strained face. Mam had never taken her eyes off the Hammonds and the Chancellors. She was craning her neck to see the coffin and the raw earth heaped up beside the grave. But in the fresh spring air in the vast park of Macclesfield Cemetery, with the scents of newly dug earth, cut grass and blossom, Lily had lost her sense of doom. The words were being carried away from those who stood at the back. As the vicar said, 'Ashes to ashes. Dust to dust. . .' Lily look around. She saw Mrs Hammond's fixed expression and Magnus, just like his father, pale and shocked by it all. Sylvia was stately, standing tall and fair and above all display of emotion.

They walked for half an hour from the graveside to the house in Park Lane, where everyone crowded into a wide hall with double doors opening on to a long dining room, making one enormous room. The big table had been taken out and through the whole length little tables were set with plates of sandwiches and cakes, tea cups and saucers. Mam didn't join in the hand-touching and murmuring condolences but slid out of the line and sat at a table near the dividing door, as far as she could be from a long, narrow table at the far end of the dining room that was set as for a speaker, with a carafe and glass and a sloped book rest.

'Are all these people mentioned in the will?' Lily asked Mam. They were piling into the house – all sorts, from grand people like the Hammonds right down to millhands in tight jackets with their cloth caps rolled into tubes and stuffed into pockets.

'It looks like it.' Mam sounded more like herself now they were seated and inconspicuous. 'Look over there!' She dipped her head in the direction of the other end of the hall, making the black eye-veil on her hat quiver. 'Nellie Plant and the Leadbetters.'

'Do you think Mrs Chancellor has left all these people something?'

'Sh!' Mam dug her elbow into her. 'Someone's going to speak.'

Mr Chancellor was standing right next to Mam in the open doorway, and when everyone was silent he said, 'Thank you, ladies and gentlemen, for being with us on this day of deep grief for my son and myself.'

There was no trace of the grieving man Lily had seen earlier. He spoke of grief but he gave a confident nod in the direction of the far end of the hall, where maids entered carrying trays laden with tea pots, sugar and milk. He stepped back a little to let them pass, and said loudly over the clatter, 'You will be served with tea, and afterwards our lawyer – here he nodded towards the long table, where a morning-suited man had seated himself – 'will read the will.'

When the tea things were cleared away, Lily's mood of calm

expanded with the air of expectancy that lit up all the faces around them. It felt as if an electric current passed through everyone in the room when the grey-whiskered lawyer got up to speak.

'Ladies and gentlemen,' he said. 'It is my duty to read the will of my client, Mrs Sarah Chancellor. It is also my duty to inform all concerned that the said will was drawn up and sealed in my presence by the testator only a week ago, when my client could not have anticipated her tragic death. However, I must warn you that should the coroner come to a different conclusion as to the cause of death from that which prevails today, this will could be revoked and the terms of the testator's previous will would apply.'

He waited for someone to speak, but you could have heard a fly walking about if there had been one. He broke the seal on the great thick envelope and pulled out another wax-sealed and ribbon-bound document, which he opened out on the sloping box before him: six or seven sheets of parchment. Then, very slowly, in a deep, unemotional voice, he read:

'This is the last will and testament of me, Sarah Elizabeth Chancellor, of Pilkington House, Park Lane, Macclesfield. I hereby revoke all former wills and codicils and declare this to be my last will.

'I appoint John Hammond and his wife Catriona Hammond, of Archerfield House, Bollington, in the county of Cheshire, to be the Executors and Trustees of this my will.'

The lawyer glanced about the room again before returning his attention to the will. Much faster, and in a higher pitch of voice, as if he wanted to get this next part over and done with, he read:

'First, to my husband, Francis Chancellor. Upon marriage my husband was made a director of the printworks and given a ten per cent holding. He also received a generous settlement of tenanted properties. Francis Chancellor is entitled by law to a proportion of my personal property. There is nothing the law allows me to do to deprive him of these benefits or the legal right he has to live in our marital home until he marries again.

'But I owe him nothing. I leave him nothing.'

There was a noise – a shocked catching of breath – before, with a crashing sound, Mr Chancellor stood, letting his chair fall to the floor.

'No! No! No! Bloody vindictive!' His face was crimson, suffused with outrage, and everyone present saw this as permission to tut and sigh and cough and blow noses.

Lily should have felt pity for him, hearing how low he was held in his wife's esteem. But to her it was exciting. She could not help being impressed with all the drama. It was better than the cinema. She'd never seen grown-up people behaving like this, for other chairs were shuffling and some of the working people were saying, 'Shame! Shame!' and Mam's eyes were ablaze with what looked like triumph but must be anger. Nellie Plant's pale eyes were round as saucers and Mr Leadbetter's mouth was gaping open.

Ray Chancellor stood and put an arm about his father's shoulders, making everyone around the room voice their approval with cries of 'That's the ticket!' and 'Good lad!' It was a right and proper demonstration, a touching show of affection. Ray Chancellor spoke words of comfort in his father's ear to persuade him to sit again and hear the rest of the will-reading.

All this happened in about a minute, and the lawyer paused for a sip or two of water before continuing in the same solemn tones.

'Chancellor Printers is a family business founded by my father and left by him in trust to his beloved grandson, my dear son, Ray Francis. If I die before Ray Francis reaches his twenty-first birthday, the thirtieth of August, nineteen hundred and thirty-six, then until that time all of the printworks will be under the joint control of my husband and the trustees I have appointed.

'In nineteen thirty a private company was formed and it was necessary to raise capital. This was done by the issuing of debentures. For the sake of privacy we chose to have the debentures payable to bearer rather than registered holder. Bearer bonds are negotiable instruments and can be transferred from person to person by the simple process of handing over the said debenture documents without registration. I have handed over ninety-five per cent of my holding to my dear son Ray Francis and these will remain in trust for him should I die before my son reaches his majority.'

After this there followed a lengthy list of earnings from

stock holdings, mortgages, pensions, investments and dividends. Lily never knew such things existed. It was taking for ever to come to the end, and throughout this long recital, which fascinated her, chairs were being scraped as people became bored and moved their positions. Only the family, the Hammonds, Mam and Lily gave this dusty list their rapt attention. Lily was enthralled. No wonder these people were powerful compared with those, like themselves, who had only what they earned or could save.

At last the lawyer came to the bit everyone had been waiting for, and another electric silence fell over the room. 'The following bequests are to be met from the remaining five per cent holding in the printworks and such monies as are deposited under my name in the District Bank.

'To the tenants of the printworks' properties, whether working or pensioned, and their dependents I bequeath the properties entire and without entail. The deeds are to be handed over when my will is proved.

'I give and bequeath to the following women who may suffer loss as a result of my death the sum of three hundred pounds each. These named legatees are as follows: Miss Ellen Plant of High Street, Macclesfield, for her loyal service as head designer at Chancellors; Mrs Elsie Stanway of Jordangate, Macclesfield, for her services as my dressmaker; Miss Winifred Mitchell of Pickford Street, Macclesfield, for her services as my hairdresser; Miss Veronica Bell of Exchange Street, Macclesfield, for her services as my personal maid; Mrs Albert Leadbetter of Hibel Road, Macclesfield, for her services as purveyor of fruit and vegetables.'

There followed a list of small bequests to house servants, but Lily could not take any more in in detail. Her mind was whirling. They were rich! Three hundred pounds! They were rich beyond their wildest dreams and Mam was not smiling. The lawyer then tapped on the table for quiet.

'To such children who are above the age of eleven years, of the above legatees, I leave their choice of personal memento from the contents of my private sitting room and bedroom. I wish to have these two rooms emptied of my effects. The entire contents are afterwards to be sold and the proceeds given to the Guardians' Institute.

'Lastly I give and bequeath to my beloved son, Ray Francis Chancellor, the whole of the residue of my property, real and personal.'

The lawyer removed his pince-nez. 'Has anyone any questions?'

'What does it mean? Deeds and such without entail?' a man at the front called out.

The lawyer said, 'It means that Mrs Chancellor has given to her workers the houses they presently rent.'

'Won't we have to pay anything?' another asked.

The lawyer tapped upon the table again. 'Insofar as this will shall be proven, the terms of it will apply.'

'Our house is going to be condemned!' shouted somebody.

'And ours!'

'And mine!'

Every week or so a list of condemned properties was published in the *Macclesfield Courier*, streams of them week after week. Whole families were being sent to live in a vast estate of new houses on the Moss. They were luxurious houses, with gardens, electricity, hot and cold running water, flushing indoor lavatories and half-tiled kitchens and bathrooms. But not everyone wanted to go. Some saw it as a mark of shame to have had their slum houses pulled down. Others, it was said, would keep their coal in the bath; they knew only how to live in squalor.

'When will we know?' someone shouted from the back.

'None of us expects any dispute,' the lawyer said. 'The inquest was held yesterday. The coroner will give his verdict tomorrow. It is expected that he will be satisfied that death was accidental. The will can then be proved and the bequests made.'

There were murmurs of 'I don't understand it all' and other such banalities, but Lily's mind was already far ahead. Mrs Chancellor had given away the company houses to save having to pull them down or repair them – and to the people whose houses were rented from her husband she had given the means to buy them. They could buy their house. Or Mam could buy the bungalow she said she had always wanted. Either way they would be property owners and could say, 'That's my house!' A man had paid £375 for two houses in Macclesfield only last week, and they were good solid houses. They could buy two houses if they wanted to – live in one and rent out the other. Or buy a whole row of cottages. Or put the money in the bank and get the interest. That was as long as nobody tried to contest the will. But who would? Mr Leadbetter? Lily saw acceptance, or it might be resignation, in his eyes. He would take his bequest and drop his threats. And if Mr Leadbetter took his share there would be no justification for Mr Chancellor to contest the will.

Mr Hammond had come up to their table. 'Elsie, my dear! May I take Lily to the private sitting room to choose a memento?'

Lily followed him to a large, airy room that was painted white and gold. It was a pretty room, with wide spaces between the yellow silk-upholstered chairs and sofas. A modern Crane piano in an alcove was set about with photographs in silver frames – no music to be seen. There were pedestal tables holding ornaments that eight or so young people were examining under the eagle eye of Mrs Hammond who was standing in front of an empty marble fireplace. Magnus was not there but Sylvia was beside the window, looking out. Lily went to her. 'Can I have anything?'

'Anything,' Sylvia said. 'What is left has to be sold off and given to the workhouse. I think she was afraid that if Mr Chancellor marries again...' Sylvia put her finger to her lips.

Lily saw Dresden figures, silver boxes with purple linings, pots and bowls in lacquer and gold; all were set out for them to make their choices. Some of the children had chosen and were pointing their objects out to Mrs Hammond, who wrapped the mementoes for them. A stack of tissue paper lay upon one of the side tables for the purpose.

Mr Hammond came back and stood beside her. 'Well, Lily? Is there anything you'd like?'

There was. Behind the locked glass doors of a splendid tall bureau bookcase in red wood that had drawers and a locking cupboard under the shelves, she had seen two books; a blue leather-bound *Every Man's Own Lawyer* which said under the title, 'By A Barrister', and a red-bound one called *The Universal Home Lawyer*. Illustrated. She wanted them. If she had them she could find out all about wills and deeds and properties – and what it meant, legally, to be illegitimate. 'Could I have two of those books?'

Mr Hammond said, 'Lily! All the others have chosen something valuable. You want books.' He put his hand on her shoulder and called to Mrs Hammond. 'Come here, my dear.'

She came and stood, frowing. 'Lily? What do you want?'

'Those two books,' she said. 'If that's all right?'

'That will be all right.' She said to Mr Hammond, 'She may as well have all the books. And that hideous old bookcase. Nobody would buy it.'

'Very well.' Mr Hammond smiled at Lily. 'Take the two books you've chosen. I will have the others and the bookcase delivered to your house. But Lily, I thought you'd have asked for the piano.'

'I wouldn't have dared,' she said, blushing.

'I won't take no for an answer,' he said. 'You shall have the piano.'

Elsie stood at the little iron gate of Pilkington House, waiting for Lily. The pains in her neck had gone. The relief was tremendous. She had barely begun to take it all in when Frank came out to join her.

'Where's our Lil?' he said and touched her hand in a secret caress.

He had not taken it badly. Elsie's last fears evaporated. She returned the pressure of his hand. 'She's inside. Choosing a memento.'

He took his hand away, looked about; then, seeing nobody, said, 'Glad you came, love. It's been an ordeal.'

'And for me. I thought she might have said...' Elsie gave a relieved laugh, seeing that Frank's bouncy air had returned. 'I nearly fainted when the lawyer came to the bit about ... ladies who might suffer...!' She had her back to the front door and he nudged her to show her that Lily was coming out. Elsie, not seeing her, went on, 'In a year's time you will be free to do what you want. You can't pretend she's left you with nowt!'

Frank said, 'You're better off than I am now!' He put his head back and laughed out loud.

Elsie had now seen Lily, who was smiling at Frank's remark. 'The money won't make any difference to me,' she said. Then, as she spotted the parcel in Lily's arms, 'What did you pick for yourself?'

'Books,' Lily answered. 'Books about the law.'

'Books?' Elsie raised laughing eyes towards Frank. 'Who does she take after?' she said. 'Books! She's into everything.'

'You're a good friend, Elsie,' Frank said. 'One of the best.'

Elsie's smile vanished. She was more than a friend. But his visits had decreased over the last year. Frank's being an alderman, buying properties, running his trading company and, as he called it, 'working his clogs off' at the mill took up most of his free time. He told her when she'd asked if his interest was waning that he loved her, but he was getting on, nearing forty, his hair was greying and his appetites were going. That much was true; it was three weeks since they had last...

Oh God! She should not think that way. Not when Frank had so much on his plate – disappointment in his civic life and scandal to brazen out with people thinking Ray might be responsible for this rotten business. She frowned and said to Lily, 'We'd best get a move on.'

They had gone a little way down Park Lane when Lily asked, 'You didn't mean it, did you, Mam? About the money making no difference?'

Elsie stopped and looked around, and when she saw that there was nobody about she laughed, loud and heartily. 'Of course it will make a difference. I was just saying it, to see what Frank would say.'

'He didn't seem heartbroken to me,' Lily said. 'And he's rich, isn't he? All that property, and the rents.'

'He's done all right for himself,' Elsie said. 'Frank's already worth more than the combined assets of Chancellor's Printworks.'

'It said in the will that he will be in charge of the works and he can live in the house until he marries,' Lily said. 'Do you think he'll get married again?'

Elsie rebuked her. 'It's in poor taste, this conversation. With Sarah Chancellor only just laid to rest!'

'I didn't mean...' Lily's face was bright red. 'I shouldn't have said it.'

But Elsie wanted to keep on talking about it. Her mood was lightening with every relieved thought. Frank was free. They were no longer committing adultery. They could marry after a decent interval and at last she'd be a respectable married woman. Elsie Chancellor!

They were at the bottom of Mill Street by this time, not talking loud enough for anyone following to hear. 'What do you think, Lil?' she said. 'Can you see Frank marrying again?'

'No,' Lily answered. 'Of course he won't. He doesn't need to marry for money. He'll catch up on all the good times he missed when he was young. I think he'll – just gallivant!'

'Gallivant?' Elsie shook her head. 'He's not the sort. He's too old to play the fool. Don't believe what his wife said. Sarah Chancellor was bitter. She never loved Frank. Her will was no surprise.'

Elsie grabbed Lily's arm and tucked it into hers as they went fast up Mill Street. Lily asked, 'What shall we do with the money? We're rich, aren't we?'

'We'll do nothing with it. At first,' Elsie said.

'After a bit?' Lily asked. 'Will we buy property? Buy the shop?'

'No. I wouldn't live in Jordangate if I didn't have to.'

'We don't have to,' Lily answered. 'You could buy that bungalow you've always wanted.'

'What would you like to do with it?' Elsie asked, expansive now that everything was going to come out right. 'Come on, out with it. What do you want that money can buy?'

'I don't know. Just to know you are not poor any more.'

They were almost at the top of Mill Street. And all of a sudden Elsie felt as if a great weight had dropped off her shoulders. Frank would be back. How stupid to think he was losing interest in her. He had been having trouble controlling Ray for a long time. This business could have been hanging over him for weeks. He'd kept it to himself, not to worry her. She said, 'Not just me. *We* are rich. You and me.'

Lily said, 'And I'm taking over, Mam. I want us to pay our way. I'll make our expenses go round. You can do what you like with the legacy.'

'I know!' Elsie looked over her shoulder again, as if there might be an eavesdropper behind. Then, softly, she said, 'We are going to spend a little bit of it, making ourselves more comfortable. Then we'll have a holiday, and new clothes.

Whatever we fancy.'

'And put the rest into investments and bonds...?'

'No. I'm thirty-nine. I'd like to get married. Next year.' She and Frank must not become careless. There must be no gossip now. But in a year's time they could be seen to...

'You don't have anyone to marry.' Lily gave a strange, humourless laugh. 'Any anyway, you don't need to marry. You are out of it now.'

'And you,' Elsie said, as she glanced at her quickly. Lily was looking straight back into her mother's face with the clear-eyed gaze that was so like Frank's it often stopped her heart.

Then, and it was as if the bottom dropped out of Elsie's world, Lily said. 'No, Mam. I won't be out of it until you tell me who my father is.'

Elsie stopped, rooted to the spot, feeling as if the blood were draining out of her, soaking through the flagstones into the ground. Lily's arm was tight, to support her in case she fell. The child was looking straight at her. 'My medical record says "*Miss* Elsie Stanway" and it says, "Father unknown". You have to tell me, Mam.'

'I can't. Not until... Give me time...'

'Will you answer one thing?' Lily sounded so matter-of-fact, so adult that Elsie was taken off guard. 'Tell me, Mam. Is he alive?'

Elsie's breath was being suffocated out of her. She could not look Lily in the face and lie to her. She had always avoided Lily's eyes when she lied. Now she looked straight into those clear grey eyes and whispered, 'Yes. Yes. He is.'

'And does he know who I am?'

'Yes.'

Elsie could have cut out her tongue. She had made a mistake. She would regret for evermore telling Lily even that much, for the girl let go of her arm and said, in a choking little voice, 'Then I hate him. He knows who I am, but he doesn't love me. If he did, he'd tell. I don't care tuppence who he is!' Tears were streaming down her face.

Chapter Twelve

Magnus twisted his face out of the water, opened his mouth, gulped air and heard the roar of voices spurring him on.

'Hammond! Hammond!' He could hear Father's voice.

Five more strokes. Keep the legs going. He reached the rail, grabbed it and he'd done it. The flag went up. The noise was deafening. They were coming in on the other lanes, second, third, fourth. But he had won. He had won the swimming cup for his house. What a way to end your school days. Only one more battle to come – the right to leave school.

He had to be helped out of the water, but that was all right. His left hip and knee, painless in the water, could not take the punishment of clambering out. He dropped down on to the form, bent double to get his breath back. In the water his body was as good as anyone's.

Father and Ian were sitting right behind the house captains. Father, proud as Punch, leaned over to touch him. 'Well done!'

'Terrific!' said Ian.

Magnus bared his teeth in a quick grimace before, shoulders hunched forward, mouth open, his breathing slowed and eased. And out of the water, the insidious, aching pains deep in his hip, knee and ankle came back to remind him of who and what he was.

He could live with the pain – he would not let it beat him, or stop him from doing anything he wanted to do. Tomorrow, with Sylvia and Mother there to see him, pain would not matter when he climbed the steps to the platform to receive the cup for his house. If only Lily were here to see his moment of triumph.

In Edinburgh that evening Father took them all to dinner at the Café Royal, where they drank champagne to honour Magnus's winning the trophy. Afterwards, back in the drawing room at Charlotte Square, Father said, 'I think it's a mistake, Magnus. Giving it all up. Why don't you continue at school? Take your School Certificate.'

Uncle Mack, in his kindly way, said, 'You are sixteen. You were years behind when you arrived here. Who knows what you might achieve.' Uncle Mack of course believed that effort in equalled results out, no matter what natural ability one had.

Father said, 'I wasn't clever, Magnus. But I stayed on until I was eighteen and...'

'You went to work with your father at Hammond Silks,' said Magnus. 'And what's good enough for you...' Magnus liked working at the mill. He liked the hustle and bustle, the noise, the sense of something done at the end of every day. Everyone liked him at the mill – the mill that would one day be his. The sooner he made himself indispensable to Father and the mill, the better. He said, 'I've made my mind up. I'm leaving school.'

Mother said, 'He should come home. Sylvia's going to finishing school.'

Sylvia butted in with her opinion, which was exactly the same as Mother's. 'I'll be in Lausanne, Father. Mother will be lost with me away and Magnus in Edinburgh.'

Mother added, 'I will have all the time in the world for him.'

Magnus said, 'I can take care of myself, Mother.'

Ian came to his rescue, 'Why does he have to make up his mind today? The summer holidays are coming up. If we all get together down in Cheshire after my week's sailing, we can see how he feels.'

In July Ian would be crewing for a friend, competing in a West Coast yacht race from Gourock on the Clyde to Formby point in Lancashire. They had asked Magnus to be fourth man, but he knew his strengths and weaknesses, and competitive sailing was beyond him. And boats – what use was sailing to a chap who would be running a mill in Macclesfield? There was not a harbour or a coastline within fifty miles.

Ian grinned at him. 'Magnus, come upstairs. I want to ask a favour.'

*

Ian stood at the window. He could see the spans and trusses of the great railway bridge from here, and the wide, glittering blue water of the Firth of Forth, with Fife and the Ochil Hills beyond. It would be good sailing next Saturday, if the weather held. But he could only spend the weekend on the water if Magnus would oblige. He said, 'How would you like to take Rowena to her school-leaving dinner and dance on Saturday?'

'Me? Does Rowena want me to take her?'

Ian said, 'I said I would take her. But look at that water! Perfect sailing weather.' He gave Magnus a smile of encouragement. 'It won't involve much dancing – but you are much better at it, dancing and larking with girls, than I am.' Then before Magnus could think of a reason not to, he added, 'Rowena would much rather show you off.'

'Would she?' Magnus straightened his shoulders. 'I am actually quite a good dancer,' he said.

Ian enjoyed teasing Magnus. 'Not promised to anyone, eh, Magnus?'

'I have a girlfriend. In Macclesfield. But it's hush-hush at present,' Magnus said.

'You mean she doesn't know you exist!'

'She knows I exist, all right,' Magnus protested. 'I just haven't got round to asking her out...'

Ian's laugh rang out. 'You are a bit of a masher on the quiet, aren't you?' Then, 'Will you do it? Can you take a whole evening on the dance floor?' He had not meant it to sound like a challenge, but he saw from Magnus's expression that that was exactly how it had sounded. He said, 'I know you like to get your head down early. But if you could ... I'd be grateful.'

'Of course I'll do it,' Magnus said. He tipped his head back and gave Ian a supercilious look. 'I'm surprised you are not interested in girls. You're not a bad-looking sort.'

Ian's laugh roared out. 'I am normal, Magnus,' he said. 'When I find one I will probably go overboard. But I haven't come across a girl yet who makes me want to dance.'

Later, in his room, Magnus thought about Ian's way of looking at girls and life and the world. It struck Magnus as odd that any male, boy or man, could be unaware, as Ian apparently was, of the opposite sex. Perhaps Ian was like Father and would one day meet a girl and fall in love headlong, without warning. No. Ian was not like Father. Magnus used to think Father was immune to the charms of any woman but Mother – until last year, when he discovered that Father, his idol, had feet of clay.

Magnus had discovered a terrible dark secret that lay heavy on him and made him see Father in a new light. And when he thought of how this knowledge had come to him, when he realised how easily it could have fallen into the hands of any of the other people involved, it must be nothing short of ordained that he should find it. It made goose pimples stand up on his body when he thought of that long arm of coincidence or misfortune. The truth of Father's past had been right under everyone's nose, and the secret had fallen into Magnus's lap.

Two months after Mrs Chancellor's funeral Magnus and Sylvia had cycled down to Lindow Farm on a Saturday morning to see Lily and her nanna. Lily slept at Lindow on Friday, as she had piano lessons on Saturday mornings.

Nanna greeted them with, 'Eeh. Look at you two. Magnus, how you've grown up. And Sylvia.'

'Is Lily in?' Magnus asked, though he could hear her playing a Clementi sonatina in the other room, going through her repertoire for the teacher.

'She'll be finished in twenty minutes,' Nanna said. 'Sit down. I'll give you something to eat.'

They were sitting round the table when Lily joined them, and Magnus stood up and made a space for her. He feasted his eyes on her. Her hair was loose, a curly cloud about her heart-shaped face, and the sight of her, delicate, quick, talented and clever – all the things he was not – made his heart leap with happiness. He said, 'We dropped by to ask you to Archerfield this evening. Some friends are coming round...'

'Thanks. I can't. I'm going back to Jordangate.' She helped herself to a scone. 'There's a lot to do. I'm trying to earn my living.' She reached for the tea pot, then, seeing Magnus's crestfallen face, said, 'I like earning my own money. But we've had so many improvements to the shop that I'm getting behind with the orders.'

Magnus said, 'Do you have to do them on a Saturday?'

She said, 'I won't have time next week. The piano and bookcase are being delivered on Monday. I got them from Mrs Chancellor, remember?'

'Haven't you had them yet?' Sylvia said. 'Father said he'd have them sent round at once.'

'It's not your father's fault. Mam and I asked him to keep them for a few weeks until the new sitting room was finished.'

In her letters she told Magnus what everything cost, saying, 'Mam has spent £8 on an Axminster carpet in autumn shades, twelve guineas on a three-piece suite in brown Rexine with velvet cushions and £1.17.6 each on two big leather things that Mam calls pouffes and I call tuffets. We have a pearl glass light bowl that hangs on chains from the ceiling and we bought a standard lamp with a fancy fringed shade which cost £19.11.'

Lily counted every penny. Magnus thought it a wonderful virtue.

Lily's letters to him were peppered with 'Mam has taken on a counter hand, Miss Duffield...' and 'Mam said...' as if he, Magnus, were as fond of her mother as she was. In fact he did not have much respect for Lily's mother. He would never tell a soul what his opinion was, but for himself he thought of Mrs Stanway as a selfish woman – a woman at the mercy of her passions, whatever they were.

Lily said, 'The books were delivered in tea chests. They have been standing in the downstairs passageway for weeks. And books being so heavy, I've had to take them up an armful at a time and stack them in a corner until the bookcase comes.'

Magnus said, 'If the bookcase is coming on Monday, can I help you sort the books out?'

'Would you, Magnus? Monday, then.'

He arrived early on Monday because Father dropped him off in Jordangate before going on to the mill. He hadn't thought Lily would be up at nine o'clock but she was already in the shop. She said, 'The furniture was delivered at eight o'clock. I've been up for two hours.'

'You've done it all?' he said.

'I've made a start,' she corrected him as they went up the stairs. 'But I keep getting bogged down. Mrs Chancellor was a true romantic.'

He had never thought of her that way. 'How do you know?'

She pushed open the sitting room door, and it was just as she had described it. 'Very cosy,' he said.

She indicated the stacks of books. 'Let's put the big reference books, *Illustrated Home Lawyer, Chambers Twentiety-Century Dictionary* and *The Book of Good Health*, on the top shelf.' She went to the heap of books, took an armful off the top and brought them to where he stood by the great bookcase. Her face was flushed with pleasure in ownership. She said, 'These books are going to open my eyes, Magnus. There's that controversial book by Sigmund Freud, *The Ego and the Id.* There are two books by Charles Darwin, *On the Origin of Species* and *Selection in Relation to Sex.*'

She said 'sex' without a blush, seeing no human sexual connotation in it, and Magnus went pink and changed the subject, stroking the wood of the bookcase. 'This is a very valuable piece of furniture, Lily. Father says it's George III – made in seventeen-seventy from flame mahogany wood. He says it's as good as having money in the bank.'

'Your father let me have it without protest.' She was surprised. 'When your mother said it was worthless.'

He laughed. 'He would.'

'Why?'

'He likes to prove that he knows more than she does. Likes to win an argument. He will tell her, one day.'

'He'll be too late,' she said. 'It's mine. I'll never part with it.' She put the books she held in the crook of her arm, stroked the wood and then said, 'Did you know that Mrs Chancellor wrote on fly leaves and end papers? She jotted things in the margins. And in place of bookmarks she used picture postcards and made notes on them. It's taking ages to sort the books out because these markers are always inserted at important passages. There are poems about unrequited love. And on one she wrote, "My life has a purpose. I think of my infant son and blind, protective love wells up in my heart. Will I ever be able to refuse him anything?"' Lily's eyes were shining. 'Isn't that beautiful, Magnus?'

He nodded, and she went on, opening a book at a sentimental poem about kindness, the page marked by a picture postcard bearing Mrs Chancellor's thoughts: "I could not go on unless I believed, as I do, that my darling Ray would not needlessly set foot upon a worm."

He loved being with Lily like this; content, helping her, watching her, asking where this volume or that should go. She said, 'By the way, if you want to borrow any of them, Magnus... You may have read them all already. But if there's anything of interest...'

There was. At the bottom of the last heap Magnus saw a slim volume bound in navy-blue leather: *Haemophilia: Clinical and Genetic Aspects.* Why would Mrs Chancellor want to know about his disease?

He picked it up and opened it, and as he did so, a letter slid out; an old letter whose envelope bore the stamp of King Edward's reign. It was addressed to Miss Sarah Pilkington and, there was no mistaking it, it was written in Father's spidery, sloping hand with flourishes on the capitals. It sent a shock – a shocking feeling – through him, just holding it.

He glanced at Lily. She had not seen it. She was busy, on her hands and knees, placing the little red leather-bound books, Oxford University Press Classics, on the bottom shelf, Magnus quickly slipped the letter into his jacket pocket and gave the book his full attention. It was an American volume that contained dozens of histories of haemophiliacs and their heredity. There were charts and family trees showing the passage of the disease down the generations. The passage Mrs Chancellor had marked in this book read: *The fact that haemophilia is transmitted through the female greatly increases the difficulty of tracing the disease, for there is a change of surname in almost every generation.* She had marked the passage and underscored '*transmitted through the female*'. There was also a large exclamation mark in the margin.

It was not until he was alone in his room that night that he withdrew the old letter from the envelope, and read it.

Archerfield House
5 January 1915

My dear Sarah,

Where have you been hiding these last weeks? My letters have gone unanswered. I have missed you. I wanted to talk to you and I have not seen you since the night last November when I came, undeserving, to your bed and you gave yourself so generously. Your love gave me such comfort.

I am glad there have been no repercussions. My one regret is that on that memorable night it was clear to both of us, from my ineptitude as a lover and the storms of tears that overcame you, that I was not the man for you.

I want you to be the first to hear, before the announcement in the papers, that Miss Catriona Mackenzie and I are to be married in Edinburgh next week. We met at Christmas and immediately lost our hearts to one another. I know you will wish us well and I hope that you, my dearest and best friend, will become as beloved a friend to Catriona as you are to me. Yours for ever in friendship,

John

Magnus read it over again, appalled. Then he sat for half an hour with it in his hands. What could he do? Show Father the letter? Of course not. How could a chap go to his father and say, 'Did you write this?' or 'Look what I have found!' or 'Explain yourself, sir!'

At first he tried to pretend that the letter meant no more than a young man's exaggerated outburst. But plainly it wasn't. No man would write a letter like that if it were not true. No matter how he tried to deceive himself, it was quite clear. Father had written this letter to Miss Sarah Pilkington. And Mrs Sarah Chancellor had left the letter in the book; probably forgotten. Ray was born nine months after the November night Father talked about – the night when he went into Miss Sarah Pilkington's bed. And, if the letter itself were not enough proof, he only had to ask why Mrs Chancellor had bought a book on haemophilia.

His own father was the natural father of Ray Chancellor. How could Father not have known? He had been away, fighting a war, that was why. And so had Mr Chancellor. Had Mrs Chancellor pulled the wool over her husband's and Father's eyes?

But worst of all – the letter could have fallen into anyone's hands. All those years on the shelf at Park Lane, under lock and key perhaps but easily obtained by a determined person.

Since then, Father had helped pack the books. Goose pimples rose on his arms as he asked himself what might have resulted if Mother had found the letter. Then the books were left in the passageway of Lily's house, where she or her mother could have discovered the letter. Nobody had found it but he. And he could do nothing about it.

Lily wished Mam had applied herself to making the money multiply by buying houses. Mam had previously said how much she admired Mr Chancellor's astuteness in buying property. But she wouldn't. She said, 'The money's safe where it is. We have a higher station in life and I've only spent a hundred pounds, all told.' Mam looked after the shop accounts and kept her legacy, and Lily put half of her private earnings into her bank account.

These improvements should have allowed Mam to take life easy. Instead she was on the go all the time and losing weight in spite of an increased appetite, waking very early, saying she had slept badly when she'd been dog tired the previous evening. Later, Lily would see the legacy as the start of Mam's decline, but she was young and knowing there was money in the bank gave her a sense of quiet satisfaction.

Mam was not satisfied. She was restless and unhappy but outwardly unchanged. Lily worried because their better living conditions had done nothing to ease Mam's mind. But there was nothing she could do to calm Mam. Mam would not be dictated to.

And she refused to give a crumb of information about Lily's father. Trying to hate did not take away the need to know. Lily could do all she had sworn to do – take responsibility for hers and Mam's daily living – but she found she could not hate the man who was her own true father. She needed to know and all she had to go on was that he was alive and had no children – and the hint that his mother's name was Lily.

The only comfort was that when she asked Howard Willey-Leigh for the name of his mother, he said, 'Eveline.'

Mr Leigh had not bought a house in Macclesfield, but all the same he spent more time in the town than before, staying at the Bull's Head Hotel in the Market Place for days on end. Mam too seemed to be playing some elaborate game, going out with Mr Leigh openly, almost defiantly. She would say, 'Last night Hah'd took me to the pictures. The Hammonds were there.' Or, 'Hah'd and I went for a run in his car. We went to the Setter Dog. Very popular with motorists. Ray Chancellor and his father were in the bar. Hah'd and I were chatting with them.'

Lily's dislike of Mr Leigh was growing. His habit of winking at her behind Mam's back as if they shared a secret was becoming more pronounced and alarming. He did it every time he saw her. It should have been obvious to him that she avoided his eye. Now that she was older, instead of blushing and looking away she put her nose in the air and gave him what she hoped was a look of contempt.

For a widower who had so much money, Mr Leigh was very interested indeed in theirs. He said to Mam, 'If it were mine, I would buy more stock, paint the shop, dress the window!' He said, 'Let me help you, dear. I have good connections with a wholesaler in Cheetham Hill in Manchester. We could buy cheap and sell...'

'We? We could buy?' Mam said, stopping him in his tracks.

He flashed his teeth. 'I mean you, Elsie. You could buy from my friend. I will bring you samples - take you to Manchester if you wish. I am sure you can trust my judgement. I know what sells.'

Mam smiled and said, 'I'll speak to John Hammond. He's the financial brains.' But Mam took advice from nobody.

And now, the mesmerising trick wasn't working. Some things would not be put to the back of Lily's mind. Every day she asked herself what she could do about her state of shame – unbaptised, illegitimate.

Nanna must have told Grandpa that Lily had learned the truth, for one Saturday afternoon, soon after Mrs Chancellor's funeral, Grandpa took her aside at Lindow. He sat in his armchair while Lily stood by the fireplace. 'Well, Lily,' he began. 'You've found out?'

'Yes, Grandpa,' she said.

'Nanna said you were ashamed of your mother.'

'No. I said things to Nanna I wouldn't say to anyone, that's all.'

He sighed, but his eyes were warm and bright with pride. 'Good lass!' He took her right hand in his hard, bony ones. 'It has been a great burden. Not being able to tell you. You must believe that.'

'I understand, Grandpa. Really I do.'

'I have prayed. And Our Lord has answered my prayers. You are a child without sin or stain.'

Her face was burning. 'But I'm not! I was born in sin, Grandpa. I can't be right until I'm baptised. I can't be baptised as Lily Stanway.'

He held fast on to her hands. 'You can! Stanway is a good name. It is my name. You can be baptised in chapel or church. Any time you want.'

'But I don't want to. I don't want Lily Stanway on my baptismal certificate. My father was not Tommy Stanway.'

He shook his head, but Lily didn't expect him ever to understand, so she asked, 'When St Paul says, "The sting of death is sin and the strength of sin is the law" – what does it mean?'

'St Paul was a Jew. He was speaking to the Corinthians of Jewish law. The commandments.'

'But what does it mean?'

'All right. Now, if you were a savage, and if you had never heard of God – and if the habit of your tribe was to make graven images, or...'

'Or break commandments?'

'Yes. If you did this and you did not know you were breaking God's law, God would not hold you responsible. Your sins would be pardonable. Once you know it is the law, that law creates the very sin it defines.'

'I don't think I see...'

'Look, our Lil , if they bring in a law in Macclesfield to say you can't do something – if they forbid you to drive a horse and cart up Churchwallgate, for instance – then if you did it you would be breaking the law. But the day before, it wasn't the law. It's knowing you broke the law that made it a sin.'

'So God won't let me or Mam into heaven?'

'No! No, lass! You are too young to be asking such questions!'

But he had clarified everything for her. She had looked up illegitimacy in *The Universal Home Lawyer*, which stated that:

A bastard is regarded in law as having no natural relationship with any person except his mother. And further on it said: *A bastard has no surname until he has acquired one by reputation; he usually takes his mother's but there is nothing to prevent his taking his father's. He may of course be christened like any other child. When his birth is registered the father's name is not to be entered in the register except at the joint request of the mother and father who then sign the register together.*

There was a lot about claims on the estates of fathers who die intestate, and over and over again it said that a bastard had no rights to anything of the father's unless he either adopted the child or, by marrying the child's mother, made the bastard child legitimate. This latter could only be done if the natural father had signed his name on the birth register. It said, 'sign the register together' specifically. And there was no father's name on her birth certificate. Her father had not wanted his name to appear. And since Mam knew about God's laws, in the eyes of the church Mam was a sinner. Lily was nobody until she was baptised, and she wasn't going to get baptised until she was legitimate. But she had her iron will. She must try harder to put that insoluble problem out of her mind.

Elsie had been patient for a year. Tonight she'd ask outright, 'When are we going to be married?' She'd go straight to the point.

Lily was at Lindow for the weekend, and for the first time ever, Frank was going to spend a whole night with her here at the shop after he'd been to the Friday-night meeting of the Licensed Victuallers in the Angel. Gossip could not hurt anyone now that a year had passed. It was time they started being seen together, little by little, preparing the way for marriage. They were breaking no commandments.

Elsie stood in front of the long mirror and cast a critical eye over her figure. She was wearing only French knickers, her suspender belt and fine silk stockings. He used to like to see her like that. In the old days, when his needs were greater. Used to...

She did a half-turn at the hips. Seams were straight. A thrill went through her. Good God, she was not a blushing bride.

Now then, what about the rest? She put her hands on her hips, drew her shoulders back and tried to appraise her body. She was in good shape for a woman of forty-one. Her waist was small. Her bosom was as full as it ever was; maybe a fraction lower – but Frank said she had the most beautiful breasts he had ever seen. When she asked how many he'd seen, he used to tell her he had seen plenty – on statues and in paintings – but never more beautiful than hers. Used to...

There was a jar of Pond's cold cream on the little table. She loved the scent of it. So did Frank. She stuck her fingers into the open jar, scooped it and massaged it into her neck and her breasts, to make herself ready. She would excite him beyond endurance tonight. She'd ask for an explanation of why his attentions had waned. These days he came round when Lily was at home and sat talking to Lily for as long as he could, content to be a friend to them. He came on Wednesday afternoons but often he was in a hurry to leave, saying he had to keep an eye on Ray – Ray, who had never returned to school but had taken to work like a duck to water. Ray was eighteen.

Remembering how demanding he used to be, she accused him of being unfaithful, but he swore to her that she was the only woman for him. However, a man who is too sure loses interest, so she'd tried to make him jealous, being seen with Howard. Last week she told him that Howard had hinted about marriage. All that had achieved was Frank's mirthless laugh and his declaration, 'Leigh doesn't want a wife. He wants an income.'

She was gratified, seeing his red face, the tight mouth, but he did not say, 'Marry me,' so she asked, 'What have you against Howard?'

'He's a fraud. A phoney – as the Americans say.'

'Phoney? No more than any man who has to keep his end up.'

He said, 'He's been chasing women with money all his life. It's your money he wants.'

'Three hundred pounds? It's pocket money to a man like Howard.' She gave a delighted laugh. 'You're jealous! Jealous because Howard has his eye on me.'

But then, stirring up jealousy was no good. She used to be light-hearted, attentive, passionate. She'd be passionate tonight. She'd wait for him, here in her bedroom. When he got to the point – the no-turning-back point – she'd stop him and tell him that their lovemaking would end unless he did his duty by her and Lily. Unless he married her.

She must stop imagining that he had someone else. She must believe him when he said his working life grew more demanding as his appetites went down. He'd said, 'Look at me. I'm grey-haired with responsibility.' Perhaps a man's desires left him as some women's did in their forties. Her desires were strong. The terrible tiredness she lived with hadn't dampened her needs.

Massaging herself and imagining his touch was exciting her. She rammed the lid down on the cold cream jar, slipped on a kimono and high-heeled shoes and went downstairs to set out crystal glasses and whisky for him, sherry for herself. She poured a sweet sherry, drank it and poured another. Tonight she would make him happy.

Frank bolted the back door and went into Elsie's living kitchen. There was a man's dressing gown laid across the fireside chair, glasses and drink set out on the kitchen table. He grinned, seeing them, and went to the stair door, calling softly, 'Elsie. . . ?'

She'd be pretending to be asleep. He'd keep her waiting for a few minutes; anticipation would inflame her. He poured a whisky and drank it neat as he undressed. He was in the mood tonight. He almost laughed at the thought that she, Elsie, was always in the mood. It was a while since he'd felt like this, what with having to keep a watch on Ray, day and night, and minding his own reputation. If he were to become a magistrate, a justice of the peace, he had to be beyond reproach, and to this end he had raised his good name since Sarah's death. He was a better man now – upright and impartial and seen as such by the people of Macclesfield.

Nobody could point a finger at him – nobody but Nellie Plant. If only he hadn't been such a fool! He tied the dressing gown tight round his waist and poured another half-glass of whisky. Then he chuckled. Why imagine trouble? Nellie was satisfied with what he was doing for her. Ray was spending the weekend at Archerfield – and upstairs, waiting for him, exclusively his, was the woman whose kisses and body could rouse him as no other woman ever had or would. All her talk about marriage, silly hints about marrying Willey-Leigh, it was ridiculous. He'd seen them together at the Setter Dog. Elsie looked as miserable as sin in Leigh's company. She was trying to make him, Frank, jealous. That was all it was.

As for marrying – surely Elsie could see that it would be the worst thing for all of them? He was on the brink of having a real place in the town. He was respected for the way he'd conducted himself over Sarah's death and the near-ruinous allegations against Ray. How could they marry without telling Lily that he was her father? It would be a terrible thing to do to her. He couldn't tell his precious lass now that he was her father; that she had a brother, and that he and her mother had deceived her all these years. It would be madness to come out into the open now.

And what would Elsie gain? They both had everything they wanted, without marriage. And the best of what he wanted was upstairs, waiting for him. He put the empty glass down. Whisky could wait. He could not.

He ran up the stairs and opened her bedroom door. There was a streetlamp outside and she had left the curtains open so that the warm, pale lamplight shone over the bed where she lay, draped, kimono open, exposing those unbelievable breasts; heavy, milky.

Her eyelids were closed but fluttering. She was pretending to be asleep. Slowly he pulled the kimono open, and as the silk touched her skin he watched her breasts firming, her dark nipples become prominent, hardening and erect. He discarded the dressing gown and lowered himself over her, closing his mouth over one breast while he fondled and teased the other. He need only touch them to rouse Elsie. She opened her eyes.

'Hello, stranger,' she said in a voice that was low and husky. Her lovely mouth was smiling and her sensuous hips were moving, writhing.

He stood up and took off his gown quickly while she slipped her arms out of the kimono and unfastened the button on her silky knickers.

'I'll do that,' he said. He liked to take his time these days. He was not as quick as he used to be, but it was better now – it lasted longer.

He grasped her ankles, lifting her off the bed as he slid the French silk thing down over her hips and cast it aside. Then he eased her legs back, bent at the knees, to put the soles of her feet flat on the bed and wide apart. Her blue eyes were narrow and inviting, her full red lips parted.

He couldn't wait. And neither could Elsie. She would be hot and slippery, and thoughts of delaying techniques were gone as he lowered himself on to the bed and went into her slowly, and felt her drawing him up and high inside while she made that lovely soft moaning.

'Elsie...' He gripped her hips, came out of her and said, 'Quick...' Then he sat up on the edge of the bed, picked her up easily and lifted her bodily on to himself so that she was facing him, straddled across him, hands on his thighs, feet splayed, knees gripping his hips.

He edged forward, deeper into her and she put her arms round his neck and wrapped her legs about his body. 'How's that?' he said, and grinned as he heard her quick in-drawing breaths, felt the movement of her muscles sliding up and down on him. 'Oh, Elsie ... Elsie...' he cried, then stopped himself. He was going too fast.

His mouth was on hers now and their tongues were moving, warm and deep, as he slowed down. He pulled away and watched her face, dark eyebrows drawing together with the heightening of her pleasure. He placed his hands on her rounded hips, gently lifted her and let her down, moving in time with him, slowly, her muscles holding and reaching for him, her beautiful sweet-scented breasts pressing into the skin of his chest and her breath coming fast and hot on his neck.

'Good girl! Not so fast...' he said, and he disentangled her and made her hollow her back and put her hands on his knees to steady herself. Then he watched her face as he closed his mouth over the firm, creamy breast. She had been rubbing stuff into herself. The scent was filling his head as he sucked gently and felt the nipple swelling on his tongue, filling his mouth. He took the other one next, and she moaned again with pleasure and contracted deep inside where he could feel her every little movement.

Her eyes were closed, her mouth was red and full and at last she was making those whimpering noises that told him she was ready; those sounds that excited him so. He loved the noises, the taste of her, his intimate knowledge of her body. He knew every inch of her, every secret part of her. He could not hold back, for blood was pounding in him as he paced his movements inside the hot slippery. . .

'Elsie . . . I love you . . . Oh God . . . I love you!' he cried out as he went harder, higher, streaming into her.

He was making her cry out for him. He gripped her fast on to him and held her there as she cried out, 'Frank . . . Oh, love . . . My God!'

And they were mingling, coming together, subsiding and tightening again and again high inside her until it was done. Then he held her there, sticky and salt-tasting, gasping for breath after release.

He was glad he was no longer a young man. When he was young he could spend himself twice and no more. Now, it would take an hour, or longer, to reach a second climax. And if she let him have his way, a third. . . And Elsie? She was more than a match for him.

He held her fast into him. When she made to move, to ease off him, he kissed deep and hard and bruising before he stopped and said, 'Stay there, woman. Until I'm ready. I'll tell you when to get off.'

Elsie had missed her chance, being too ready to please. It was four o'clock in the morning before they sat, she in her kimono, he in the dressing gown, in the kitchen, eating cheese butties and drinking the sherry and whisky. Frank was relaxed and happy when he had taken all he wanted of her. She had always been able to ask anything of him, so now she replenished their glasses, held hers towards him and said, 'Well, drink to us.'

'To us? What do you mean?'

'I think it's time you made an honest woman of me. Married me. I'm willing.' She said it like that; flat and bald. When it was said she added, 'I've waited a long time.'

'For marriage? To me?' He looked surprised, as if it was the last thing he expected. 'The only reason to marry is to bring up children.'

'I've brought your daughter up without a husband.'

'She's nearly grown up. So's Ray.' He made a sheepish

smile and took a sip of his drink. 'It would do nothing but harm, to all of us, telling them now.'

A lump came into the back of Elsie's throat. 'You want me to wait till our Lil's grown up?'

'And Ray's off my hands.' He was not smiling. He was brisk and decided. He stood, put his glass down and reached for his clothes.

Elsie was dumbfounded. 'Going home?' she asked. 'I thought you were going to stop...'

'I never stop overnight. Can't afford to get caught.'

Elsie held back her tears of disappointment as he threw his clothes on as fast as he could, tied his shoelaces with great ferocity and bent down to kiss her on the nape of her neck. Then he was gone. He slipped out at the back door. She heard his careful tread across the yard, the back gate closing and his footsteps growing fainter down the entryway with the confident cautiousness perfected over the years.

Elsie's tears fell. He had promised nothing, said nothing significant. Did he expect her to wait until Lily and Ray were off their hands? Until their children were married? Was he asking her to wait at all?

Chapter Thirteen

Mam's forecast about the money making no difference to their way of life was not the only one that had been wrong. She said they would have a holiday, and they didn't have that until Lily was fifteen, in 1934. Some of her friends were working. Magnus was helping his father in the mill. Shandy had left school willingly to keep house for her father and brothers.

Lily had passed six RSA exams. Her ambition was to pass the School Certificate exams and think of a career. She was drawn to the law but didn't know whether there were lady lawyers – or, being illegitimate, whether she could become one. Doreen was still at school, doing a commercial course; bookkeeping and typewriting. She was also getting a name for herself. The older girls spoke about her as a 'bad girl'. They were both, Doreen and Shandy, ahead of Lily in physical development. Doreen was tall, broad-shouldered and busty. Shandy was small and athletic, but both of them had 'started' and Lily hadn't. Nanna said it would happen in time, and if she started later she'd keep her good looks for longer, like Mam.

Mam had kept her slim figure and was proud of her appearance, but in the two years since the legacy she had grown harder, and it showed in the sharp lines on her face that made her appear older and slightly desperate. It was as if she'd had a disappointment that had made her bitter, not the unexpected windfall that had made Lily so pleased with life.

Mam and she walked arm in arm through the Shambles in the market one warm, summery Saturday afternoon in April. The eighty stalls were crammed between the Town Hall and Sparrow Park and reached through the arched Unicorn

Gateway which separated two pubs, the Unicorn and the Unicorn Gateway.

'We're going to Nanna's after dinner.' Mam stopped in front of a stall selling honey and big round oatcakes. 'Buy a dozen. We'll take them with us.'

'We?' Mam hadn't been to Lindow and stayed overnight for ages.

'Yes. I want to talk to Nanna and Grandpa,' she said. 'I've decided it's time we had that holiday we've been promising ourselves.'

'Where are we going? Can we afford it? How long for?' Lily asked. They talked about holidays but always the plans fizzled out, as Mam never would tear herself away from Macclesfield when everyone else was away at Barnaby or October Wakes week.

'We're going to Southport.' Mam put the honey and rolled-up oatcakes in her shopping basket.

Lily's high spirits plummeted again. 'Mr Leigh lives in Southport,' she said. 'We're not staying at his house...?'

'No!' Mam smiled. 'That wouldn't be right. But Southport's a better class of place than Blackpool. Half of Macc goes to Blackpool. I want to get away. We're going to take some money out of the bank. Stay in a hotel.' She went back towards the Market Place, through the gateway, walking fast, Lily dawdling behind, ignoring the cries of vendors, the aroma of roasted meat, lost in a dream of hotels, sand and sea and sunshine. 'Come on, Lil,' Mam said over her shoulder. 'I don't want to hang about.'

Lily caught up with her. 'You're not tired already, are you?' It was worrying, the way Mam flagged; lost her energy. But that wasn't the problem.

Mam had spotted someone she didn't want to speak to. She set her face in the direction of Jordangate. 'Come on!' she said, tugging Lily's arm. 'Look behind in a minute. Not now. Don't let her see you looking!' Mam's expression was fixed, furious.

Lily adjusted her shoe buttons and, looking back, saw the cause of Mam's anger. Nellie Plant and the little boy she had recently adopted were standing in front of the Bull's Head. Nellie was corseted into a tight pale-blue costume with, ridiculously for the warm day, a huge fur coat wide open to show off the suit and coat. She and the little blond boy, who was about five, were laughing out loud with a bunch of the ne'er-do-well men who gathered outside the Bull's Head on market days. Lily stood and hurried to catch Mam.

'Common as muck!' Mam whispered. 'Filthy little piece! Brothel-keeper! That's what she is!'

Lily was used to Mam's tongue-lashing Nellie Plant, but this was going too far. 'Mam! What's brought this on?'

'You know Frank Chancellor's bought the Unicorn?'

'Yes. It's no secret.'

'He's blatant!' Mam replied. 'He's set his fancy woman up now.'

'Nellie Plant?'

'I don't know how he gets away with it. And him a JP.'

'Being a magistrate doesn't stop you from buying property, does it?'

'He's bought a licence for her. She's the landlady of the Ring O'Bells up Backwallgate.' Mam was spitting fire. 'He'll be ringing her bell, all right!'

That must be an insult. Lily tried another tack. 'Does it matter?'

Mam replied by gripping Lily's arm tight without revealing her mood to passers-by. 'Matter? Of course it matters! Hah'd is trying to decide between buying a house and taking a room at the Ring O'Bells. He says that all the talk about Nellie Plant's ministering to her residents is salacious rumour. He says the Ring O'Bells has a good reputation for food and accommodation.'

'There you are, then.'

'Well, I've told him, if he moves in with Nellie Plant he can court her an' all! I'm sick of this town. I'd get out now, if I could.'

Doreen Grimshaw, sullen and bad-tempered and dressed up to look more like a twenty-year-old than her fifteen years, glared at Lily across the compartment. Lily ignored her. They were on the first leg of the journey to Southport, and she didn't want any part of her holiday ruined by Doreen. The Grimshaws were going to Manchester.

Lily tried to switch off the listening part of her brain as she gazed over the flat fields where the Bollin looped and curled. She thought about her four brand-new bought dresses. Today she was wearing a blue and white striped dress of linen. It had a dropped waist, short sleeves and a finely pleated skirt. The wheels' regular rhythm, 'chatta-ta-tom... chatta-ta-tom', was music to her ears as she breathed what was to her the stimulating smell – sulphurous fumes and tobacco smoke – of the compartment.

Mam was speaking to Mr Grimshaw. 'What were you saying, Bert? About Chancellor's?'

'I said, Ray doesn't believe in fixed wages, regular hours,' Mr Grimshaw said. 'The factory is going on to piece rate and shift work.'

Mrs Grimshaw nodded agreement. 'They are lucky to be in work. Not signing on at the labour exchange every day.'

It was impossible to concentrate on the view. Mam should have had her fill of Macclesfield gossip, but she was working up to finding out the latest scandal about Nellie Plant. She was much too good at investigating with that feigned casualness to let the Grimshaws guess what she was after. Mam's face was animated as she and Mr and Mrs Grimshaw talked about Chancellor's, the depression and the closure of other Macclesfield mills.

'It's getting worse,' Mam agreed. 'You'd think with so many out of work, the pubs would be doing badly. But there you are. The Ring O'Bells must be doing well if Nellie Plant can afford to adopt a child. Swanking round the town, dressed up like a tart with that lad done out in his posh school uniform. St Bride's indeed! And him only five years old!'

'You are off to Southport, Elsie?' Mrs Grimshaw said. 'Miss Plant comes from Southport.'

'So she says!' Mam said.

Doreen had a sly expression on her face. 'Are you going to stay with Mr Willey? Mr Willey comes from Southport, doesn't he?'

'Willey-Leigh!' said Mam. 'Mr Willey-Leigh has a very large house in Southport. We are staying at the Beach View. On the prom.'

'Oh, I see,' said Doreen.

'No you don't,' Mam snapped back.

Mr Grimshaw, whose mind had not hopped from the original subject, said, 'Miss Plant used to go back to Southport. She went once a month for a long weekend. Her mother died recently.'

'Well I never,' Mam replied.

Lily sighed. Mam did know that Nellie Plant went to Southport. She always wanted to know what Nellie Plant was up to. She asked Howard Leigh about her all the time. Lily glanced at Mam, who was wearing her red-spotted artificial silk two-piece with the flat-brimmed white straw hat. Mam opened her vanity case and inspected her mouth to see to her lipstick.

'She nearly lost her mother a few years back,' said Mr Grimshaw. 'She took six months off. Compassionate leave. Mr Chancellor said her job would be waiting for her.'

'I don't remember Nellie Plant leaving Macclesfield for all that time,' Mam said. 'How long ago?'

'It's over five years since,' said Mr Grimshaw.

'Oh! Heavens! Why on earth are we wasting our breath on Nellie Plant?' Mam snapped down the lid of her compact in a dismissive way that covered a burning interest. 'She's of no interest to us.'

'Everyone's saying...' Mrs Grimshaw leaned towards Mam, 'it's her child. they say her mother looked after it, but when her mother died Nellie cracked on she'd adopted him!'

'Well, I never heard the like,' Mam replied. 'I wonder who...?'

Mam said she was sick of Macclesfield and would get out of it if she could. Lily would never fathom Mam out.

After leaving the Grimshaws in Piccadilly they crossed Manchester by tram, caught the train at Exchange and arrived in Southport at midday, stepping on to a long sunny platform where porters bustled for business and Mam gave her orders in her posh voice to the taxicab driver. Lily could hardly contain herself for pleasure in the salt-scented air, the sun, the wide streets and the prospect of the drive on the tree-lined boulevard of Lord Street.

'Look!' she said in the taxi as one sight after another unfolded. 'A fountain. A bandstand with a band playing, and it isn't Sunday.' At the sight of the flower-decked glass canopies over the shops she was at last silenced. 'Have you ever seen anything like it?'

Mam said to the driver, 'Please drive slowly along Cambridge Road before you take us to the promenade.' Then, to Lily, 'Hah'd has a house in Cambridge Road. We'll have a nosy!'

They left Lord Street and were being driven past houses such as Lily had never seen, huge houses standing in great tree-filled gardens, four-storey shiny red-brick mansions with towers and turrets and bay windows you could fit Mam's whole shop into. They had grand sweeps of steps up to ornate front doors, and wide gravel drives with dazzling cars threading in and out.

'I wonder which it is?' Mam said.

'The Beach View's this end of the promenade,' the taxi driver said. 'Not far from Cambridge Road. Soon be there.'

'Can you tell me where the registrar's office is?' Mam asked him next. 'I have to make a few enquiries.'

'Cambridge Arcade. Opposite Christ Church school.'

Lily said, 'Is Mr Leigh going to show us round his house?'

'No. He's coming to see us, though,' Mam dropped her voice to a whisper. 'Don't tell Hah'd we've been nosying.'

When they reached the hotel Mam was not a bit fazed. She sailed in, giving her orders in her best voice, and soon they were unpacking in a great big bedroom that had two double beds in it – and both piled high with eiderdowns over rose-embossed silk bedspreads. Lily couldn't tear herself away from the bay window and the view of the sea and the second longest pier in England. 'Oh, Mam!' she said. 'I'll never want to leave.'

Mr Leigh put in an appearance on the second day, and after that he called for Mam every morning, leaving Lily to her own devices. She and Mam spent the afternoons wandering under the glass canopies in Lord Street, inspecting the gown shops. They sometimes spent ten minutes or more looking at the kind of outfit they would never see in Macclesfield, before they wandered up to the Floral Hall gardens, paid for deckchairs and sat, breathing in sea air that was laden with the scent of flowers, listening to the band while Lily drew in her notebook, all kinds of variations on the clothes.

Her mornings took on a routine. After breakfast every day she walked down the pier and rode the tram back, then in the fresh salt air she strolled back to the Beach View by way of all the little booths and kiosks where the snappers' photographs were displayed. Casual photographers stood at the pier entrance or walked along the promenade and the Marine Parade, snapping without invitation. The photographs were displayed in the windows of the kiosks, and she was half expecting to see one of herself, for people were snapped indiscriminately and sometimes didn't know they had been taken until they saw the picture in a window. Afterwards she'd stroll in the side streets where buckets and spades and shrimping nets spilled on to the pavement from the gift shops, and she'd linger, laughing at the funny postcards, looking for gifts for Nanna, Grandpa and Shandy.

Then, near the end of the week, they spotted Sylvia and Magnus in Woodhead's Café where they went most days for tea. Sylvia was seventeen, beautiful and elegant, scented with cool Atkinson's lavender and wearing a lime-green sleeveless dress. She was tall and slender like Magnus, and her face and arms were covered in pale freckles. A sun tan made her eyes seem larger and bluer. Her hair had been bobbed, and it slanted in waves over her brow, curling towards her cheek.

'What are you doing here?' Lily asked.

Magnus got to his feet, exclaiming on the surprise of it all. He looked taller in his striped blazer and was evidently trying to grow a little blond moustache; the hairs shone like golden prickles over his smiling mouth. 'We're staying at the Palace Hotel in Birkdale. Where...?'

'Beach View. On the prom,' Lily said.

Sylvia gave Mam one of her sweet, well-bred smiles. 'It is good to see you, Mrs Stanway. Are you enjoying the holiday?'

'Yes,' Mam said. 'It's a nice town.' She sounded off-hand, and Lily looked at her quickly. Mam pushed her chair back. 'But I'll leave you young ones. I'll nip over to the Cambridge Arcade while I've got a minute.'

Lily ordered. Magnus said, 'What do you do in the evenings, Lily?'

'There are ten cinemas,' she said, 'that change their programmes three times a week. We can't keep up. What do you do?'

Sylvia laughed. 'Uncle Kenneth and Mama sit over dinner and talk non-stop about Edinburgh. They don't dance. There's a band and cabaret every night at our hotel.'

'Is your uncle with you? From Edinburgh?'

Magnus answered, 'Yes. And Ian and Rowena. Ian came in at Formby yesterday. He crews for a friend who has a twenty-seven-foot boat at Gourock. But it's a bit of a swizz having no young things at the Palace. Imagine having to dance with your cousins every night! Now we've bumped into you,' he went on, 'let's bring our swimming costumes tomorrow. Meet us here at two o'clock, Lily?'

'All right. I'm sure Mam won't mind,' she said, before settling down to enjoy a delicious cream tea. Afterwards, Lily had to leave them there, waiting for the taxi that was to take them back to the Palace. It didn't occur to her to wonder why they needed a taxi when there were motor buses and trams galore running between Lord Street and Birkdale.

Her only concern was that Mam might be drinking in secret in the bedroom. She had already polished off two bottles of port and one of sherry since they'd arrived. Twice she'd missed her dinner, so Lily had eaten alone, giving her apologies and saying Mam had gone to bed early and could she have a plate of something cold to take upstairs for later? Lily was afraid Mam might stagger downstairs, desperate with hunger after drink.

Her feet went faster and faster until, turning the corner of Nevill Street at a trot, she went haring down the promenade to the hotel. She found Mam in the room, sitting sober and quiet, staring at her hands.

The following afternoon Sylvia and Magnus were waiting for her at Woodhead's Café, Sylvia holding a crocheted bag with swimming things inside. Lily had hers in a little string bag. It was hotter than ever. Sylvia and she both wore cream shantung dresses with low waists, and both wore straw hats.

'Snap!' they said together, although they were not at all alike – Sylvia tall and blonde, Lily five feet four only, with dark curly hair worn long and fastened with a scarlet silk bow at the back of her neck.

'I'll call a taxi,' said Magnus.

Lily was about to protest, but Sylvia shot a warning glance as Magnus made towards the kerb. It was then Lily saw, by his rambling gait, that Magnus could barely walk. She had last seen him walking normally at Easter. Now his left leg was bent and drawn up so that only his turned-in toes touched the ground. He leaned against one of the plane trees that bordered the wide pavement as he attempted to hail a cab.

Sylvia took her arm and whispered, 'He won't be stopped. His left knee and hip are dreadful. He won't use sticks. Pretend not to notice.'

'All right,' Lily squeezed Sylvia's arm but wondered why it seemed like treachery, to talk about Magnus's affliction. His family had no need to lie. Everyone could see that Magnus was a cripple.

Sylvia said, 'Yesterday we went to the cinema. And on the newsreel we saw that dreadful Herr Hitler. And I know that these things could never happen here, but Magnus was upset because they are forcibly sterilising people with deformities and diseases, feeble citizens, the blind and the deaf. They were herding Jewish people on to trains for concentration camps, and if they resisted, they charged them with "fighting the storm troopers".'

Lily held her hand tight. 'Don't Sylvia...!'

Magnus had stopped a taxi and called them over. To the driver he said, 'Pleasureland, please. Wait outside for us.'

They made an odd trio going under the archway into Pleasureland, where all the attractions were set out in a walled-in area behind the sand hills. Magnus, in the centre, had a girl on each arm, but it was they who supported him, though he did look debonair in his flannels, blazer and straw boater. His pale face was animated as he played up to them, saying, 'My sweet! My sweet!...' and 'Oh, dah...ling! You are *di-vine!* as he passed other young men and their lady friends. And, 'We're the cynosure of all eyes!'

Lily wanted to cry for him to stop it because she could see that he was in pain. There were deep creases between his eyebrows, and above the smiling mouth his eyes were filled with terrible fear. But he was older and she couldn't speak to him as once she had.

'I'll sit in the sun while you two go in,' he'd say as they neared one of the attractions. And every time, at his insistence, they went to a nearby bench together so that they could keep the charade going until Magnus let go of their arms and sat down, leaning back lazily, to wait for them to return from their frolics. After an hour Magnus said, 'Who wants a swim?'

By half past three they were sitting in the conservatory café of the Sea Bathing Lake, eating strawberries and drinking dandelion and burdock that wore a head of foaming and frothing ice cream. The oval lake, nearly half an acre in area, was a natural sun trap for the hundreds of young people who baked their faces, oiled bronzed limbs, displayed and watched. Surrounding the pool, in little rocky beds, geraniums and palm trees grew. The pool had high diving boards, a water chute and a raft moored facing the café. In front of the café, on rose-bordered terraces around ornamental waterfalls, were set canvas folding chairs. Magnus nodded his head in their direction. 'I've reserved three. When you've had your swim you can sit with me.'

Lily had a great welling-up of sympathy for him. 'I don't feel much like swimming,' she said. 'I'll have a quick dip and sit out with you, Magnus. I keep getting attacks of the cramps.'

They helped Magnus to the canvas chair. Lily was expert now at making these critical manoeuvres seem like casual behaviour. When Magnus was seated and had put his boater on one seat and his blazer on the other, he leaned back, eyes closed, to enjoy the heat of the sun, and said, 'If your nanna hadn't told us you were coming we'd never have had such fun.'

'Is that true?' Lily asked as she and Sylvia headed for the ladies' changing rooms. 'Did you come here because of me?'

'Yes.' Sylvia laughed as they picked their way through the sun-worshippers who were stretched out on towels all along the way. 'When Magnus heard you were in Southport the very week Ian and his sailing friends would be here, he pestered Mama to death to bring us.'

'I'm worried about Magnus. He can hardly walk...' Lily said. She dared not say more because Sylvia's expression told her that Magnus must not be discussed out of earshot. They were at the queue outside the ladies' pavilion. The pool was crowded and she was longing to get into the water.

'Don't worry about Magnus,' Sylvia said. 'They're coming for us.'

'Who?'

'Father and all.' Then, in a quiet voice, 'Magnus is only happy when you're near. You know that, don't you, Lily?'

It sounded like a warning, so Lily gave a laugh, to make light of it. She didn't want to be anyone's only source of happiness. They were at the head of the line and it was her turn to be given a cubicle. 'See you in the water!'

As soon as they were changed they ran to the pool and headed for the water chute, plunging one after the other into the chilly green sea water. Lily lost sight of Sylvia and swam towards the raft, where a dozen or so bathers were dangling their legs and diving with great splashings and horseplay. She struck out, but it was farther than she thought and there was the inky, nine-feet-deep area to swim through to reach it. She was almost there when the cramping pain came, low down in her belly, with such piercing strength she almost passed out. Frightened, she rolled on to her back, dropped her head back and felt the air trapped beneath her rubber cap buoying her up. Then came another cramp, making her bring her knees up. She was deaf with the cap pulled down over her ears, strapped tight under her chin; perhaps that was why she never heard the warning shouts of 'Look out!' as somebody leaped off the raft on top of her.

Sylvia told her later that she'd reached the raft ahead of Lily and seen it all. Lily went under, screaming in pain, swallowing and breathing in water. It was lucky Sylvia had seen her – and shouted to her rescuer, who was sitting on the raft beside her, 'Quickly! Lily's gone under. She hasn't come up!'

They say that when you are near death you see everything slowly, as in a slow cinema reel; bright lights pull you forward out of the darkness and you hear and think but cannot speak. The only thing Lily could recall afterwards was turning on to her back, the cramping pain – then nothing, nothing at all until she came to, face down on the wet rope matting of the café floor.

Someone was holding her ankles down, another her wrists

up. Hairy male legs were astride her hips. Strong hands were pressing rhythmically and painfully down on her ribs. She was being crushed into the coarse coir matting, coughing, choking, spewing great gushes of salt water from her mouth and nose between every desperate breath she fought to take. The hands stopped pressing. Someone said, 'Pull her up. Into a sitting position! Push her head down. Hold her there!'

Through the wet curtain of hair that hung forward, she saw Magnus, squatting awkwardly, cradling his arm about her, crying, 'Lily! Thank God!'

Sylvia said, 'Sh! Magnus! Lily's going to be all right. Isn't she...?'

And then Lily recognised the deep, warm Scottish voice of her rescuer – he who had been kneeling astride her, pumping air into her lungs with firm, capable hands. 'She'll have to be examined. In case there's any fluid on her lungs. probably all she'll have is a sore throat. And a sore head.'

Ian Mackenzie was on his feet, calling for towels, her clothes, a blanket. She was coughing and spluttering under the curtain of hair as Ian said to a waiter who was hovering near, 'A hot sweet drink, please.' He said to Magnus, 'Tell your father to bring the car round to the back.' Magnus got up and hobbled away as Ian said to Sylvia, 'We'll find her mother. Make sure she gets home and into bed. And sees a doctor. Do you know who she is?'

Sylvia gave a lovely relieved laugh. 'It's Lily! You remember Lily. At our Christmas party – she accompanied you when you played.'

Then Ian crouched in front of her and gently lifted the soaking hair away from her face. 'My wee accompanist? The piano-player?'

Lily tried to say 'thank you', but no words came. She was crying and coughing and being seated on a long cane bench seat where someone had placed her big striped towel. Ian was wrapping it firmly about her waist and legs and gently tucking another towel round her shoulders. A cup of sweet tea was being offered, and as the hot liquid ran burning over her tongue Lily knew she'd be all right. Her nose and throat were raw, but life was tingling through her with every breath. She shivered and opened her eyes, but she was conscious as never before of every sinew and nerve in her body.

Ian, dressed in his swimming costume, sat beside her, holding her with strong brown arms. It was odd that the first thing she noticed was the black curly hair on his muscular thighs and arms and how it went thicker like a mat into the scooped-out neck of the low-cut man's bathing costume. The hair thinned out but was still visible at the wrist of his hand that was holding the cup to her lips. His black hair fell forward over sun-crunkled eyes and he gave a great delighted grin as she took the cup from him and drank. When she had drunk it all and passed the cup back, he put his face close to hers and said softly, so none of the others could hear, 'I'll put another towel around you before I carry you out to the car. Don't be embarrassed.'

Lily glanced down and saw the red bloodstain of her first period seeping through the stripy towel – and to her undying shame she looked into the handsome face of the boy she loved and passed out cold.

'Sit up. Here's the doctor!'

There was tight elastic round her waist and a wodge of padding between her legs. Mam's drink-drenched breath was on her face and her thin arms were trying to raise Lily up the bed. Then the deep Scottish voice of Ian's father brought her round. 'Mrs Stanway. Allow me...'

Lily was helped up into a sitting position and opened her eyes to find Dr Mackenzie taking her pulse while Mam, at the head of the bed, fussed with the pillow, saying, 'You shouldn't have put yourself to any trouble... Our Lil's been sleeping on and off since they brought her back...' in a drunken voice. Lily averted her head. The smell made her sick. Mam used to suck strong mints to disguise her breath; today it smelled of pear drops.

'No trouble at all, Mrs Stanway,' the doctor replied. 'Well, young miss? How do you feel?'

She would always be able to date precisely the moment she grew up. It was the day she almost drowned, when she came back to consciousness in the late afternoon to find she was aware of every inch of her body. 'All right. I'll be all right.' She was shivering with cold when the covers were off, and her head was pounding. 'If I could get rid of the headache.'

'I'll give you a sleeping draught. As soon as I've listened to your chest,' the doctor said. 'Open your eyes wide ... Good. Let me feel your neck glands ... Good. Open your mouth. Good!' he said to Mam, 'Remove her nightgown, please.'

Mam fumbled while the doctor placed his bag on the bed. Did they carry their bags with them on their holidays? Lily pushed Mam's hand away and dragged the nightdress off, for once not caring if anyone saw her slight shoulders and ribs and the bouncy round breasts with rigid dark tips that appeared to belong to a much larger frame than hers.

Dr Mackenzie warmed the stethoscope in his hand and placed it firmly under her right breast, listening intently. Then he went slowly and thoroughly all over her front before turning her and making her call out loudly as the instrument touched her.

'Ah! Poor girl!' said the doctor.

'What's up?' Mam leaned, tipsy, over her.

'My son has been rough, Mrs Stanway. See the bruising?'

Lily moved her head sharply. 'He only saved my life,' she said fiercely, as the cold instrument on painful bruises made her draw a sharp breath.

She heard the doctor chuckle. 'I'll have to give him some advice,' he said to Mam. 'He's in his second year of medical school. Overzealous.' Then, to Lily. 'There.' He held out the nightdress. 'All clear. Have a good sleep and you can be up and about tomorrow. In fact it is much better if you are.' He put away the stethoscope and brought a small corked phial from the bag before asking for a drinking glass.

Mam went slowly to the washstand and brought a glass, which he took from her trembling hand. 'I'd like a word with you, Mrs Stanway,' he said softly. 'When we settle your daughter to sleep.' He poured a strong-smelling dose and held it out.

'What is it?' Lily said. 'I like to know.'

'A cholorodynum preparation.' He gave a hearty laugh. 'That means nothing to you, does it?'

She closed her mouth tight shut, making him say. 'An elixir, my dear girl – of chloroform, morphine, Indian hemp, capsicum, treacle, liquorice and glycerine, alcohol, peppermint...'

'I'll take it.' She didn't really believe that the medicine contained all those powerful ingredients. Quickly she swallowed the dose and leaned her head back as if she were ready to drop off to sleep. But she wanted to hear what he'd say to Mam. She closed her eyes, aware that they were waiting for her breathing to slow down.

Lily heard them go quietly to the window end of the room, heard Mam whisper, 'She'll be all right, won't she, Doctor?' and his assurance, 'She'll be fully recovered by tomorrow.'

Mam's speech was slurred. 'How much do I owe you...?'

'Nothing. Your daughter is in perfect health. It has been a pleasure to attend...' His voice changed. 'But *your* health concerns me, Mrs Stanway.'

'Me?' Mam was sharp, defensive. 'There's nothing the matter.'

'Are you normally this colour?' he asked.

'I've been sunbathing. Getting a tan.' She sounded surprised.

'Do you tire easily?'

'Lately, yes. I used to be on the go all the time. Why?'

'Have you an increased thirst?'

Lily prayed to God fast that Mam didn't give the good doctor the edge of her tongue.

Mam did not answer, and Lily heard him say, 'You may not be aware of it, but your breath has a strong odour of acetone. This is a clear indication of diabetes. Seek treatment, Mrs Stanway.'

Mam said, 'Sugar diabetes? It killed my mother's mother.'

'Treatment is different now,' he replied. 'We have discovered insulin. Patients are able to inject themselves. Diabetics can live as long as anyone else. But delay can be fatal. I suggest you consult an old Scottish colleague of mine at the Infirmary.'

'I'll see him tomorrow,' Mam answered.

'In the meantime,' said Dr Mackenzie, 'I advise you to be very careful not to drink alcohol. A diabetic person on the verge of coma can become bewildered, confused and unable to stand upright. It looks remarkably like inebriation but in fact is a symptom of something far more dangerous.'

In spite of her will to stay awake, Lily was loosening, drifting off to sleep, grateful that the doctor had warned Mam off the alcohol that had sustained her all these years; glad that Mam was going to seek medical advice; glad to know at last that Mam's symptoms were not those of a drunkard.

Chapter Fourteen

Howard would be downstairs and Elsie didn't want to keep him hanging about. She wouldn't have anyone say, in the hotel, that she'd neglected her daughter. But Lily was fast asleep. Elsie leaned over the bed. 'Lil? Lil – are you all right?'

'Mm ...? Goo ... nigh ... Mam ...'

'I'm going out. The maids will keep an eye on you.'

'Mmm. Go ... way ...'

Elsie checked her appearance before she opened the door. Her dress of black and white dog's-tooth check was mid-calf and had a bright-red belt and white collar. It was as smart as anything she'd seen on Lord Street. But knowing she looked good was no help. Her mother said that troubles came three at a time, but to have them follow so quickly was incredible. For yesterday's shocking discovery to be followed by Lily's near-drowning was as much as she could take. Now she was to believe that she had sugar diabetes, but that at least was nothing, these days.

Elsie put a pin in her black hat, picked up her red bag and gloves, slipped her feet into patent shoes then went out, closing the door quietly behind her. After food and a sherry she'd be all right. She had suspected for a while that something was up with her, and had been worried in case it was the worst.

Howard was waiting. 'You are very chic, my dear. How is Lily?'

'The doctor says she's all right,' said Elsie, gratified that Howard was fond of Lily.

He led her out. 'She was with the Hammonds, wasn't she?'

They crossed the road to the Lanchester. Elsie did not reply until she was seated. She said, 'Just as well the Hammonds were there. Lily fainted in the water. John Hammond brought her back.'

Howard made a sound of irritation. 'Tsch!' He did not like John Hammond. Elsie had told him, years ago, about the natural photographs, as John called them. The prude in Howard had been outraged. He swung the car into Bold Street. Elsie said, 'Where are we going?'

'Cottons. A country club. About ten miles from Southport.' He leaned towards her, patted her knee and smiled, the smile he thought winning and which Lily hated.

It was not the smile, it was the nervous little intimate gestures which put Elsie off. It was the lightness, the hesitancy of them. But then, compared with Frank ... No! She would not compare. She'd done with Frank. She let her hand rest under Howard's. 'Would you mind if we went somewhere nearer?' she said. 'It has been a shock. Our Lil.'

'We'll go to the Prince of Wales. I have a question to ask.'

She knew what he was going to ask. He'd been leading up to it all week, driving her past his splendid house, to show off. He hadn't been able to take her inside because it had been rented out on a three-year lease after his wife died. She had been dead for two years.

The Prince of Wales was the best hotel in town, and there Howard ordered a table and gave her sherry – two sherries – in the cocktail bar. Then, over dinner, with the waiter out of earshot, he put his hand on top of hers. She pulled her hand away smartly.

'Have I been hasty, Elsie?' he said.

'It's not that. It's the shock.'

'Lily?'

'Not only that,' she said. Then, after a second's pause, she lowered her voice and looked away. 'I went to the registry office yesterday.'

He started to tackle his food. 'To ask about ...?'

Elsie toyed with her quenelles of chicken. Her appetite had gone. She took another sip of wine. 'I was looking something up.' She pushed a tiny piece of chicken on to her fork. Then she put it down again. She must talk about it. But she must try to speak dispassionately. She tried to say it in a conversational tone but it didn't come out the way she meant it to.

'I discovered that Nellie Plant gave birth to a boy. Five years ago.' It was agony, putting it into words. Almost as painful as reading the registers. Her words came fast and high-pitched in protest. 'Frank Chancellor was the father. He signed his name! He had the brass neck to sign his name!'

Howard had not noticed her agitation. He smiled. 'Didn't you suspect? Miss Plant told me that Frank Chancellor—'

'I knew she was free with her favours,' said Elsie, cutting and sharp. 'But I didn't think you were so pally with Nellie Plant.'

'Not pally. She did some braid designs for a friend in the trade.'

'And she told you her secrets?' Elsie interrupted. She was not interested in the how and why of his meeting Nellie Plant. It had been the worst moment of her life, turning the register's pages. Seeing Frank's name. She said, 'The boy she says she adopted is hers and Frank Chancellor's! She told you?'

He smiled again. 'People tell me things, you know. They confide.'

She dared not raise her voice or show her wounded feelings. 'Why didn't you tell me?'

'Miss Plant would hardly want it spreading about. She told me in confidence, some years ago. When she heard that I came from Southport.' He returned, cheerfully, to his plate.

'Why?'

'I expect she thought it better to say, at once. In case I'd heard that she had a child. She swore me to secrecy.'

'And what did you think about it? Weren't you disgusted? As I am?' Elsie was toying with her food again. It was giving her a pain in the stomach; Frank's betrayal of her.

He put his knife and fork down and gave her his attention. 'I'm not as innocent as you seem to think, my dear. I know you had only a brief married life. You've had no experience with men. But there are certain men, Elsie – I and I am afraid that Frank Chancellor is one of them – who ...' He began to bounce his hands on the edge of the table while he thought how best to say it. 'I don't want to shock you. Some men have a physical ... dare I say, sexual hold over women. One woman is not enough, Mrs Chancellor was alive at the time. Men like that satisfy their basest desires wherever they can.'

She came back quickly with, 'Nellie Plant must have been over the moon when his wife died.'

'Oh, no. Frank Chancellor told her he would not marry her. He said she could never be his wife ...'

Frank had said the same to Elsie. Was she on a par with Nellie Plant? She took a gulp of wine.

' ... Miss Plant asked for my advice. She said, "Do you think he'll marry me?"' Howard gave a light, polite cough here.

'And ...?' said Elsie.

'I said, "Miss Plant. The only advice I can give is that which I would say to any woman. For heaven's sake, believe a man who tells you to your face that he will never marry you. Chancellor means it or he would never say such a thing."' Howard was full of his own importance. 'I said, "He must provide for you and the child. You should not be in his employ, my dear, when you are bringing up his child."'

The knot in her stomach was so tight she could be sick. She was sick, sick to the heart. How could he come to her, after he'd been with Nellie Plant? Nellie who, rumour had it, would 'give pleasure and relief', whatever that meant, for half a crown.

She must get even. She would let anger claim her now. Frank must not get away with treating her and Lily like nobodies; signing the register for Nellie Plant's child. He'd set Nellie up as landlady in her own right, with furs and a private school for the child. What had he done for her and Lily? Nothing. The shop was his. She, Elsie, only had what she earned and that which Frank provided: rent and rates and a few groceries. They had nothing to show for her years of toil. Heat was rising in her face. 'That's enough, Howard. I don't want to hear any more.'

He was pleased with himself; moistness glistened in his eye as he glanced round the room to be sure they could not be overheard. 'That's what I love about you, Elsie,' he said. 'Your innocence. But the world is full of men like Frank Chancellor. And women like Miss Plant.'

'Then how do they become justices of the peace, magistrates, landladies of public houses?'

'Adultery is not a crime, Elsie.' He smiled and patted her hand as he said. 'A woman such as you needs a man as protector. A woman can spend her energies on a man who gives her his protection.'

Elsie did not reply. He was leading up to it, again. He was going to tell her how much he longed to be her protector.

He went quiet for a second or two, then in a low, earnest voice said, 'Elsie, dear. A man needs a woman to care for him. Her gentle touch, her gentle hands. I have found it most difficult trying to live as a single man since my dear wife died.'

She said, 'Howard. If you are going to ask what I think you are, please, wait.' She put her knife and fork down. She could eat nothing. 'There's something I have to tell you.'

He talked tripe at times. As if looking after a man would be a full-time job! She'd done a full-time job, kept house, brought up a child *and* kept a demanding man happy. But she put a sweet, secret expression on her face and said, 'There's something you don't know, Howard. Before you ask your question, we'd better have a little talk.'

It would give him the shock of his life. But it must be done. Certificates would have to be produced if she married. She glanced round the room again. The waiters were nowhere near. Elsie pushed her plate aside and, demurely casting her eyes down, said, in a small, pathetic little voice, 'I was never married, Howard.'

There was silence. She heard the click of a knife on his plate. She half expected to see a sympathetic expression on his face. Instead she saw that he had taken umbrage. 'I take it that it was a single fall from grace? Did he force himself upon you? I wish you had told me the truth at the time ...'

'Oh, dear.'

'Letting me think you had fallen in love with a cousin you had never mentioned before. You know that it was because I was disappointed in you that I married on the rebound?'

Why did he always make the subject under discussion himself? His feelings? Not hers. Elsie said, 'That is all in the past, Howard. I won't tell you who Lily's father was. I'm telling you this in confidence. Please keep my secret just as you kept Nellie Plant's.'

'You need not tell me.' His face was red. He leaned a little way over the table and said, 'I think I know. There's only one man. Only one over whom you'd so lower yourself. Only one you'd so let yourself down as to ...'

Lower yourself? Let yourself down? He was such a prude. He might not propose now. Elsie dabbed the corner of her mouth with the napkin. And even if he did she'd make him wait until tomorrow for her answer. She had never felt the faintest stirring of desire for Howard. He had kissed her twice; chaste, respectful kisses that seemed to pain him.

She'd have to think it out, ask herself if it would be possible for a woman to respond to a man she felt nothing for – a man who had no passion in him. Howard had juvenile ways; he had the impulses of a boy of thirteen, not a man of fifty-one. He liked to tickle, tease, pretend to have fires he'd no inkling of. Did other women feel this way? She thought not – otherwise how could they let their husbands touch them? Bert Grimshaw, Albert Leadbetter – no, their wives must not be able to feel anything. But they had not known passionate love, as she had with Frank. But how many other women had known passionate love with Frank?

She was beginning to feel faint. She said, 'Howard? Do you think I might have a large brandy. I think reaction to all these shocks is setting in.'

The first thing Lily saw when she woke up was a ruby-red silk dress hanging over the wardrobe door. Its deep V neck was trimmed with ecru lace, as was the narrow shawl collar that came from the hip seam and went up, skimming the shoulder of the sleeveless top, fastening with a jet clasp at the back of the neck. The bias-cut skirt was ankle-length. Her first long dress was the prettiest she'd ever seen.

Beside the bed was a note in Mam's wobbly handwriting, the important words emphasised by capital letters. 'Gone to Doctor's. Howard is meeting me out. Will buy your Towels. Two more on Dressing Table.' Lily glanced over to where two Southalls were laid out. Then she blushed, remembering Ian. The rest of the note said, 'Do not have a Bath. Do not Wash your Hair. Do not stand with Bare Feet on a cold floor. When you are Unwell bad blood rushes to the head. We are going to a Dinner Dance tonight. Try on the dress. Your loving Mam.'

She hopped out of bed, slipped off her nightdress and tried on the ruby dress. It was a perfect fit, and when she lifted her hair into a cascade at the back and whirled round in front of the mirror it startled her, seeing that she looked seventeen, at last.

No sooner had she dressed and eaten breakfast than there came a knock at the bedroom door. 'Coo-ee, you there?'

It was Sylvia and Rowena, holding armfuls of flowers and fruit which they dumped on the bed. 'Ian said you'd live to tell the tale!' Rowena was tall and dark like Ian, and evidently as direct and unaffected. 'I didn't think you were the sort to have the vapours,' she said. 'I'm learning all about it at nursing school.'

'I've never been given flowers before.'

'Are you well enough to go out?' Sylvia asked.

'Course she is!' Rowena poked her finger into the soft upper part of Lily's arm. 'Put your jacket on. Where do you want to go?'

Lily picked up her long cardigan, slid her arms in and said. 'Floral Hall gardens. Listen to the band.'

'I'd have thought a brisk walk . . .' Rowena said.

'Rowena!' Sylvia said, 'This is a sedate English seaside town. Not the rugged highlands, you know.'

They went out on to the promenade. 'Any other time I'd love to walk,' Lily said happily to Rowena as they went in the crowd towards the Floral Hall. 'I love walking on the hills above Archerfield.'

'Good! Then when you come to Edinburgh we'll walk over the Pentlands when I'm not on duty,' Rowena said.

They had joined the queue. 'When I come to Edinburgh?'

'Yes. Why not? Ian wants you to come with Sylvia!'

They hired deckchairs a few rows back from the brass band. Sylvia said, 'Will you, Lily? Come with me to Edinburgh?'

'If I'm invited,' she said. 'I'm sure Mam won't mind.'

Sylvia said, 'Oh! You are a good friend. I always feel so out of place at Uncle Kenneth's. Everyone's so dedicated.'

Rowena had heard the remark and said, as she adjusted the deckchair, 'We don't have a conventional family life.'

'Oh dear!' Sylvia said. 'It's not that. You make everyone welcome.'

'Dad's always spurring us on.' Rowena was louder than anyone else around them. 'He has no time for slackers. "Forward! Onward and upward by your own efforts!" is Dad's motto.' She paid no heed to the people who were watching her. Her black hair was flying about her face as she tugged off her jacket and threw it over the back of the deckchair. 'A bit of advice, Lily, for when you come to stay. Never say you are bored. Dad sees it as his duty to "fill the unforgiving minute with sixty seconds' worth of distance run . . . "'

'Rowena! Sit down!' Sylvia ordered. 'You're making a spectacle of yourself.'

Rowena dropped on to the canvas chair with an apologetic sigh. 'I've probably put you off coming to Edinburgh.'

'You haven't. Not in the least,' Lily said. It would be an education in itself, spending time with an assured, uncomplicated girl like Rowena. And it sounded a marvellous family to her – a household with a good, kind dad who encouraged his children forward, onward and upward.

When Rowena and Sylvia had caught their tram to Birkdale, Lily bought Shandy a pokerwork motto: 'Friendship is Golden.' She took it back and was wrapping it, standing in the window recess, when she saw Mam and Howard Willey-Leigh coming along the promenade, arm in arm in broad daylight.

Mam came in and Lily said, 'I saw you! Spooning with him!'

'That's enough!' Mam sat, and put her bag on to the bed.

'I'm worried,' Lily said. 'What did the doctor say?'

'It's diabetes but I've not got it badly.'

'What's he given you for it?'

'The needle. In my arm. I have to watch what I eat.'

'And drink? Did you tell him you drink?'

'He said a little drink every day won't harm me as long as I count it in as one of my sugars. I can have four ounces of bread a day but if I don't want the bread I can have a sherry instead.' Mam said, 'I have to see him every morning and teatime and take a specimen.'

'A specimen?'

'Of my water. I have to test my water. Get the needle twice a day until they've got the dose right. Then I shall have to do it myself. The trouble is, I'm a coward. I'll never be able to give myself the needle.'

Lily was relieved that an injection was all that was necessary to cure Mam. 'I'll learn how to do it. Don't worry.'

'It's going to be a new lease of life. The doctor said, "The needles will transform you, Mrs Stanway."' She studied her hands, went quiet for a minute, then said, 'Lil, I've something to tell you ...' Her face was pale and determined and immediately Lily got the familiar, sinking feeling in her stomach. She was about to hear something she'd rather not know.

Mam went to sit by the window, pointed to the other chair and said, 'Come here. Sit and listen.'

Lily went to sit facing her, but Mam stared out of the window before, carefully choosing her words. 'You remember what I said, when we walked home from the will-reading?'

Lily's stomach turned over. Mam was going to tell her the truth at last. She had no control over her mouth, but sat looking intently at Mam, who averted her eyes again and stared out to sea. Lily waited for the bombshell, barely breathing, in an agony of suspense.

In a flat, expressionless voice Mam said, 'Hah'd has asked me to marry him. I told him I'd ask you first.' She glanced at Lily and away again. 'Well? What do you say?'

It was a slap in the face. Lily's mouth was as dry as dust. She jumped to her feet and went to stand between Mam's chair and the window so Mam would have to face her. 'You don't love him. You can't marry him.'

Mam said, 'I can. I asked what you thought.'

'I can't abide him,' Lily said defiantly. 'How can you think of it?'

Suddenly Mam's eyes blazed. 'Because I've been the world's biggest fool. I've been treated like ...' She took a deep breath.

'Like what?' Lily said. 'Not by me, you haven't.'

Mam had control of her voice again. 'I want us to live the way we ought to be living. In a nice house. Looked up to.'

'His house? In Southport?'

'No. A new house, in Macc. Hah'd wants to take on my responsibilities when I marry him.' Mam said it in a flat voice, without any feeling whatever.

The sick feeling was back. '*When* you marry him? I don't have a choice then, do I?'

Mam was not going to give an inch. 'You do have a choice. Hah'd wants to adopt you. I want to get you away from the Central School and those medical records. Send you to a private school. St Ursula's in Southport. You can be a boarder. Learn to be a lady. You'll have a new birth certificate. You will be the legitimate daughter of a man of means.'

She waited for a few seconds, then, as if to dangle another carrot, said, 'You could choose your own name. Start afresh. If you don't want to be Lily Willey-Leigh ...'

Lily could just picture the delight Doreen would take in taunting, Silly Lily ... Her eyes filled with tears. 'Or what? What's the alternative?'

'Keep on being illegitimate. Keep the name of Stanway. Keep on at the Central School. And go to live with Nanna and Grandpa. Hah'd won't take you on any other terms!'

Tears were brimming over. They had it all planned. If she kept her mother she'd lose her home, her name and her school. She made a foolish appeal to Mam's motherly love. 'Who do you love? Him or me?'

She ought to have known better. It sparked off the tinder. Mam said, 'I won't be given an ultimatum! It's my life. The Stanways have been cheated out of everything! First the mill. Then my chance of marriage was snatched from under my nose by that Scotch ...!' She stopped and made an effort to control her temper. 'A man must be master in his house. Hah'd – you'll call him Father – has always wanted a daughter. He can't have one with a different name from his.' She was red in the face. 'Unless you can give me a good, solid reason for saying no, I'm going to accept his proposal.'

The thought of calling that man Father was repulsive to Lily. The seconds dragged by as Mam waited. Then Mam touched her shoulder affectionately, rather shyly, softened and said, 'I don't want to lose you, Lil. We've been through thick and thin together. Go on! Say yes. Let me tell Hah'd you want him for a father. Go on, Lil!'

Mam was pleading with her. She had asked her to give her a good, solid reason why she shouldn't marry. If Lily told her about the time Howard Leigh had put his hand on her bare bottom Mam would call it off and never have the happiness she wanted. Or she'd think Lily was lying. Either way, as it was for Mam, this was Lily's only chance of legitimacy.

'Well?' Mam said. 'What have you got to say?'

Lily blew her nose hard. 'I can't think straight.'

'And you can't give me a straight answer, is that it? You don't want me to be happy?'

'Give me time. It's not that . . .'

'What then?'

Lily swallowed hard. 'I can't choose between you and Nanna.'

At last Mam let her anger show. Her face was set, her mouth tight. 'We all have to make choices. I've made mine.'

Lily was glad they were going out that evening. Mam didn't expect her to make up her mind in a hurry, and they were too busy getting ready for the dinner and dance to argue.

Mam pinned Lily's hair up so that it looked as if it fell naturally that way. She lent her her shoes and a touch of lipstick, did her nose with a fluff of powder, showed her how to put boot-blacking on her eyelashes and gave her a spray of her precious Lanvin scent, My Sin.

They set off at seven o'clock in Mr Leigh's Lanchester. 'Where are we going?' Lily asked him. He was dressed in tail suit and white tie.

'Palace Hotel.' His teeth flashed and his eyes glinted in the reflected face in the driving mirror. 'The biggest and best. Nothing but the best for my two lovely ladies.'

Mam giggled at the compliments. She had evidently forgotten that the Hammonds were staying at the Palace.

'You're going to meet some of my business associates,' he said. 'There will be seven of us, with Lily.'

It was a splendid, grand hotel. Uniformed men ushered them into the ballroom, which was the biggest room Lily had ever seen in her life. Scores of tables, round and oval, were laid with white damask and laden down with silver and crystal under the great chandeliers.

They followed the head waiter past women in silver lamé dresses with low-cut backs, *grandes dames* in black satin with feather trims and men in tail suits, wing collars and white bow ties. Gold glistened and diamonds flashed, and over all was the hum of male voices and the tinkling of ladies' laughter.

Lily was pink and self-conscious as they were shown to their table, where two middle-aged couples sat. Their table was next to the dance floor, where couples were gliding to the tune of 'Blue Moon', a foxtrot played by a dance band: five men in white suits. It was like the Hollywood pictures she'd seen at the Majestic. Waiters pulled at their chairs and seated them, and Lily's knees were weak with nervous excitement for she had spotted them at the next table – the Hammonds and the Mackenzies. Her heart almost stopped. She wanted to curl up and die of embarrassment at the thought of Ian having carried her, covered in blood.

Mam smiled and nodded in their direction with an air of indifference, and Lily tried to sneak a quick look at Ian. He grinned broadly and lifted his hand in a welcoming gesture. Lily's face burned fierce, fiery red.

They brought iced lemonade to the table for Lily and red and white wines for the others. Lily noticed that Mam was merely toying with her glass as the hors d'oeuvres, the first of seven courses, were wheeled to them on a great trolley. She had never seen such food and had to watch what Mr Leigh did so she wouldn't make a fool of herself.

Mr Leigh was being the fine gentleman, switching his smile on and off, being extravagant in flattery to the other two ladies in the party as well as to Mam and herself. Prim from embarrassment, Lily blushed whenever she caught Ian's eye, which she did every time she looked across at his table.

Mam was occupied – sparkling for Mr Leigh, making him laugh so much he had to dab at those droopy-corner eyes with his table napkin. After the fish they brought fillet steaks with a béarnaise sauce and tiny new potatoes, roasted onion and buttered peas.

There was a pause after the meat, and Mr Leigh asked Mam to dance. People had been taking to the floor all through the meal. There were about eight couples dancing when he took Mam in his arms while the band played 'Embraceable You'.

Mam was *soignée* in a low-backed black dress of crushed velvet with a headband of sparkling stones. Jet beads at the hem and neckline twinkled under the revolving glitter ball as they danced. The chandeliers were dimmed. Only on the dance floor was there light and movement.

And all this time Lily sensed Ian's eyes on her. She dared not look him in the face, but out of the corner of her eye she saw that he had stopped eating, he was very still and his eyes were fixed on her.

When Mam and Mr Leigh came back from the dance floor they were served with meringues glacées with chantilly cream. Mr Leigh called out for champagne and asked that a glass be brought for Lily. When it was poured he tapped his hand on the table and stood up. He was the only person standing up to speak at a table in that vast room. Heads turned towards them. Lily noticed that the Hammonds' table had gone quiet.

And then she realised, too late, the purpose of this celebration. 'Friends!' he said. 'Friends! My dear friends.' He made a little high-pitched throat-clearing noise. 'It is with pride and joy that I am able to say that ...' He patted Mam's shoulder. '... that Elsie and I are to be married.' He lifted his glass and said, 'She will make me a very happy man! To Elsie!' then, abruptly, he sat down again.

'To Elsie!' Everyone but Mam and Lily raised their glasses. Mam nudged her, and reluctantly, Lily raised hers, but there was a lump in her throat and she could not swallow a single sip of the sparkling champagne. Tears blurred her eyes. Her chin and mouth were being pulled down in misery as she wondered why she had not seen it coming. She couldn't speak, though everyone at the table was congratulating Mr Leigh and wishing Mam every happiness, making Mam's face go all pink and self-conscious.

Lily remembered Nanna's words. She must shift for herself, try to find something good that could come out of the dreadful decision Mam had made. Everyone at their table had gone to stand by Mr Leigh and offer their hands for shaking, because their table was too wide to reach over. But it was graceless behaviour, in Lily's eyes. Nobody else in the ballroom stood up and walked round the table. Everyone was watching them, and as Mam fumbled in her bag for a handkerchief to dab her eyes, which were watering, she pleaded, 'Give us a hand, Lil! For heavens' sake find my hankie!'

Lily handed hers over. 'Here.'

Mam didn't want the others to hear. 'I told you we'd be out of it. Have you made up your mind?'

'Not yet.'

'You wanted a father! You told Grandpa you wanted it all made legal,' she whispered. 'You're an ungrateful . . . !' Mam stopped whispering rebukes, because the others were seated again.

Lily felt herself growing faint. She put her elbows on the table and cupped her face in her hands. Was Mam was doing this for her? Did Mam want Mr Leigh to adopt her? She could be legitimate. She could be baptised and confirmed. She drank her glass of champagne in one go.

Everyone was getting up from their table, making for the dance floor. Only Lily was left. She looked towards the Hammonds' table where Magnus, Sylvia and Ian were talking. Ian looked across the two tables and again their eyes met and locked. Lily tried to avert hers but couldn't, because Ian was smiling at her. Despite the embarrassing blush, Lily's low spirits began to lift.

Ian got to his feet, said something to Magnus and Sylvia, all the time watching Lily. A warm, tingling sensation came rippling through her as he came towards the table; tall and handsome in his evening dress suit. Then he stood in front of her, correct and formal. He held out his hand. 'May I have the pleasure of this dance?'

His level, steady blue eyes were not cool or formal – they were blazing with life. Something as old as life, the magnetism that draws lovers together, sparked between them as Lily held his hand and went to the dance floor.

'Better?' he asked as his right hand went firmly into the small of her back and she felt the pressure of his fingers, through the ruby dress. Her left hand rested on his shoulder and she was moving like an automaton, but her face was flaming. As they joined hands he looked into her shining eyes and said, 'You don't look like a girl who was at death's door yesterday.'

'I'm all right.' She coughed, to catch her breath. 'I feel such an idiot.'

'So do I!' Ian's straight eyebrows almost met. 'I'm sorry I hurt you.'

'Oh. It's nothing.' She was breathless. 'I feel an idiot because ...'

They moved across the floor together, and he said, 'You don't appear an idiot. You seem at home in' – he smiled – 'this milieu!'

She was concentrating like mad, and the smell of him the faint man and coal tar soap smell, was making her aware of all her senses. 'I mean yesterday. You rescuing me and ...'

They were dancing, turning at the corners, all the difficult steps, but Ian pressed his hand in the small of her back and turned expertly. 'Don't give it a thought,' he said. Then he tightened his hold on her. 'I could dance the night away with you.'

He made a little frown of concentration. 'I'm trying to look couth – not uncouth – as if I'm used to this ...' he said as they did a smooth reverse turn. 'Trying to impress you so you'll think I'm a ... a ...'

Lily laughed at last, because her nerves were gone and because, though he meant what he said, Ian was so obviously enjoying himself.

'Not a very convincing lounge lizard, am I?' he said. 'I spend all my free time out of doors.' They danced past Mr Hammond and Rowena, Mrs Hammond and Ian's father. Their feet matched in perfect step. They had not missed a beat. Next he said, 'The important thing is ... are you recovered from the water? From the bruising I gave you?'

'Good as new.' She laughed softly, and her laugh had changed, gone lower and huskier with the thrill that was coming from dancing; from being held in a man's arms for the first time in her grown-up life. Their eyes met again, his blue and steady, hers wide and gazing up into his in the naive, adoring expression that fifteen-year-olds cannot hide.

'We make a good partnership,' he said. 'Everyone's watching us ...' He danced faster, did another reverse turn. 'Do you remember playing the piano when I played accordion? At Archerfield?'

'Oh, yes!'

'And we said we'd make music together?'

'Of course I do.'

He twirled her round in the corner of the floor. 'We are making it!'

Ian might not realise it, but to Lily he was an expert dancer. His firm hands were guiding her so that they never touched or bumped into anyone, but she was aware of every muscle in his arms, every movement of his strong legs against hers. He laughed softly as he did another complicated step. Then he said, 'Do you still play the piano?'

'Yes,' she said. 'And you?'

'It's my greatest pleasure ...' He couldn't stop the deep, chuckling laugh, not caring who was watching them. 'Playing the piano is my greatest pleasure. The next best thing to dancing with my pretty wee accompanist.'

This was the most romantic conversation she could ever have dreamed of. Words and answers were slipping out of her mind. The ruby-red dress was swirling round her ankles, her head was whirling and spinning and a great big smile was fixed on her face as she looked into honest blue eyes that had no guile, no pretence, no insincerity in them. The band was playing a quickstep and Ian was singing, 'Grab – your coat – and get – your hat. Leave your worries on the door – step. Just – direct – your feet, to the sunny side of the street.'

Lily looked up into his eyes, wishing the dance might last forever.

Ian said, 'I keep forgetting your name. I always thought of you as my wee accompanist.' He pulled her a bit closer, bent his head towards hers and in a voice that had lost all traces of its former buoyancy and had become tender and hesitant said, 'Now I'm with you again I don't know how I could have forgotten. What is it? Tell me, I promise I'll remember it for ever.'

She was not a child any longer. She was making her own decisions and choices. Onwards and upward! She couldn't go back. She'd go forward, with Mam, into a new life. She went on tiptoe and whispered in his ear, 'I used to be called Lil. Short for Lily Isobel. Just call me Isobel!' she said. 'soon I'm going to be Isobel Leigh.'

'Isobel Leigh. Isobel Leigh. What a lovely name.' He leaned back a little and held her at arm's length, smiling appreciatively. Then he pulled her towards his strong, broad chest and said, 'Magnus hasn't taken his eyes off us. I once told him I hadn't met a girl I'd care to waste time dancing with.'

'You did? Why?'

'I hadn't met you, Isobel.'

She looked over her shoulder at the table where Magnus sat. And suddenly her heart felt as if it were being torn in two, seeing Magnus, white-faced with pain and suffering, watching her dancing with the boy she loved.

Part Two

Chapter Fifteen

'Isobel?'

'Isobel,' she said to everyone on their return from holiday. 'I want to be known as Isobel.'

Mam and Nanna kept forgetting, Shandy had to think twice and Doreen said she could only think of her as Silly Lily, but Isobel refused to answer to her old name and it turned out that a change of name was not at all unusual. At the Central School there was an Elizabeth who was no longer Betty, two Margarets who used to be Peggies and a Bunty who cried if anyone remembered that her real name was Jane.

But the new name was not the only difference in her life. Since she'd taken charge of the housekeeping money, her responsibilities had snowballed, to the point where Mam would say, 'Sometimes I wonder who is the mother and who the daughter.' Mam had begun to look to her for advice, and Isobel determined to learn about diabetes and its treatment.

They had never subscribed to the penny-a-week scheme where families could consult a doctor free, so Isobel had to squeeze out of the housekeeping purse the money for Mam's treatment as well as half a crown for a private consultation with the doctor. She was shown into Dr Russell's surgery a week later.

He had the reputation of not suffering fools at all. People lowered their voices when they said his name. Others boasted that he was the best doctor in Macclesfield and that he called them by their Christian names. He said sternly, 'It cannot be cured.'

'I haven't come here hoping you can cure her,' she said.

'Tell me how to look after her, please.'

He looked over the top of his wire-framed glasses. 'The greatest danger is coma. You know there are two sorts of coma?'

She didn't know. 'They are?'

'Diabetic coma resulting from high blood sugar is the lesser of two evils. A patient's blood sugar levels can rise steadily through years, yet they carry on with nothing more than bouts of depression or lethargy. The danger here comes from infection or, worse, injury. Poor circulation and unhealthy tissues. Cuts that won't heal become gangrenous . . .'

'How do I make sure this doesn't happen?' Isobel asked quickly.

'You make sure she takes her insulin.'

Isobel felt her mouth starting to pull at the corners as it did when she was trying to appear more confident than she was. She pressed her lips tight. 'And the other sort of coma? You said there were two.'

'Hypoglycaemic coma results from high insulin levels. It can be lethal if not treated quickly. Sugar has to be ingested at once, to save the patient.'

This was far worse than Mam made out. Isobel swallowed hard. 'How will I recognise which is which?'

'Your mother must not be left alone. She must be watched.' He spoke in a serious voice to impress the dangers upon her. 'An insulin-dependent diabetic may have taken too high a dose of insulin, may not have eaten enough, have exercised too much or be suffering from anxiety which depletes the blood sugar rapidly. First she will be combative or disoriented; then she may have a seizure.' He said, 'Shall I continue?'

Isobel pressed her fingers tight together. 'Continue. Please.'

'Blood sugar drops – this can happen in minutes – and the patient falls into what looks like deep sleep. Frequently he can still hear. Hearing is the last sense to go.'

'And the treatment?'

'The treatment is to get glucose into the bloodstream, by ingestion. Once the patient is unconscious, ingestion is no longer an option. The patient must be taken to hospital, where glucose will be given directly into the stomach, through a tube.'

'How do I recognise the difference?' Isobel asked.

Now at last his expression softened. 'I will give you full instructions.' He paused, then as if on impulse came round to her side of the desk and placed a hand on her shoulder. 'I don't think that your mother has anything to worry about. With such a devoted daughter she could live to a ripe old age.'

'I intend that she shall,' said Isobel. She listened intently, and took away booklets and medicine and warnings of what to look out for. Diabetes, the doctor said, made its victims bone-weary one minute and full of life the next. This then was why Mam was erratic.

Isobel threw herself into getting Mam's diabetes under control. Mam didn't want it advertised, she said. People might think it was catching and would stay away from her. So a tray was hidden on an empty shelf in the scullery cupboard; on it was a spirit lamp and test tubes for boiling urine, two syringes, four needles, methylated spirit in a flask containing a ready-primed syringe, gauze and spirit to clean the skin. There was also a collection of phials of insulin with different-coloured labels showing the various strengths. Isobel became an expert, and a bossy one, recording the dosage and the sugar levels, and every day she saw Mam improving.

Mr Leigh came round to the house more often than before but there was no mention of wedding plans and Isobel came to hope that Mam was having second thoughts. Her behaviour surely could not all be due to the blood sugar levels. She swung from black moods, when she fumed about everything and could barely speak to Mr Leigh, to being girlish and frivolous, when she'd try to make him unsure of her. She'd say, 'Can't see you tomorrow, Hah'd! Our Lil and I – I mean, our Isobel and I – are going to the pictures. I've fallen madly in love with Fred Astaire.'

Then Mr Chancellor came round for the rent one Friday. Isobel had not seen him for months, but before she could speak Mam said, 'Hello, stranger!' in a sarcastic voice. 'Avoiding me? I thought you'd passed on.'

'Don't be like that,' he said. 'I said I'd have to leave it a while.'

Isobel thought it shocking, what Mam did next. She came to stand in front of Mr Chancellor, close and provocative, and said, 'When are you and Nellie Plant going to tie the knot, then?'

He gave her a cold, hard look before putting his hand out for the rent money Mam was holding. 'I'll not marry again.'

Mam handed it over and put her hands on her hips. 'You're only forty-four. No age. Why! You could marry and rear another family.'

What Mam was saying was suggestive and presumptuous, and a hot blush of embarrassment rushed to Isobel's cheeks. How could Mam behave like a low gossip-monger and bear false witness? There was a hostile silence. Mr Chancellor looked from Mam to herself and then down at the book. 'I've enough on my plate, with the family I've got,' he said. And there was a new, dreadful distance between them all.

Frank was furious. If he didn't go now he'd lose his temper, strike Elsie or say something he'd regret. He slapped the rent book down on the kitchen table. Then he gave her a look that could turn a gorgon to stone, before giving a painful attempt at a smile in the direction of his sweet, precious daughter. He went fast and angrily out of the shop on to Jordangate.

The usuals were in the Swan: a butcher and a few taxi-drivers. They hailed him, broad smiles on their faces, but Frank ordered a pint of Adshead's and went to sit in the far corner. He wanted to be left alone, to brood about Elsie. How could she? How dared she? Putting him down in front of Lily, and weeks since they'd had that big quarrel.

When she and Lily were on holiday he'd missed them. Then, a couple of days after she got back from Southport, he went round to the shop on Wednesday half-closing day. For two weeks they had been out of his life and he'd done nothing but think about them, missing Lily and hungering for Elsie. It was the first time that Elsie had not been available to him; her first absence since he came home from the war. And it came to him, when she was not there, that he needed her.

Elsie was the biggest part of his life. Always had been. Ray was a trial, a worry, but he was growing up fast. In two or three years' time he would settle down, marry or want to live away from his father. When all risks of Ray and Lily's being thrown together were over, Elsie was the only person he could share his life with. It would even be seen in the town in a year or two as a good thing for a respectable widow to marry a man of substance, a JP. He was on the point of telling her this when he went to the shop in high spirits. If Lily was there he'd enjoy their company for an hour or two and return to Elsie late at night. If Lily was out he'd make love to Elsie. He was as eager as a young blood for an afternoon in bed with his woman.

Elsie was waiting for him, dressed in red; a close-fitting, high-buttoned dress that showed off every curve of her beautiful body. She also had the haughty look on her face that told him she was annoyed about something. He grinned and went to her with arms wide.

'Don't touch me!' She backed away, spitting the words.

'What?' He dropped his arms. 'What have I done?'

'You dare ask?' The blue eyes flashed. 'You make me sick!'

He stood still. 'Now then,' he said. 'What is it?'

'Nellie Plant. That's what. And your son. Nellie Plant's son.'

'Oh, hell.' He pulled out one of the kitchen chairs and thumped down on to it. There was nothing he could do but tell the truth. Elsie stood with her back to the fireplace like a commanding officer, waiting, eyes glinting. He chose his words with care. 'Listen, Elsie. I made a mistake. Once. And I regretted it as soon as I'd ...' He stopped and looked at her, hoping to see some understanding in her eyes. Seeing only scorn, he looked down at his hands, abjectly. 'I spent a foolish evening drinking with Nellie. I hadn't gone round there with the intention ... One thing led to another ...'

'My word! Didn't it lead to something? I'll say it led to something.'

'I'm sorry. I was sorry then.'

'Five years ago,' she said. 'That takes us back to when you and I were seeing ...' She gave a contemptuous laugh. 'When we were seeing a lot of one another. You were coming round three nights a week. Wednesdays. Sundays if Lily was away.' Her eyes were blazing. 'Wasn't I enough for you?'

He had to be straight. 'I didn't tell you because you'd be upset ...'

'Upset? You thought I'd only be upset?' She waited for a

few moments before she reached for a cigarette, struck a match and lit it. Then she sent a stream of smoke out, fast, right in front of his nose. 'I tell you, Frank, I was sick! I saw your signature and hers on that register and I went outside and vomited!'

'Nellie means nothing to me!' he said. Then because she looked away, 'It only happened once. I've taken care of them.'

'Haven't you just?' She came to stand by the table. 'Well, you can start taking care of your first indiscretion, can't you?'

He could not continue to apologise for something that was over and done with while she refused to show understanding. She had not asked why he'd signed the register for Nellie's child and not for Lily. He'd been in Germany, clearing up the aftermath of a war, when Lily was born. Hadn't she remembered that? The army didn't give compassionate leave to a man whose mistress gave birth. He said, 'If you mean you and our Lil, I take care of you.' There was an edge to his voice. 'You want for nothing.'

'We want a lot. The difference this time is we're going to get it.'

'Get what? What can I do?'

She didn't speak for a moment, but her head went high as she looked down her nose at him. 'You always said you wouldn't stand in my way. Well, I'm going to get married.' She waited a second or two, then, 'Did you hear me? I said I'm getting married to a man who loves me. To Howard.'

Hot, jealous rage swept through him. He jumped to his feet. 'Willey-Leigh? He'll bleed you white. Then he'll be off, after bigger fish. You are not going to marry him.'

'Oh, but I am. I'm going to have a husband. And a house!'

'You can have a house any time you want!' His fingernails were sharp as he clenched his fist. 'You don't need to get married to that—' Now, his pride wouldn't let him ask her to wait until the time was right. The mood she was in she'd delight in refusing.

'Our Lil's going to have a proper father. At last.' She was triumphant.

'I'm her father.'

'Prove it!' She tossed back her head, but her eyes never wavered.

'I'll tell her myself,' he snapped back though he knew that he would not. How could he speak up now? It was far too late.

'Too late,' Elsie said. 'She doesn't want to know. She'd hate you for it. She wants Howard for her father. Howard is going to adopt her. *Isobel*, by the way. She doesn't like the name Lily. She's already changed that.' She came a step nearer, put her face close to his. 'It's over, Frank. Finished!' Then, because he made no reply, she said, louder, '*Kaput*! Ended!'

He had never seen her like this. 'What can I do?' he asked, as a hot tide of anger rose in him. 'What do you want?'

'You are not going to get away with it scot-free.'

He had never before wanted to hit a woman. She continued, her face flushed with vengeance, 'You'll pay for her to go to a good school. St Ursula's in Southport. They only take upper-class girls.'

'I'd do that anyway.' Jealousy, raw and painful, made him say, 'Does Leigh know she's mine?'

'Nobody knows the truth except you and me,' she said. 'And I've a mind to tell Isobel that Howard is her real father.'

He was shaking. 'My God! You are vindictive.'

She ignored him. 'The money has to be found for the school. Howard's having business troubles at present.'

'At present?' He gave a cynical laugh. Willey-Leigh had been borrowing through Cheshire Trading for years and still did not know Frank was his creditor. Nobody borrowed from a trading company if he could get a cheaper loan. Cheshire Trading charged ten per cent to high-risk customers like Leigh. Frank now said, 'Come to your senses, woman. Leigh hasn't the means to keep a dog, let alone a wife and family.'

'Not like you, eh? Keeping three families going and never missing the money. Setting women up in business. Paying for expensive schools . . .'

Frank knew he must wait until Elsie saw through Leigh. There would be no cautioning her now. He said, 'How do you think you'll explain the little matter of school fees to Willey-Leigh? Where will he think the money is coming from?'

She had the nerve to smile at him. 'I'm going to keep working, though Howard doesn't want me to. He wants to take the shop over.'

At last, he could retaliate. 'Like hell he will! The shop is my property. Always was. You are the lessee. The lease is not transferable.' He returned her smile, with interest. He had enjoyed saying that.

Elsie carried on as if he'd never spoken. 'I've no intention of giving my shop up. But it doesn't take as much as people think ...'

He gave a dry laugh. 'No. Willey-Leigh thinks he's marrying into money again. The only attraction for that type is money.' She went on smiling. He repeated, 'What are you asking of me?'

'You can pay the school fees. I'll tell John Hammond that we've come to an arrangement whereby I pay you more rent so the money's always there for the start of the term.'

'It's not your bank manager you'll have to explain to. Stupid woman! I pay many a bill for my tenants under those arrangements. It's your *husband* who'll be asking the questions.'

'I'll make it look as if the shop takes more.'

'False accounting?' He gave a dry laugh.

'Don't talk daft. I've never had to account for what I do.'

'Evidently.'

Now, here in the Swan, he thought it all through again. Elsie was going to go through with this marriage. He'd stayed away, hoping she'd come to her senses. It was William Congreve who wrote, in *The Mourning Bride*, 'Heaven hath no rage like love to hatred turned. Nor Hell a fury like a woman scorned.' Elsie had more fury than hell. She'd refused to listen when he tried to tell her the truth – that, though he'd signed the register rather than risk the scandal Nellie had threatened, he didn't believe for a minute that Nellie Plant's child was his.

He had spent one foolish evening with Nellie, one foolish, drunken night, and even drunk as he was, he thought he had taken the ultimate precaution of *coitus interruptus*. He'd gone to Nellie, low in spirits, when he thought his drives were fading. Would it be different with someone else? Would it increase his potency? Could he let a woman give him pleasure and relief without him wanting to finish the job?

All it had done was prove that he and Elsie were a perfect match and that, no, he couldn't let a woman merely give him pleasure and relief. Nellie wouldn't let a chance like that pass her by. She had made a night of it, cooking a meal for him, wine and brandy too, and she had tempted him again and again, made him ready for more and more until he was sick with the food and the wine and sick with disgust at his own body.

He signed the birth register under the threat that unless he did, Nellie would tell Sarah. Then, when Sarah died and marriage was not on offer, Nellie made him dance.

He'd have to see Elsie again and beg her to reconsider this mad idea of marriage. Surely she could see through Willey-Leigh. Leigh was a penniless humbug. He was nothing worse than that, thank God. He'd be a good stepfather to Lily. Elsie wouldn't consider him otherwise. But as for means – he was a strawman.

Then jealous blood rose again as he imagined Elsie in bed with Willey-Leigh. He thought of those sapphire eyes, heavy-lidded with desire, the softest skin in the world, the little noises she made ... Would she make them for Leigh? He gave an ironic laugh. Elsie would soon find out what she'd married. Willey-Leigh was no use to a woman, Nellie Plant said.

There was a flurry of dressmaking and packing for a quiet wedding in Grandpa's chapel at the end of November. Isobel wanted to know who was providing what in all these wedding arrangements because Mam, though professing rapture, had been going about with a worried look on her face, talking to Isobel about what Mr Leigh could afford. She had even mentioned mortgages. In Isobel's book the man provided the house and looked after his family, and here was Mam talking about running her shop and taking out a mortgage.

Isobel pointed out the facts to Mam. Mr Leigh had a house of his own, in Southport. He must sell his house and buy one in Macclesfield, or else they must all go to live in his house in Southport. Mama was becoming exasperated. 'You silly girl. People are losing hundreds of pounds, on houses. It's the wrong time to sell, Howard says.'

But Mam was looking forward to her new standing as a married woman. She said, 'I'll show 'em! A woman needs a man at the back of her.'

'You've managed without so far,' Isobel said.

'That's all in the past. We'll be looked up to when I'm married. We'll be respected, a proper family with a man at the head. You need a background, too. You'll be taken advantage of without a good background.'

'Taken advantage of? Who would? And how?'

'You're growing. Soon men will be chasing you,' Mam said.

'Mam!' Isobel retaliated. 'Don't be disgusting! I'd never . . .!'

'Never do what I did? Is that what you mean?'

Isobel blushed, then she saw that Mam had not taken it as a criticism. 'I didn't mean that.'

'Well, I did,' Mam said. 'It's the old, old story. You'll fall for it as well. It's the easiest thing in the world to fall for the wrong man. You only have a few years for picking and choosing,' Mam spoke in her sharp, don't-argue-with-me voice. 'A girl's life is made or broken by the man she marries.'

'Nowadays girls make their own lives!' Isobel said. 'I'm going to try for law school. Put myself forward for a bursary if we can't afford . . .'

Mam wasn't paying attention. She had that eager look about her. 'You must meet the best people. To do that you have to have a good family background, or you'll never be invited anywhere.'

'I meet the best people already,' Isobel protested. 'At Archerfield.'

'Hah'd doesn't like the Hammonds,' Mam replied sharply. 'He doesn't want you to spend your time with them once he's your father.'

Isobel was dreading the day Mr Leigh became her stepfather, for he was presuming his future powers, winking at her and standing close, letting his hand linger on her shoulder as if he had rights. This was the moment to put a stop to it, to tell Mam. But how could she tell, ruin Mam's happiness? Wouldn't she too be worse off – illegitimate? Should she keep quiet, become adopted and legitimate, with the new name she wanted and the prospect of university? She'd be out of Mr Leigh's way at St Ursula's in Southport.

Miss Duffield was a treasure, discreet and loyal, though Elsie knew full well that her sights were set higher than being a counter hand. Miss Duffield wanted to buy the business for her niece. She had said as much, hinting that now Mrs Stanway was going to get married, and it being unusual for a married woman to continue to work, if at any time Mrs Stanway thought of giving up the shop, would she give Miss Duffield first refusal? Elsie merely smiled and said she'd keep it in mind.

But she would not give the shop up. She couldn't now. Howard was having business troubles. He had taken her to Buxton last Wednesday afternoon and there, after they had taken tea in the Winter Gardens, they walked up to the old baths and drank the waters and Howard told her that they must postpone their marriage for a little while because his business partner had been cheating him. Elsie did not know about the partnership.

There were tears in his eyes as he said, 'I cannot swallow my pride, Elsie, and go begging for a loan.'

'I don't want you to borrow money, Howard,' she said. 'And I don't want to start married life under an obligation to anyone.'

'Then perhaps your father could contribute,' he said.

'Contribute to what?' she asked.

'Our marriage, dear. We will need a house. If your father contributed and I obtained a mortgage from a building society ...'

'I can't ask Dad,' she said. Howard would not have suggested it if he knew Dad. Dad thought that building societies were lower than money-lenders. You paid your honourable rent, in Dad's book. The workhouses were full of people destitute through debt. Elsie said, 'We could live at the shop for a year or two. Until your business is on its feet.'

'The shop is not your property, Elsie. I can't be expected to live under Chancellor's roof. Pay rent to that lecher? No. Unless we find somewhere suitable, it is our marriage that must wait for a year or two.'

So, either Elsie raised the money herself, or the marriage was off. She must not let all she had ever wanted – a husband, social standing and respectability – slip through her fingers. 'Leave it with me,' she said, 'I've seen a house I like, in Bollinbrook Road.'

*

One morning, early in November, Mam said, 'Don't go to school today, love.'

'Why?'

'I've got the keys to a house in Bollinbrook Road.'

'Opposite the cemetery? I didn't think there were any houses ...'

'There's only one or two. Ours is ever so pretty from the outside. Half house, half bungalow. Pebbledash. A big garden, surrounded by farmland.'

'Ours? Have we got it, then?'

'Not yet. I want to see if you like it.' Mam smiled, seeing Isobel's excited face. 'We'll go to the solicitor's office afterwards.'

Isobel went upstairs to change, and Elsie gave instructions to the elderly Miss Duffield.

She and Isobel reached Bollinbrook Road before ten o'clock, with Isobel chattering gaily all the way. 'I never knew there was a house here,' she said, for it was hidden from the road by a thicket of overgrown scented rosemary and hawthorn hedging. Woodland trees surrounded the garden, separating and sheltering it from the farmer's fields. There was a little orchard, where apples and pears lay rotting and scented in the dead long grass, and the lawns either side of the crumbling gravel drive had become meadows full of weed, but there it was, in mock-Tudor splendour, a chalet-bungalow with the sun glancing off red pantiles and shining on leaded glass panes. Isobel's face wreathed in smiles that would not go down. 'I've fallen in love at first sight,' she said.

She turned the key in the front door with trembling fingers, and once inside almost ran from room to room, exclaiming with delight. Downstairs were three rooms, a square hall and a kitchen. From the hall a flight of polished oak stairs went to three pretty bedrooms with sloping ceilings and dormer windows, and a bathroom, a white-tiled bathroom with a black and white tiled border. Isobel said, 'Oh Mam! Look at this,' at every turn until at last, done with the house, they went out of the back door.

Isobel said, 'It's so beautiful.' Then she left Mam sitting on a wooden bench in the garden, where the only sound was the insects buzzing about the dropped golden fruit. She went slowly round the house again, standing at windows to feast her eyes on fields and trees and to delight in there not being another dwelling in sight. No shops or passers-by. It was utterly private; perfect in every detail.

Half an hour later she thumped down on to the seat. 'It's the nicest house I've ever seen.' She gave a great satisfied sigh. 'We are going to live here, aren't we?'

Mam said. 'Not unless we pay for it. Poor Hah'd's factory has gone.'

Isobel's euphoria was wiped out in an instant. Familiar sensations hit the pit of her stomach as she snapped out of her dreams of living here. 'Gone where? Factories can't go anywhere. What are you talking about?'

Mam got to her feet. 'Hah'd has to start all over again, borrow money from a trading company.' Then, as they set off towards the gate and the way home, 'He is a very determined man.'

Isobel's heart was sinking to her very boots. Something awful was coming. She let go of Mam's arm and stood still, facing her. 'Why have you kept me off school to look at the house when we won't be living there?'

They had reached the corner where a red pillar box stood. Mam leaned against it and took Isobel's hands. 'I'm asking an awful lot. I couldn't ask Nanna or Grandpa for money. And I wouldn't do it unless I had to . . .'

'Do what?'

'Will you sell your furniture? Your piano and bookcase? You said they are worth a lot. If I put in two hundred pounds and you put in the rest . . .'

Isobel felt sick. She had never owned anything of value until she came into her furniture. She looked away. She could not look at Mam but said, in a small voice. 'Would the house be half mine?'

Mam smiled. 'You are a little mercenary. Of course it would be half yours. It will be all yours one day. I'll pay you back for the furniture as soon as I've got the money.'

Isobel looked at her feet. 'You do love him, don't you? You aren't marrying just to be respectable or to put things right for me?'

Mam didn't answer at once, and now Isobel looked up and

saw that her eyes were very bright. Mam held fast on to her hands and said, 'I want to put things right for both of us. Howard loves me. I'll be a good wife. We'll go to church every Sunday like a proper happy family.' Then, shyly, 'I want to be baptised and confirmed as well, love. We can be done together. I might even join the Mothers' Union.'

Isobel gabbled now. 'Don't let him talk you into anything! He's a lot older than you. Don't sign anything, will you? Don't sign away the property?' It was all she could think of, without the law books to refer to.

A dealer was called in to view the pieces, and to Isobel's secret delight the piano was only worth three pounds. She was allowed to keep it, and the piano stool which was worth three pounds, ten shillings. But the honest dealer called in an expert to value the bookcase. He offered two hundred pounds. Mam sold it like a shot. Isobel ran to her room and wept.

Howard needed to take out a mortgage for the remaining hundred pounds. But the repayments were *nothing*, Mam told Isobel. Then, three weeks later, the knot was tied and they went directly to the new house after the wedding service. No honeymoon. No reception. They were going to get the house straight, her stepfather said, though he didn't say how, now he was ruined.

Chapter Sixteen

Isobel loved the house that her stepfather called his but which she and Mam had paid for. If he had allowed them to treat it like a proper home, like Lindow, Isobel might have been content, but Mr Leigh made it clear that they were not going to keep open house. Even Nanna would come by invitation only.

Mr Leigh arranged the furniture. The front room was allowed to be filled with their belongings from Jordangate. The rest of the furniture was his. The dining room was soon crammed full, with a big oak table and a modern light oak sideboard loaded down with the 'Willey-Leigh family silver', as her stepfather called his collection of dented, black-speckled EPNS. They would never use this room. Meals were to be taken in the kitchen, on his orders.

The last room, to the right of the front door, had originally been a small study. Isobel was allowed to call it hers, and she was truly grateful for this. She could keep out of her stepfather's way in her room, where her piano and a table Nanna had given her took up nearly all the space. She managed to squeeze in a little padded tub chair and the piano stool. She paid, from her own savings, for a carpenter to put up bookshelves, floor to ceiling, on the narrow wall. Opposite her room was a hall table on which stood the telephone. Mr Leigh needed it for his customers. They were not to make calls, unless in an emergency.

Control of the money was taken from Isobel. A man must be master in his own house, Mam said, so her stepfather paid the bills by cheque. Mam had a chequebook too. She was inordinately proud of it but had been told only to use it for shop transactions.

Control of Mam had also gone to him. He'd say, 'Time for your injections, dear; and when Isobel made to get up and check that Mam was doing it right, 'No need for you to do it, Isobel. Your mother will have to attend to them when you are no longer here.'

Their first Christmas came, but there were no decorations, no mince pies and no presents. Mam bought a chicken and an iced fruit cake. Every crumb was counted and there was no pleasing her stepfather, who looked down his nose at their preparations as if he were used to something better. Normally they went to Lindow and Isobel would be free to visit Sylvia and Magnus. She kept thinking of Nanna and Grandpa celebrating by themselves at Lindow, missing her as she missed them. The thought of the Hammond family gathering with Ian and Rowena made her want to cry. Mr Leigh had forbidden any contact with the Hammond family.

She tried to please, and she told God in her prayers that it was dishonest to take Mr Leigh's name and let him become her father without treating him with respect. She tried very hard to like and respect him – and being almost grown-up, she'd have to convince the judge at the court that she wanted to be Mr Leigh's adopted daughter – but she discovered that it was one thing to say she would love and respect someone and quite another to stop her flesh from cringing when he squeezed past her in a narrow doorway or winked at her behind Mam's back.

It soon became obvious to Isobel that marriage was not bringing contentment to Mam nor pleasure to Mr Leigh, who was clearly a disappointed man. His moods changed, at the least opposition to his will, from overfamiliarity and false *bonhomie* to complaint, bullying and more and more rules.

'Isobel! No invitations to be accepted without my approval.' She had to be in the house by six o'clock and would not be allowed out in the evenings. He could not stop her weekends at Nanna's, because they were established, but Isobel knew better than to mention the Saturday afternoons she spent with Sylvia and Magnus.

Isobel often sat alone in her room, for she couldn't stand being cooped up with them while Mam did cut-work embroidery – an accomplishment she had previously despised – and her stepfather read aloud from the *Macclesfield Courier*, sneering at Macclesfield while giving his opinions an airing. 'I see the workers at the Neckwear factory are striking. I know what I'd do with them!' He would go on at length about strikes: 'If there's one thing I can't stand it's the feckless poor,' he said one evening.

'Yesterday it was the idle rich you hated,' Isobel reminded him. She would not let him get away with any more poisonous observations about Macclesfield and its people. 'Why do you live in Macclesfield if you can't say anything good about us?'

He spluttered with temper. 'I said it was the idle poor I have no time for,' he said. 'Nor has your mother. Have you, Elsie?'

Before Mam could answer, Isobel said, 'Last night you called the Hammonds idle parasites. They have the biggest silk mill in Macclesfield.'

He turned on her. 'What do you know about it?' He could not stand for her to disagree with him. He demanded of Elsie. 'Did you hear what she said?'

Mam said, 'Isobel's been practically brought up with them, Hah'd,' and went on smiling and sewing, acting the role of the little wife. As she sewed she sipped the sherry he'd poured for her. She never had more than two, but she told Isobel that they went to her head very quickly since she'd been on insulin. Her stepfather never recognised the signs. Mam would appear sober and quiet, the level of sherry in her glass barely dropping, excusing herself from the room every fifteen minutes or so, saying, 'Won't be a minute, Hah'd. Just going to put a light on,' or to check some unimportant thing somewhere. After each exit she came back into the room grown steadily more and more drunk and wobbly, avoiding Isobel's eye and muttering, 'Oops, Lil! I mean, Isobel! Nearly tripped over you then.' Isobel knew the difference between low levels of insulin and plain drunkenness.

But in all of this new way of being the subservient little woman, Mam kept a hold on her old life. She would not give up her business, though Mr Leigh was desperate for control and Miss Duffield hinted that her dressmaker niece would like a partnership. Mam did not want a partner. Keeping the shop was the only sensible thing Mam had done, in Isobel's opinion.

For herself, Isobel was counting the days until she would be out of it at her new school in Southport.

'Isobel Leigh?'

'Isobel Leigh,' she repeated mechanically as the register was called. She tried to show some interest, but the biology lessons at St Ursula's were a thorough waste of a perfect afternoon. St Ursula's was a pettifogging, tuppence-ha'penny school, and after almost a year Isobel hated it.

'Isobel Leigh! I'm surprised at you!'

She had sneezed very loudly, and before she could find a handkerchief, stood up quickly. 'Pardon me ... Oh, I mean, beg pardon!' There was a burst of tittering laughter from the others.

'Isobel! Don't stand up. Well-brought-up girls never beg anyone's pardon. Find your handkerchief, sneeze quietly and if you feel you have to draw attention to it, simply say, "Sorry."'

'Yes, Miss Porter.' Isobel sat down.

'Pay attention, Isobel!' Miss Porter tapped her ruler on the table and the room went quiet again. She gave a little cough before turning to the book on the table in front of her. 'When the male stickleback wishes to attract a female, his, er ... underside becomes an attractive shade of pink. He dances and displays before her – just as the peacock did, girls, if you remember.' She glanced around to see that nobody was giggling, and went on, 'He too, the peacock, tempted his ... his mate –' she said 'mate' very fast and hurried on – 'by the splendid fan of his tail feathers.'

This was supposed to be a lesson on reproduction. Isobel's eyes wandered to the window again, where an expanse of inviting blue sky soared above the sycamore trees, making her long for escape, for with every day that passed the feeling was growing in her that she was in the wrong place. Was she homesick, even though she received a letter from Magnus every week and, regularly spoke to Mam on the telephone? Or was her anxiety a sixth sense that all was not well? She had to close her ears to the impelling voice that told her to break out, get back to Macclesfield where she belonged, looking after Mam. Mam's diabetes was out of control, because her stepfather ignored the signs and Mam was careless and forgetful, leaving it until the last minute to take a glucose drink or give herself an injection.

She was no use to Mam here at St Ursula's, where the only thing that counted was your father's position and bank balance. It was not good value for money, and that offended. Everything they were given over the basic tutoring and board was charged for. Little chits had to be signed for repayment if they broke a plate or lost a pencil. Cakes at Sunday tea were an extra. The beds were cold. There was not enough to eat and a kind of stifling politeness of manner was expected at all times, especially when allowed out on Wednesday afternoons in twos, unaccompanied but conspicuous in long plum-coloured barathea coats with matching velour hats. How could Mam afford it? Mam had less money not more since she married. Isobel was sure her stepfather didn't pay the school fees, so this school must be taking every penny Mam earned.

The chasm between her and the other girls was unbridgeable. They were rich. She was not. They had money in the bank – some had as much as ten pounds in pocket money each month. Mam sent her a five-shilling postal order once a fortnight, to 'keep her end up'. The other girls invited one another home for weekends of fun. Isobel stayed at school.

There were only about six of them in school on Saturdays and Sundays, the rules were slack and, when they had only one inattentive teacher to watch them, Isobel would seize her chance, sneak over the garden wall and dash down to town. She'd ring Mam, as if she were ringing from school, then, satisfied that Mam was well, she'd buy a quarter-pound of chocolate gingers and a ticket for one of the Saturday matinées at a picture house.

After the first time, it was easy. Isobel knew it was wrong, but it became a challenge, to get away with it again and again. She'd sit in the darkness, amazed at her own daring, lost in the wonder of the cinema. She saw the dashing Clark Gable in *Mutiny on the Bounty* and Greta Garbo in *Anna Karenina*. She saw the funeral procession of their beloved King George. And she told herself that the worrying things that were shown on the newsreels – the Tannenberg rally and the Nuremberg decrees, what Adolf Hitler was doing in Germany in this modern, enlightened year of 1936 – could only happen abroad.

Jews and Aryans were forbidden to marry. Couples of mixed blood were called race-defilers and could be arrested on the spot. Race-defilers, diabetics and haemophiliacs were being put down like animals. Sterilisation was too good for them. There was no mercy. If this were Germany they would have to resist the arrest of her diabetic Mam, and probably Magnus.

Magnus would soon be nineteen. He had been working responsibly, doing a man's job for years, and he would not put up with it again. He was not prepared to sit like an imbecile whilst Mother talked to Mr Meiklejohn over his head. He insisted on seeing the specialist by himself this time.

And here, in the consulting room at Edinburgh's Royal Infirmary, Magnus sat, dressed only in a gown, waiting with bated breath for the expert's opinion. His joints had been checked, urine samples had been taken and analysed and he'd been weighed and measured.

'Well, Magnus.' Mr Meiklejohn smiled. 'I think you can look forward to a period of good health.'

'No traces?' It was a year since he'd bled, anywhere.

'None.' Then, 'The only worry is your joints. You have special shoes?'

'Yes.' Magnus, sitting awkwardly because of his hip, looked down at his in-turned foot and misshapen knee. 'The shoes make a difference.'

'There has been deterioration in your joints. Are you aware of it?'

He was. There were things he'd never do again: dance, ride a bicycle, walk any distance. But these were minor problems as far as Magnus was concerned. He said, 'I don't think much about it. I wanted to ask ...' He drew in his breath, to give himself courage. 'I want to ...'

'What?'

He'd ask the question. His voice was steady, but he prayed as he spoke, *Don't laugh at me, please*. 'I know I'm only young but I want to get married.'

Mr Meiklejohn did not answer for a few seconds, then, as calmly as if Magnus had asked the time of day, he said, 'Your girlfriend knows the risks, does she? She knows you may become progressively disabled? You have told her about the risk of having children – though we don't have all the answers yet?'

'She has always known.'

He was silent for a moment. Then he smiled. 'There are preventatives to conception. When are you thinking of?'

Relief made Magnus laugh. 'I haven't exactly proposed. Not formally. I wanted to ask your opinion.'

'Then my advice is, don't waste any time. Go ahead.' He nodded to Magnus to indicate that he might dress himself.

Magnus struggled into his clothes, stuck his foot on the chair and attempted to fasten his shoelace. He had been treated like a man. Taken seriously. He could marry. And he could not control the great silly grin that was plastered across his face. He stood up, tried to straighten his face and went to stand in front of the desk.

Mr Meiklejohn said, 'Is your lady friend here with you in Edinburgh?'

'No. I wish she were.' Then the grin went. He did not wish that Isobel were here. The family was going out this evening, to the Caledonian Ball at the Assembly Rooms in George Street. It was one of the big social events of the Edinburgh calendar and the Hammond and Mackenzie families were celebrating Ian's birthday. If Isobel were here, and Ian set eyes on her again, then Magnus's hopes would be dashed. He must try to keep them apart in the same way that he kept Sylvia from Ray Chancellor. His first nightmare was that Ray and Sylvia would fall in love and he'd have to tell them why they must not marry. His second was that Ian would fall in love with Isobel.

Ian took Sylvia on his right hand and Rowena on his left for the dance. Facing them in the great ballroom were Dad, Uncle John and Aunt Catriona. Other groups of six were forming, the men in kilts, velvet jackets, knee socks and laced dancing shoes, all holding their ladies by the hand. And the girls ... He looked at Sylvia, then at Rowena, both in pale silk with tartan sashes. It was a grand spectacle, this happy crowd in the ballroom, with white lace jabots, brilliants and silver brooches flashing under three great candle chandeliers. There was a quick introduction and they were off, hands joined in a circle, fiddles soaring in the rousing 'Dashing White Sergeant'. A great sweep of sound and Ian's heavy kilt in the dark Mackenzie tartan swung against his knees as they circled for eight bars in the pas de Basque; four to the left, then back again. Set to Sylvia. Turn. Set to Rowena and figure of eight with both girls looking over their shoulders at him.

The girls were beautiful, laughing when he linked arms and twirled them around. He could do these dance sequences blindfold. They had been drilled into them since early school days. He took their hands again and faced the parents. Three forward. Three back. Advance and stamp the feet. Ian made a blood-curdling 'Yoooop!' before he raised the girls' hands to let the parents pass under as they advanced to the next group of three. With a quick shock it brought back to him the memory of having Isobel in his arms. He said to Sylvia, 'The last time I danced was at the Palace Hotel.'

'I remember. You danced with Isobel.'

It was Rowena's turn. He said, 'I thought you were going to invite Isobel to Edinburgh. What happened?'

Rowena was laughing. 'Sylvia hasn't seen her for ages.'

He was hotter. This outfit was ridiculous for dancing. Highland dress was more suited to marching in the chilly Scottish air. 'Sit the next one out?' he asked the girls.

They had agreed not to leave Magnus alone for long, so they went back to the table. Magnus could not dance, nor could he wear the kilt or dancing shoes because of his knee and foot. He might make it round the floor to a foxtrot, but he moved clumsily and didn't want people to stare.

Ian said, 'Phew! That's kicked the stuffing out of me,' to please Magnus. 'Shall I order another bottle of whisky?' The one on the table was empty. They were knocking it back tonight. He said to Magnus, 'Have you seen Isobel? I'd like to meet her again.'

Magnus affected a bored expression. 'Not much hope of that. She's got a heavy father. He says we're not good enough for her.'

Magnus's mother said, 'What did you say?'

Magnus repeated it in the same bored voice and she tapped his father's arm to get his attention. 'Did you ever hear such effrontery, John? Elsie Stanway's husband thinks we're not good enough.'

'Aren't you pleased?' John smiled. 'You have no time for them.'

She said, to Sylvia, 'Is this why Lily didn't come to see us at Christmas?'

'Isobel.'

'I mean Isobel. Is this why?'

'Probably. That and the fact that she thinks you don't like her.'

'What ever gave her that impression? When did I say I didn't like her? It's her mother I dislike.' Nobody answered, and she said, 'The silly woman. Marrying that awful man.'

'What do you know about him?' asked Magnus.

'Your father says he's a crook!'

They laughed, hearing her use the slang word she'd learned from the American cinema. John Hammond held up his hand. 'Catriona! I said the man was a pretender. Not a swindler.'

'It's the same thing,' she answered. 'He wanted to borrow from the bank. Thousands – to buy a factory. He has no security. Nothing.'

'That's enough, dear,' said John. 'I tell you these things in confidence. Don't speak so freely.'

Magnus said, 'I'll ask Isobel to come to see us when we're home.'

Ian said, 'Can I come?'

'As if you needed to ask!' they chorused – all but Magnus, who drank his whisky very fast and got up from the table, saying, 'I'm going outside for a breath of fresh air.'

Isobel was officially Isobel Leigh, legitimate and adopted. They had been to the county court in Knutsford, where the assizes were held, to have her adoption order passed in her new, legitimate name. And though she was grateful to him for her legal status, the words stuck in her throat when she tried to call Mr Leigh Father. He wanted her to; one of his grievances was that she lacked respect for him. He said, 'When a man comes home from work he expects his wife and daughter to be standing up, waiting to greet him.'

They were sitting at the kitchen table. Mam had discovered Symington's soup powder and every night made a pan of soup which they took before the tinned Skippers or cold meat they were to call dinner.

He dumped his attaché case of samples in the middle of the floor. 'Aren't you two aware that a man is demeaned if the women are seated when he comes home?'

They didn't know. How could they? Isobel glared.

'You, Elsie, should say, "Dearest, you're home!" and you, Isobel, should say, "Welcome home, Papa!"'

Mam jumped up. 'Dearest! You are home!' she laughed gaily. She could jump up when he came in and call him dearest if she wished. Isobel would go through great verbal convolutions to avoid using any name.

Her stepfather went away on business every week, from Monday until Friday, leaving Mam alone in the house, and this worried Isobel to death because the diabetes was making Mam pale and thin. It was obvious that something was going wrong with Mam's sugar and energy levels. Then, when he was at home, her stepfather was short-tempered and critical, finding fault with both of them; demanding of Isobel, 'Out? Why do you want to go out?' and saying of Mam's cooking, 'What do you call this?' as if he'd never eaten toast with the burn scraped off, and of her unsteady walk when an injection was due, 'Why do you keep tripping over your feet?' Then he'd flash his teeth so that if challenged he could tut-tut and say, 'Can't even take a joke.'

Isobel had only one defence, a sarcastic tongue. When he said to her, 'Why can't you be more like Doreen? She's a strapping girl. You're becoming thinner and more miserable every day,' she rose to the bait and answered with the chilly politeness she was learning at her snobbish school, 'How very kind of you to point out my failings. I might never have known.'

Doreen was the only person her adoptive father made welcome, and he encouraged her, taking her aside, fawning, revelling in her flattery, so much so that Isobel asked Mam if she was hurt by his behaviour. Mam said, 'No. Your father isn't the kind of man who'd flirt with a child like Doreen.'

But Doreen had gone past childhood. She appeared much older than her years; overdressed and painted up to the nines, with thick lipstick in Cupid's bows of theatrical red. Isobel and

Doreen never met outside the house, but it was Isobel's turn to feel envious, for Doreen could come and go as she pleased, and it pleased her to visit Mam in the evenings once a week. She earned twelve and sixpence a week as an invoice clerk in the counting-house at Chancellor's. She was never short of money for clothes and cheap jewellery and scent. Most young people handed over their pay packets and were given a few shillings back. Doreen kept it all.

Doreen loved her job. She told them that the girls and women who worked in the mill were in love with Ray Chancellor and wanted him to take them for a ride. She said, 'He came into his inheritance. Bought a Delage.'

'What on earth's a Delage?' Isobel asked.

'Just about the most expensive motor car in the world!' said Doreen, as if Isobel were an ignoramus. 'Haile Selassie has one. So does the Aga Khan.'

Mam laughed at this and Doreen said, 'He teases the mill girls, telling them he can't choose between them. Telling them if he could decide which one was the prettiest, he'd take her up in the hills for a ride.' She made the staccato laugh that Isobel hated. 'The mill girls will do anything for a ride.'

'Anything?' Mam was laughing fit to burst.

'That's what they say, but Ray treats them all alike,' said Doreen. 'I've even got a crush on him myself.' A self-satisfied look came across Doreen's face. 'Fancy! I've got a crush on Ray Chancellor! Me! The girl every man in Macc wants to go with!'

Mam said, 'Don't talk like that, Doreen. Don't say "wants to go with" – it's cheap. Find a young man of your own age. Watch your reputation.'

'I do,' Doreen said. 'I've got my eyes on one or two others . . .'

Isobel looked with disgust at Doreen. Her stepfather scowled furiously but Mam laughed at Doreen's impudence. She would never have allowed Isobel to talk like that.

Towards the end of the spring term, shortly before her seventeenth birthday, Isobel sneaked out of school to go to the pictures and treat herself to tea and cakes in the Grand Cinema's café. She had received a letter from Sylvia, and when she finished her tea she went to the public telephone box and dialled the operator. Soon she was speaking to Sylvia, whose clear, musical voice came ringing back. 'Rowena wants us to go up to Scotland at the end of July. Will your parents let you come this time?'

'No. Send my apologies?'

Sylvia said, 'Would it help if I got Father to ask?'

'Oh, no! That's the last thing.'

'I'm sorry.'

Isobel had no hope of going to Edinburgh. She had not seen Ian since they danced at the Palace Hotel. He would have forgotten her.

'Are you there . . . ?'

'Yes.'

'Pity you aren't home this weekend,' Sylvia said.

'Why?'

'Didn't Magnus tell you? In his letter?'

'No. Tell me what?'

'I'm finished! I don't go back to Lausanne. Ian and Rowena are staying with us for a week. We're having a party on Saturday night. Mama says it's time I found a rich husband.' Her silvery laugh rang out again. 'Magnus must have forgotten to invite you.'

Isobel's escapes to the cinema had given her practice in being rash and impulsive. Hot blood rushed up to her head, blotting out all inclination to caution. 'Sylvia?' She would play truant on a grand scale this time. 'Will you to go Nanna's for me? Tell her I'm coming to Lindow for the weekend.'

'Yes, of course,' Sylvia hesitated. 'Are you my best friend?'

'Yes,' Isobel assured her. 'Can you lend me something to wear for the party or shall I ask Shandy?'

'I'll send some things round to your Nanna's. Take your pick. See you on Saturday night. Bye!'

Isobel put down the receiver and caught sight of her face in the dusty little mirror. Her cheeks were pink, her eyes sparkled with devilment. She was going to do it. Nothing must stop her. She had saved enough – just – to pay her train fare. It's nothing short of outright rebellion, she thought as she plotted her escape.

She'd sneak out in her ordinary clothes, climb over the garden wall and run down to Lord Street as fast as she could.

If she did it after tea on Friday nobody would miss her until supper, and then it would only be the assistant matron. It would be Saturday before the girl could inform the headmistress about the note she'd leave in the dormitory: 'Forgot to say I am expected at home this weekend. Back Monday. Isobel Leigh.'

In the kitchen Nanna was packing Isobel's rucksack. 'No stockings?' She frowned in the direction of her legs – slim but brown and muscular under the flared check skirt that she kept at Lindow for walking. She wore heavy leather walking shoes and turned-over socks that made her skinny ankles look more like a boy's than a young woman's.

'Nanna! Modern girls don't have to be given a hand to get over stiles!' A smile began to play about the corners of Nanna's mouth as Isobel said, 'I won't be molested. Or drive passing tramps wild with passion. I probably won't see a soul all day.'

Nanna said, 'Why didn't you tell your mother you were coming? Won't you slip home for an hour?'

If she'd thought it out, she'd have seen that she was dropping Nanna into a pickle. 'I can't. There isn't time.' Her stepfather would never have allowed her to go to the Hammonds' party. 'I'll tell her later.'

Nanna stuffed the rucksack full, then took down a medicine bottle from the dresser and filled it with milk before she banged the cork down hard with the heel of her hand. 'There! Keep it right way up else it'll spill.' She held the sack up. 'Put your arms in. Where are you off to?'

Isobel pushed her hands through the straps and Nanna settled the bag between her shoulder blades. 'Up the hill to White Nancy. Saddle of Kerridge. Past the quarry, through the kissing gate, Rainow ...' She smiled at Nanna. 'Any more?'

'We'll want to come looking, if anything should happen,' Nanna said solemnly.

She kissed Nanna's dear worried face again. 'Over the Dean. Slack-o'th-Moor ... The turnpike road to Derbyshire. Hayles Clough ... Past the old mill pool and back to Archerfield. Seven miles. How's that?'

Twenty minutes later she'd climbed stiles over drystone

walls and walked the steep footpath to White Nancy, where she stopped on the top for a while to let the cooling breeze blow through her hair while she enjoyed the magnificent view of Bollington sprawled out below. She could see the whole town from here: Grimshaw Lane, which Doreen claimed was named after her ancestors, the cotton mills, the railway, the canal and the churches and chapels that punctuated the rows of stone cottages. Her misgivings about fleeing school were receding, here in the hills above Archerfield.

She was warm and the rucksack was heavy, so she opened the iron door of White Nancy and hid the sack by the stone slab table. She'd not want all that food. She'd collect it on the way back.

The breeze sighing through golden gorse was the only sound that accompanied her until, after another half-hour, when the first stiffness had gone out of her legs and she was striding out faster towards the three ways at Penny Lane, she heard faintly, then coming closer, someone calling out, 'Isobel Leigh! Isobel Leigh! Not so fast, Isobel Leigh.'

She stopped, put her hand above her eyes to shade them as she looked back – and saw a tall, broad man, dressed in cord trousers and a Fair Isle pullover, running with long, loping strides. As he came nearer her heart leaped. It was Ian Mackenzie.

'You're a fast walker,' he said as he came to a stop, panting for breath, hair awry and damp. 'I thought I'd catch you a mile back. Your grandmother said you'd only been gone ten minutes.'

'Were you looking for me?'

'Sylvia asked me to drop some frocks and things at Lindow.' His blue eyes were merry. 'Your grandmother said, "You've just missed our Isobel!"'

She could not keep her face straight. 'I bet she didn't. I'll bet she said, "You've just missed our Lil."'

Ian put out his left hand to her and for a moment Isobel thought he wanted to shake hands, so she put her right hand into his. He grinned and held fast. 'Let's take the path up through the fields and into the pine woods.'

His hand was warm and dry and firm and it sent the same tingling sensation up her arm as the very first time he'd shaken her hand. 'And let's get to know one another, Isobel – or Lily, whichever you prefer.' He tugged gently on her hand. 'Which *do* you prefer?'

'Isobel, please.' They set off over the field path to where steps in the wall led to a track into the pine forest, Isobel's heart singing with happiness, holding his hand, walking in step with him, sensing his keen blue eyes on her.

'You changed your name when your mother remarried?'

'Yes. Lily doesn't go with Willey-Leigh. So I dropped the Lily . . .'

He stopped in his tracks and roared with laughter. 'And then you dropped the Willey?'

He had a loud, straight-as-a-die laugh and a candid, outspoken way that was infectious. They saw humour in the same things and now they laughed together until tears came rolling down their faces. Every time they tried to stop or straighten their faces they lost the battle until finally they ran the last few yards to the summit of the hill where the pine woods were mere yards away, threw themselves down on the short, yellowed grass, and rolled, heads in hands, crying with laughter until they were done. Then they lay, growing calmer, faces pressed close to the earth, watching one another.

'I've not laughed so hard for ages.' Ian propped himself up on one elbow and smiled at her.

'Nor I,' Isobel said, breathing softly, merriment gone.

And all at once, as spontaneously as the laughter had overcome them, Ian stretched out his arm along the grass in invitation; his blue eyes and her grey ones met and held. Slowly Isobel rolled over into the crook of his arm. Then, as if it were the most natural thing in the world, she put her arms up and drew his face down to feel his mouth moving, locked into hers as they held one another fast, bodies close, melting.

She could taste the sweetness of his mouth after he pulled away and looked into her eyes. His blue eyes were alight with the same passion that had set her ablaze. Then his cheek was against hers and his firm, tender hands were sliding inside the navy-blue jumper and touching her bouncing round breasts, where they stood proud of the fine wool vest that was being slipped down until the shoulder ribbon straps were pinning her arms close to her sides. The breeze was cool on her bare breasts as they rose and fell under the touch of gentle fingers and an enveloping warm mouth. And she was quickening, melting inside as he rolled on top of her, hard and urgent through the layers and layers of serge and tweed that separated them. Then her hands fastened behind his neck and his mouth was sealed into hers again and all her senses became one sweet longing to be loved. She didn't want it to end.

It could not have been the first time he'd kissed a girl – and he must see female bodies every day – and yet it felt as if it were a new discovery to him. Quickly then he pulled away and they lay, side by side, Ian breathing very fast. She heard him say, 'My sainted aunt. This is it ...' She lay very still, eyes closed, because she could not bear any more without crying out; struggling to calm the fast breathing and banging heart-beat she was sure he must hear thundering around her body, that had left her shaken to her core.

It felt like eternity before he sat up, took hold of her hand and said softly, 'Isobel?' For a moment she thought he was going to kiss her again and a great aching was in her arms. She opened her eyes slowly and gazed into those blue eyes that were narrowed against the glare of the sun, making him appear serious and vigilant. She was on the point of tears and he bent over her, stroked her cheek and said, 'I've fallen in love. With a beautiful girl called Isobel Leigh. And if I kiss you again I'll be lost.'

She couldn't control the catching breath that was almost a cry as she said, 'I've been in love with you since I was twelve.'

He smiled and gently brushed the tears from her face. 'Fourteen,' he said. 'You were thirteen or fourteen when we first met. Remember?' He held her hands and tugged her up into a sitting position.

'Eleven,' Isobel said. 'Nearly twelve.'

'So now you are ...?' A frown of disbelief crossed his face.

'Sixteen. Nearly seventeen.'

He closed his eyes and put his hands up to his face. 'My God!' he said. 'Sixteen! I'm twenty-two.' He sat for a few moments, his hands covering his face. Then he stood, put his hand out and helped her to her feet. 'You are much too young. I'm sorry. I wouldn't have done ...'

'But I love you. I love you just as much as before.' She had to make him understand. 'I'm not too young to be in love with you.'

He put his arms around her and clasped his hands at the back of her waist, smiling at her ingenuous declaration of love which, Isobel realised, might sound forward or brazen. He said, 'You're sixteen. You can't know, at sixteen. Let's walk. And talk.' He kissed her on the forehead and held her close. 'Tonight we'll spend an hour at the piano, shall we? Come to Archerfield early. I want to get to know you. If I have to wait two years to kiss you like that again, we'd better find some other passion in common.'

They went into the green silence of the pine woods, hand in hand, and as they walked on the springy needle-strewn ground that muffled every sound, she found that she could talk – and talk – and talk to him. All of her secrets came spilling out, the secrets of her heart – that she had been born without a legal name or a legal right, that she was afraid for her beautiful diabetic mother, that she would forever feel herself to be an outsider and a nobody until she knew who her father was, for she was certain that the stepfather she mistrusted was not her real, true father. She couldn't stop talking, yet she had never spoken as openly before.

She could not tell him why she mistrusted her stepfather. She could not talk about such things, and that was something she had to bury, for Mam's sake as well as her own. But she told him that many of her heart's desires had come with Mam's marriage, and she told him that she no longer had a vile pink record card that followed her from one council school to another. She was adopted, legitimate. She had chosen a name she loved. He listened intently to her outpourings. They were out of the pine woods, dropping through fields of clover and mayflowers, over ancient stiles to the River Dean, past stone-walled farms to the turnpike road to Derbyshire. She kept on talking and talking: she and Mam had been baptised at a little midweek ceremony at St Michael and All Angels – 'Publick Baptism of such as are of Riper Years' it was called – and soon they would be confirmed and able to take Holy Communion. She ought to be happy that she was, in the eyes of the church, 'a member of Christ, a child of God, and an inheritor of the kingdom of Heaven'. But there was something missing. Something was wrong.

When finally she finished she was exhausted. They were sitting on a drystone wall by an old mill pond. Ian put his arms about her again and said, 'Oh, Isobel! It was your father you were seeking – not legal status. It won't go away, the need to know. I hope you find him one day. But it's what kind of a person you are, not the mistakes your parents made, that matters. We can't blame our parents, our background, our past for everything. Life goes forward and we're all going in the same direction, no matter where we came from. We have to look ahead. Not back.'

'I've talked too much,' she said. 'I'm usually the one who listens.'

'I'm glad. I know what has made you what you are.' He slid his arm round her waist and held her close. 'You're the girl I want.'

They walked on in the spring sunshine, and as they went he told her about his own life – that it had been just as hard when he was a child, having no mother, as it had been for her without a father. It was hard to live up to a father you loved and admired. He loved the challenge and the freedom of sailing. He'd have liked to join the Royal Navy – but his father had refused his permission. His father had insisted on his studying medicine, and Ian was glad; glad he'd been made to study in his early years because out of that had come self-discipline. He needed to use his brain. Great achievements were expected of him – and of his dear sister, who had no mother to teach her womanly graces. Rowena, he said, was an odd mixture of enthusiasm, tactless confidences and long silences. He said, 'But my father's not to blame for the stout-hearted way Rowena and I behave – any more than your mam is to blame for the way you are.'

He was absolutely right. Isobel said, 'I don't blame them.'

Ian helped her down, laughing. 'I sound like a blinking preacher.'

They went along the stony cart tracks, side by side, hands free. Isobel said, 'What will you do? When you are a doctor? Specialise or be a family doctor like your father?'

'I'm drawn to genetics – what's in the blood, as you might say.'

'Because of Magnus?'

'Because Magnus's haemophilia comes from the Mackenzie family. I don't have it, and as long as my wife doesn't carry it my children will be normal. But Rowena may be a carrier. Sylvia almost certainly is. Magnus dare not risk marrying and having children. I want to know more.'

He went quiet, then he said, 'I may not get the chance.'

'Why not?'

'Our generation are not going to have an easy ride. There will be another war. And we'll be in it.'

A shiver went down Isobel's back. 'Someone's going to have to stand up to Hitler. Don't you think?'

He took her hand again. 'the French want us to stand up to him and we do nothing. We've let his Nazi jackbooters march into the Rhineland.' He went along, silent for a few more paces, before he said, 'Sorry. I do go on a bit. What about you?'

'The law.' She held tight on to his hand. Perhaps it was a dream – a dream of escape, just as her adoption had been. 'I used to say that all I wanted was to be a mam, to have a happy home – a big house in the hills – married to a good man and with loads of children.'

Ian's eyes were bright with approval. 'I think that's a wonderful ambition. It's my goal in life. To be the father of a big, happy family.'

They fell quiet, embarrassed. They were approaching Archerfield but high above it. Isobel said, 'Are you hungry?'

'Ravenous.'

'Then we'll have a picnic. In White Nancy.'

Inside the round picnic room of White Nancy, Ian said, when they had eaten, 'It's going to be the best party ever. I'll come for you in Dad's car.'

'I can walk!'

'I'll come for you. It will give us an excuse to be alone.'

Chapter Seventeen

Sylvia had sent down to Lindow three dresses, silk stockings, artificial flowers and ribbon. She had also sent her spare pair of gold sandals, knowing they both took size five.

Isobel chose a long dress of bias-cut amber silk that had one shoulder bare and the other tied with wide silk bow straps. It was a much older style than she'd worn before, but Sylvia was taller, and with this one she could adjust the straps to make it shorter. She pinned on to the shoulder a little bunch of velvet violets and silk snowdrops with trailing stems of green silk.

At six o'clock she was dressed and ready and sitting patiently in the living room while Nanna brushed her hair. 'If I could take my head off,' she said, 'I'd try a Grecian bun.'

'Impossible!' Nanna went on brushing it, back and up. 'These curls will spring back again in no time. I'll get it smooth and fasten it with my ivory clasp.' She went on brushing with long strokes for another five minutes while Grandpa sat watching from his armchair by the fire.

'There,' said Nanna when she'd finished. 'Eeh! Spit and image of your mother. Isn't she, Dad?'

Grandpa nodded. 'Pretty as a picture.'

'Take a peep.' Nanna held up a long-handled mirror.

Isobel was startled by her reflection – milky-white skin with a sheen, high cheekbones touched with Nanna's ancient rouge. Her naturally thick eyelashes were silky from a feathering with Vaseline. Nanna had told her that when she was young one of her beauty secrets was, of all things, soot. So Isobel blackened a mole near the outer corner of her eye into a beauty spot, then dipped her toothbrush in soot and scrubbed her teeth until, with all traces of black gone, they gleamed against naturally red lips that were full and sharply defined.

But it was the shining grey eyes, with the amber flecks dancing when she glanced this way and that, that made her see that her looks were out of the ordinary. She had a light in the eye, a turn of the head that could bewitch and beguile. She was as pretty as Mam.

'That's enough primping, miss.' Nanna took her hand-mirror away. 'Put your other shoes on for going down the lane in.'

Grandpa said, 'I'll walk down with her.'

'Ian's coming for me.'

Grandpa said, 'I don't approve of a young lass being alone with a man. Make sure he treats you with proper respect.'

'Grandpa! I'm sixteen,' Isobel said as Ian's knock came on the back door and she leaped to her feet.

'All right. All right.' Grandpa was smiling as he went to open the door. 'I'm an old-fashioned old man!'

Then Ian was inside, filling the little room because he was so tall and full of life and presence, shaking hands with Grandpa and promising to take care of her, asking Nanna if it was she who played the piano. Nanna and Grandpa were won over. Nanna began to flutter and dimple with pleasure as he admired her piano, asked, 'May I?' and sat down and played 'Over the Sea to Skye' for them, remarking on the fine tone.

When he had done, Nanna said, 'Will you stay a little while?'

'No. But may I come tomorrow?' Ian took Isobel's hand. 'It will give me another chance to see Isobel ...'

'None of that! Don't hold hands with a girl until you're courting her properly,' Grandpa said. Then, seeing embarrassment on Ian's face, he said, 'After morning chapel tomorrow. Come at two o'clock. You'll be able to meet Isobel's mother and father as well.'

Isobel went hot and cold. She hadn't thought so far ahead. The web of lies was growing. 'Oh! I don't think I'll be here by then, Grandpa. I have to get an early train ...'

'Never mind,' Ian said. He had not been embarrassed by Grandpa's rebuke because he lifted her hand, this time for all to see, gave a little bow and said, 'Your carriage awaits, ma'am!'

In the car he said, 'What was all that about your going back to school? I thought you said Monday . . . ?'

'No.' she said quickly, ashamed that she was having to lie to Ian. 'Sunday. I have to be back for Monday.'

'I can drive you, if you like. We could leave early in the morning – be in Southport for two. It's about sixty miles, isn't it?'

'Would you?'

The driveway was not long, and Sylvia and Magnus were waiting at the open door. Sylvia, fair and ethereal in white, with a camelia clipped into her bobbed hair, came down the steps. 'You look marvellous in that colour, Isobel,' she said. 'So glad you're here. It's going to be a wonderful evening . . .'

Magnus, who was lounging against the doorpost, gave a long, appreciative whistle.

'Magnus! Don't whistle!' Sylvia chided him, and took his arm. 'Mother and Father will be down later. We'll have an hour to ourselves in the drawing room before the guests arrive. Rowena is in there already – arranging everything to her liking.'

The room was ready. The piano stood in its position, where the band would play in an hour's time. Rowena was setting out glasses, fruit cup and cocktail shakers on the high semi-circular bar in the far corner of the room.

'Goody! You're here!' Rowena called out before coming to the piano. 'Give us something lively, will you, Ian?'

First Ian played 'Three Little Maids' from *The Mikado*, while Sylvia, Rowena and Isobel tried to sing and act it out. But he stopped and said he'd have to cover his ears, they were making such a caterwauling. He played jazz for a few minutes, then stopped and said, 'Isobel, I saw your music on the piano. Play the Chopin waltz for us.'

'I've never been able to get it right,' she said. 'I'll have a go but my playing sounds mechanical – compared with yours.'

She played it through, then Ian drew up a chair beside the stool and said, 'You start off a bit fast. Try it with less speed and less pedal . . .'

She tried again. He said, 'Good . . . Do it again. Up to the tenth bar. Go on. Make it exciting . . . !'

Excitement was mounting in her. She was concentrating on

the music but aware of his face close to hers, his breath near her cheek.

'Don't scramble those big skips ... Go on ... Good ...'

He was a natural teacher. She was playing better than she'd ever done and her mouth was pushing in and out, and when she got to the *Cantabile* her eyebrows were going up and down and she knew she looked silly, but Ian was tapping his foot.

'*Meno mosso*! Make that piano sing!' He was singing in tune with the music, 'Come on ... I'm going to there ... to there ... to there ... to there! I'm going to there! ... I'm going to there!' Then, 'Sh! Tempo one. *Molto vivace*! Keep that fingering clean and crisp. Brilliant!'

When she ended she felt as if she'd run a mile. Ian put his arm across her shoulder and said to the others. 'What a performance!'

Then Isobel heard Mrs Hammond's voice, clear and haughty. 'Is that my daughter's dress you are wearing, Lily Stanway?'

She whirled round. Mrs Hammond was behind her. Isobel's face flamed as she got to her feet. Not knowing how to answer, she could only look in desperation at Sylvia, who quickly came to her rescue.

'Mama! I'm furious with you.' She faced her mother. 'I told you that I was going to lend my dress ...'

Ian blazed, 'Aunt Catriona! I know it's your house, but ...!'

Magnus, in a fury shouted. 'Don't you dare upset Isobel, Mama!'

And Isobel hung her head in shame, just as she had as a five-year-old; forcing back tears and wishing for the ground to swallow her.

'Oh, dear! I didn't mean to be rude. I thought I was being witty,' Mrs Hammond said, 'I was taken aback, seeing Lily ... Isobel in the dress I bought for Sylvia.' She gave a careless laugh. 'Please accept my apologies, Isobel.'

'Yes. Yes,' Isobel stammered. It would take ages for her to calm down.

'Good. Let's go to the door. The guests will be here at any minute. Your father is waiting.'

There were fifty guests, young people and friends of the Hammonds, and of course Ian and Sylvia couldn't talk only to her all evening, but at last Isobel's embarrassment began to dissolve. The band started to play and couples took to dancing. The lights were low, and although hard drink was not served, the cocktails had a punch and the Pimm's was delicious and the guests became gayer and noisier. Isobel chatted and laughed and sipped the fizzing iced fruity drinks that made her head light.

Magnus, unable to dance, settled himself behind the bar and was happily shaking cocktails and making Pimm's for everyone who asked, trying to be the sophisticate he'd never be, saying, 'I say, old boy!' to the men and, 'Dah ... ling, you look di ... vine!' to the girls. And they all knew that it was a wonderful act of his, because he had just read *The Great Gatsby*.

An hour later Rowena and Isobel sat on high chromium-plated stools, facing Magnus. Rowena leaned both elbows on the bar, urging Magnus to pour a double helping of something or other into her glass. Isobel swung her crossed legs like film stars did, holding a coolie-hat cocktail glass by the stem, dipping the cherry in to suck the sharp martini cocktail off slowly while Magnus went on with his nonsense – making them laugh, saying that he was ready for marriage and soon would propose to the prettiest girl in Macc, and inviting them to guess who she might be.

There was a tap on the shoulder. Isobel looked up into the handsome face of a redhaired young man with a devilish smile: Ray Chancellor.

'Magnus,' he said. 'Don't keep all the pretty ones to yourself.' He placed his hand on her bare shoulder. Isobel felt his fingers moving gently, tightening over her collar bone so that she nearly lost her hold on the glass.

'Oops!' she said as she wobbled on the stool and stretched out to save the cocktail.

Ray was quick. His hand came over hers to steady the glass. 'I've never had a pretty girl fall for me so quickly before ...'

Then they were all laughing together, and his hand was on her elbow. 'May I have the pleasure of this dance, please, Miss ... Miss ...?'

Isobel put the glass on the counter, tilted her head to one side for all the world like her mother did, and said, 'Isobel Leigh. Thank you, Ray Chancellor. Yes, I'd like to dance.'

They went zipping around the floor to a quickstep while Ray questioned her and she flirted, practising her new charms.

'How do you know my name?' he said. 'Have we met before?'

'Many a time. I used to see you here at Archerfield when I was little,' she teased, pleased with the way the cocktail had given her confidence, pleased that Ray Chancellor was flirting and dancing with her – because Doreen said that every girl in Macclesfield was crazy for him. 'I sometimes see you in church. But I sit at the side and you are on the front row. And I go to evensong instead of morning service.'

'Do you?' He laughed and held her tighter. 'I'd remember if we had met,' he said. 'You're the prettiest girl in the room.'

She was enjoying this, though she knew he was spinning a yarn and dancing close and fast so that everyone would have to get out of his way and all eyes would be on him. She tilted her head again to make him say more. 'No. I'm not. Sylvia's the prettiest.'

He held her closer and leaned his head down to speak in her ear, so nobody should hear him. 'Sylvia's beautiful and charming. The kind of girl men want to marry. *You* are a dazzler! The kind of girl men fall madly in love with.' Then he straightened up, gave that wicked grin again, looked into her eyes and said very softly, so that only she should hear him, 'I want to kiss you.'

Isobel could not think of an answer, but his bold, suggestive words brought a response in the very pit of her stomach. Fancy a boy daring to say such a thing in public – on a dance floor, with everyone looking on. She glanced about the room. Everyone was looking, and somehow she knew that Ray wanted to make somebody in particular watch his performance, because he held her close and whirled her round faster and faster. So this was flirtation! Ray Chancellor was very, very daring.

Her head was spinning. 'Can you slow down a bit . . .?' He hadn't heard. He was full of devilment.

But she did not have a chance to ask him again or wait for him to stop, because Ian, a determined look on his face, came striding across the floor and grabbed Ray by the shoulder, halting him, nearly knocking him off his feet. He said, in a furious voice, 'Find yourself another partner. You're dancing with my girl!' Then he took hold of Isobel with a roughness she'd not seen in him before, and those level blue eyes flashed with anger as he said, 'Have nothing to do with that fellow. He's no good.'

'I wasn't . . .'

He held her fast. 'Consider yourself spoken for.'

Isobel tried the flirtatious tilt of the head to see if it would take the heat out of him, make him laugh. 'Yes, master.'

'Don't play games, Isobel. I'm a plain-speaking Scotsman. Not Prince Charming.' But all the love in the world was in his eyes as he said, 'When you're eighteen we'll have a proper courtship, as your Grandpa calls it. I'll be a qualified doctor by then. We can wait.'

Later they seated themselves near to the bar, Magnus, Ian and she, eating a buffet supper. Isobel's plate was piled high with smoked salmon rolls, ham sandwiches, sausage rolls and pork pie. Magnus was teasing her about the amount of food she could eat and yet stay slim.

'I don't get the chance to eat as much as I'd like every day,' she said, as she tried to decide what to eat next. 'I think I'll have . . .'

She never finished the sentence because behind her she overheard Mrs Hammond talking to Ian's father. Perhaps it was the loud voice – but Ian and Magnus didn't hear – perhaps Isobel's sense of hearing was heightened when Mrs Hammond was near. Or did Mrs Hammond intend that only Isobel should hear?

'Did you see that girl's behaviour?' she said.

'Who? What?' Dr Mackenzie said.

'Ian nearly hit poor Ray. And all because of a brazen . . .'

'Och! Calm down. You're imagining . . .'

'I am not imagining. She's exactly like her mother.'

The food turned to ashes in Isobel's mouth. She took another sip of the drink to help it down. What had she done? Had Ray held her too close? Was she making a spectacle of herself as Mam had done in the photographs?

'Are you all right, Isobel?' Magnus was worried. 'You're not going to faint, are you?'

'I'm not going to faint,' she said, trying to appear normal.

She pushed her plate away. 'I've had enough.'

Ian said, 'You're pale. Do you need fresh air? Shall I take you outside?'

'Yes. Yes, please,' she said. But before she could get to her feet Mr Hammond came to her side.

'Isobel,' he said, 'your – I suppose you call him your stepfather is at the door. Will you go to him? He won't come in.'

Her knees had gone to water. Her face was chalk white as she followed Mr Hammond down the hall. There was a coppery taste in her dry mouth when she saw him; her stepfather standing inside the open front door, hands clenching and unclenching, red in the face with proprietorial outrage.

'Come home at once, Isobel,' he said in that high voice that could sound hysterical when he was annoyed. 'Where's your coat?'

She felt sick, Mr Hammond took her elbow. 'Isobel can be brought home by one of the guests, Mr Leigh,' he said in the lovely, courteous way he had. 'We are in the middle of supper. Would you like to join us?'

'No.' Her stepfather grabbed her arm and pushed her towards the big front door, ignoring the butler, who was standing back, waiting for orders. 'Your mother is ill. Get into the car.'

Mr Hammond, all concern, nodded to the butler and said, 'Is there anything I can do?'

But she was being handled roughly into the chill night air, down the steps and into the front seat of the Lanchester. Her stepfather slammed the door before he turned back and shouted. 'There's nothing I want from you, Hammond! Isobel won't come here again.'

He flung himself into the driving seat and pressed the starting button. The Lanchester's engine burst into life and he drove hard enough to make channels in the fine gravel driveway, all the time repeating, 'I won't allow you to go there again!'

Isobel didn't want to go back. She never wanted to be under the same roof as Mrs Hammond, ever again. She said angrily. 'It's just an excuse, isn't it? Saying Mam's ill?'

'Your mother has gone to bed with a blinding headache. Brought on by shock. I can't wake her.'

Mam was probably dead drunk. 'What shock?'

'A telephone call at noon. To say you were missing from school.'

'Not until midday? My God! What a school!' She must have got her second wind, to say such a thing.

He ignored her rudeness and said, 'We waited all afternoon for you to arrive. When you didn't come I said, "I'll bet I know where she is!" And what did I find? That your grandmother had allowed you to stay with her – without my knowledge!'

'Don't blame Nanna. She didn't know I was going to the party until yesterday,' Isobel said. 'Can you go a bit faster?' He put his foot down and they went speeding towards Macclesfield. After twenty minutes Isobel said, 'If Mam's not well I'll stay home with her.' He didn't answer, so she glanced at him. He was smiling. 'You said Mam was ill.'

'She'll be all right. She's been unconscious for ten hours at a stretch. She'll come round by morning.'

'Unconscious?' Isobel was horrified. 'Mam's never unconscious.' She'd seen Mam asleep, in a drunken sleep, many a time, but never unconscious. 'You are supposed to watch. See she injects herself.'

He looked smug. 'I remind her. I can't be expected to do *everything*.'

Anxiety sharpened, making Isobel turn on him and say, 'You *have* to.' They were bumping down the short, pot-holed drive. The house was in darkness but a storm lantern lit the way to the garage. He stopped the car and Isobel put her hand on the handle. It was locked. She turned to her stepfather to ask him to unlock it, quickly. And as she turned, his leering face came towards her.

He reached over her lap and with his right hand clutched the amber dress and pulled it up above her knee – and finding the top of her stocking he slid cold, thin, probing fingers along the soft skin inside her thigh. Instantly all her fear of him came back. This time she would not sit and cry. She shied back a little, then, just before his face could come closer, she used all the strength she had to bring her left fist up and land it straight in his eye.

At the same moment that he dragged his hand back from her

thigh and clapped it to his face she bared her teeth to him, just as a wild animal does. 'Don't you ever do that again!' she snarled. She wanted to scratch and mark that sneering face. Instead, lips curled back like a fighting dog, she darted her head forward and literally snapped her teeth. She could hear them gnashing as she threatened, 'I'll bite you!'

'You silly girl,' he whined. 'I wasn't going to ... I lost my balance and my hand ...' But he backed towards his door and struggled to open it as Isobel lashed at him across the wheel. 'Let me out of this car!' she screeched. The door on his side flew open and he toppled on to the grass, protesting as first his head, then his knees hit the ground.

She jumped, missing him by inches, and ran to the front door. It was locked. The man was mad. Fancy locking an unconscious woman in the house. What might have happened? She yelled, 'Give me the key or I'll break a window.'

He was on his feet, fumbling in his pocket, coming closer, holding out the key. 'Say nothing to your mother ...!' Isobel pushed him away, turned the key, hurled herself through the door and ran up the stairs to the bedroom.

Mam lay on the bed, fully dressed, mouth open, eyes closed, her deep, sighing breathing telling Isobel that she was in a coma. Her stepfather had been taught by the doctors what to look for. Mam's pulse was feeble and her hands were limp and cold. Furious now, Isobel faced her stepfather, who stood at the door of the bedroom. 'You hateful beast!' she said through gritted teeth. 'Mam's in a coma! Ring for a doctor! This is an emergency!'

'It's all your fault,' he said. 'If we hadn't had the telephone call she would never have—'

'Don't you dare blame me!' Isobel put her face close to Mam's, but she knew what she'd smell. 'She's not been taking her injections! You are supposed to see to it.'

He sniffed. 'How am I supposed to know a coma from a heavy sleep? I didn't know what to do ...'

She pushed past him and went to the bathroom, took the tray down and checked the record book. Mam had taken no insulin since breakfast. Her stepfather knew how to give injections and how to recognise the difference between hypoglycaemia and the diabetic coma she was now in.

He was behind her. 'What are you doing . . . ?'

'If she doesn't have the insulin – and a high dose at that – she'll die.' He was blocking the doorway. 'Get out of my way!'

She went to the bedside, plunged the needle into the phial and drew up fifty units. The injection would have to be given under the skin of the abdomen, where it would be absorbed fast. She pulled up Mam's dress and slid her hand under her light body, unfastened the waist button on her knickers and rolled them down.

'I can't be expected to do everything . . .' She heard his whining voice behind her. 'It's not as if she'd eaten a lot of sugary—'

'Be quiet!' Isobel wiped Mam's abdomen with spirit and pinched the flesh to give her something to push into. She winced as the skin resisted the blunted point. There was a sharpening wheel in the cupboard but Mam had not been doing the needles regularly. Slowly she pushed the plunger. 'If Mam doesn't come round in a minute or two you'll have killed her,' she said.

'If I'd known it was going to turn out like this – married to another sick woman – I'd never have risked . . .'

'Risked? You?' She must try to keep her voice low, in case Mam could hear. 'It wasn't you who risked! You gained a wife, a daughter – and our house. If you hadn't married her I'd have been watching. Not stuck away in Southport where I can't see what's going on. Was she sick?'

'All over the place. I can't be expected to clean up all . . .'

Mam's eyelids moved. Her pulse beat stronger. Isobel stood and faced her stepfather, and all the loathing she'd tried to suppress was in her face. 'If you let Mam go into a coma again,' she threatened, 'I'll kill you. I'll wait until you are asleep and . . .' She waved the syringe at him. 'I'll fill you so full of this you'll never wake again!'

He had the nerve the flash his teeth. 'I don't think that is likely. You'll be expelled. Then you will be here, looking after your mother day and night. I'm damned sure I can't! Telephone the doctor yourself. I'll spend the night at the Ring O'Bells where someone knows how to please a man. Your grandmother can move to Bollinbrook Road to take care of my so-called wife!'

*

Frank set off early to walk to Bollinbrook Road. It was a baking-hot morning and years since the weather had been like this for the Barnaby holidays. Most years in Macclesfield their hot weather came in late May or the beginning of June, and here they were, in the dog-days of early July, with the temperature in the eighties at only ten o'clock in the morning. He'd left the car at home to walk to Elsie's house in the state of shivering excitement that was growing in him the nearer he came to her house. He had not felt like this for so long: his head was light; his legs were fragile and felt as if they might snap under him. He halted alongside the cemetery and peered through the iron railings and hawthorn hedges, trying to see if Leigh's car was at the front of Elsie's house.

Elsie had been married for over a year and had given every impression of being happy, but there was not a woman in the world who excited him as she did. And last week, unless he'd completely misinterpreted the situation, she'd let him know that she wanted . . . Oh God! He hoped he wasn't imagining it.

He would not cause her any embarrassment, but if he knew Elsie – and if anyone knew what lay beneath that sparkling, unpredictable exterior, it was he – she had planned everything. He could not have imagined it.

Under his collar a tiny rivulet of sweat ran between his shoulder blades. He was sure Elsie would not have said what she did unless she meant it. So why go through it in his mind like an overanxious young swain? He was a mature, experienced man. He sat on the magistrates' bench and made judgments. And Elsie was not a hothead. She'd known what she was saying, last Friday when he'd called in at the shop for the rent.

Miss Duffield was in the shop, so he went straight to Elsie in the kitchen, where the rent book and money lay weighted down in the centre of the table, under the teapot stand. It was hot, and the door was wedged wide to let the cooler air in, and he was annoyed with himself because the minute he set eyes on her he knew again the tightening in his loins she always raised in him. She would know it, too. She'd guess the state he was in.

She was reading at the table, one leg crossed loosely over the other so that her skirt was raised above her knee. She wore an ivory blouse that had the top three buttons undone – not her usual style. The sunlight streaming into the room gave her face a warm glow and made the shadow between those beautiful breasts gleam on her bronzed skin. He said, 'Been sunbathing?' though it was risky, being familiar since she had gone up in the world.

'Yes.' She looked at him with eyes full of laughter and promise – exactly as she used to do when they were lovers. His senses leaped. She'd undone those buttons deliberately, to be provocative. She said, 'I like to stretch out in the garden whenever I can. Hidden away in private at the back.' Even her words were chosen for effect; stretching, hidden, private.

He would not be flirted with, treated lightly, after all these years. He picked up the rent book. 'You and hubby?' he said, sharply.

It was then she said, 'The only sensible thing I did was to keep the shop on, Frank.' He looked up from the rent book quickly. Their eyes met and held, his full of heat; hers promise. She was offering herself. But he could not reply, because Isobel came into the kitchen and, seeing him, said, 'Hello Mr Chancellor. Rent again? It doesn't seem five minutes since . . .'

'Hello, Isobel.' He smiled at his precious lass, who had grown so quickly into a beautiful young girl, unaware of her charms, natural and unspoilt. He looked at the cloud of dark hair, the translucent grey eyes, her dancer's deportment, and he saw again what he had lost. Nothing would make him prouder than to recognise them as his women or walk down Chestergate and Mill Street with the whole of Macclesfield looking on, with his precious lass on one arm and Elsie on the other. And it was too late. He was on the outside, looking in, not pulling the strings. He said, 'Not at school?'

'Home for the weekend,' she said. 'I go back on Sunday night.'

'How do you like St Ursula's?'

'Do you know it?' she asked, surprised.

Frank felt colour rising in his face as he tried to cover his mistake. He said, 'Your mother said. Is it a good school?'

Isobel pulled a face. 'It's very snobby. And expensive for the standard of teaching. But I can take School Certificate. When I asked the headmistress, she said – here she mimicked Miss Colclough's genteel voice – "St Ursula's girls go to finishing school. They don't take state examinations and go on to university, Isobel." Such a snob.'

Frank grinned. 'What did you say to that?'

'I said, "I'm not the usual St Ursula's girl."'

Elsie smiled proudly. 'She's picking up a lot, though. She's learned how to answer back. Nobody gets the better of our Lil. Sorry, Isobel.'

At ten o'clock in the morning, Elsie lay naked in the orchard on the little square of grass she had persuaded Howard to cut for her. So early an hour and the sun was biting into the back of her thighs. With half-closed eyes she peered through the long grass. She could see the house, though had there been anyone at home she could not be seen. She rolled on to her back and reached for the medicine bottle. She'd read somewhere that an application of olive oil was the secret of acquiring a deep sun tan. She ran a little warm oil into the palm of her hand before stroking it first into her neck and breasts and then along her thighs.

She lay down and the heat of the sun, the oiliness of her body and her longings aroused her so much that she made an effort to turn her thoughts to contemplation of her unhappiness – the disaster that married love with Howard had turned out to be. If she had never known perfectly matched passion with Frank, would she be able to tolerate what passed for a lover's technique with Howard?

She was a disappointment to Howard. He said as much last night. She had gone to bed early, hoping that if she feigned sleep he would leave her alone. Sometimes it worked. Last night he came into the bedroom carrying a tray with sherry and two glasses upon it. He found her lying on top of the sheets, with the window open to let in the cooler night air. He said, in the mocking tone he used, 'Don't go to sleep, Elsie. Your husband demands his conjugal rights.' He brought sherry to the bed and shook her shoulder.

Elsie drank her sherry while Howard undressed. She looked away, unable to stand the sight of his bony, naked body. It repulsed her, yet she must go along with this charade of lovemaking. It was only fair. Howard had married her. Frank had not.

He took away her empty glass and lay down beside her, turned to face her and without a word, much less a look of love, began to clutch at her breast and squeeze it slowly, trapping the nipple between bony fingers. The other hand slid inside her thigh and set to work, clawing and pinching. Where had he learned these painful tricks?

'Isn't my wife in the mood tonight?' he said as she recoiled. 'Then perhaps she could give her husband a little happiness instead?' He wanted her to take that limp thing in her hand and excite him to the point where he might be able to use it – if she were quick and ready.

He took his right hand from her thigh, grabbed her hand and tried to force her to hold his flaccid part while Elsie struggled not to. Then, with eyes closed, he continued for a few moments longer to squeeze her breast, saying irritably when she did not respond, 'I'll be gone for a week. Don't be selfish. Let me at least go satisfied.'

Elsie moved his hand away from her breast and rolled on to her side, facing him. She would have to do it, though she'd had no experience of this performance and always got it wrong. Howard was going to teach her something more adventurous, he told her, when she'd mastered the manual skill. If he was thinking of what she suspected he was – the skills people hinted were Nellie Plant's own speciality – then it would be all over between them. But he took her hand and placed it where he wanted it. 'There,' he said. 'Now don't be afraid. You can't break it, you know . . .' as she ran her cupped hand about it and felt it give a little jerk as she got to work.

'Not so fast!' he said. Then, when she slowed, 'Harder! come on.' His bony fingers plucked at her breast, then squeezed. 'Keep going. Kiss me.'

Elsie put her lips against his tight-closed mouth. She could feel the clenched teeth behind his lips. He liked it if she moved her lips slowly against his. As long as her lips were dry. He hated 'sloppiness'. She could hear his breath coming faster now he was becoming rigid. Quickly she rolled on to her back and pulled him on top of her and felt him pushing against her, against her pubic bone. She eased up a little so that he sank down. He was not inside but he'd think only that he had made it and that she was not ready – and he didn't concern himself with her pleasure. He told her that she was a hopeless wife who compared unfavourably with his first, invalid wife. The refusal of her body to respond to his touch – to remain dry and guarded – had made her believe that her own passion was spent.

At last he came to his own climax with a terrible drawing together of his eyebrows, indrawn breath hissing between clenched teeth as if the whole business were a painful, disgusting agony. Elsie did her wifely duty by giving a small groan that he would take to be delight, and waited for a few seconds for him to roll away and fall into a deep sleep. Then she got up and went to the bathroom, to wash away all traces of her husband and to pray for sleep.

Today, lying in the sun, she knew her own passions were not dead. Last week, in the heat of June, they had burst into life again. She had started to dream, night after night, that Frank was making love to her – so strong were the dreams that she woke up, shivering for his touch, wanting him back. It was an agonising decision she must make. She had always wanted marriage. Now she had it – and was in danger of throwing it all away. Howard would leave her, divorce her if he found out. She was contemplating breaking the seventh commandment. It would finish Dad if he thought that his daughter could so easily break the commandments he lived by. And this time it would not be Frank but she who'd be committing adultery. If she gave in to her desires then God would punish her.

She must have fallen asleep, for she was dreaming about Frank again, dreaming that he was touching her and she was on fire for him and he was whispering in her ear, 'I can't go on without you, Elsie. You know there was never anyone but you . . .'

She came up, out of the dream, and found herself looking into those hot hazel eyes and feeling Frank's hands sliding over her body, holding her at the hips while his mouth closed over her breast. Instantly all her senses came leaping into life.

'Frank . . . Oh, Frank . . .' she whispered. 'I want you, too.' When he brought his face up from her breast she slid tender arms about his neck and sought his mouth until they went rolling into the long cool grass under the trees.

He stood up, took off his clothes and draped them over a low branch of the apple tree. He smiled down and said, 'Adam and Eve, eh? Temptress!'

She reached out to grab his hand and pull him down, and as he squatted beside her he said, 'Does he keep you short, Elsie? Can't you go on without me?'

Elsie tried to control the churning, stirring inside herself. She was faint with need of him but she would not admit that she had been lying here, longing for him to come to her. She tried to be nonchalant, and looked away so he should not see the truth in her eyes.

'I'm not complaining,' she said. 'I'm glad I'm a married woman.' But even as she spoke she wanted him to grasp her tight, to force himself upon her, take her roughly and hard so she had no chance to waver.

He began to stroke her oiled thighs so that she would quicken and shiver. 'I'm not going to be your plaything, Elsie. We go back to where we were before – or not at all.'

Still she would not admit to her need but said softly, 'I want you back.'

'How often can we be together?' he asked. He might be arranging a lease on one of his properties.

She was not to be allowed the excuse of being overcome, then? He expected her to devise their arrangement. She said, 'Howard goes away early on Monday mornings . . . You could telephone about eight o'clock . . . there's nobody here . . .'

'And you are alone in the shop on Wednesday afternoons?' He ran his hands lightly across her breasts, his face serious, though he must see the response in her body. He wanted to have it all back as before, with his woman available for him three times a week as she had always been. She tried to regain the high ground. She looked up at him. 'I'm not miserable, Frank. I want to stay married. And I'm not going to give you the satisfaction of hearing all the intimate details . . .'

But instead of the burning desire she thought she'd find in his eyes, she saw amusement. He threw back his head and laughed loud as he straddled her, making her hold on to him for support. 'Intimate details?' he said. 'What intimate details?'

Elsie's hands slid round his waist. She moved in close and put her cheek against his muscular chest, and bit her lip to stop herself from losing control too fast. But his hands were caressing the heavy breasts she was thrusting forward for him and she caught her breath and tried to keep her balance and stop herself from falling back where he wanted her, flat on the grass with her hips lifting to receive him.

He stopped, laughed again and said, 'There aren't any intimate details worth hearing, are there?'

'No ...' she whispered.

'Not like us ... is it? Not like this with anyone else, Elsie?'

She lay back on the grass and reached out her arms for him as he came down on top of her with the little grunting noise he always made when he knew she was ready for him. Then he wiped the tears away from the corners of her eyes with his fingers and very softly said, 'If you had waited for me, love ... If you'd married me ...'

'Are you proposing?' Elsie's voice was low-pitched with love for him. 'Now you are safe?'

He planted little kisses all over her face and neck and said, 'You've always been my wife, Elsie ...' Then his mouth was on hers and everything but fiery need was being blotted out as she melted inside. He stopped kissing her and looked at her for a moment with burning eyes. 'I love you, Elsie.'

'I love ...' Elsie said, but he had not heard, for his mouth was fastening on to hers again and his hands were sliding over her hips, moving her legs apart, and he was going deep, deep into her, making her cry out for him and grasp him into herself.

And it was as if they had spent ten years apart and could never be filled nor their thirst slaked, for she was whimpering even as he drove himself hard into her, and she was crying out, 'Frank. Oh my God!' as they spent themselves and repeated their spending in an orgy, a gluttony of love.

Chapter Eighteen

Isobel was denied all privileges for the summer. They told her that she should be thankful she had not been expelled after 'letting down the good name of St Ursula's last term. She was forbidden to go to town or to use the school's telephone once a week as the other girls did. But she was allowed pen and paper and she wrote to Sylvia and Magnus, apologising for everything – for borrowing Sylvia's dress and tearing it, for provoking a scene between Ian and Ray Chancellor, for leaving the party without saying goodbye. She thought she had ruined everything, thought that Sylvia and Magnus would want to end their friendship. But she asked them to remember her to Ian and Rowena, then she sealed the letter and posted it. The next move was up to Sylvia and Magnus, because she would not go to Archerfield again since she knew what Mrs Hammond thought of her.

She wrote to Nanna:

'Dearest Nanna,
I'm sorry that I got you into trouble. We break up at the end of July. I'll come up to Lindow to study every weekend, if that's all right. I'm allowed to sit the School Certificate next year and I am desperate to pass. During the week I'll be at the shop, making things to sell, where I can watch over Mam.'

Back in Macclesfield, she and Mam sewed at Jordangate every morning. They took the sewing machine and a table upstairs to the old sitting room where there was plenty of space and light. The room looked almost inviting now that Mam had put down a carpet and placed an enormous leather and horsehair sofa before the fireplace.

Her stepfather was seldom at home because his new factory, which neither Isobel nor Mam had seen, was not yet breaking even and, he said, it took all his time to keep his head above water.

Isobel was happy that summer. With or without her stepfather, she and Mam went to evensong at St Michael's. Isobel knew a warm contentment, seeing Mam praying and joining in the responses,saying the Confession so fervently: *Almighty and Most Merciful Father; We have erred and strayed from Thy ways like lost sheep. We have followed too much the devices and desires of our own hearts. We have offended against thy holy laws* ... It was at this point that Ma always closed her eyes, knowing how Grandpa lived by the holy laws. *We have left undone those things which we ought to have done; And we have done those things which we ought not to have done; And there is no health in us*. There was health in Mam, though. Mam's brush with death had given her a fright and now she took great care. She was healthy and pretty again. *But Thou, O Lord, have mercy upon us, miserable offenders. Spare Thou them, O God, which confess their faults. Restore Thou them that are penitent; According to thy promises declared unto mankind in Christ Jesus our Lord*. Isobel was aware that Mam meant every word - and especially these last: *And grant O most merciful Father, for his sake; That we may hereafter live a godly, righteous and sober life. To the glory of thy holy Name. Amen*. For Mam had stopped drinking.

It was like old times on Fridays. Mam would be in the shop, laughing and hearing all the gossip about Nellie Plant, who was soon to marry a rich widower from Wilmslow - Mr Chancellor had introduced them - and while Mam was 'haw-hawing' and 'hem-hemming' Isobel would be doing a bit of hand stitching, making tea for old friends and planning her afternoons, which she spent with Shandy.

Isobel was surprised one morning when Shandy ran into the shop to say, 'I'll treat you to afternoon tea at the Corner Café. I have something important to tell,' and ran away before Mam or she could question her.

The Corner Café on Castle Street was only yards from the grocery shop, the doley shop, where the poor exchanged their Public Assistance vouchers for groceries. Isobel felt guilty walking past that long line of patient people. Always there would be people she recognised, and as she passed they'd look away, embarrassed. Inside the café, seeing the price, one and sixpence, on the menu she said to Shandy, 'You can't afford to pay for all this. You only get a few shillings a week.'

'Four and six,' Shandy said. 'But I get free board and lodgings, don't I?'

'You'd get that anyway,' she told her firmly. 'You ought to be paid as much as a housekeeper – and get your board and lodgings. Tell your father to give you a rise.'

'He would, if I asked. We've got the contract to supply the doley shop and the feeding centre. They give two hundred children free dinners every day. It's a lot of bread.' Isobel passed the toasted teacakes. Shandy said, 'I wanted to talk to you here where it's private ...' She glanced about but there was nobody near. All the same she leaned across the table and whispered, 'Doreen Grimshaw's got her claws into our Cyril!'

The three older Anderson brothers were married. The idea of Doreen taking a shine to the handsome but immature Cyril was ludicrous. Isobel almost laughed but, seeing Shandy's worried face, didn't. She said, 'I'd have thought she'd go for someone older, more her sort – not a nice lad like your Cyril.'

'He's daft about her. Do you know what my brothers are saying?'

Isobel shook her head. 'They say they all had a turn before they got married. Doreen's been charging men, for years. Jack said, "She's a whore, Cyril. What's worse, she's a box-of-chocolates-and-a-florin whore!"'

Imagine men saying things like that about a girl, even a girl as fast as Doreen. 'It can't be true,' Isobel said, 'You couldn't keep something like that quiet in Macclesfield. Cyril would never marry a girl with a reputation.'

'He says my brothers are jealous. He's going to ask her to marry him. He says there's plenty of room for him and Doreen in our house. They are going to live with us. If she says yes, I'm leaving home!'

'It won't come to anything.' Isobel smiled at Shandy's

furious freckled face. 'Doreen doesn't want to get married. She told Mam she's having a good time with every man in Macc after her.'

'I hope you're right,' Shandy said. 'She'll lead her husband a merry dance. I don't want it to be one of my brothers.'

Magnus and Sylvia had gone to Scotland for two weeks in July but had not come back by the time Isobel returned to school. Then Sylvia wrote to Isobel. There was no mention of the party. She wrote:

> Magnus was taken into hospital after he cut himself. It was a blade of grass, Isobel. A simple thing like that. He plucked a blade of grass to suck the sweet end and when he pulled it out of his mouth the grass sliced his finger. It is terrifying, knowing that such a tiny injury can threaten his life.
>
> We have prayed so hard that his illness would be cured. It is a cruel fate and Magnus knows it. He's usually so brave but this time he broke down and cried, 'It puts the fear of God into my heart, seeing my life blood flowing away from me.' They tied his hand to the headpost of the bed to elevate it. It took a week to stop bleeding and all the time blood was oozing out from where a clot was forming very slowly. He is out of hospital, but weak and low in spirits. He says he doesn't want to go home and let anyone (he means you, of course) see him like this. He says he may as well stay until the end of September. Mama and I will stay with him.

She also had a letter from Ian. It was a matter-of-fact letter without a single tender word. He talked about his studies. This year he was very busy, spending most of his time working in a hospital. His handwriting was a scrawl. It seemed that doctors must always be inscrutable when they put pen to paper. Then, at the bottom, after he had signed himself 'Yours, Ian', he had added a postscript that sent her spirits soaring to heaven: 'PS: You have an appointment with a doctor, 14 March 1937.' This would be her eighteenth birthday. 'Meet me. White Nancy. 3pm.'

*

She had not wanted to go back to St Ursula's after the weeks spent with Mam. She had been back less than a fortnight when, in the middle of a maths lesson, the school secretary came into the classroom and crooked her finger to call Isobel out to the front and say, 'The headmistress wishes to speak to you, Isobel Leigh.'

Her heart pounding in alarm, wondering what on earth she had done, Isobel followed the secretary to the oak-panelled study where Miss Colclough was seated behind her desk, facing the door. In front of her lay Isobel's school file with copies of her three school reports. Attached to the top report was a large pink cheque, drawn on the District Bank, Jordangate, Macclesfield. Isobel could not see if it was Mam or her stepfather who had signed it, because the signature was obscured by an opened-out telegram.

'I've received a telegram,' Miss Colclough said. 'From Mrs Isobel Stanway. Who . . . ?'

'My grandmother,' Isobel said quickly. Her heart beat faster. Why would Nanna send a telegram?

'It says, "Please send Isobel home. Mother is ill."'

Her knees went weak. 'Mam wasn't ill ten days ago.'

Miss Colclough winced when she said 'Mam' instead of 'Mother'. 'Take the train. Can you make your own way to the station?'

'Yes . . .' She stared at the telegram. It said 'seriously ill'.

'Have you money enough for the fare?'

'No.' Of course she hadn't enough money for the fare. There was a great fat cheque for a term's fees on the desk. The knot of anxiety twisted in Isobel's stomach. 'Will you lend me . . . ?'

Displeasure was all over Miss Colclough's stern face. 'I must ask you to sign for fifteen shillings,' she said. 'If you intend to travel first class as our girls—'

'Please.'

Isobel's hands were shaking as she signed the note and took the money. Then she ran to the dormitory to fling on her gabardine and outdoor shoes. Mam was ill. She couldn't believe it.

She ran like the wind to Lord Street, and when she arrived at Chapel Street, an express train to Manchester was leaving in two minutes' time. She went third class and had to stand all the way, all the time asking herself, *What's the matter with Mam? Nanna wouldn't send for me unless Mam needed me*. Mam was seriously ill. The old churning feeling was back in her stomach as she crossed from Manchester's Exchange Station to London Road for the train home to Macclesfield, where the only person waiting on the platform was Mr Chancellor.

Frank felt the tears springing behind his eyes when his precious lass came down the platform towards him, white-faced with dread. He wanted to protect and console her yet he must appear to be merely a family friend.

She put out a hand. 'Were you waiting for me?'

He held on to her fingers. 'Thank God you're here. I'll drive you up to the Infirmary.'

'The Infirmary? What happened?' She pulled her hand back quickly. 'How did you know . . .?'

'In a minute.' He took her ticket and handed it to the station master, then placed an arm across her shoulder as they walked to his car. He said quietly, 'I found your mother unconscious in bed this morning.'

'Why were you at our house?' She shrugged free and he dropped his arm. 'Mam's going to be all right, is she? Where's Nanna?'

'Your grandparents are with your mam,' he said. They had reached the car. 'The doctors don't know if she will pull through. She's unconscious . . .'

'But how did you know . . .?' She was choking with tears in the privacy of the car. 'What made you go to the house?'

'I went to the shop. She wasn't there. She's never not there at nine o'clock in the morning.'

They were passing the shop and he said, 'I knew something was wrong. I can't explain. I went to the telephone box and rang your home. There was no answer. I panicked.'

Isobel turned to face him. She touched his arm. She was crying hard now. 'Thank God you did.'

He gave her a wan smile. He dared not touch her again, even to give comfort, though he ached to take her in his arms, cry on her shoulder, unburden himself, tell her all he had found. He could not tell his precious lass that he'd telephoned

Elsie from his house to check that the coast was clear and say that he was on his way to her. They had only last week resumed their lovemaking after Isobel's return to school. They had not been able to get enough of one another after the six-weeks separation, even though Elsie believed she was committing adultery and that heavenly retribution was impending. This weekend, with Willey-Leigh at home, had seemed like a month to Frank. He had even gone to church on Sunday evening to get a glimpse of her, and seeing her there, standing beside Willey-Leigh, had brought it home to him again that it was he who should be at her side. But their eyes met across the aisle and he knew, as he had always known, that in her heart she was his.

This morning, when she should have been as eager as he was, Elsie did not answer the phone. And he'd known that something was wrong. He threw himself into the car and drove hell for leather for Bollinbrook Road, panic rising with every turn of the wheels. The house was silent. The back door was locked. He ran to the front, hammered at the door and heard the sound echoing up the hallway. She was in there. He knew it. His hands were weak, nerveless as he picked up an edging stone and smashed it through the coloured glass beside the front door. The glass shattered and he put his hand through the diamond-shaped hole in the leaded pane. He undid the catch, opened the door and tore up the stairs, and for a moment relief flooded through him when he saw her peacefully asleep.

'Elsie?' He shook her shoulder and instantly his fear returned. There was no resistance in her. She rolled on to her back, her head lolling to the side, yet her breathing was quiet and regular. He ran down the stairs and called his own doctor. Strange that he didn't know which of the town's three doctors Elsie used. But she was as strong as an ox. She was never ill.

Then he sat holding Elsie's hand for five minutes until Dr Russell arrived. He had to make excuses to the doctor, too, to explain his presence at Elsie's home, just as now he must explain to his precious lass, who was crying beside him as the car nosed through the open iron gates of Macclesfield Infirmary.

'I called Dr Russell. He's my doctor. We brought her here.' His heart was pounding with fear for Elsie now. The doctor told him that every minute was vital – that Elsie would have been dead in another hour.

Isobel was trying to control herself before she went inside; her shoulders lifted under lurching sobs. He said quietly, 'Wait here for a minute, lass. Go in when you are ready.' It was agony to him, when he wanted to take the responsibility for both Elsie and Isobel, that he had no right to be at Elsie's side when she most needed him.

Isobel stopped weeping. She put her head up and squared her shoulders. 'Where's my stepfather? Have you told him?'

'I don't know. He wasn't there. He must have left for work.' How could he say more? He said, 'Does he know that your mother is diabetic?'

'He knows.' She pressed her lips tight.

Had he gone too far? Did his precious lass see his questioning as interference in their private lives?

She said, 'We've been taught what to do in an emergency.' She turned her big grey eyes on to him and said in an icy voice, 'How did you know? Mam kept it secret from everyone but the family.'

Was she telling him not to overstep the boundaries? 'Dr Russell told me. Your mother is in a hypoglycaemic coma. She must have given herself a dose of insulin when she needed sugar.'

'My stepfather must be found.'

'I'll take care of it, lass.' Frank would go straight to the police and tell them to find Willey-Leigh.

'Why are you doing so much?' she asked. 'It really isn't your . . .'

'My business?' He touched her arm tenderly. 'I'm your mother's best friend. Remember that.'

'I didn't mean to be rude. I'm ready to go in. Thank you, Mr Chancellor. You are very kind.'

He said, 'I'll go and tell Miss Duffield. Telephone if you need me.'

Mam was in a small side ward. The window curtains were drawn and Isobel's heart skipped a beat. Grandpa, old and worn, was at the far side of the room with Nanna, watching the elderly doctor who stood at the foot of the bed; ponderous, eyes fixed on what looked like a little doll.

For a moment Isobel thought there must be a mistake, then, as she came a step closer, a great lump lodged in her throat and sobs came jerking through her chest as she saw that it was Mam. It was Mam as Isobel had never before seen her. Mam's eyes were closed and the once-heavy lids were thin and stretched tight over sunken eyes in deep, dark sockets. Her right arm was outstretched and splinted with a needle contraption attached to a rubber tube with a bottle suspended above. Mam's nose was pinched and high-bridged and the mouth that could curl at the corners in merriment or scorn was straight and flat. Isobel raised tearful eyes to Nanna. Mam took a deep, noisy breath, then fell silent again.

A quivering-jelly sensation was in Isobel's stomach as the doctor gave details. 'Blood and urine have been tested. Glucose and insulin are now in balance. Your mother is not responding. Unless she shows any vital signs—'

Isobel interrupted in a broken voice, 'Which vital signs?'

'Any. If she opened her eyes, if she could co-operate and was holding on to life ... we could pass a tube into her stomach to feed her.' The doctor said, 'We have reported the matter to the police.'

'Police?' Grandpa sat down quickly on the edge of the bed. 'Surely you don't suspect ...?'

'I do not believe that a diabetic patient would make such a mistake. She would not inject a high dose of insulin when she needed glucose. Her husband must give an explanation.' Then he said gently, to all of them, I am afraid it is too late to hope for a recovery.'

Grandpa's face went grey as he sagged against Nanna, saying softly, 'It's no use. My poor lass.'

Isobel took Mam's little ice-cold hand in hers. 'Mam ... Mam ... Don't die, Mam ... Please don't die.' There was no response. She put Mam's hand close to her own cheek to warm it, then held it loose and placed her index finger in Mam's palm. The doctor had told her once that hearing was the last thing to go. 'Mam ... if you can hear me, squeeze my finger.'

There was nothing.

'She can hear,' Isobel whispered. 'But how can she let me know?' She couldn't let Mam die without everything being tried. She turned to the doctor. 'Why can't you feed her into her stomach?'

'Your mother cannot swallow the tube, my dear. It's as simple as that. The tube would pass into her lungs. Pneumonia would follow.'

'If I can get Mam to swallow the tube ...?'

The doctor brought his hands up, opened his fingers and shrugged. 'If you can get a response, I will try.'

'Help me prop her up,' Isobel pleaded, and when they had Mam lifted high she placed pillows behind Mam's shoulders and took her hand again. 'Mam, it's Isobel. Can you hear me?' There was no movement.

What was it she had read, in the Darwin and Freud books? Humans had no instincts left – only learned behaviour and reflexes. Then what was the first reflex? Which reflex followed the in-drawing of a baby's first breath? It came to her, 'Mam ... if you can't move your hands ... if you can't open your eyes ... can you suck? Can you put your tongue out?'

Isobel watched, holding her breath, until at last a muscle moved under Mam's bottom lip. Then slowly, so painfully slowly that tears were coursing down Isobel's cheeks, she saw Mam's mouth begin to open and the tip of a pink, wet tongue push through.

At once the doctor left the room and returned with a nurse, who wheeled a trolley loaded down with fearsome equipment: rubber tubes and syringes, glycerine for lubrication, funnels and huge white enamel jugs and vomit bowls. He said to Isobel, 'You won't want to watch this. There is no guarantee that she will come round. But now she has a chance.'

The doctor said gently to Grandpa, 'Please I must ask you to leave.' Grandpa was ashen-faced and had to be helped to his feet by Nanna, who took his arm and led him out of the room, Isobel looked at the doctor, who nodded to her to indicate that she must follow. Shaking like a straw, Isobel went out of the room.

Nanna and Grandpa were a long way ahead, Grandpa's walk slow and unsure. Nanna supported him but she appeared to be flagging. Isobel stood in the tiled corridor outside the ward, watching Nanna and Grandpa go, whilst she herself was rooted to the spot with dread as she heard Mam gurgling like a drain and the hollow noise of her retching as the tube was passed into her stomach.

A ward sister came to her. Nobody was to return until the visiting hour at six. No exceptions were made to this hospital rule. If Mam took a turn for the worse, the sister would telephone Isobel at the house. She turned Isobel away, telling her to take heart. Mam was alive.

Nanna and Grandpa had gone now, and Isobel walked home in fear, desperate to wake up and find that it was all a horrible nightmare. But everything was normal. The September sun beamed down, warm and golden on the leaves at her feet as she went home to Bollinbrook Road. People stopped her in the street to say, 'I'm sorry to hear about your mother, love. If there's anything I can do ...'

It had only happened a few hours ago and they were talking about it already. But it was a comfort, seeing how many people wanted to show their affection for Mam. Isobel answered, like a repeated prayer, 'Mam's going to get better. It will take a bit of time. I don't mind how long it takes ...'

It was two o'clock. Weary now, she went upstairs to change out of her school clothes, but before she could do this a postman came to the door, asking her to sign for three registered letters. And because she'd signed for them, she opened them. The first was a final demand notice for a £15 rates bill. If it were not paid within ten days their goods would be distrained. The second was a demand notice from the coal merchant: a year's bills totalling £5.17.11 was outstanding. The third was from the building society to say that unless the sum of £16 was deposited before the end of the month, the whole outstanding mortgage would fall due.

Isobel sat down at the kitchen table and put her head in her hands. Where was her stepfather? Surely he would come home at once, explain what had happened this morning, take charge, shoulder his responsibilities. How could one family be struck by two disasters in a single day?

The telephone rang. Isobel jumped at the sound and dashed to the hall to answer it, heart hammering in her tight, painful chest. Was it the Infirmary? Her stepfather? she picked up the receiver and gulping back her tears said, 'Hello ...'

Mr Hammond's voice came hesitant, soothing. 'Isobel?

Please sit down. Prepare yourself for bad news. Your grandfather collapsed and died half an hour ago. It was a heart attack. He would have known nothing. It happened in seconds. I am so very sorry, my dear.'

Mam was alternating between a diabetic state and hypoglycaemia from day to day; coming out of it for brief periods, disoriented. The doctors warned that she must be treated gently and not told about Grandpa's death yet. So Isobel had to stand in for Mam at Grandpa's funeral.

Grandpa was buried at ten o'clock on Thursday in the churchyard in Bollington. There was not room in the sunlit graveyard for all the mourners. They crowded between the gravestones and stood on the pavement beyond the stone walls. They came in droves – the chapel congregation, friends, acquaintances, the doctor, Macclesfield's shopkeepers and traders, the Grimshaws and Doreen, the Hammond family and Mr Chancellor.

Throughout the service in Grandpa's chapel, Mr Chancellor used a large white handkerchief, holding it to his face. His eyes were red and puffed, Mr Hammond's eyes were bright with tears. Mrs Hammond was stony. Magnus – poor Magnus on two sticks – and Sylvia stood, pale and shocked. Mr and Mrs Grimshaw were sad and silent, Doreen dabbed at her eyes with her left hand where she wore a diamond ring. Isobel's stepfather kept looking at his watch. He had been questioned by the police and told them that Mam was conscious when he left for work last Monday. He had not yet spent a night at the house.

The burial service was over. The family and chief mourners were to go for tea and sandwiches to Lindow. Nanna and Isobel did not want to be driven. They walked together, the others fifty paces behind them.

Nanna took Isobel's arm, and because as soon as she was with Nanna she could let go, Isobel was immediately overcome with tears. As they went, Nanna told her that if Mam died it would bring her close to losing her faith. 'I loved my parents and I've always loved Our Lord, Lil. I tried to love Him with all my heart and soul. And I loved your Grandpa. But I never understood the meaning of true love until I had Elsie. They put my baby into my arms and from that moment on I was a changed woman.'

Isobel could let her tears fall unchecked now. Silent, she held Nanna's little square hand. Nanna needed to put her anguish into words, and only with her could she do it. 'You'll never understand love, our Lil, until you have a child,' she said. 'You'll think you've found love when you meet your man. But it's nothing like love you'll have for your child. It's an ancient and primitive emotion that can turn heads of mildest women. A mother will kill. A mother will sacrifice her own life to protect her child.'

She stopped speaking for the ten minutes it took her to climb the hill, then, just as they got to the lane end, she clutched Isobel's arm and cried out loud enough for heaven itself to hear. 'It's all wrong for a mother to outlive her child. I want to die before Elsie!'

'Nanna. Please. No more tears. We have to be strong today . . .' Isobel swallowed the great wodge of pain in her throat. 'Mam isn't going to die. Stop crying, please, Nanna.'

They didn't cry again. Not even when in Nanna's crowded living room they discovered that Howard had left the funeral at the churchyard. People spoke in hushed voices, placed hands on their arms and said nice things about Grandpa and how much he had meant to them.

When they had finished eating and nobody wanted more Isobel took the used crockery into the scullery and started to stack everything for washing. It was there that Doreen found her. Doreen was wearing a black dress, her face was thick in powder and paint and she came to stand very close and in a new, unctuous voice said, 'I've been to see your mother. Oh, I was shocked. She used to be the most beautiful woman in the world.'

Isobel said coldly, 'Used to be? Mam is getting better every day.'

Doreen's voice went high and insistent as she added, 'Your mother used to confide in me, you know. She told me things she'd never tell you!'

Isobel had nothing to fear from Doreen, so it must have been the old reaction that made her hands shake and her adrenaline surge as Doreen pinched her hard on the elbow. 'Why aren't you crying?'

Then, calmly, Doreen looked at herself in the kitchen overmantel mirror, took out a handkerchief and dabbed at her eye corners where her eye-black had streaked. After she had put her face to rights she taunted, 'You'll have to cut your cloth. Come down to earth and work for your living. You won't be kept on at that fancy school. Howard Leigh wasn't paying for it, that's for certain. He spends his money on other women. Good job he adopted you, though. He'll have to provide for your mother and you. He wouldn't if you'd still been a ...' Seeing the horror on Isobel's face, she gave a spluttering laugh before she went back to inspecting her face. She said, 'Anyway, it's common knowledge. He's up to his ears in debt. Everyone knows he's made a fool of your mother. Money was all he wanted.'

Then she made a calculating face and watched for Isobel's reaction through the mirror as she said, 'He used to meet me out of work. He'd say, "Fancy seeing you, Doreen!" But he always brought me a box of chocolates and' – she spluttered with laughter again – 'took me for a drive down the country lanes.'

Isobel's face drained of colour. She could be sick on the spot, thinking of her stepfather fondling Doreen. She clasped her hands tight to stop herself from striking the girl. 'You know how to put the knife in, don't you?' she said. 'And twist it.'

The explosive laugh came. Glee was all over Doreen's face. 'Me? What have I done? I've done nothing but tell you the truth ...'

Isobel's black coat and hat were hanging up behind the kitchen door, and she pushed past Doreen, knocking her off-balance as she reached for her coat, buttoned it with trembling hands, grabbed the hat and pulled it on. 'I'll have to get some good, clean air,' she said. 'There's a nasty smell in here.'

Doreen screeched with laughter. 'It's coming from your mouth!'

'Rot in hell!' She flung the words, slammed the door and started to run, tears streaming down her face, down the lane to Bollington.

She was crying, running and a hundred yards past the lane

end when a car drew up and she heard a man calling, 'Isobel? Isobel Leigh?'

Isobel halted, wiped her eyes on the backs of her leather gloves and saw Ray Chancellor, one arm resting along the top of the door of his motor car – a long navy and ice-blue Delage open-top car that almost filled the narrow lane. 'It is Isobel!' He gave that devilish smile. 'Why all in black?'

He must be the only person in Macclesfield who did not know. 'My grandfather,' she said quietly. 'It was his funeral today.'

His face fell. 'Isobel, I'm sorry.' He pulled on the brake and came to stand beside her, placing a comforting arm about her shoulder. 'I'm so very sorry. Where are you going?'

'Home. I couldn't stand another minute up there.' She waved her arm in the direction of Lindow. 'With all those weeping people who weren't there when my mother needed help.'

'Oh, no!' He took her hands in his; holding on to them. 'Your mother? Is it your mother who is in a coma? I can't leave you here like this, Isobel. I lost my own dear mother, and now ...' Tears welled in his greeny-grey eyes. He blinked rapidly, clenched his jaw, then smiled and said, 'Dad said he was going to a funeral. Isobel, I'm sorry. I didn't connect you with the Elsie Stanway Dad and Mother spoke about.' He led her round to the passenger side of the Delage. 'Get in. I won't go to Archerfield. It was an impulse visit. I like to keep up the friendship my mother had with the Hammonds. I'll take you home.'

Isobel got in gratefully and leaned back against the deep-blue leather while Ray closed the door and went to the driver's seat.

'Home first – or would you feel better if I took you for a short drive?' he asked.

'A short drive, please.' A drive would help her to stop thinking and worrying about facing her stepfather.

'Then we'll drive up into the hills. I'll take you to Buxton. We'll go out for tea and I'll have you back in Macc before the mills come out.' His face was all concern. 'Throw your hat in the back. There's a ladies' scarf if you need something for your hair. It's not very breezy.'

Isobel threw the hat in and shook her hair out so that the

wind might blow through it.

They were travelling fast, heading for Macclesfield along the road from Manchester, and the fresh wind was catching her hair over the split glass windscreen that had chrome catches and all sorts of clever devices to open and hold and wipe the glass. Ray pointed them out to her as he drove. 'The windscreen glass is hinged,' he said. 'See the Jaeger instrument panel?'

'Yes. All those clocks and dials. How do you know what they are for? It's a quiet engine,' she added. 'I can hear everything you say.'

'It's a four thousand cc engine, designed by Maurice Gaultier,' he said, and he was laughing at her questions, showing off about his beautiful motor car. Passers-by were stopping to stare because few in Macclesfield had seen anything half as grand.

'French, of course,' he said. 'I drove it home from Paris. The Delage showroom is on the Champs-Elysées.'

They had gone under the bridge in Waters Green and were heading up the steep Buxton Road, into the hills. Ray was delighted with himself, impressing her with technical talk. 'She can do eighty-six miles an hour with ease,' he said, and he laughed and put his foot down so they went skimming forward, faster than before.

'It's lovely inside,' Isobel ventured and, away from Macclesfield she smiled, and not least for the sudden impression she had that she was sitting next to a peacock, or a red-bellied stickleback.

'Should be! Fernandez et Darrin coachwork,' he said. Then, seeing her face, 'You're not pulling my leg, are you?'

'No. Honestly! It's just that I can't help smiling all at once.' She should feel guilty, enjoying herself today. 'Tell me more.'

He laughed and put his foot down hard. 'All right. She's got coil ignition on a straight eight engine. A hundred and eighteen BHP produced at three thousand eight hundred rpm, with a Smith Barraquand carburetor . . .'

Isobel was laughing as they bowled along the empty road, heather-clad moorland either side of them and the wild scent strong in the air. Her hair blew across her face and trailed out behind. She thought his profile was so like his mother's. She said, 'And . . . ?'

He said, 'And? If you don't stop looking at me with those smouldering eyes, Isobel Leigh, I shall halt this magnificent car and take you into the heather and ravish you!' Then he must have seen that his words, instead of delighting her, had dispelled her light mood, for she stared, stony cold, at the road ahead. 'Please don't talk that way,' she said. 'I'm not used to it.'

'I'm sorry,' he said, softly. 'I didn't mean it. I wanted to tell you that you're an extraordinary person. The prettiest girl in Macclesfield.'

He said that to all the girls but she was sure he hadn't meant to upset her. 'All right,' she said. 'I won't take offence.'

They sped through the wild moors until they pulled up at last in front of the Cat and Fiddle, reputed to be the highest public house in England. And she went laughing from there because the sheep on the moors were so tame that they pestered people for titbits and scraps, and all at once Ray became agitated, shouting, 'Watch their feet! They'll kick the paint off my bodywork!' angry with the sheep – as if they could help being tame – and as if by watching them, Isobel could help where they put their feet.

They had tea in a café and Ray made her feel, for the first time in a year, that she was interesting, good company and attractive. He asked her questions and she told him what she'd want a stranger to think. She didn't feel free, as she had with Ian, to tell all. But she was at ease and Ray was charming and flattering. Only in the mildest way was he flirtatious, saying things like, 'Oh, those eyes, Isobel Leigh. Little sparks and golden flames are burning in the ashes.' And, 'I'll dream about your eyes tonight.'

He drove home fast so that they should arrive before the mills closed. He said, 'We don't want anyone to see us – or set tongues wagging.'

'Not on this of all days,' Isobel said quietly, because her spirits were sinking the closer they got to Bollinbrook Road.

'Don't tell anyone,' he said. 'Keep it to yourself. I'll go the back way.'

It was the wrong thing to say if he'd meant to sound considerate. It sounded more as if he had something to hide. But when they reached the house and had not seen anyone in particular he placed his hand on the back of her seat and, very gently, kissed her cheek.

'Thank you,' she said.

Like a gentleman he leaped out of the car and opened her door. 'I'll give you a ring.'

'Oh no! Don't!' Isobel blurted out, and felt her face growing red.

'Then, for now, goodbye,' he said.

'Thank you. Goodbye!'

The telephone rang before she'd taken her coat off. The sound echoed through the uncarpeted hall in the empty house. Ian's voice came burling down the line.

'Isobel? I've only just heard. What can I say?'

Hope and longing welled up. 'Where are you?'

'Edinburgh. I have five minutes before I go on duty at the Infirmary. How are you?'

He sounded so near she'd believed he was in Macclesfield. Now she was cast down again. 'I'll be OK. I'll find a job.'

'What about your future? University?'

'I can't.'

'Why not?'

'My stepfather. I don't think he can pay for Mam,' was all she could say. How could she tell the boy she loved that there was no money for school or university? There was no chance for her to go onwards and upwards as he and Rowena were doing. And how could she say, to such a boy, that they were, with the lowest of the low, in debt? She said, 'I'm going to earn money.'

There was a moment's silence, then he said, 'Isobel, it's presumptuous of me – and possibly in bad taste – but can't you ask your grandmother for help? There must be money put aside for you.'

It was presumptuous. She was offended, but she answered, 'Mam would never ask Nanna. Neither will I. I shall earn my own money. Grandpa hadn't much to leave – only Lindow and whatever he had in the bank. Nanna is going to need security.'

'Go to see a lawyer tomorrow. The money for your education should be in trust for you. If your mother dies intestate your stepfather is entitled to it all. House. Money. Everything.'

How could Ian say such a thing? Her throat was tight as she

blurted out, 'Mam's not dead! I'm going to visit her in half an hour. Grandpa was buried today! Don't ask me to fight for my rights!'

'I'm sorry.' Ian sounded sorry this time. 'But try to think this out. The most important thing is that you go to university. Finish your education. Your stepfather adopted you. He must act in your best interests. And Isobel ...'

'What?'

'Tell me if I can help?'

She wanted to cry, to shout, 'Don't advise me! Come for me! Save me!' But she couldn't. She needed to see him, touch him. She needed a protector. She needed him now and she needed to hear him say, loud and clear, that she was his girl. If he didn't speak she'd know he didn't care.

There was a long silence.

Then he said, in a softer voice, 'Are you there, Isobel?'

He had not said the words she wanted to hear. She was talking to a stranger. She did not answer, and after a few moments he said, 'See a lawyer. Speak to my uncle about your legal position. I'll ring you tomorrow. All right?'

'All right,' she said in a cold little voice. She could not tell anyone anything. Especially she would not tell Mr Hammond about Mam's debts. It was part of her burden of shame.

Chapter Nineteen

Elsie came out of blackness as hands pulled her into a sitting position. She opened her eyes. A nurse's bosom – a crisp white apron, starched and smelling of carbolic – reared up in front, then slowly moved away from her face. She was in hospital. Voices came to her from a long way off.

'She's come round again.' The nurse leaned over. 'Can you hear me?'

'Mmm ...' She could hear. She couldn't talk. Her tongue stuck like a lead weight in her mouth. There was something painful at the back of her throat and high in her nose. She put a hand to her face and felt soft rubber tubing coming from her nostril, taped to her cheek. If they would give her a drink ... If only they would give her ...

'Don't be alarmed, Mrs Leigh. We're feeding you ...' Another nurse.

The second nurse was holding Elsie's arms tight to her sides. Elsie tried to struggle. The stout one was taking the rubber tube, holding it down on her lap, taking out the stopper, attaching a steel injection. Those plunger things – what were they called? That thing – the last thing she remembered. Howard standing over her, plunging the needle in so hard and she wanting to say he'd got it wrong. She didn't need the insulin. She needed something sweet.

Elsie stopped struggling. It was no use. The nurse's arms gripped like a vice. The steel plunger thing was being pushed in and she felt the liquid run light and tickling and warm into her stomach.

'You'll start to feel better in a minute.' The nurse filled the syringe again from an enamel mug. 'You're coming round now, Mrs Leigh.'

'Mmm?' Her head was clearing. There was a jug of water at her bedside. And some fruit in a bowl. Grapes. Oranges. A banana. The nurse loosened her grip and let Elsie's shoulders sag against the pillows. It felt good. Her head was fuzzy, but now she didn't want to sleep.

The stout nurse fixed the rubber piping somewhere to the back of and above Elsie's head. 'There's a bell pull, Mrs Leigh. You might feel better sitting up.' The nurse drew back the curtains.

It was a big room. Twenty or more beds. She reached for the banana but her fingers were weak. The banana was heavy. She dug her fingers through the skin, split it, put it to her mouth and sucked. Then she tore back the peel and stuffed the fruit greedily into her mouth. It was manna from heaven – that was what Dad called it – manna from heaven. Her tongue was working. There was a rumbling in her stomach. Now, a drink of water.

'Let me ...' Frank's voice.

'S'a'right ...' But he had his arm about her shoulders and was holding the glass to her lips. And the cool, sweet water was running over her tongue and down her throat.

'You're better!' Frank's beloved face, relieved and pleased as he laid her back against the pillows. 'When did you come round, love?'

She opened her eyes. 'Long I been ... here ...?'

'Best part of a week.' He was dressed in a dark suit. Black tie.

The older nurse was back. 'She's talking.' Then, to Frank, 'This is the first time she's spoken. The nurse, who evidently did not know who he was, was officious. 'Are you a relative?'

Elsie smiled. 'S'a'right. Good friend ...'

'Five minutes. That's all. Don't want Mrs Leigh to overtire herself.'

Elsie could not help it that her words were slurring. It would pass. It happened when she had too much sugar. This time she'd had too much of the other. Insulin. It was all coming back to her. She said, 'Where Hah'd? Is ... is ... bel? Where's ee ...?'

'At Lindow. I left after the funeral service.'
'Funeral? Who funeral . . . ?'
'Your dad. It was his funeral today.'
'Dad?' Her voice cracked and broke. She sat bolt upright, and felt the blood draining from her face. Then she fell back against the pillows and clapped her hands to her face. 'Killed him . . . I kill . . .' She wailed and rocked herself back and to against the pillow. 'Dad . . . Dad . . .'
Frank looked at her in horror. 'It's not you, Elsie. It's not your fault. He was an old, old man . . .'
And Elsie heard her own screams coming from a long way off. Screaming, a terrible, agonising screaming. Nurses were running, holding her up. Frank was crying, begging to know, 'What's wrong, Elsie? Oh my God. What's gone wrong? Get the doctors. Quick. She's in pain.' But they were dragging Frank away and pulling curtains round her bed and holding her down until at last she went under into the merciful black state of unconsciousness.

Her stepfather must have come home late in the night. Early next morning Isobel heard him, clattering about the kitchen. She would wait until the front door slammed before going down for breakfast.
There were footsteps on the stairs. Isobel held her breath, waiting for him to pass the door. Instead, to her alarm, she saw the door knob turn, the door open slowly, and in he came, dressed only in striped pyjamas, carefully holding a cup and saucer and a plate of biscuits. He came right up to her bed.
'Here you are, Isobel,' he said, and flashed his teeth at her.
She sat, pulling the sheet up to her chin so he could not see down the sweetheart neck of her nightdress. 'What's all this?' she said. 'You don't allow breakfast in bed.'
He held the cup out and Isobel had to let go of the sheet to take it. 'A fresh start,' he said. 'For both of us.' He leered, 'Isobel, we have to live together, my dear. May as well be nice to one another.'
She handed the tea back. 'I don't want it. Leave my bedroom.'
Smiling eerily, he placed the tea things on the chest of drawers and, looking pleased with himself came and sat on the

bed. 'Now then, Isobel. I *am* your father.'

'You are not! You adopted me. That's all.'

'I am your father. Your father in the eyes of the law. I have legal rights!' Here he flashed his teeth again and the voice went high, silly and wheedling as he asked, 'And if you play ball with me – I'll play ball with you.'

'Play ball? What do you mean?'

'I mean that you will not go back to school. I cannot pay the fees. You will remain here, in your father's house. And I will make a home for my little Jordangate Lily.'

'Mam's house! Mam's and mine!' Isobel heard herself shouting.

'Mine.' His voice was hard. 'The house is mine. The shop is mine. You are mine. Your mother will have to go to the Institute of Guardians. I cannot pay for expensive hospitals.'

'Mam is getting better. She will never go into the workhouse.' How could he be so cruel? 'Have you no heart? No feelings?'

He came to sit close beside her and put his hand over the back of her neck. And as a knot tightened in her stomach and her legs trembled with fright he let his hand slide slowly down the front of her nightdress. She tried to raise her left hand but his arm was in the way. Her right arm was immobilised by the weight of his body as he pressed closer to her. And Isobel knew in the few seconds all this had taken that she had to fight him. He pulled back a little way, looking for approval. Not taking her eyes off his face, she let her head drop forward. Her cheek brushed against his forearm – and he wiggled his fingers playfully on her bare breast.

Then, quick as a python striking, Isobel darted her head down to close her teeth on the loose skin over his thin wrist. He yelped but she held fast, like a terrier on the neck of its prey, and the weight had gone from her arm as he tried to pull himself upright and bring his other hand up under her chin to push her head away. But this increased the twist on the skin and nerves of his wrist.

He screamed in agony, 'Get off, bitch!' while he tried to force her head back, but Isobel held on and fetched her hand up, clawing for his eyes. She let go as soon as she drew blood, tasting it salt and sticky on her tongue. Then she spat it out fast and straight into his face and watched it run, saliva streaked red, down his face.

'Get out of my room! Get out! Get out!' Isobel shouted, and he went, gripping his injured wrist, staggering to the bathroom.

She leaped out of bed and shoved the chest of drawers in front of the door. Then went back to lie on the bed, gasping for breath, faint with fright and anger. Would she have to fight him off again and again? What was it that drove a man to terrify a girl? Isobel lay there thinking desolate thoughts of what her future held. She could not tell anybody about this. Only Mam's presence had protected her.

Frank woke at five o'clock in the morning and went to stand by the window that overlooked Park Lane. Outside it was pouring with rain. The shiny wet pavement under the lamppost reflected light into the deserted street. There was no use trying to get back to sleep. The house was quiet. His ma, who sometimes rambled around in the night, had been in bed for hours. Ray slept as sound as a bell. Frank put on his dressing gown and went downstairs to the silent kitchen.

The fire was laid. He would not go up the back stairs and wake the kitchen girl who slept in the attic. He struck a match and held it to the paper in the grate. He dragged forward a kitchen chair and watched the fire while he thought about this impossible situation. His women belonged to Leigh, and despite all he knew of Leigh's enormous debts he must assume that the man was looking after them well but that Elsie and Isobel were proving an expensive pair to maintain.

The flames, blue and orange, sparked and crackled on the sticks. He dragged his chair back, making an unholy noise as wood scraped on the flagged kitchen floor. He didn't want to disturb the young kitchen lass. She had a hard time of it, working from six in the morning until late at night. He took the kettle to the sink and ran the tap. What a racket everything made when you were trying to be quiet. He dropped the kettle lid and it went rolling over the floor. He picked it up and banged it on, then carried the kettle carefully to the range. Could he keep Isobel on at school without Leigh knowing who was paying? He'd woken the lass. He heard the stair door open and waited for her to come pattering into the kitchen.

There was no sound. He went to the kitchen door and opened it just in time to see Ray, barefoot and wearing only a towel like a loincloth, creeping along the kitchen corridor, close to the wall.

'Come here!' Frank's fury had reversed itself, full blast on to Ray, who stopped and gave a sheepish grin.

'It's all right, Dad. It's not what you think. I heard you. I went to wake Jenny ...' He hopped on to the carpet runner.

'Come here, I said!' Frank held the kitchen door wide, and as Ray went past him – he could not help it – he clouted him hard across the back of the head. It was the first time in his life he'd raised his hand to anyone.

Ray turned swiftly, red in the face, arm raised to strike. But then he gave a weak grin, held on to his head and said, 'Deserved that.'

'How long has this been going on?' Frank was holding himself back from laying into his son.

'It was the first time. I swear it.' Ray sat down on the kitchen chair. Then, seeing his father's angry face, 'Look here. I – I'm not like you, Dad. You and Mother didn't ... I can't go without ...'

'Can't? What did you say?' Frank came to stand next to him and shake him by the bare shoulder. 'Don't tell me that you can't help yourself! We are not going to be dragged through the mud again.'

'Again?'

'You know what I'm talking about. If you can't keep your hands off young girls, it's time you got yourself a wife.' Ray looked away and Frank said, 'You can't keep your hands off, can you? Well, you'll marry the next one. Kitchen maid or not. Just get down on your knees and pray to God that you haven't given her a baby. I'll not bail you out again. And I'll not be dragged down with you. I'll disown you. I may not be able to control your finances but you'll not dare show your face in Macclesfield when I've finished with you.'

Ray held his head in his hands. 'I'm sorry, Dad. I'll never do it again.'

'You won't. I'll make damned sure you don't.'

Ray did not reply. Frank said, 'What's got into you?'

'I want to marry Sylvia Hammond. But I can't get five minutes alone with her. If her mother isn't watching her, Magnus is.'

'Sylvia Hammond? First I've heard of it.' Ray made no move, and it occurred to Frank that he was being thrown a red herring. He said, 'It's Hammond Silks you're after, isn't it?'

'No.'

'Yes it is. Well, forget it.'

'It's all right for you. Property and financing.' Ray had lost the sheepish look. 'We are losing money month by month. The printworks will go under unless something is done.'

'Hammond Silks is doing no better. Textiles are being over-produced. The markets are dwindling.' Frank said, 'Don't imagine that you and Sylvia will be allowed to go a-courting. Your reputation's not worth much.'

Ray smiled. 'I'll have to find a way around it, then. If my name's mud.'

Frank said, 'I mean it, Ray! I meant it when I said the next one, you marry her! Don't let it happen again.'

'It won't. I want to get married. Have a home of my own.'

'Do you?' Frank said.

All trace of remorse was gone from Ray's face now. He said, 'Well, I can't live for ever with you and that mad old woman.'

He laughed – but it was not the first time he'd said it, and Frank's temper rose again. 'Mad old woman? My mother?'

'She's nothing to me. Dad. Just a crazy old . . .'

Frank made a move towards him and Ray backed away, dodging his head as if he expected a blow. Then, as no blow came, he gave a laugh, a tactful, apologetic laugh to break the tension. 'Sorry,' he said. 'It was thoughtless of me. But we have to thrash this out, Dad. You may have a lot of authority in the town. You're used to being obeyed and listened to. But it's time you stopped trying to run my life.' Then he sauntered off, out of the kitchen.

The sooner Ray was married off, the better. In the meantime there was the question of the kitchen lass. Frank would find her another place and look for a middle-aged housekeeper. He looked through the window. It was coming light but still raining. In an hour or two he'd be with his daughter. Why couldn't his relationship with Ray be as easy as it had always been with the lass he'd lay down his life for?

It was pouring with rain when Isobel went from the house, umbrella close to her head, coat collar high, her stepfather's words going round in her mind: 'My house ... My shop ... My daughter ...' He never said, 'My wife.' Was there enough money to pay the debts? How could she get her stepfather out of their lives – hers and Mam's? She walked fast and arrived half an hour after Miss Duffield had opened up.

Miss Duffield was in a state. She followed Isobel through to the kitchen, where a fire was burning in the grate, and while Isobel spread her coat over a chair and put it in front of the fire to dry, Miss Duffield said, 'Who is in control now? I can't work for a man like that. I want my wages.'

Isobel's heart sank. 'What's the trouble?'

'It's your father.' Miss Duffield's face was bright pink. 'Came in and raked in the cupboards, looking for your mother's cash box. Pushed me aside. Emptied the till ...'

'When?'

'This morning. He said, "You are working for me, Miss Duffield. You will be paid monthly, in arrears. I'm off to Manchester for stock. We're going to sell the latest in ladies' dresses." He tried it before. Brought in dresses with hems sagging, side seams crooked, sleeves put in back to front. Your mother said, "I can't sell them! It's slop trade. They went wrong at the making-up factory. They are past redemption."'

Miss Duffield tucked her handkerchief back up the wristband of her black dress, sniffed and said, 'I'll not find another job, but I have my pride. I want my wages.'

'Is there enough to pay you for this week. How much ...?'

'Twenty-five shillings. That's how much.'

Isobel went into the shop and opened the till. It was empty. She had six shillings in her purse and ten pounds in the bank, but she said, 'Please will you stay? I'll find the wages money.'

When Miss Duffield was in the shop Isobel took the duplicate bunch of keys and went upstairs to Mam's old bedroom, unlocked the cupboard and found the big metal cash box, black with red and gold lines around the handle on the lid. Mam never let anyone see inside the box, and Isobel was nervous as she carried it downstairs and set it upon the table.

On top was a chequebook and a bank passbook with a credit balance of £30. She scrutinised the transactions. Every week Mam paid in the mortgage money, and on the twelfth of every month drew out the payment. The bank book was not used for school fees. Nevertheless Isobel would write today to Miss Colclough and demand that the term's fees were repaid. That would bring in at least another £60. Even if her stepfather paid the fees she was not cheating. He should be paying the mortgage.

Under the bank passbook was another envelope, and inside it eight white five-pound notes. Another £40. Underneath the notes was her old birth certificate – without a father's name. Under that was a brown envelope addressed to 'Our Lil', containing two Chancellor Printworks share certificates each for a hundred pounds. Isobel stared. Why had Mam bought shares for her? Had Mr Chancellor got them for her at cost or cheap? Attached to the certificates were long sheets of tear-off slips. And at the bottom of the box was a school exercise book with 'Poems' written on in Mam's handwriting.

There were some Mam had copied out. Isobel had read them before: 'Little Jim', 'Over the Hill from the Poor House' and 'Praying for Shoes'. And there were Mam's own compositions, melodramatic in the way of the Victorians. But the one she read three times and which set up a host of questions in her mind was the one Mam had written to the man who must be her father:

Our Lil has eyes like yours, my love,
And sometimes, when she looks at me,
I touch your heart and feel the fire
Of love that she will never see.

Our Lil has hands like yours, my love,
And sometimes, when she touches me,
The memory of your loving arms
Disturbs my false serenity.

Our Lil, whose ways are yours, my love,
Has never once played false with me.
And my heart breaks to see her truth
And contemplate your treachery.

She read it again, hoping for some blinding flash of insight or revelation, but she was no wiser than before, though she had the oddest feeling that somehow the answer to all her questions was staring her in the face. She read the poem again, and again she looked at the bank book and the share certificates – and nothing came to her.

Frank faced his precious lass over the table. She had a determined look. 'What do you want to do, lass? When are you going back to school?'

'I'm going to stay in Macclesfield. Close to Mam,' she said.

He said, 'What about School Certificate?'

'I can't. Not now,' she said, apologising. 'My stepfather can't afford it.'

Frank understood that she would not want to seem disloyal. 'Listen, lass. I was in the same boat as you. No money to go on with my education.' He gave a sigh. 'I do some charity work. If you want to stay on and take your exams, I'll make sure the funds are raised.'

'I won't. Thank you. I don't want charity,' she said. She hesitated for a moment, then, 'I have to work. There's no other way. The shop's the only way to pay Mam's hospital bills. My stepfather isn't rich.'

Frank wanted to say that neither school expenses nor hospital bills were her worry, but he could not. 'I said, "What do you want?" not, "What do you think you must do?"'

She leaned her elbows on the table and said, 'My stepfather says the shop is his. I want responsibility. I owe him a duty.'

'You owe him nowt!' He saw shock in her eyes and realised that he'd said the wrong thing.

She went to the fireplace and took down a brown envelope. She drew out the certificates that he'd given to Elsie to make a little extra provision for his precious lass. 'What are these?'

He reached for them. His hand was shaking. 'They are bearer bonds.'

'Why did Mam buy them for me?'

He said, 'Bearer bonds are negotiable instruments. Property, ordinary shares would not come to you if she died. Your stepfather would have lifelong interest on any capital or property that your mother left to you.'

She said, 'How could these benefit me?'

'They are payable to the bearer. You can buy and sell bearer bonds without declaring ownership,' he said. 'Like paper money, they can be handed over. Except that their value fluctuates as the company does. Paper money is always worth its face value.'

'Then why would anyone buy bonds?'

'They are speculative. They're normally kept in a safe deposit at a bank. When dividends are declared the bank presents them for payment.' He pointed to the tear-off coupons. 'Your mother never cashed the last one. It's too late.' He tore it off, saying, 'Your mother has no head for money.'

'Mam is straight. She settles her bills every month.' She had a tight, determined expression on her face; one hand was clenched into a fist. She said, 'Will you buy them back? I need the money.'

'Not so fast, Isobel.' He'd better draw parallels with something she might more easily grasp. 'Our economy, like America's, is in recession. If Chancellor's goes under, the bonds won't be worth the paper they are printed on. Today they are worth less than face value. But as Chancellor's rises it could go on to the stock market. If it amalgamates with a bigger company or is bought out, your bonds will be worth a lot more. Things will change. Improve. Hold on to them.'

'I can't afford to speculate,' she said. 'How much? What are they worth on the open market?'

'Fifty pounds,' he said. 'Each.' He had to tell her that much of the truth, but she had gone very white, so he smiled and added, 'But not to me. I'll buy them back at face value if you'd rather have the money.'

She said, 'I'd rather. I want to look after the shop until Mam's better. The doctors say it could take months. I'll take over. Pay the rent if I can find the book. I think my stepfather took it.'

He took the bonds from her and then brought out his chequebook. She watched him make out a cheque for two hundred pounds. He handed it over to her and said, 'Put that in your own account. Not your mother's. Anything that's in your mother's account will be frozen until she's well.'

'My stepfather can't take this, can he?' She blinked hard, then said, in a rush, 'I don't want you to think I'm not grateful. I don't mean to be disloyal. But I have to pay Mam's hospital bills and everything.'

'It's your money,' he said.

'And if my stepfather holds the rent book?'

This at least was something he could control. 'It's my property. My business. Always was. It was a private arrangement.'

'What sort of arrangement?' She said it in a high-handed way. She was very like Elsie.

He put on his no-nonsense voice. 'An arrangement whereby Elsie paid ten shillings a week in rent – a lot less than the normal rent for a shop – and I paid the rates, the gas and the electricity. I also got your mother her materials at cost. She came to me when she needed help.'

'Then can I take over? Will you pass the business over to me, not my stepfather? I'll pay a proper rent and pay for my cloth.'

'You couldn't run a shop. Could you? You're too young.' He pondered for a few moments and saw that she was biting her lip, holding her breath as if her life depended upon it. 'But, no reason at all why you shouldn't have *charge* of a shop. You'd be working for yourself as far as the money goes. But you'd be working for me to all other intents and purposes. I was doing a man's work at your age. Keep Miss Duffield. A shop – a business – needs someone older than you out in front to be taken seriously.'

When he'd finished, her cheeks were bright pink and her eyes were dancing. 'The shop won't be my stepfather's?'

'No.' He grinned and put out his hand. 'Ten shillings a week in advance. I'll transfer the lease to you in your mother's absence.' He biffed her on the arm, laughed and said, 'I'll fetch a new rent book next week. When you want anything no matter what – material, or anything troubling you – you know where to find me.'

'You can do something,' she said. 'Send round a locksmith. I want to put a new lock on the shop and on a safekeeping cupboard.'

The locksmith's first job would be at Bollinbrook Road. He

could put one of those fancy Yale locks on her bedroom door. The shop locks could be done later.

Isobel was ready for the confrontation with her stepfather when he came back the following day. She said, 'I'm in charge of the shop.'

'Don't talk silly . . . !'

'Mr Chancellor has given it to me.'

He lost his temper. 'He can't override me. I'm the husband of the leaseholder. I'm your father. I have rights!'

'You have no rights. Not to me or the shop,' she said.

His eyebrows shot up. He had a disdainful look on his face. But at least he didn't flash his teeth at her or try to lay a finger on her. Isobel thought she had the upper hand.

But face-to-face confrontations with him and the real fear she had of him, the fear that lay behind her bravado, took their toll. She was uneasy when he was home; jumpy unless she knew exactly whereabouts in the house he was. It was a cat-and-mouse existence, though it appeared that she had put a stop to his advances. Every evening she went to visit Mam, and always she returned home despondent after sitting for an hour, chatting at Mam's bedside while Mam went off into a dream and occasionally looked at her as if she were a stranger. It was costing three pounds a week now for Mam to be treated in privacy. And they could not let her home yet because she had lost all interest in life. The doctors said, 'She will not co-operate. Your mother wants to die. She will not take part in anything. She won't get out of bed, or walk. We are afraid that if we send her home, without constant medical care she will neglect her treatment.'

As the weeks passed she and her stepfather began more and more to live separate lives, only speaking enough to acknowledge the other's presence. Isobel believed he had found bigger fish to fry. A huge effort was going into his appearance – visits to the barber, hair-oiling, new suits – and he continued his regular Monday-to-Thursday business trips.

At Lindow, on Sundays she answered Nanna's anxious 'Are you managing, lass?' with 'Everything is going beautifully,' when the truth was that the shop was bringing in only enough to pay the bills.

Nanna suggested that she gave up the shop and came to live at Lindow, but Isobel refused to leave the house. It was her house – hers and Mam's – and she would not leave it to her stepfather. She had a legal right to live there, and had it not been for her presence, she knew that her stepfather would first abandon and then sell it. He could not afford to run it and it was for her to work to pay the bills and do anything that was necessary to keep her property. But she was lonely. When she came home to a silent, empty house after a long day in the shop a great weight of loneliness came over her. She'd light a fire, tidy up, but always alert for the crunch of wheels on gravel, ready to run upstairs and lock herself in her room.

She lost her appetite and slept badly. And odd little jumping nerves started in her eyelids, at the corner of her mouth, at the back of her neck, so that if anyone spoke to her for more than a few seconds her head shuddered on her neck and she was afraid they would think she was mad.

She stopped writing to Ian, whose letters were full of his own progress. In a few months' time he would be a doctor. He wrote of Rowena, who had passed her nursing exams and now worked in their father's practice. In the face of all this advancement Isobel could not put pen to paper and write about her wasteland of a life. Nor could she put pen to paper and tell lies.

He wrote to ask why but she did not reply.

Their beloved King died at the beginning of the year. Now a popular new young King would soon be crowned, and the newspapers showed his smiling face, but Isobel knew that he had nothing to be happy about because the world was going wrong all about them. She became inward-looking, melancholy. At the piano, instead of playing 'Dancing With My Shadow' and the light romantic pieces she used to like, she played wistful music by Debussy and the ponderous slow movements from the Beethoven sonatas. Then she'd punish herself, playing scales for an hour.

Every day she listened to the one o'clock news on the radio in the living kitchen at the shop. 'This is the BBC news on Wednesday the fourteenth of October. The two hundred unemployed men of Jarrow who started their march to London ten days ago have reached . . .' and hearing these things, and seeing the dole queues and tales of suffering all around her, she told herself that beyond the confines of her life a harsher world existed. She was lucky to be able to earn her living and keep hold of the house. She told herself that she was ungrateful, but then she had never wanted any of it in the first place.

She was sensitive to everything. She saw Hitler on the cinema newsreels saluting and smiling, while at the same time the Jews in Germany had been deprived of their citizenship, their jobs and their pensions. Hitler was a fiend, and where once Isobel had thought it exaggerated, this time she knew it was true. Mr Chancellor told her that one of the town's dyeworks had been given a big government contract to dye cloth khaki. Soldiers wore khaki. They were heading for war.

Elsie dreaded seeing Howard. He expected her to have pulled herself together. He said so. 'Pull yourself together, woman,' he said, every time they were left alone in the private room that was costing him a fortune. 'We have to sell the house. I can't afford all this.' He made a sweep with his arm to indicate the world beyond the hospital. 'Everyone pities me. What can I say? That my wife would rather skulk in a hospital bed than take up her duties?'

She was ashamed of being such a liability to him – and ashamed that she now detested him without reason. He was working hard to keep the house, he told her. Isobel was running the shop and looking after him well, he said. He said that they were content without her, and certainly Isobel never voiced any contrary opinion. So she, Elsie, was perhaps giving in to base and selfish fears; afraid now that Howard had control of everything that she held dear. And try as she might, she could not shake off the dreadful lethargy, nor could she reason her way past the terrors that alternated with weariness. She was silent, frightened of everyone when she was awake, yet asleep she had dreams of violence; dreams of arming herself with the sharp kitchen knife, of stalking Howard, of stabbing him straight through the heart whilst he mocked her efforts to kill him until her limbs grew heavy and she sank to the ground, weeping, weeping until she awoke, lathered in sweat, with nurses around her, brisk and impatient. As now.

'Mrs Leigh! Come, come!' A sister pulled her up the bed

then said to Howard, 'What brought it on?'

Furious, Howard replied, 'I can't take any more of this. Tell the medical superintendent that my wife must be certified insane. She will go to the asylum. I will sign the necessary consent.'

'It is not quite that simple, Mr Leigh,' the sister said sharply. 'There has to be an independent signatory to certification.'

'Who, besides me and the doctor?'

'A justice of the peace. A magistrate.'

'Frank ...' Elsie wept. 'Frank won't let you put me away ...'

Chapter Twenty

Mam was not sent away to the asylum as her stepfather had threatened. She was sent home, and it was only right that she should go to Lindow, where Nanna could watch over her and nurse her back to health. Nanna wanted Isobel to live at Lindow with them, begged her to give up the lease of the shop, saying, 'Your mam will never want it back, lass.'

'But we need the money. I have to keep the house going,' Isobel answered. She was stubborn. She would not be diverted in her determination to hang on to the house. She need only remember her bookcase and the legacy and the fact that she or Mam had paid every penny of mortgage and deposit. But she was smarting underneath, because Mam ought to pull her weight instead of languishing at Lindow, being mothered by Nanna. Still, no matter how low she felt or how she despised Mam's spinelessness, Isobel would not budge. She would hold on to the house at all costs.

Sylvia and Magnus sometimes dropped in to see her at Lindow on a Sunday when they were at home, but Isobel never wavered in her decision not to accept invitations to Archerfield. Mrs Hammond had meant every word when she'd called Isobel brazen, 'exactly like her mother', and Isobel would not allow her to be rude about her or Mam ever again.

Once every fortnight she received a phone call from Ian. In spite of her cold-shouldering he continued to call her. Yet he was a complete stranger, someone she used to know long ago. He said that he wanted her to talk to him. He told her he understood that she was unhappy and worried about her mother. He said he had made enquiries and that Mam was suffering from a shock which had caused a temporary unreason known as melancholia. He assured her that Mam's faculties would return. He asked her to try, little by little, to look outside herself, not in. And he said he would not hold her to any promises she thought she had made to him. He did not say more than this, and from then on he talked about his work, the challenge of it, the long hours. He spoke now and again of sailing his boat or crewing for a friend. He told her about Rowena and about his beloved Edinburgh. But he never spoke a word of love.

Isobel thought of him not as a sweetheart, but as Magnus's cousin whom she did not expect to see again, and it was a surprise when, two hours after she arrived at Lindow on Christmas Eve, Ian came to the house.

Mam had gone early to bed when Isobel heard Ian talking to Nanna at the back door. To her dismay her heart hammered in her chest. Until now her feelings had been under control. She did not want them reawakened. Then when Nanna brought him into the living room and she saw him – so tall, darkly handsome and yet much older, remote and commanding – she was overcome with shyness. She felt as well a hideous embarrassment. She didn't want him to see her like this; thin and pale and drab. And her mouth would not be still and her head jerked as pangs of doubt and fear and inadequacy swept through her.

Ian had on a heavy overcoat, and when Nanna offered to take it, he refused, saying, 'We're having a get-together at Archerfield. I thought Isobel would be there. I want to take her for an hour or two, if you will allow . . .'

It was a particularly cold night and Nanna, standing close to the fire with a shawl about her shoulders, said, 'Get your coat on, lass.' And to Ian, 'Bring her back before ten o'clock.'

'Ready?' Ian came to her, smiled and put out a hand. 'You don't need to change. It's very informal. A family gathering. Music and singing. Mince pies and mulled wine round the tree. Come on!'

She knew they were going to have a party. They would all be dressed up and the talk would be clever and witty. The blue Delage had passed Lindow half an hour ago. But she had not been invited. She had seen Magnus only two days ago and he had not mentioned that Ian was coming for Christmas. Mrs Hammond certainly would not want her there. And Isobel was afraid of being alone with Ian. She couldn't go. But she was trembling, being so near to him. Even so, she stood back and heard her voice, rebuffing, saying, 'I don't want to go to Archerfield with you. Thank you.'

There was a dreadful, painful silence and if she had known how to do so she would have apologised, begged his pardon for her rudeness. If they had been close, as they had been nine months ago, she could have explained. But she stared somewhere to the left of his ear.

'Isobel?' he said in the warm voice that had suddenly lost its authority. 'Do you mean that?'

'Yes!' She made a hard little face to cover her wretchedness. It was her age, her circumstances, her inexperience, but it made her say what could not be unsaid. 'I can think of nothing worse than spending Christmas Eve with the Hammond family.'

Ian looked puzzled and hurt, and as realisation came burning into his eyes he said, 'Forgive me. I won't ask you again.'

He turned away from her to say to Nanna, 'I'm sorry. I misunderstood. When you told me this morning that Isobel would be here, I naturally thought she'd want to see me.'

He left. Isobel ran upstairs and cried herself to sleep.

Later, at Archerfield, with everyone seated round the fire, mellow with wine, and Ray returned to Macclesfield, Ian said quietly to Magnus, 'Isobel refused to come tonight. I didn't realise that she was so run down. Why didn't you tell me?'

'I did,' said Magnus. 'I thought I did . . .' and crossed his fingers. He would not act as go-between for Ian, who could easily get any girl in the world to fall for him.

Sylvia, in a long dress of green velvet, burst into happy laughter. 'Magnus would have liked Isobel to come. Silly Ian! He'd just love to get Isobel under the mistletoe. Wouldn't you, Magnus?'

They all laughed, and Magnus's face burned. He wanted to tell them to stop making sport of him. They saw him as a child, with childish impulses and no desires. One day he'd prove to them just what kind of a man he was. But he made his mouth into a stiff smile and said to Sylvia, 'You were enjoying yourself with Ray under the mistletoe!'

Ray had kissed Sylvia and Rowena. He had even given Mother a gleeful peck on the lips. But to Magnus's alarm. Ray's kiss with Sylvia was the one he'd lingered over. And afterwards it took all Magnus's ingenuity to keep them apart.

Rowena said, 'Well, I didn't enjoy mine. I'd have preferred another glass of wine! And I shall go down to Isobel's house on Boxing Day and tell her she didn't miss a thing.'

The wireless was on and Rowena asked them to be quiet because it was being announced that the Duke of York would be broadcasting the Christmas message to the nation tomorrow. He was shy, inward-looking, the opposite of his brother who had abdicated only two weeks ago. People had talked of little else since.

Rowena said, 'Can you turn it up a little? I want to hear the abdication speech again. They're playing it.' Ian obliged and soon they were all quiet, intent on the now familiar words of the young King who could not 'carry the heavy burden of state and discharge my duties as King, as *I* would wish to do, without the help and support of the woman I love'.

Rowena sighed at the end. 'What do you think, Sylvia?'

'I suppose he's doing the honourable thing, marrying Mrs Simpson. His grandfather had a wife for keeping the line going, mistresses for pleasure.' Sylvia looked at her uncle and avoided Magnus's eye as she spoke. 'What do you think, Uncle?'

'Och! He's been spoiled – wasted, we call it in Scotland. He's been given the earth. He's done nothing in return. He should have behaved himself. Set a good example.'

Rowena said, 'What would *you* have done, Ian?'

Ian said quietly, 'Duty first. I should put it behind me. "And I should find some girl perhaps . . . "'

Rowena said hotly, 'You wouldn't! Don't quote Rupert Brooke. He's my favourite poet!' She stood up in front of them all and said, 'I'm going to bed. To have a cry!'

Magnus used crutches, not the under-the-armpit ones that the men who'd had amputations used, but short-handled crutches a little thicker and stronger than walking sticks, for getting about on foot. But his life had changed since Father had bought him a motor car – and his freedom. Magnus could go wherever he wanted – and the place he wanted to visit most often was Isobel Leigh's, as the shop was known. His darling had gone into a decline since her grandfather died.

Magnus knew instinctively that if he stayed by her side, always there for her, one day she would turn to him, in gratitude if not in love, as he was. He always went on a pretext, and he always went at one o'clock, when Miss Duffield had gone home and Isobel was about to prepare a quick lunch. Often he took something to eat – hot pies or cold meat – and he'd bring samples of silk and say, 'I wondered if you'd like to see these swatches of silk, Isobel. If there's anything that takes your fancy, we can let you have some on sale-or-return.' He said, 'I'd like to show you round the mill some time.' And on the day she was to see round the mill, he went there at ten o'clock in the morning, saying, 'Are you sure? Do you really want to see over the mill?'

'You know I do.'

'Don't say anything to Mother.'

She stopped him with a lift of her hand. 'I never see your mother. But why should she be kept in the dark? There's nothing to hide . . .!' Then, seeing his hurt expression, 'You invited me, Magnus.'

'Sorry, dah-ling!' He made a face and laughed to disarm her. 'It's just that Mother says, "Why do you see her *every* day!" She thinks we're courting.'

'Whatever gave her that idea?'

She did not think it funny, and quickly he tried to pretend that it meant nothing. 'Me. I suppose.' He made an apologetic face. 'Coming here for lunch every day, instead of going home.'

'I don't give you the impression that we are courting, do I?'

'Oh! Mother would keep me in a glass case if she could.' He kept on smiling so she shouldn't take it seriously.

'You'll have to assert yourself one day,' she said, though she could not be cross with him for long, for he sang her praises without being too pressing, saying, 'I love coming to see you. You are such a dear, good-hearted girl.'

She said, 'Where do you get your ideas from, Magnus? If you knew how much ill-will I bear to some people . . . !'

'No you don't. You're speaking to Doreen again. And she's always been beastly to you. Why didn't you tell her to take a running jump?' Magnus said. 'I would.'

'For a hundred reasons. She's marrying my friend's brother. Her mother and mine were friends, and most of all I can't afford to make enemies.'

Recently Isobel had tried to exercise her will, forcing herself to stop dwelling on misfortunes. The vicar came to see her, to ask her to play the piano for Sunday School – and Isobel would hurry back from Lindow at two o'clock on Sundays, looking forward to the afternoons with the little children in Beech Lane School where the classes were held. After a few weeks of enjoyable Sundays she made a bit more effort at the shop.

Then, when she was just picking up, Doreen's wedding invitation arrived: *Doreen Millicent Grimshaw, to Cyril Ernest Anderson, at 12 noon on Saturday 3 April at the church of St Michael and All Angels. Reception afterwards at the Macclesfield Arms Hotel will be followed by a supper and dance at the Parish Hall*. Doreen wanted her to make the dress and going-away outfit. Her biggest order yet.

Isobel was grateful for Doreen's custom. She was slowly coming out of the depression. She was glad to see Magnus and talk to him because he always offered her encouragement and praise, saying things like, 'I've told Sylvia to come to you for her clothes. But she says you are her best friend, not her dressmaker.'

'I am. Her best friend. Sylvia and I made a pact, when we were babies. To share everything, for ever.' She laughed. 'Especially Nanna.'

Magnus laughed too, 'You don't know the latest. She's got a boyfriend.'

'Sylvia?' Isobel had seen Sylvia only last week. 'She never said.'

'It's top secret. But I have a feeling there'll be an announcement.'

'Really, Magnus? Who?'

'I don't know. Something's happened. I think it's someone she's met at these weekend gatherings. I don't go any more.'

'Don't you suspect?'

'No. I thought at one time she was going to get tangled up with someone unsuitable. I was worried.' He laughed. 'This time she's besotted. She's in Edinburgh for a month, pretending to play 'hard to get' so he'll miss her so much he'll fall to his knees as soon as she comes home.'

'She'll tell me when I see her,' Isobel said.

'She's spending a fortune on clothes,' Magnus went on. 'And they aren't a patch on your designs.' Then, wistfully, 'You are so clever! You made that beautiful wedding dress for Doreen.'

She had made them all, the wedding dress and Shandy's bridesmaid dress. Doreen's going-away outfits, two the same but in different colours, had been the very devil to make. Doreen had chosen striped silk and a dress pattern that had eight gores in the skirt. She had insisted on the gores being cut on the cross to produce chevrons from the stripes. It made Isobel dizzy matching stripes, making sure they all fell properly and the hems were level.

If only her biggest order had come from anyone else. Doreen was at her worst during her engagement. If she came for a fitting when Shandy was at the shop she was not so outspoken – dared not be, for she was marrying into the up-and-coming Anderson Bakery family – but when she and Isobel were alone she was wicked. While Isobel fitted and pinned, Doreen jabbered away, saying, 'Make it good. We're going to London for the honeymoon. Try that lace on the neck – no, not that! The other stuff.'

It was a real test, of both her skills and her self-control, making these clothes for Doreen, listening to her and getting satisfaction at seeing how well she looked in them. And putting up with Doreen's foul mouth, having to listen while she revealed such intimate details about Cyril and their courtship as would have made a navvy blush.

At her final fitting for the ankle-length wedding dress, that made her appear statuesque, a Greek goddess – for she had a marvellous figure – Doreen ruined the effect as soon as she opened her mouth.

'He's not very experienced. Poor Cyril. Doesn't get me worked up first!' She exploded with laughter, then looked sideways at Isobel. 'Don't suppose you know what I'm talking about, eh?'

'I get the gist of it, Doreen,' she said. 'I've not had any experience – but I know all about it.'

This delighted Doreen. 'I've had a lot of practice!' She pushed her lips out in the common-as-muck way she had and said, 'Ooh! I can't go long without it. It takes a lot to satisfy me. That's my trouble . . . !'

Isobel tried a weary expression, but such talk always upset her. 'Why *are* you marrying Cyril?' she asked. 'If you make fun of him for loving you?'

'"Fun of him for loving you"? Hark at you!' She had not dropped her taunting tricks. 'Prim little miss, aren't you?'

Isobel was going pink, as she always did when she made a fool of herself in front of Doreen. 'How else could I put it? I take it that's why you are marrying so young. Because you love Cyril?'

Doreen screeched with laughter and then kicked out with the toe of her shoe. 'Have you nearly done?'

Miss Duffield and her dressmaker niece were going to run the shop all day on the Saturday of Doreen's wedding. Mam was not well enough to go, and to Isobel's relief her stepfather refused his invitation on the grounds of being away that weekend. He had to go away to make his excuse valid; even he would not have dared show his face in Macclesfield when he'd refused the invitation. Isobel was going to have a weekend to herself.

It was going to be a 'right good do', Mr Grimshaw said. 'No expense spared for our Doreen.' And Doreen said that everybody who was anybody in the town had been invited. The Chancellors were going, as Doreen and her father were the printworks mainstays. Doreen was so needed at Chancellor's that she was going to continue working after she was married. It was very rare, even in Macclesfield, for a married woman who was not a mill-worker to stay in paid employment after she was married.

On the eve of the wedding, Isobel took round to Doreen's house the dresses and her present – a smart Ewbank carpet sweeper in polished wood with detachable handle and white rubber tyres.

'Doreen's at work. She's getting everything in her office up to date,' Mr Grimshaw said. 'How will Chancellor's manage without her for a week?'

'I expect you will miss her,' Isobel said with careful politeness.

Mrs Grimshaw said to her husband, 'We'll be a lot happier when tomorrow's over. Won't we, Bert?'

When Isobel awoke and saw the sun streaming into the bedroom, it occurred to her that she was in a happy mood and had been so for a week. Was she coming out of the depression? It was going to be a perfect day.

She ate breakfast and lit the gas geyser to heat the water for her bath. She hung her dress up in the bathroom and luxuriated in the hot water as she looked at it. She had made a slim-fitting mid-calf-length tailored dress in a dusky-pink, cream-embroidered Spot Angolaine – a new wool fabric. It had wide, padded shoulders with long, narrow sleeves and fine pleating that fanned out from just above the knee. To finish off the neckline she had made a cream-coloured berthe – a silk georgette scarf collar with double frills. She had used the same georgette to trim a cream hat of fine straw. She had new shoes; high-heeled and pink, with an instep strap and chisel-toes.

She dressed and brushed her hair until it shone and was soft enough to pin into a chignon. Then she used all her best stuff – *poudre* Mattever, Laleek Longlash, Natural Rose lipstick and My Sin scent. She rang for a taxi.

The church was half-full. Isobel was seated on the fourth row back, behind Mr Chancellor and Ray. Ray kept turning round to smile at her. And looking at him, standing so upright and clean – and in church – she wondered how anyone could ever think that Ray was a bounder.

Doreen came down the aisle on her father's arm, pale and veiled and mysterious. Cyril was a nervous heap until Doreen came to his side, and Mr Grimshaw was bright-eyed with pride and love. Doreen was his most treasured creation.

After the church came a whirl of photo-taking and laughing and shaking hands and sipping sherry, until at last Isobel found herself at the wedding feast table between Ray Chancellor and John Anderson, Shandy's big brother. Good manners made Isobel spend half the time in conversation with dull John Anderson and only half in the delight of listening to Ray

Chancellor's flirtations and witty comments.

'Isobel Leigh! You've grown up,' he said early on in the meal.

'I haven't. I've grown an inch taller. It makes me seem older,' she said.

'Mmmm! Don't look at me like that, Isobel. Your eyes are sending shivers down my spine,' he said.

This time she didn't object. Light-hearted banter and a handsome young man's flattery had been missing from her life. Champagne was poured into her glass every time she emptied it and Isobel, who had vowed as a child never to touch strong drink and become like Mam, forgot her childhood promises. 'Doreen looks lovely, doesn't she?' she said to Ray.

Ray grinned. 'Yes, amazing – if you'd seen her last night.'

'I went to her house, but she was working late,' Isobel said.

He chuckled. 'Doreen worked her hardest last night.'

'Her father said she was tying up the loose ends.'

He almost laughed out loud. His eyes sparkled. 'Oh Isobel!' he said. 'You are priceless. How long have you known Doreen?'

'All my life.' She drank the champagne down in one go.

With the speeches and toasts they drank more champagne, and afterwards came a whirl of meeting Shandy's relations and being flattered by Ray and Shandy's brothers' attentions. Then it was half past four and everyone trooped down to Hibel Road station to see Doreen and Cyril off on the five o'clock train to London.

Doreen looked splendid in the chevron-striped dress, which she wore with a blue coat and matching hat. Isobel had never seen her so elegant, though by this time Doreen was well on the way to being tipsy; effusive in her farewells, especially to the men. One or two of the older cousins were embarrassed at being kissed so hard in public on a station platform with everyone cheering Doreen on.

Ray was not embarrassed. He gave Doreen a great smacker until everyone called, 'that's enough!' and when they pulled apart there were cries of, 'Remember! You're a married woman!' to shrieks of raucous laughter. At any other time Isobel might have been embarrassed, but she was merry for the first time in her life – and the behaviour of everyone felt like uninhibited fun. She joined in the larking around with the rest and let herself be chased up the platform by Ray to shouts of encouragement from the others – until she fled into the ladies' waiting room to compose herself for the send-off.

She had sobered up, walking back to the Parish Hall, when Ray caught up with her and whispered, 'Do you *really* want to spend the evening jigging round a dusty hall?' He tucked her hand into his and said, 'I'd like to take you out to dinner. What d'you say?' And when she couldn't think of a reply. 'Meet me at the West Park gates in half an hour.' And he was gone, airily waving goodbye to everyone.

She reached the Parish Hall, but somehow the sparkle had gone. The more senior people, like Mr Chancellor and the Manchester Andersons, had already gone home. Fifty or so guests, waiting for the band to arrive, sat on the wooden benches that went round the dusty floor.

Shandy said, 'Isobel? Are you staying for the dance? I thought you'd be going to your grandmother's.'

The old rebellious impulse came over her; the going haywire feeling that had plagued her at school. 'No.' she said, 'I'm not staying for the dance. Nanna and Mam are expecting me. I don't like leaving, but ...' Then she was out and speeding down Cumberland Street, through the Infirmary grounds, out on to Prestbury Road past the workhouse, and running down to the park where Ray Chancellor stood, leaning against the gates.

He took her hand and they ran like escapees to where the Delage was parked. 'Into the back until we're out of town,' Ray said. Isobel dropped on to the back seat. Would her name be mud if anyone saw her in the Delage?

They were a mile out of town when Ray stopped the car and opened the door for her to come into the front. Then, when she was seated beside him, his eyes took in every little detail of her before he said in a different, softer voice, 'Isobel ... Isobel ...'

And before she could think of anything to say, he leaned over and kissed her full on the mouth, gently for a few seconds until she relaxed, then closer, his lips moving soft and warm and sweet-tasting on hers until she opened her mouth a little way. And something happened inside Isobel's head as all the pent-up passion that had been simmering under her frozen exterior – all the love and longing she'd put into the kisses with Ian – came spilling over. Her arms went up and wound around Ray's neck. She tasted the mouth that was hard and searching in hers and hot blood rushed to her head as her whole body sprang to eager life. His hands slid from her back to rest one on her waist and the other on the bosom that felt as if it wanted to break free from the camisole and the pink dress and know the touch of his hands.

They pulled apart.

'Phew! Isobel.' Ray was evidently delighted. His arm was about her shoulder and he leaned back against the driving seat with closed eyes.

She was breathing fast. She closed her eyes and rested her head against his arm and felt silky, warm sensations running over her skin. For Ray to have kissed her she must have been behaving provocatively without knowing she was 'asking for it'. But her face was wreathed in smiles, for all thoughts of Macclesfield – of the shop, of worries – were gone. She could think only of when, of if, he would kiss her again.

He gave a devilish smile. 'Full steam ahead?' Then he laughed at her for having no answer but the silly delight that wouldn't be wiped off her face. With one arm about her shoulder, his long fingers stroking her skin inside the georgette collar, he pressed the starter button.

Soon they were sailing down long, sweeping bends on the road to Alderley Edge, seeing ploughed fields behind hawthorn hedges. She was bursting with affection. She was eighteen and a bit and had spent too many long months alone. This was her first date and she wanted him to think her sophisticated, not the gauche girl she was. She said, in an uppity voice, 'Where are we dining tonight, Ray?'

'The de Trafford Arms at Alderley,' he said. 'That all right, your ladyship?'

'Did you ring and reserve a table?' Isobel knew that she was behaving provocatively again, because his hand kept straying back from the gear lever to her neck and her knees, and though his slightest touch set her skin on fire, she pretended that nothing was happening. She felt elegant and bold.

Ray said, 'I have a standing reservation. I dine here every Saturday.'

She thought about the other time she had been out for dinner and said, 'The last time I dined out was at the Palace Hotel in Southport. Will we be dancing tonight?'

He put his hands back on the wheel because the road was full of bends. 'No,' he said. 'Just you and me. Good food. Good wines. A night of promise.'

Isobel looked at the countryside and kept her nose in the air when they passed anyone on foot. Perhaps it was because of the champagne that she didn't care if the whole world saw her, sitting next to Ray Chancellor, bold and brazen, looking down her nose at everyone. But there were no poor people, no doley shops in those few miles. There were beautiful country houses with rose gardens and pony paddocks behind high hedges, and nobody to see them sailing by.

Soon they were speeding down the long hill that led to the village and pulling up in front of a black and white and red-brick half-timbered old hostelry, the de Trafford Arms.

They were shown to a little alcove, where a table was set apart from the other diners. Lighted red candles flickered over the table where a bottle of champagne rested in a bucket of crushed ice. And as soon as they were seated and left with the menus, for the first time in her life, Isobel realised, her appetite had gone. She said, 'I can't eat a thing.'

Ray reached for her hands across the table. It was like being in a film, where the handsome hero says, 'Darling ... you know ... you know that I ...?' Ray said, 'I'll order. Relax and enjoy it. We have the night ahead of us.'

He taught her how to swallow oysters, downing them with the champagne – while he touched her knee under the table. They ate filet de boeuf and drank claret while Ray made kissing mouths at her and held her glance until she could barely swallow. And all the time he was saying, 'Those smouldering eyes, Isobel. Did I say they send shivers up and down my spine?'

It was exciting, seeing the effect her 'smouldering eyes' had upon him. Isobel kept looking at him when he told her not to, because she loved the warm, churning feeling that stirred in the pit of her stomach when his own greeny-grey eyes smouldered into hers. She tipped her head, laughing a little, letting the champagne from the second bottle slide easily down with the ice cream and brandy peaches. But after the coffee and cognac all she wanted was to melt in his arms and be kissed again and again.

They went out into the dark, velvet spring night scented with fully blown leaves that were spread like a leafy canopy over the silent, empty road home. And all the time Isobel was willing him to stop and take her in his arms and kiss her. She leaned back, anticipation tightening in her, eyes closed while his hand fingered her hair and throat and slid lightly inside the neckline of her dress to where her full breasts were firming for him. She waited, trembling, for more.

He didn't speak until they reached Bollinbrook Road and came to a crunching halt in front of the garage. The house was in darkness, Isobel faced him and put her arms up.

'Not here.' He sounded annoyed. 'Let's go inside.'

'No. We can't do that!' she said. It was wrong to be alone in a house with a man. He'd know it was wrong. A shiver ran, cooling, over her. She reached for her bag and searched for her keys. But her fingertips had lost all sensation. The keys were not there. She said, 'My fingers and my brain don't seem to be doing things together ...'

He put out his hand. 'Here. I'll find them.'

He found the keys and he held her hand to help her from the car. But her knees were weak. And the champagne that she thought had not affected her all day, in the colder air outside the car suddenly made her head so light that she lost her balance. 'You've had too much to drink,' he said. 'I'll help you in.' And he half carried her to the front door, where she fell against him heavily while he put the key in the lock.

The door closed behind them and Isobel leaned back to steady herself. She could not grasp, keep hold of any thought, while all the time questions and possibilities were crowding into her mind. Had she crossed a threshold that was not just the front doorstep? A minute ago she could have said 'Enough!' Now she had no strength.

She was holding on to his shoulders in case she fell over. Her breath was hot and shallow and her knees were like jelly. Here, in the hallway, her back to the front door, she was letting him push her arms down, letting him unbutton the front of her dress, undo the ties of her camisole and expose her full, milky-white breasts. She had no strength to stop him from dragging down the bodice of her dress, nor could she speak when his open mouth fastened on to one side of her while his free hand teased the other breast. Her head was dizzy. She was faint, but tantalising sensations were tangling between his sucking mouth, caressing fingers and a place deep inside her. She was swooning, faint from the champagne or the pleasure; she was moaning and giving at the knees. And her hips were pushing towards him as he slid his arms under her legs and carried her, easily, up the stairs.

He kicked open the door to Mam's bedroom, carried her to the bed without stopping to put on the light, pushed away the eiderdown with his elbow and dropped her down on to the sheets. And all the time, somewhere at the back of her dizzy mind, came the warning that she was behaving like a trollop. But he was strong and he was searching for her mouth, making hard kisses that set her on fire, made her melt and run liquid fire inside.

'Isobel . . . ?'

'Yes.'

'You know what's going to happen, don't you?'

She tried to get up but he held her down with one hand while he pulled the pins out of her hair, throwing them on to the floor, literally letting her dark hair down until it fanned out all over the pillow. Then he kissed her again, long and hard until, head spinning, she almost fainted. His hands were stroking her neck and her breasts and before she could catch up with what was happening he was ripping her clothes away, throwing them to the floor until all but her silk stockings were gone. She lay back in the darkness, quaking but stilled in suspense, immobilised, her iron will gone, the room spinning around her whirling head if she tried to close her eyes . . .

He was taking off his clothes. It took seconds before he said, 'Look!'

In the silvery-white moonlight she saw his raw aggressiveness standing over her – a tall, strong, big man, aroused. She had never seen a naked man before. And now she was afraid, for there was nothing of love or gentleness in Ray. But it was too late to go back to how she was half an hour ago, because her limbs were as weak as her will – and fright was mixed up with sick excitement and a new hunger that was burning through her.

She whispered, 'Don't ... don't let me. Don't do anything ... I don't want to ...' but he was lowering himself on to her and pushing her hips down to hold her, spreading her legs wide. He was making grunting noises, coming closer, and his mouth was on hers and his big hands were holding fast on to her breasts.

'I can't give you a baby, Isobel. I'm wearing a ...'

She didn't want to know. And she could not stop him, for his mouth was on hers again and now his fingers were sliding inside her and moving in a way that made her make a strange noise in the back of her throat. He forced his fingers wide, stretching inside her, hurting her. He stopped kissing her then, and leaned back a little and looked into her barely focused eyes, and in a low, husky voice he said, 'This is going to hurt. It always does, the first time.'

'Stop, please ... Please. Stop! Don't ...!' she said. She wanted to cry out loud but his hands were holding on to her hair and a great heaviness was on her and every nerve in her body was stretched against the quick, sharp pain as he drove fast and hard inside her.

Isobel felt him slide tight inside, filling her, and the pain was gone and only strength and a pushing higher into her was happening. Then came weakness with unbearable tension until he moved faster. And she heard herself calling out, over and over, 'Oh, no ... Oh, no ... Please stop ...' until, just before she cried out again, he stopped, held back and looked into her eyes as if he were asking did she want him to go on. But he did not stop. Suddenly he made the grunting sound louder than before and toughly he forced her knees up wide about his muscular hips before he threw back his head and thrust himself, hurting her, hard, fast and deep until she cried out. Then it was too late to stop him, for it was all going so fast ... so fast. He was taking her into that breaking, pulsing need that brought her, crying out with the force of it, into and over the edge of a pleasure that was all mixed up with pain, and Isobel was holding on to him for dear life until, deep inside, a grasping, desperate passion was spending itself in wave upon agonising wave.

Then it was over and she was subsiding down into nightmares of violent pleasure and pain and bitterness and acid rising into her mouth and a dread of waking into the reality of tomorrow.

Chapter Twenty-One

She woke up on top of her own bed – naked, alone and cold. She pulled the eiderdown about herself and sat up, wide awake as realisation dawned and last night came flooding back.

She must have dreamed it – surely she had dreamed it – that Ray had done it again and again, and made her do all those things – made her kneel down while behind her he . . . Oh, no! they had behaved like beasts of the field. And surely she imagined that she'd let Ray out of the house at four am and waved to him with not a stitch of clothing on? Then, in her dream, she'd staggered back upstairs, been sick in the lavatory pan, lurched into her own bedroom and fallen on to the bed. Her head was splitting. She was shivering with cold. Her thighs were stuck together; sitting up was painful. Then it all came back, and this time she crawled under the covers, closed her eyes and tried not to think. It was 11.30 and she had two hours for sleep before she would get dressed and ready for Sunday School.

'Brightly gleams our banner, Pointing to the sky . . .' The children were singing at the tops of their lungs as Isobel hammered away at the keys, feet pedalling like a pianola player. She looked at the innocent little faces all around her and prayed, not as they were for a 'home on high', but for Ray Chancellor to come to her. She wanted him to say that it was all right – he wanted to marry her, she had not behaved like a trollop. 'Dear God,' she prayed, 'let him ring tonight.'

When the children went home the teachers and Isobel stayed behind to tidy away the crayons and chalks and the stencilled pictures of the mud huts and brown children of the African mission. She worked fast as thoughts of all she had to do came crowding in. She must clean the big bedroom, change the bed and put the soiled sheets in the laundry bag. She must have a bath. She went home fast, running past the cemetery and on flying feet into Bollinbrook Road – and she reached the gate just in time to see her stepfather closing the front door behind him.

For a full two minutes she stood, rooted to the spot in fear, while all the evasive actions she might take flashed into her mind. Could she persuade him to stay downstairs ...? She could dash up and ... With throbbing pulse and a sick sense of doom, Isobel went slowly to the front door and opened it.

He was coming down the stairs, in his hands the blood-stained, incriminating sheet. 'Go upstairs at once. Remove that disgusting ...' He leered. 'Dispose of your seducer's rubber accoutrement from my bedroom. Then tell me who it was you spent the night fornicating with – in my bed!'

She ran past him, crying, to the bedroom. A wave of nausea came over her as she picked up the knotted rubber thing Ray had used. She went to the bathroom, put it down the pan and pulled the chain, then ran the tap to scrub her hands and wash her face. The thing was there in the lavatory. She flushed it again and saw it come bobbing back to the surface.

Her stepfather was standing in the bathroom doorway, leaning against the jamb, one arm barring the way. 'I hope he did it only the once,' he sneered. 'Careless if you let him take his pleasure twice ...'

'Go away! Go away!' she begged. 'Please leave me alone.'

He stayed where he was. 'All that mess on the sheets makes me think he must have been very careless ...' he said. 'Who was the lucky fellow?'

She couldn't speak.

'Can I guess? Someone you picked up at the wedding?'

'Let me get past!' Isobel cried again, but as she went to the door he caught hold of her upper arm and held it in a pinching, bruising grip. 'You'll have something to cry for,' he jeered. 'You'll be crying for more! Once you have tasted the fruits of ...'

She screeched and swung her other arm over, but he

grabbed that one and, lifting her by the arms, carried her, kicking, to her room.

'You'll be looking forward to the next time. Is he coming again? Coming again tonight?' He was strong and he pushed her down on to the bed but did not let go of her arms. His face came down close to hers and Isobel caught the full blast of that bad-cheese breath as he said, 'I could have you put away, Isobel. That's what they do with naughty girls like you. Reformatories and correction houses ...' His face was very near and his spittle was dropping into her mouth as she struggled to breathe.

He said, 'Your daddy won't have you put away, not if you give him a kiss – a little bit of what you gave to ...' His mouth came down over hers as she heard the telephone ringing.

It was ringing when she bit him and brought her knees up and kicked out with both feet, sending him reeling backwards, out of the door, to crash into the banister rail. It was ringing when she flew across the room to bang the door to and let down the brass snib to make sure she was safe. Then she leaned against the door, faint and sick, as she heard him speaking.

'Who's that?'

The caller spoke and her stepfather said, 'Ray Chancellor indeed! So you're the lucky fellow who's ...'

There was another pause before Isobel heard, 'No, you may not speak to Isobel.' Again a few moments of quiet while he listened to Ray, before, his voice rising with every word, he said, 'Don't come near this house again! There's a law against entering a house without permission!' He listened again, then, 'Not worth all the damn bother? Who's not worth all your damn bother? I'll sue! You'll rue the day ...'

Ray must have put the phone down. Isobel heard the hiss of fury as her stepfather banged down the receiver. Then she heard the front door slam, heard an engine starting up and crunching tyres on the gravel. Would he go to the Chancellors and confront Ray and his father? Crying, she ran downstairs, dialled the operator and asked for Ray's number. The operator answered. 'The line is engaged. Shall I try again? who is calling, please ...?'

All this had taken minutes – precious minutes – but during

them Isobel forced herself to quieten. Self-preservation, or the iron in her soul, was coming to the surface. Slowly, she put the receiver down. She could not speak to Ray about such things. He must be the one who came to her aid, not the other way round. She went back towards the stairs. Ray Chancellor was big enough to take care of himself.

Her stepfather had gone away. Isobel knew that he was not ashamed of himself but rather he was afraid she would tell Mam and Nanna. Then, less than a week later, a letter came from him, addressed to her at the shop and delivered by hand.

> Dear Isobel
> After all I have suffered at the hands of the Stanways you cannot expect me to say that I am sorry about the break-up of the family.
>
> I have left Macclesfield for good and have returned to live in Southport where, as you have always known, I have a large house. However, I have sunk a considerable amount into the Bollinbrook Road property and I do not intend to maintain two establishments. I cannot continue to provide a home for you and your mother.
>
> I expect that you and she will return to live in Jordangate. I intend to sell the Bollinbook Road house soon and I ask you to remove any small items of personal property from the house. The furniture, linen and silver are mine.

Isobel packed all her stepfather's clothes, then dragged out into the garage his sideboard and dining table, and on top she put the silver and his case. She nailed a notice to the garage door: *Mr Howard Leigh. Your belongings are inside the garage, waiting for collection*. Then she had the locks changed again and went to see a lawyer, who said that as long as she had possession, her stepfather could not turn her out.

Darling Nanna cried when Mam received the same letter from Howard and took to her bed for a week. But Isobel could not join them in tears over Willey-Leigh. In the space of a year Nanna had lost her husband and, almost, her daughter. Isobel was all she had left. And Isobel . . . ?

It was eight days since the night of debauchery, and it had

taken all that time for her silly brain to accept the truth, that Ray Chancellor had no further use for her. They were eight days of shame when she asked herself, had she lost all sense? All her pride? She had resorted to subterfuge, altering her voice if his father answered the telephone when she asked to speak to Ray; pretending to herself that all she wanted was a chance to explain that the threats her stepfather had made were idle. Ray had prevaricated at first, then finally he had made excuses not to see her.

She had been used, abused. And cast aside.

Isobel stood at the shop counter, counting the morning's takings before locking up for half-day closing. It was the Wednesday of their May Fair week and all the mills had closed on Monday, when excursions by train left for Blackpool, Rhyl and Southport. Isobel had been to Southport yesterday.

She had stopped asking, 'Have you given up your pride?' weeks ago – her pride was not a consideration any more. She had not had a period since the fifteenth of March and she had barely been able to swallow solid food since the day of Doreen's wedding. Nausea washed over her as she thought about it. She clutched on to the counter until it passed, closed her eyes and waited for the going-down-in-lift sensation that would follow.

Ray must see her. She had telephoned his house yesterday and the housekeeper said she would pass the message on. If Ray's call did not come this evening she would see his father and tell all. Mr Chancellor had said, 'When you want anything ...' She would throw herself on his mercy. Pregnancy could not be put out of her mind.

Through the back door of the shop she heard the lunchtime news: 'Thirty thousand London bus workers have started their strike ...' She barely listened. She was looking out for Magnus, who wanted to take her to the fair in the afternoon.

Two pounds, seventeen shillings and eightpence was all she had taken. She might just as well close for the rest of the week. She wrote the amount in her cash book, slammed the drawer and locked it. Then she went into the kitchen and switched the radio off. She bolted the back door and turned the great iron key, and as she did so she caught sight of herself in the little cracked mirror that hung over the sink. She was pale. She was thin. There were dark shadows under her eyes. Her nose and cheeks were pinched. She shivered and patted her face to bring blood to the surface. But it was no use. Ice was growing in her heart, growing into a hard little stone. She went back into the kitchen and dropped down on to the chair by the unlit range, and went over and over again in her head the awfulness of the last two days.

On Monday, May Fair Monday and the shop closed for the day, she had slept in at Lindow until half past ten, something she never did, and so as not to alert Nanna to anything unusual, she suggested they go for a long walk in the afternoon while Mam had a nap. It was one of those deep, sunny days when Nanna's legs were at their most supple. The air was soft and still and the mellow colours of the hills fooled them into going a long distance before they turned back. They walked miles until they came to a country café where they stopped for tea, sharing a trestle table with a crowd of hikers. Then they walked home along the low road, and it was then that Nanna referred to her lie-a-bed. She said, 'It's not like you to get up late.'

'I was tired.'

Nanna said, 'It's too much for you. The shop. The house.'

'Mam's in no state to go back, though,' Isobel said. 'I wish she'd pull herself together. She's fretting, ashamed and disgraced. She can't face everyone in Macclesfield.'

Nanna lifted her hand to stop her from saying more. 'First things first, lass. You'll get up early tomorrow to get to Southport in time. Remember what you've to say to Howard Leigh?'

'I'm to ask how much he wants for the house,' Isobel said. 'And how much he'll reduce the price to, for a quick sale.' She saw Nanna's determined face and added, 'Are you sure you want to do it, Nanna?'

Nanna strode out firmly and her face showed no trace of doubt. 'Your grandpa was a careful man. What are savings for, anyroad? I allus wanted a house. I might come and live with you and your mam in Macclesfield. It's not a big decision. There would be no need for you to work.'

*

Isobel got up early the next day to catch the 8.30 train to Manchester, and there, in the post office in Piccadilly, she sent a telegram to her stepfather: *Coming to discuss house sale today 2 p.m. Isobel.* When that was done she went by tram down Oxford Street to Exchange station, where she caught the 10.30 to Southport so that it was noon when she arrived.

Leaving Chapel Street station Isobel cut through the Cambridge Arcade on to Lord Street, and her spirits lifted a little as she walked in the sunshine down that wide, tree-lined street where shoppers strolled under flower-decked glass canopies that shaded the shop fronts. She wore a grey linen dress relieved by a wide blue belt and blue hat, and she tried to use her will and not think of the frightening prospect of pregnancy. She stared at the beautiful displays in the fashion house windows. There were long, cross-cut summer dresses, and lightweight coats with fancy linings that matched hats and skirts in the fashionable shades of maroon and eau-de-Nil. She tried to absorb the detail and not to dwell on what faced her – being forced into marriage with Ray, shame and more disgrace brought to Mam and Nanna.

Afterwards she walked back along the other side of Lord Street, under trees beside the newly dug gardens with their pungent earthy scent. She felt better for the walk. Perhaps she wasn't pregnant. She hadn't fainted or been sick this morning. Was it true, not an old wives' tale, that you could miss your period because of fright? On a wave of hope she went into the Kardomah and bought herself a pot of coffee and a plate of biscuits.

At two o'clock she arrived at the Cambridge Road house where her stepfather's Lanchester was parked in the drive. He must have been watching out for her, because seconds after she rapped on the great oak door he opened it. 'Come in, dear,' he said, and made to peck her cheek.

Isobel side-stepped him. 'I'm not here on a social call.'

'Follow me.' He went into a wide tiled hall that had five great polished doors with pilasters and pediments. The place had a seedy air. There were no pictures, no curtains at the high stained-glass windows. A threadbare carpet was laid on the splendid oak staircase. Her stepfather had gone down the hallway and was standing, holding open a door at the end of this corridor. And then Isobel noticed that all the doors had little nameplates, and realised that of course the house had been divided into flats.

He took her into a big room where three large windows overlooked a neglected garden. The room was crammed with furniture – a bed, dresser, table, chairs, wardrobe – all placed, as men place furniture, about the walls of the room, leaving only a small space in the centre. There were no plants; the pictures hanging with deadly symmetry from the rail were of ships and maps. No feminine hand or eye had been at work in this room.

'So this is your mansion?' Isobel said. 'Do you own the whole place? Do you get the rents?'

'Yes. But the maintenance costs, my dear ... I should sell if ...'

She didn't believe a word he said, and she was not afraid of him any longer. He was an imposter. He had no money, no big house and she had no interest in his life of pretence and deceit. 'Nanna wants to buy our house. How much do you want for it?'

He had a far-away, calculating air. 'It's worth at least five hundred and fifty pounds.'

'We can only give you three hundred,' Isobel said.

'I was offered five hundred for it yesterday.'

'With me in possession? I'm not leaving.'

He said, 'I could force you to go.'

'I've seen a lawyer,' Isobel said. 'You can do nothing. Mam put in all but one hundred pounds to buy the house. It is four-fifths ours. Three hundred pounds for your share is a lot more than you deserve.'

Now he gave the supercilious look that came so readily. 'You can tell your mother,' he said, 'that I want a divorce. I will give her grounds. Then I will accept four hundred pounds for the house.'

Mam cried every day because she thought she had lost face in Macclesfield. She believed that people were gossiping, asking why she and her husband did not live together. Now he was prepared to make an outcast of her. Isobel's insides were churning but she gave a look of icy contempt. 'You are prepared to shame my mother for the price of the house? You disgust me. You are the most contemptible creature on God's earth. I never want to see you again.'

She made her way back to the station slowly. Her train did not leave for an hour, and as she walked she tried to make sense of it all. She walked the whole length of the promenade on the landward side, passing the hotels, the Victoria Baths and the Promenade Hospital. Then she crossed over to the seaward side, stopping now and again to gaze over the sands, the Floral Hall Gardens and the lake. And standing there in the sunshine, on a day when everything was going wrong, she made a silent little prayer and a promise. If she were not pregnant – if it were only imagination and fear that had stopped her periods – then she would work harder, save more money, sell her piano, anything, anything to keep the house for herself and Mam. She would ask Mr Chancellor if she might help him in his charity work – anything. Anything, she prayed, only, 'Please God, make the period come soon. Please God, don't let me be pregnant.' She crossed over to the pier entrance and walked by the flowerbeds, and then she stopped, more from habit than curiosity, at one of the snapper's booths to look at the photographs.

Her insides did a somersault. There, in the centre of the window, was a photograph of Ray Chancellor – with his arm wrapped about Doreen's waist. They were walking down the promenade, oblivious of the camera, of everyone, their heads together, like lovers. There was no mistake. It was Doreen – Doreen wearing the very chevron-striped dress Isobel had made for her wedding. It had been taken on Monday, the mills' spring holiday.

She went to the nearest bench and sat down. Then her insides did a somersault again – and this time she had to run for the hedge behind her and was horribly, violently sick. This was not sickness such as she got when she had a fever. Her insides were rising up, throwing up everything she had eaten today. She was shaking and cold when it stopped. There was an iron drinking fountain nearby and she managed to get to it and rinse her handkerchief in the cold water before she could bend her knees to drink and take away the bitter bile that was burning her mouth. Then she dropped on to the bench again and wiped her face and wrists to stop herself from shaking. She had to control herself. She concentrated harder than she ever had in her life before. Face it, Lil! she kept saying to herself. Come on, Lil! as if it were only through her old name that she could summon up her iron will. Your mam faced it. What's coming to you won't pass you by! It's how you fettle it that matters!

After a few minutes she had steeled herself. That iron will – the stubborn streak, whatever it was – had returned, and Isobel went into the kiosk and asked to buy the photograph.

'My cousin,' she explained as bold as brass. 'She didn't have the time to collect them yesterday.' She paid the exorbitant price of three shillings and sixpence for the three photographs, and tucked them into her handbag.

Magnus was outside, blowing the horn, so Isobel locked the shop and went out on to Jordangate. Magnus poked his head out of the side window. 'Ready? Hop in.'

Magnus made heavy weather of driving. He snatched the gear lever and made the car leap forward. 'We're meeting Sylvia at the fair,' he said. Then, because she looked indifferent, 'You want to go, don't you?'

'Yes.' The fair would be a way of filling in the hours until she could go home to Bollinbrook Road and ring Ray in a last-ditch attempt to get him to speak to her. If he would not see her, she would call on Mr Chancellor and tell him what had happened.

Magnus steered down Hibel Road then along Gas Road, past the swingboats, rifle ranges and coconut shies that were strung out under the railway bridge to the Waters where the big rides and booths were. 'You're a bit peaky. I thought you'd be all agog!'

'Why should I be?'

'You haven't seen Sylvia for ages. She's dying to tell you her news.' He steered past the big Hobbyhorse ride in the Waters and nosed uphill, coming to rest at the kerbside in Queen Victoria Street.

Isobel didn't dare speak until he was safely parked – he always told her to keep quiet while he made his parking manoeuvres, in case he hit the kerb – so she waited until he pulled on the brake. 'What news?'

'Haven't the foggiest. It's all a great mystery. You know Sylvia.' He smiled in relief, having parked the car safely. He reached over into the back of the Riley for his sticks. 'Help me, will you?'

Isobel got out and was enveloped – eyes, nose and ears – by the sights, smells and sounds of the fair. The shouts of gypsy men and vendors were all mixed up with dozens of clashing musical tunes from hurdy-gurdies and mechanical steam organs. She took Magnus's crutches round to his side and helped him on to his feet to totter down the cobbled hill towards the bottom market and the fair rides.

'Take my arm,' she said. He would not, and Isobel admired him for the heroic effort it must be to go to work every day in such pain – and thought how unfair it was that Magnus, whose disability made him appear weak and dependent on others, should have such devotion in him when Ray, with all the advantages life could offer, had none.

The air thickened with the aroma of fried potatoes and waffles and the hot oil of the engines. All ranks of society crowded into the fair: respectable clerks, their wives and children, dirty children tugging at the skirts of dowdy women, squealing adolescents attracting attention to themselves, and ruddy-faced farmers' lads from Wildboarclough and Gawsworth. Older men sized themselves up against the fighters in front of the boxers' booths.

Magnus wouldn't be able to go on the rides but he made a great hirpling dash for the big games. There was a new game, lit up with electric bulbs and powered by a noisy generator that stood behind the tents of the freak shows. It was a big booth where a round board counter surrounded a mountain of prizes that were stacked nearly to the canvas roof. Between the prizes and the counter a gypsy man circled, taking money and handing out slips of paper, calling, 'A winner every time! The Wheel of Fortune!' under a great revolving drum that was covered in back-lit mirrors. A ring of players had gathered and Magnus edged in. The drum had ten facets, on which, three deep, were the names of towns.

'Which town do you want?' Magnus shouted above the noise.

'Coventry!' Isobel chose it from the few that were not yet lit up. Magnus paid over his shilling and she said, 'It's a lot of money, Magnus! The odds are low. There's twenty-nine people playing against us.'

Magnus was beside himself with excitement. He'd have bought every ticket if he'd been allowed to. 'Look at the prizes! What will you choose?'

The lights flicked from town to town as the drum revolved: Coventry – Bath – Glasgow had clacked and clicked by as Isobel studied the great bank of prizes – dolls with celluloid faces, ugly plaster dogs and enormous brown-glazed plant pots. Magnus's excitement was catching. Isobel had forgotten her worries for the moment. Dangling from thick elastic were furry monkeys with glass eyes. There were velvet cushions wrapped in cellophane. But at the back, on the top shelf, was a small table lamp with a china crinoline lady for a base. She'd choose that if they won. The drum was turning faster, noisily whirring in such a dizzying flash of lights she could no longer read the names.

Magnus, when he stood, transferred both crutch handles to his left hand to leave his right free. He clenched and unclenched his right hand fast as if he had a fortune invested. His face was pink, his blond hair had a life of its own, falling softly over his eye and yet standing up at the back of his head. The drum was slowing. The lighted names were coming round to their side. It stopped. They sighed. It moved again: Birmingham – Manchester – Brighton and almost stopped. Then – Coventry – and it finally came to rest. Isobel shouted out, 'We've won!'

'What would the lady like?' called the gypsy man.

'The crinoline lady lamp, please.' She squeezed Magnus's hand gently as they waited for the man to get the prize down.

Magnus, beaming proudly, said, 'It's our lucky day.'

She had taken the lamp from the gypsy when a light touch fell on her shoulder. Isobel turned round. Then she froze as she saw the bright face of Sylvia who, dressed in a cream-coloured coat and a white hat, was holding tight on to the arm of Ray Chancellor. Isobel's knee and elbow joints went to oil as her stomach tightened into a hard knot.

'Isobel. I wanted to tell you first!' Sylvia let go of Ray and put both arms out to her. She kissed Isobel's frozen face, then held her at arm's-length. Laughing and excited she prattled on, 'Ray and I are engaged ... We've been for the ring ... It's being altered so I can't show it ... on our way to Archerfield to tell Mama ... Ray's going to do all the formal stuff – asking Father for my hand. We'll invite all our friends to a party ... You'll come, won't you? Ray's going to speak to Father before we announce it ... I'm so thrilled ...'

Sylvia chattered eagerly while Ray pretended to be the fond lover, and every time Sylvia looked away from him, Ray watched Isobel's face intently, waiting for a sign that she might spoil his game. Isobel's face drained of blood but with a tremendous effort of will she made all the right noises, saying, 'What a surprise, Sylvia. I had no idea ...'

'I wasn't absolutely sure myself. Ray has been saying for years, "Sylvia Hammond is the only girl I'd dream of marrying!"' She switched those dazzling blue eyes on to Ray. 'I thought he'd never ask! I've been in love with him for absolutely ever, of course ...'

If she confronted Sylvia with the truth about Ray – if she opened her handbag and showed Sylvia the photographs of her betrothed, arm in arm with Doreen – would it make the slightest difference? Isobel could do nothing. She was rooted to the spot.

Ray took Sylvia's hand, lifted it to his lips and gave Isobel a knowing look as he said, 'The only person who won't be pleased, darling, is Magnus.' Magnus's face was taut. His knuckles were white where he gripped on to his crutches. 'Isn't that right, Magnus? You've been doing your best to keep us apart. We've had to do all our romancing in secret.' He kissed Sylvia's hand.

Sylvia's silvery laugh rang out and her eyes were shining with happiness as she said, 'You're delighted as well, aren't you, Magnus?'

Magnus's face was drawn and white. He said, 'I think you should speak to Father before you announce it.'

Ray shot a warning glance at Isobel and said, 'Don't say a word, any of you, until I've plucked up my courage. Gone down on my knees.' He put his head back and laughed as if it were all a great joke. 'I shall beg very humbly for his daughter's hand.'

Seeing him take it all so carelessly, ruthless seducer that he was, Isobel's knees buckled. She had a few seconds' presence of mind, when she shoved the china lamp at Magnus and said, 'Take it. I feel a bit . . .' before she slumped on to the dirty old cobblestones of the Waters at Magnus's feet.

Magnus cried out as she fell, 'Help her! For God's sake . . .' then they were all, all at once, alarmed. Ray pulled her up on to her feet and Sylvia touched her face, all concern, saying, 'Why, Isobel, you're as pale as death!'

Magnus was frightened, frightened for Isobel whose eyes were opening and closing again as if she were dizzy and her world was spinning. He said, 'Hold on to her. I'll get the car and take her home. I'll get the doctor to her.' Then he went lurching on his sticks, twisted to one side with the lamp tucked under his armpit, through the crowd to get to the Riley. And every step was agony, hurrying up the hill, his ankles jerking and turning on the cobbles. What was he to do? He'd not known that Sylvia and Ray were having a secret courtship. What could he do?

He reached the Riley, put the lamp in the back and took out a rug for Isobel. Then he opened the door wide as they half carried, half dragged his darling up the hill and lifted her into the passenger seat. Magnus could hear their voices as he pulled the car away from the kerb and headed uphill towards Mill Street. 'Take care of her!' Sylvia called. And Ray shouted, 'I'll call in tonight, Isobel . . . On my way home . . .'

Magnus glanced at her. Her eyes were open and she was blinking to get them back into focus. 'I'm all right, Magnus. I don't want to go home,' she said. 'Will you drive up into the hills? Let me get a breath of fresh air.'

Magnus saw his face in the driving mirror, tight with anxiety as he drove down the steep, cobbled Mill Street. He reached the wide square of Park Green before he could speak, then he pulled up. 'I can turn up Park Lane. Take you home to Lindow if you'd rather.' He could be at Archerfield before Ray and Sylvia got there. If he went now he could tell Father why Ray and Sylvia must not marry. He would have to tell Father the conclusion he'd drawn from the letter. The dreadful secret would be out. And what would Father say? He would think him a traitorous son.

He looked at his darling again. Her eyes were closed and the lashes were wet. She said, with a great effort, 'Please – drive out of town and find somewhere quiet. I've something to tell you.'

The Riley jumped forward again. 'We'll go to Wincle.'

She leaned her head back against the leather. They had been going for a few minutes before he saw that she was holding back tears that were brimming in her grey eyes. She said, 'Can you drive in a state of shock?'

They were climbing, pulling uphill towards Wincle, the local beauty spot, a hamlet high in the hills that had a clutch of stone cottages, farms and the ancient Ship Inn. Magnus had to concentrate on steering up the narrow, rough road. He could not look at her. 'How will you shock me, Isobel?' There was nothing she could do or say to shock him. He loved her so much. If she had murdered someone, he would hang for her.

Chapter Twenty-Two

Isobel felt her mouth pulling down at the corners, like a child who is trying not to cry. She closed her eyes and said in a miserable voice, 'I don't know if I've been raped. Or seduced. But I'm going to have a baby, Magnus.' She let the words hang in the air for a second or two. 'I don't want a baby. I wish it had never happened. Don't hate me. Help me, please.'

She didn't want to see the hurt and pain on Magnus's face, so she put her head back, hoping to hang on to her self-control. But now that she had told him, said the words she'd been frightened to say, a change was coming over her. The hopelessness she'd felt was slipping away. She was filling with sadness and a lonely understanding that she must never say those words again.

For she didn't mean it when she said 'I don't want a baby.' She had told Magnus of her trouble but in the very moment she spoke she knew that she wanted her baby. She had always wanted children. And if no man would marry a girl with a baby, then this might be the only child she would ever have. As she came to this realisation, slow, steady and silent came rolling tears under her closed eyelids, while at the same time she recognised a steely resolve that was hardening in her. She would see it through, just as Mam had. She didn't want any help from Ray Chancellor.

It had taken twenty minutes of driving on narrow, rough lanes where every turn in the road revealed a breathtaking vista of hills and meadows, but at last they had reached Wincle.

Magnus was silent. His fine-featured, sensitive face had an angry flush, his eyes were narrowed and his mouth was compressed in concentration. His bony hands on the wheel were white-knuckled and clumsy. She had shocked him, and angered him, but he didn't speak or look at her until he drove the Riley into the little flagged courtyard behind the Ship Inn.

He braked and switched the engine off. His eyes were full of pity as he leaned over and took her cold hand in his. 'Who's responsible, Isobel?'

Isobel said, very fast, 'I'll never tell! I wish I hadn't told you. It's my secret. And that's how it's going to be. Don't ask me who . . . !'

He drew in his breath. 'You asked me for help. You can keep the name of the father a secret. But you can't hide the fact that you're having a baby.'

She took her hand away and stared through the windscreen at the steep green hill behind the inn. 'Don't worry about me, Magnus. I'll survive. I come from a long line of determined women. There's nothing I can't do, if I set my mind to it.' The painful lump was still lodged in her throat but she meant every word. 'Nanna will stand by me.'

Magnus's eyes were full of tears. He whispered, 'Marry me . . . ?'

When she made no answer he said it louder. 'Marry me. You could always marry me.'

Love and hurt had made him offer. Isobel must be careful, so she said, very softly. 'I know you mean it, Magnus. And I don't want you to think I'm ungrateful. I don't want pity.' She couldn't bear to see him cry, so she looked down at her hands, folded in her lap. 'I wish I hadn't told you. But you're the only person I know who . . .'

'You don't love me? Not a little?'

Her throat was hurting from the effort to control herself, but she kept her gaze steady as she told him the truth. 'I do love you, Magnus. But I've never loved you in that way. The way a wife should love her husband.'

'I love you in that way.'

Her self-control was slipping, and yet she tried to be practical and sensible and honest and look him in the eyes while she said, 'I know you do. I've known for a long time. But if we married, I'd be cheating. You deserve better than that.'

She remained looking at him and helplessly heard the

throaty swallowing and saw tears come rolling down his thin cheeks, under the sharp jaw, dripping inside the hard white collar. Strange how she noticed every little detail, the solitude and silence all about them, the smell of the leather upholstery, the windscreen going cloudy, the river of warm tears sliding down Magnus's bony nose that was bright pink at the tip. Isobel fished her handkerchief out of her pocket and dabbed at his face, but he grabbed it and pulled away from her, swallowing fast to get a grip on himself, turning his face to the side window so that she shouldn't see his distress. Then, choking back tears, in a desolate voice he said, 'I can't live without you. I love you. It isn't pity. You are the love of my life. I'm no use for anything else but loving you.'

Her throat constricted hard and tight and her voice was breaking. All she could do was whisper, 'Magnus ... I'm sorry. You said, ages ago, that you wanted to be a good man. Do good things. You don't have to marry me ...'

He said, 'It's not just because you are having a baby. I'll tell everyone it is my baby. I've always been told I can't have children because of haemophilia. You'd be giving up everything if you'd marry me.'

Control had gone. Hot tears were streaming down her face. 'Ask me again ... Please.'

He still had not heard what she was saying. 'I've enough love for two. Couldn't you come to love me?'

'Look at me, Magnus! Yes, I'll marry you.'

He turned his face back from the window, saw her tears and reached out as she went into his arms and felt his thin, soft cheek wet against her own. And it was she who had to make the move to kiss him, because his eyes were blind with tears and he was trembling so violently as he tried to hold her to him. His soft mouth was hesitant and light and unpractised and he was shaking because he so wanted to do everything right.

And a fierce, protective love welled up in Isobel – a love that had nothing of physical passion in it, a love that made her want to make Magnus happy, made her want to be deserving of his great love and the sacrifice he was making for her.

They were crying and laughing and Isobel tried to be practical. 'We won't be allowed to marry. You are under twenty-one.

I'm eighteen. Your mother is afraid of losing you and I'd have to ask my stepfather.'

He slid his fingers under her jaw and lifted her face to look into his eyes. Behind his tears they were full of pride and love. He said, 'I don't care about anyone else in the world – not my mother, not my father. Only you. We won't ask. We'll elope tomorrow.'

Magnus planned it over bowls of chicken soup and plates of meat-and-potato pie in the Ship Inn. 'We'll run away to Scotland,' he said.

'Gretna Green?'

'Anywhere in Scotland as long as we can prove we're over sixteen.' He was like an excited child. 'Bring your birth certificate.'

The colour drained from Isobel's face again. Her spoon clattered into the soup plate. 'Do I have to?'

'What's the matter?'

The shame of her birth would have to be shared with Magnus. Her lips were numb as she pushed the bowl away and looked down at the checked tablecloth. 'You don't know everything, Magnus,' she said. 'You can change your mind if you don't want to marry me when I tell you this . . .' and then she told him, quickly, that her birth certificate was her adoption certificate, that her mother had never married. 'It has been the scourge of my life, Magnus. You can't imagine how it feels, to have no father.'

Every time he made to say something she lifted her hand to stop him, until the tale was told and she could look at him.

His eyes were shining as he reached for her hand. 'Don't apologise for your mother, Isobel. And I won't apologise for my father. I found something out about him. God knows what our parents got up to when they were young. Mine as well as yours.'

Magnus must have discovered the photographs of Mam. Isobel said quickly, 'Don't tell me, Magnus.'

'They all have a past. Your mother. My father.' He smiled. 'Now us.'

She said. 'It won't matter, when we're married.'

'You said it, "when we're married". I'm going to burst with

pride.'

Now they must get back to reality. Isobel said, 'How can you go missing?'

'I have a medical appointment in Edinburgh in the middle of next week. I'll say I haven't had a holiday for ages. I'll tell them that I'm going to stay with my uncle.'

'You can't expect your uncle to tell lies for you to his own sister.'

'We won't tell Uncle Mack. We'll stay in the North British Hotel on Princes Street. I'll ring Father from there. He'll think I'm at uncle's.' He put his hand over hers. 'Let's go into town and buy your rings.'

She must come down to earth again. 'What will I do about the shop?'

Magnus said, 'Will Miss Duffield look after it for a week while we elope? The shop is your mother's worry. Not yours.' He lifted her hand again and this time held fast. 'You can't go on working any longer.'

A little nerve started to pull at the corner of her mouth. 'How much will it all cost? Have you enough money?'

'I love your practical ways. I'll go to the bank and draw out enough cash. I haven't a lot of money – about four hundred pounds all told.' He smiled broadly, hugely pleased with himself. 'Can we live off my wages at present? I come into a trust next year, when I'm twenty-one – it should bring in about ten pounds a week at three per cent, less tax.'

'We can manage on much less,' she said. 'I've got a hundred pounds. We may have to live off our savings if you get the sack.'

For the journey Isobel wore a green linen dress and high-heeled shoes of tan leather. She appeared older and more sophisticated, but her nerves were jangling when she left Macclesfield for Manchester the next morning. Magnus, bold as brass, was going to ask his father to drive him to the station to catch the eight o'clock express to Manchester. Yesterday he had given her ten pounds to book first-class seats on the eleven o'clock Flying Scotsman. When she'd done this, and put her case on the train, she stood on the platform, waiting for him, sick with fright at what they were doing and afraid too that

Mam or Nanna might come looking for her and start a police hunt. Then she saw him, struggling along with his two sticks, red-faced, trying to keep up with the porter who strode ahead of him carrying two leather cases that were monogrammed MJH. Relief and love flooded through her as she ran to him and stood on tiptoe to kiss his cheek.

'Have you had to walk far?' She had to shout, there were so many people on the platform. 'No hitches?'

'Too far. I'm not used to it.' He was out of breath but he had a great silly smile on his face. 'Everything according to plan. Got your rings on?'

Isobel pulled off her glove and showed him her left hand, where a thin gold band shone new and bright under the antique opal and diamond ring he'd bought yesterday. Then she insisted that he took her arm and leaned on her to walk the last fifty yards to their carriage.

Six hours later the train drew in to Edinburgh's Waverley station, and they followed a porter into a lift behind the taxi rank on the station. The lift whisked them up to the hotel, where they trekked along miles of corridors and steps to the reception. Magnus booked them in as man and wife – before ordering afternoon tea to be sent up in half an hour.

The strain was starting to tell on Magnus. He was pale and there were deep shadows under his eyes when they reached their suite of rooms. There was a large marble bathroom, with a claw-footed bath that had brass taps and a showering contraption, and a huge heated towel rail in shiny chrome that was big enough to dry a week's washing. In the sitting room was a table, writing desk and three deep armchairs. Magnus dropped, fatigued, into one of the chairs and fell back, eyes closed.

Isobel followed the porter into the bedroom, which overlooked Waterloo Place and the enormous bronze statue of the Iron Duke on a rearing horse in front of Register House.

She unpacked, all the time wanting to pinch herself, to keep looking in the glass to be sure she really was here in a Scottish hotel bedroom. The high bed was made up with white starched linen. Would Magnus want to wait until they were legally man and wife before he took her to himself?

Magnus came in. 'The tea's just arrived,' he said.

'Did they ask for proof that we were married?'

'No.' It was an effort for him to speak. He was weary and drawn. Being strong and determined all day had taken its toll.

She said, 'All right?'

He got on to the bed and put his head back against the pillows. 'I'm tired. I have to rest.' It was five o'clock in the evening. His eyes were closed 'Come here. Give me a kiss. Then let me sleep for a couple of hours,' he said.

She was afraid for him now. 'What do they do at home, Magnus? If you get overtired?'

'Mother fusses,' he said. 'I only need rest . . .'

Isobel had a stab of fear as she kissed his cheek. He was asleep. What if harm came to him? His mother fussed, he said, but there was a need for fuss. She was strong and energetic and her sickness and fainting spells would pass. Soon she'd want to walk for miles. Magnus had no stamina.

He slept on while she untied his shoes and discovered that they were specially made. She saw his poor, twisted feet and deformed ankles. His feet were cold and she warmed them in her hands. Then she took his jacket off, unfastened the studs on his high starched collar and slipped off his shirt. She pulled off his trousers and left the woollen vests and long underpants on to keep his bony frame warm. Still he slept. She rolled him over, wrapped a warm pullover round those feet and pulled the covers and eiderdown over him. He was making contented, gruff little sounds as she did all this but he didn't open his eyes, or speak. When all was done Isobel went to the window to close the curtains before she tiptoed out of the room.

In the sitting room she sat at the window for half an hour, eating ham sandwiches and drinking tea, gazing out at the houses and tenements, churches and university all huddled and piled on a steep rocky crag – and the New Town that was fronted by the shops of Princes Street on her right. It was more beautiful than she had imagined it.

She went into the bedroom to check on him and found him sleeping soundly, his breathing deep and regular. Relief flooded through her. Sleep, good food and fresh air should do the trick. She tried to read but could not stop thinking about the shop and Mam and Nanna. She would send letters to them on the day she married Magnus. And it was on her mind the whole time that Ray Chancellor must be stopped before he wrecked the lives of any more girls. But who would believe her?

There was only one person she could tell – only one who would know she was telling the truth because she had nothing whatever to gain and everything to lose by opening her heart. She went to the desk, found pen and paper and began: *Dear Mr Chancellor* . . . She would post it with Mam's letter.

At nine o'clock she tried to wake Magnus, but he muttered, 'I'm so tired . . .' and fell asleep again. She stood at the window again, watching the sun go down behind the great grey castle on its purple rock high above the city. She prayed for Magnus, that he would be well and standing beside her tomorrow, and as she prayed the clouds went from white and pewter to molten gold and copper. The setting sun cast long shadows over the well of the gardens below. Lights were twinkling on the darkening hill while the sun's last rays flashed orange fire off the hundreds of windows on Princes Street.

The next morning her prayers were answered. Magnus was better. They went to the registry office and discovered that they could marry, by special licence, the day before Magnus's hospital appointment. And Magnus said, 'Don't worry, darling. I'll ring Father tonight. If you have been missed, he will have heard about it.'

'When will you tell your parents?' she asked.

'When we get home.'

'Won't you write. Or speak to your father on the telephone?'

'No,' he said. 'I know what I'm doing. Mother would try to stop me.'

That night Magnus made love to her. He was gentle and had been told, Isobel supposed, that a wife was usually slow to respond, so they spent hours embracing and kissing and whispering loving words before he decided that she was ready for him. He spent another ten minutes fiddling about with himself and then with her. She had to ask him to stop what was becoming an irritation because she wanted him to get on with it – get it over and done with. It was all over in seconds once the final act was commenced.

Magnus was very proud of himself. He kissed her warmly and patted her belly, saying, 'Mother was told by a specialist that I'd never be able to do this. And here I am! Married. And our baby growing in there,' as if he really were the father.

Afterwards, Isobel lay for an hour, unable to rest, glad that Magnus was pleased with her; wishing with all her heart that he *were* the father of her baby. And wishing that her first experience of lovemaking had been with her husband, on their wedding night; that she had never known the fiery need that Ian had aroused in her and that Ray had so callously satisfied.

But she made a promise to God, in her prayers that night, that she would not think about fires and passions. She was Magnus's wife. Theirs might not be a love match but she would repay Magnus a thousandfold for saving her child from the shame and disgrace of bastardy. Her child would grow up with a father who was a good, kind man.

When her prayers were said she felt better. After all, how big a part of marriage was it one spent loving and thinking of love? Five per cent? She would put her heart and soul into the other ninety-five per cent – the important things, the parts of marriage that mattered to her; a home, a child and a father for that child.

The seven days flew. They spent the weekday mornings in travelling by tram or train to fishing villages, where they'd walk for a little way along sedate sea fronts or stand on rocky headlands outside harbour walls, where high, powerful waves crashed and broke. But a quarter-mile walk in the breezy air on the coast was enough to tire Magnus, so they'd search for a café with seats by the window and over cups of coffee, pancakes and treacle scones would sit and talk about the young King's abdication last December or about the newly crowned King, his brother, the Duke of York. Then they would read *The Scotsman* and talk about the terrifying Adolf Hitler. They were like an old couple who had been married for years.

In the afternoons, while Magnus lay down, Isobel explored the city. She was entranced with Edinburgh, the city where you turned a corner and found unexpected spectacular views of hills and mountains and the wide sweep of the River Forth. She walked in the Old Town of tiny, old-fashioned shops and steep, cobbled and stepped wynds and closes. She ran down steep streets and steps from the castle to the ancient Grassmarket where the gallows used to stand. And walking and climbing under clear blue skies brought colour to her cheeks and her appetite back in force. The cool summer air that went to the head like wine suited her, gave her tremendous energy. She was glowing with health.

But Magnus seemed to be losing his strength. The good food, sea air and exercise should have made him fitter, yet he could barely keep his eyes open after supper. And on their wedding night, the night before his hospital appointment, he said, 'I'll be glad when tomorrow is here. I'm done for.'

For the first time in his life Frank had been unable to work for a whole week. He felt as if he were a step behind everyone else. The doctors said gastroenteritis, and his ma said, 'It's all the nast!' To his intense irritation she kept repeating, 'The nast will out, Frank. Nast has to come out.' When he asked what she meant, she just muttered, 'Nast – like nasty,' and he wondered how much longer she could go on. She was bed-ridden but she kept everyone awake at night, laughing and singing in a croaky old voice. She had to be fed and washed and nursed round the clock by two nurses. He'd have Sarah's old sitting room done out for her. Put two beds in there – one for the nurse. And he'd ask the doctor to come and prescribe sleeping draughts so they might all get some rest.

Today, he felt better. It was a fine day. One of those hot, early-summer days that can burst out of a warm, wet month.

He went downstairs and found on the hall table the letter that was going to change everything. He turned it over – a large brown envelope, addressed to him in Isobel's forceful, sloping handwriting. On the back was embossed 'North British Hotel, Edinburgh'. It had been posted in Edinburgh, yesterday. He slit it open, but pleasure had already changed to apprehension. There was a smaller square envelope inside, and a two-page letter. He pulled out the pages and started to read.

Dear Mr Chancellor,

When you receive this letter I will be married to Magnus Hammond. We have eloped to Scotland because we have no time to waste. Magnus has married me and saved me from certain condemnation. I am expecting a baby in December and I cannot tell anybody, not even Magnus, the name of my baby's father.

The only person I can tell is you. I want you to know that your son is responsible. I cannot tell if he raped me but I did ask him to stop. Perhaps I did not fight him off hard enough but I was very drunk from the wine and brandy and champagne Ray gave to me. Ray has enormous strength and can hold a girl down easily. I do know that had I been sober, had I been asked, I would never have consented to what went on, in my mother's bed, on the night of Doreen Grimshaw's wedding.

You may choose to do nothing. You may not even believe me, but if you have any doubts about your corrupt son please see the enclosed photograph, taken two weeks ago, in Southport.

You certainly cannot do anything about my disgrace – not with Ray engaged to Sylvia Hammond and with me, another of Ray's cast-offs, married to Magnus Hammond. You must destroy this letter when you have read it. I do not wish to talk about it, ever again, to anyone, especially to you.

But you have often spoken about the good name of Chancellor and I want you to know what your son is capable of. What kind of people are you? What kind of name is Chancellor?

Yours truthfully,
Isobel Leigh

The pages were shaking in his hands. Far worse than the thing he had dreaded had happened. His own son had raped his daughter. He looked at the photograph – Ray and the Grimshaw girl canoodling – it meant nothing. The Grimshaw girl had earned her reputation long ago. His feet were blocks of ice, his fingers were numb as he folded it all back into the envelope and rang the printworks. 'Tell Ray to come home immediately,' he said, and he put down the receiver and waited. He was ice cold, inside and out.

Fifteen minutes later the Delage drew up and Ray, full of smiles, came into the drawing room. 'There you are, Dad. What's the matter?' he said.

Frank got out of his chair. 'Close the door,' he said coldly.

Ray looked surprised but he pushed the door as his father

launched himself across the room and hit him under the chin with a closed fist that sent Ray staggering backwards, on weakened legs that gave under him as his head struck the door.

Frank crouched over him, hands up and ready. 'Get up!' he snarled.

Ray rolled to one side, and muttering, 'For God's sake! I give up!' he snatched an arm cover from the chair and spat into it, a spatter of dark-red drops of blood staining the white linen. He looked up at Frank, bewildered. 'What the hell . . . ?' Then he came slowly to his feet to lean back against the door, the cloth held to his mouth. 'Don't try that again,' he said in a voice thick with phlegm and blood. 'What in God's name is the matter . . . ?'

Frank went to the sofa table for the letter and thrust it at Ray. 'Read this. Then you tell me what's the matter.'

Ray took the letter and after the first few lines looked at his father. 'She's in Edinburgh? Married to Magnus? His mother and father know nothing about this.'

'Read on!'

When he came to the end Ray looked at the photograph and smiled. Then, casually, he threw the letter and photograph into the empty grate. He looked Frank straight in the eye. 'Lies,' he said. 'The girl's mad.'

'You deny it?' Frank came towards him, burning with anger. 'No girl makes up a story like that.'

Ray calmly put the flat of his hand on Frank's upraised arm. 'Calm down. I don't deny I was with her. But as for forcing myself, raping her – giving her a baby. Bloody lies!'

Frank knocked his arm away, and with his face inches from Ray's and every impulse in him wanting to smash the smug look off his face, said, 'Tell me the truth. Convince me – or you'll not get out of this room in one piece.'

Ray gave him a contemptuous push, but he held Frank's wrists and 'I don't want to hit you,' he said. 'The girl's a liar! I took her out to dinner. She was knocking the drink back like lemonade. I had to take her home, put her to bed and get out before—'

'And you didn't . . . ?'

Ray let go of his father's wrists and gave him a push, making Frank drop into an armchair. 'No, I damn well didn't.

If that girl has a baby it's not mine. I'm getting married in November. Sylvia won't live here with you and a crazy old woman. We want the place to ourselves. You've four months to get out and find yourselves a house.'

Frank threw himself into the car and headed for Lindow, and as he went his anger turned against Elsie and grew like a fiery bush in his chest. His precious daughter had been neglected, the prey of Magnus Hammond.

Frank put his foot down hard. The car leaped and he raced down the Manchester Road to the Bollington turn-off. He must believe Ray. Ray would not jeopardise his chance of marriage to Sylvia Hammond. He was speaking the truth. Frank could not even contemplate the thought that Ray was responsible. But why would Isobel lie?

Young girls had hysterics, didn't they? Did she see Ray's attention, putting her to bed, as interference? Believing oneself pregnant was a frequent delusion in young girls who had merely been kissed. Isobel imagined she had been seduced and was having a baby. It was a common enough self-deception.

He had to slow down on the winding road through Bollington, and his anger simmered inside him as he asked himself what the hell had been going on while Elsie wallowed in self-pity. Well, she had wallowed for long enough; taken leave of her mind. She had no interest in her child, her business, her home. It was time she pulled herself together.

He glanced right as he passed the churchyard and saw Elsie, sitting on the marble fender of her father's grave, looking wistful, removing dead flowers from the urn. He pulled up on the grass verge, got out of the car and vaulted over the stone wall. Elsie looked up briefly without acknowledging his presence, then went back to her task.

Frank heard himself say, harsh and demanding, 'What are you doing here? Why aren't you where you should be? In Macclesfield, looking after your family? What the hell are you doing? What kind of mother is it who lets this happen?'

She stood, the dead flowers in her hands. 'I suppose the Hammonds told you.' She put down the dead tulips beside a bunch of fresh primroses, brushed her hands one against the other and reached into her pocket for a letter which she handed to him. He read:

Dear Nanna and Mam,
Magnus and I will be married by the time you receive this letter. We ran away to Scotland last week.

Please forgive me for doing it this way but I am expecting a baby in December and we would not be allowed to marry if we asked permission. I love you very much and I would never willingly deceive you. I hope Magnus's parents don't make trouble and upset you.

We will come home as soon as Magnus has seen the specialist. We will live at Bollinbrook Road for the time being until we find a place of our own. But I can't carry on with the shop, Mam.

Love from Isobel

Fury rose in Frank again. Elsie did not even appear to be concerned. He wanted to shake her. 'Aren't you ashamed of yourself? How could you let this happen?'

'It's not my doing. She's only done what I did.' Then, calmly, she said, 'I'm not ashamed of Isobel. At least Magnus loves her. He has married her. You never loved me. You made me into an adulteress.'

Was this all she cared about? His anger made him shout. 'My precious lass has eloped with a crippled boy with a transmissible disease. And you are moping about here, feeling sorry for yourself, wallowing in misery because your old father died?'

'Any my husband left me.'

'Left you? He's gone?'

'He said we had to move out of the house because he wants to sell it. That's why Isobel wouldn't leave. She was hanging on to the house.'

'It's your house.'

'I paid four hundred. Howard had to borrow the rest on mortgage.'

'So if you paid him a hundred, the house would be yours?'

'Isobel went to see him a week ago. He says he wants four hundred. And he wants a divorce.'

Frank got hold of her arm and gripped it hard. 'Why didn't you tell me? I'd have seen to Leigh.'

Suddenly she drew back and shook his hand away as if he were a leper. Then she put her shoulders back and faced him, as bold as she used to be when she was a young lass herself. She tilted her head back in the challenging way she used to do, and her voice was sharp and quick. 'I've had enough of you. And enough of everyone else. And I'm telling you now ...' The old fiery light was in her eye as she continued, 'I came down here to say goodbye to Dad. Not to listen to you, Frank.'

He looked at her in astonishment.

'Everything's different now. I've changed. I don't want Howard. And I don't want you. I have to get my courage up and go home. The only people who matter are Isobel, my mother, my grandchild.'

Then she put the primroses in the urn on her father's grave and stood back. Very softly she said, 'Dad, I'm not coming back. As one light goes out another little light comes in, burning bright. Your great-grandchild, Dad. I'll be a better grandmother than I was a mother. Goodbye.'

Frank's anger against her drained away as his heart turned over. He had never loved her as much as he did now. Her head was bowed, her eyes closed. She picked up the old tulips and went towards the heap of dead flowers. Then she turned and said, 'I think you should tell Isobel now. Tell her that you are her father. It would mean a lot to her to know. I can't do it.'

But he could not do it. Not now. Not with his precious lass believing she had been raped and was expecting Ray's child. It could drive her to suicide. He said, 'No. We can't tell her. She must never know.'

The premises Willey-Leigh called his Manchester factory were nothing more than a storeroom above a shop. It was not even a large storeroom and it was cramped with trestle tables, at which sat a couple of women, attaching cloth buttons to cards. Willey-Leigh was in a small adjoining office.

Frank threw open the door and Willey-Leigh got to his feet, blustering, 'What on earth ...?' Then, seeing the anger in Frank's face, he said more quietly, 'Why are you here?'

'I'm going to give you a thrashing, Leigh.' Frank slammed

the door closed behind him and advanced.

'Will you leave my premises.'

'My premises.'

'Are you off your head? I said, leave my premises.'

'And I am telling you, Leigh, that I own these premises. My company financed you. Cheshire Trading. I am calling in the loan.'

'You can't do this.'

'I can. I'm going to ruin you. If it were not for Elsie I'd have you declared bankrupt. Elsie can't face the fact that you want a divorce. So, Leigh, you are not going to get a divorce. You are going to sign away any interest you have in Elsie's house. I will purchase the outstanding loan and have the transfer deeds drawn up.'

'You can't do this ...'

'Oh, but I can. And when the property is returned to Elsie I am going to squeeze you dry.' He laughed. 'No, I haven't finished with you.'

'Get out. Get out or I'll call the police.

Frank went a step closer. 'Call the police? I don't think you'll be in any state to call the police when I'm done with you. We'll find a solicitor's office. Right now.' He gripped Leigh's arm tight. 'Then when you've signed over the transfer deeds I will have the greatest delight in smashing that face of yours off the wall.'

'You are mad! What have I done to deserve this?'

Frank pushed Leigh hard against the desk, hearing the crack as his backbone struck the oak. Frank said, through gritted teeth, 'You know what you've done!' His anger was about to erupt. He must save it, though, until he had forced Leigh into signing the transfer deeds. 'You tell your wife that you want a divorce. What other dirty deeds have you done?' He pressed harder on Leigh's arms, forcing him back.

Leigh was squealing. 'It's your son you want to threaten, Chancellor, not me!'

Frank wrenched Leigh's arm and pushing his face close to Leigh's said, through gritted teeth, 'What's that? What's my son got to do with it?

Leigh seemed suddenly to find strength. He jerked forward towards Frank, butting Frank's face with his forehead, freeing his grip, making Frank reel backwards until he came up against a cupboard, caught his elbow on the edge and crashed down heavily on the dusty floor.

Frank put his hand to his nose. There was no blood. He was not hurt, but by the time he had sprung to his feet Leigh was away, past the women in the workroom, running like a frightened deer down the staircase.

The street door was open, and from the top of the staircase Frank saw Leigh run through into the crowd. Frank reached the street at the same moment as a shout went up, 'Watch out!' The crowd parted, stopped at the sight of a man running crazily across the tram terminus and acres of square that was Piccadilly.

'He's gone berserk!' 'What the Dickens?' 'Look out!' came the shouts.

But it was too late. Leigh's zig-zagging progress was halted. He had been struck by an oncoming tram whose driver was wildly clanging the warning bell. Frank pushed through to him. Leigh had tried to scramble to his feet but had collapsed again and was being carried to the transport manager's office, blood streaming down his face, crying and sniffing loudly and pitifully.

Chapter Twenty-Three

On the day of Magnus's appointment they went in the morning, by taxi, to the Royal Infirmary. And Isobel was off-guard when, in Mr Meiklejohn's consulting room, she found herself, with an electric sense of attraction that alarmed her, face to face with Ian Mackenzie. He stood before her, tall and handsome in the dark suit and white coat that the pre-registration doctors wore.

'How did you guess I was coming today?' Magnus asked as the two cousins shook hands.

'I didn't guess. I looked up your next appointment.' Hope and delight had leaped into Ian's blue eyes as he held out his hand to Isobel. 'How nice to see you, Isobel.'

She put her hand in his, heard the deep, educated Scottish voice, felt the shock of contact and said, because it had to be said at once, 'Magnus and I were married yesterday. We are staying at the North British.'

The light of welcome went out of Ian's face as Mr Meiklejohn hustled her towards the door, saying, 'All the same, I must ask you to leave your husband with us. We have lengthy tests to do. Perhaps you could return at four o'clock.'

Isobel walked slowly back to the hotel, her confidence shaken by her involuntary response to Ian's presence. She had no appetite for lunch but sat at the window waiting.

The telephone rang in the sitting room at two o'clock.

'Isobel? Ian here.' There was urgency in his voice. 'Can you come to the Infirmary immediately? Magnus is having a blood transfusion.'

Fear, a sharp stabbing pain of fear, gripped her. 'No! Why . . . ?'

'There has been considerable blood loss since he was seen a year ago. We don't know where it's coming from – the tests aren't complete.'

Her hands were trembling, her mouth was dry. 'Do you think that the journey – getting married – the strain has been too much?'

'Nothing like that,' he said. 'There's no reason why haemophilia should prevent Magnus from marrying.' There was a pause, then he said, 'I've never seen him so happy. You have nothing to reproach yourself with.'

'Ian . . . ?' She wanted to say something, to explain something – but what could she say? Her voice wavered. 'Thank you.'

He hesitated for a moment before he said, 'I may have done the wrong thing. Perhaps I should warn you.'

'What have you done?'

'Last night I rang my uncle and aunt to check that Magus had not forgotten his appointment. He has always come to us, in Charlotte Square.'

'Magnus hasn't told them.' Isobel bumped down into the nearest armchair, weak with fright and panic. 'Would it be better if you rang . . . ?'

'No. It wouldn't.' He was brisk and professional. 'And I couldn't. They are on their way to Edinburgh. They'll go straight to Charlotte Square and Rowena will tell them that Magnus is in the Infirmary. I think that will be shock enough to greet them with.'

'I'm sorry.' She had been rebuked. 'I don't know why I said that.'

His voice softened a little. 'And Isobel?'

'Yes.'

'When my uncle and aunt return to Macclesfield, please have your things sent round to Charlotte Square. You are Magnus's wife. We can't have you living in a hotel for three or four weeks.'

'Three or four weeks?'

'If all goes well.'

*

Magnus was attached at his bandaged forearm to a contraption of rubber tubes and metal and glass pipes on a high tripod stand, where an upended bottle of blood was being dripped into his veins. There was nobody in attendance and Isobel went to the bed and touched his cheek tenderly. 'All right, are you?'

'I'm used to it,' he said. 'Don't be frightened.'

'What's gone wrong? Has it been too much ... our marrying ...?'

He put his free hand out to take hers and his eyes shone with happiness. 'Marrying you is the best thing that's ever happened to me.' He made a kissing mouth. 'Our nights of love! I can't wait to get out of here.'

Isobel let go of his hand. 'Lie as quietly as you can, darling. You'll weary from talk.' She put her finger over his lips to hush him. 'Rest.'

'You love me in that way now, don't you?'

'Always. Forever,' She *would* love Magnus forever, and she'd be a faithful and devoted wife. But she had seen Ian behind the glass panel in the door and her heart was pounding. She kissed Magnus's face. 'I have to go and talk to the doctors.'

Ian led her to the consulting room, but it was Mr Meiklejohn who said, 'How much have you been told about your husband's disease?'

'Nothing,' she said. 'Tell me everything. I'm a good nurse.'

'You should have been told,' he said gravely, 'Magnus has bled into the joints since he was a child. Now he is bleeding internally.'

A shiver of fear ran through Isobel. 'What does it mean?'

Mr Meiklejohn said, 'We can detect blood in the bowel, stomach, kidneys and bladder, but when blood is lost into the lungs or peritoneum there is no effective treatment. There is no cure.' He looked at her over the top of his glasses. 'In Magnus's case internal bleeding will recur.'

Isobel was numb inside but she spoke in a determined voice. 'I can nurse him. I have a diabetic mother.'

He said, 'I'll ask Dr Mackenzie to show you how to make observations and do the tests. This time it's blood you'll be looking for, not sugar.'

'If I find blood?'

'Transfusions are the only answer. The patient stays in bed

until it stops.'

Isobel tried desperately to think of questions she might wish she had asked, but all she could think of was to say, 'What if he cuts himself shaving?'

He spoke sharply. 'You must learn to shave him yourself.'

She persisted. 'But what if he does injure himself? Bleed?'

Mr Meiklejohn said, 'You call a doctor. At once.'

She would watch Magnus every minute, she promised herself. If anything should happen when they were on their own ... She said, 'Do you want to see Magnus here in Edinburgh every time?'

'There are specialists in Manchester. Every bit as good as here.' He put his hand out at this point, to shake hers. The interview was over. He said, 'Dr Mackenzie will take you to the laboratory. He'll show you how to collect specimens for testing.'

There was nobody else in the little laboratory where Ian taught her what to look for in urine samples. 'A smoky appearance indicates a slight loss of blood,' he said. 'If there are traces of pink or red you'll know what it is.'

'What else?'

'Magnus must use a commode. I'll tell you how to collect a sample with a wooden spatula. Seal it in a waxed box and send it promptly to the Infirmary for analysis. Do this daily.'

He watched her closely and Isobel wondered if he were looking for signs that she would find it all revolting. He said, 'If he vomits you must look at it. If there are signs of altered blood – it looks like coffee grounds – then you have an emergency on your hands.'

'Very well. Anything else?'

'I'll show you how to take a temperature and pulse accurately,' he said. He took off his wristwatch and found a thermometer. Then he took her hand and placed her fingers on his pulse. 'Can you feel it?'

'Yes.' Her face was burning. He popped a thermometer under his tongue. And Isobel had to look away from his face and concentrate on the wristwatch because warm ripples were running up her arm and she couldn't stop her hand from shaking. When she had counted his pulse she let his arm drop and glanced quickly around the room.

When she looked back at him, his blue eyes were alive with laughter. The long lines at the sides of his mouth were deep and the black hair had fallen forwards so that he looked exactly as he had the first time they met. He pulled the thermometer out of his mouth, read it and said, 'Ninety-eight point four. Perfect.' Then Isobel's eyes flew wide open as he said, 'Do it again. And this time don't take your eyes off me.'

Her face flamed – but he was smiling. He said, 'Observation, Isobel! Observe! You were supposed to count my breathing. Twelve to fourteen breaths a minute is within the normal range. Remember?'

She put the thermometer under his tongue, took his watch from him again and held his wrist to feel for his pulse. She watched his face to count his breaths, their eyes met and held, and in an instant the old attraction came flaring into life again. When she had done counting she was shaking.

They walked down the corridors of the Royal Infirmary, back to Magnus's room, discussing the safe subject of Magnus's care. Isobel was calmer and Ian had never lost his control, but hers was to flee a few seconds later when she saw, through the glass panel of the door, Mr and Mrs Hammond standing one either side of Magnus's bed.

She stopped with her hand on the door knob, white-faced and faint with dread. If ever she needed a father, a man beside her, it was now. Ian must have seen her reaction, for he grabbed her hand and said quietly and firmly, 'Come on! Get it over with. I'm here.' She squeezed his hand tight before she let go and opened the door, to face her in-laws.

Mrs Hammond's face wore a look that told Isobel at once that Magnus had not spoken. 'What on earth . . . ? What are you doing here?'

Isobel stood near to the door, stock still. 'I'm here with my husband.' She did not flinch. 'Magnus and I were married yesterday.'

Mr Hammond went pale but did not speak.

'Don't talk rubbish!' Mrs Hammond said sharply to Ian, 'What did you know?'

Ian, close beside Isobel, said, 'I knew nothing until this morning.' Then he went to Magnus's bed and made some adjustments to the transfusion equipment.

At this point Mr Hammond came towards Isobel where she was standing like an outcast away from the family group. There was no anger, just sadness, as he said to Mrs Hammond, 'Well, Catriona? Our son has the gumption to elope with the prettiest . . .' but here he stopped.

'It is not a marriage!' She was all but shouting. 'It must be annulled, immediately.'

Magnus beckoned Isobel to his side, where she took his hand, summoned all her courage and faced Mrs Hammond. 'It is very much a marriage.'

Mrs Hammond turned her full wrath on to Magnus's father. 'No wonder I find him at death's door!'

Ian said, 'Magnus has been bleeding into the bowel for at least three months.'

Mrs Hammond's eyes were narrowed, her hands balled into fists. 'It cannot be a marriage in the full sense. Magnus has haemorrhages into his hip joints! His left knee is enlarged. There is muscular atrophy. I was told when he was a small boy and there were haemorrhages into the—'

'Hold your tongue, Mama!' Magnus shouted from the bed.

Mr Hammond had gone to stand by her. 'Calm down, dear!' He put an arm about her shoulder. 'You'll regret anything you say in haste. Let us leave the young ones alone. We can talk about it – make provision for when they come home to us in Macclesfield . . .'

She would not be hushed. She shook off his arm. 'How can Magnus support a wife?' Then she leaned right across Magnus's body, so that she could get her face as close to Isobel's as possible. 'Don't imagine you will be welcome in my house. You are a grasping, brazen hussy!'

Ian's voice came loud and burling. 'And you are in a hospital! Magnus must have quiet.'

Isobel was on the point of tears. Magnus pulled his hand out of hers and heaved himself into a sitting position so fast that Ian had to grab the stand and steady it. Magnus brushed aside his mother's restraining hand and said to her in a voice thick with fury. 'Hold your tongue, I said! You are speaking to my wife. And my wife is expecting a baby.'

Isobel heard Ian's in-drawn breath at the same moment that Mrs Hammond burst into a rage of tears and ran from the room, leaving them all shocked and silent. Then Mr Hammond came to Magnus's side. 'Get better, son,' he said. He put out his hand to Isobel and she took it. 'Make allowances for Magnus's mother. Give us a little time to get used to it. I welcome you into the Hammond family.' He touched Magnus's hand again and left the room.

When the door closed Isobel was sick to the stomach but she heaped Magnus's pillows to help him to lie back. 'Come on, darling. Don't upset yourself. Your mama will be back, full of apologies, at evening visiting.'

'She'd better not be.' He leaned back against the pillows, happy as a sandboy. 'I feel like a man. For the first time in my life.'

After the high passions of Mrs Hammond and Magnus it was a relief to Isobel to hear Rowena's voice, forthright and uncomplicated, shouting down the phone. 'I'm Dad's dispenser. I work two days a week at a children's clinic.' Her laugh came bouncing down the line. 'We want you to come here, to Charlotte Square. When I'm off duty we'll have splendid fun. Do you still want to walk on the Pentlands? In your condition ... Oh! Was that tactless of me?'

Isobel was thrilled to hear her. 'Sure I'm not putting you to trouble?'

'Good heavens, No! Can't wait to have female company. I said to Ian when he was so cut up about Magnus grabbing you for himself ...'

Isobel's heart came thundering up into her throat.

'... I said, "You should have swept her off her feet when she was sixteen – told her you wanted to marry her. Magnus has always been dotty about her. Magnus was on the spot. She needs a man to depend on. Too much of a gentleman, that's your trouble!"' There was a dreadful little silence, then, 'Shouldn't have said that, probably! Are you still listening?'

'Yes.'

'Anyway, I said to Ian, "I'm going to make the most of having her as a – what are we? – Cousins-in-law?' Again the hearty laugh.

Isobel couldn't talk about Ian. The familiar breathlessness

was upon her as she asked, 'Was your father shocked? The baby and everything.'

'It happens all the time,' she said. 'Even in the West End of Edinburgh.'

'Did Mrs Hammond simmer down? She was very angry.'

'Auntie Catty? She hates being called that – she was *livid* at first. But by the time Dad and Uncle John had talked to her – assured her that Magnus isn't the first young man to get a girl into troub ... Sorry, Isobel! Anyway she calmed and finally said, "Wouldn't it be wonderful if we have a Hammond grandson? Sylvia's will be Chancellors. They'll have bright-red hair!"'

Isobel sat down before her knees gave way. She hadn't thought that the baby might look like Ray Chancellor. In six months' time, the world – or everyone in their little world – might see at once who had fathered the child. The truth would be out in the open if she bore a red-headed baby.

She heard herself saying to Rowena, 'Keep the news until tomorrow or we'll have nothing to talk about.' Then she shivered as the full weight of this deception came home to her. Every move she had made to put matters right had only made them worse.

Magnus had been in hospital for a month but today they were going home. His father had reserved a compartment on the train for them.

Isobel said goodbye to Rowena and Dr Mackenzie after breakfast, then rushed upstairs before she cried. She hated saying goodbye and soon she'd have to say it again, to Ian, who was going to collect Magnus from hospital and see them on to the train. She was tearful as she fastened the big suitcases and pushed them out on to the landing to be taken downstairs. She was confident about nursing Magnus, but he couldn't walk more than a few paces and she was worried in case he fell and injured himself. She made running repairs to her eye-black and lipstick. The eye-black was streaked and she licked her finger and ran it under the lower lid – she must have resembled a clown, tearful and ridiculous all through breakfast when the tears had started.

Isobel cried at everything. Rowena said it was her condition.

Rowena could always tell, she said, when women were expecting because they spent half their time weeping about how happy they were. If Rowena was right, then tearfulness and a three-pound increase in weight were the only signs of her condition, though she was three months into her pregnancy.

Ian knocked on the door. 'Are you ready?'

'Come in.' Her heart leaped at his nearness, so full of life and health. She had not admitted to herself that she did not want to leave Edinburgh – leave Ian, who seemed to her to be a giant in every way. He had wit and intelligence and, like her, enjoyed the simple pleasures of music and walking. She would miss the serious after-dinner talks around the table and the musical evening hours when he was home and they played duets on the grand piano in the drawing room. Her eyes filled with tears again.

'You are very smart,' he said.

She was wearing a grey dress with a white puritan collar and a navy-blue linen coat. She blinked back her tears. 'Thank you. So do you. I haven't seen you in tweeds since . . .' She stopped and went pink with embarrassment.

'Since I told you that you were the girl for me?' he said, but there was nothing in his manner to show that he was disturbed by her leaving Edinburgh or the hours they had spent together yesterday.

Isobel picked up her handbag and fastened her coat. 'All right,' she said. 'Let's go for Magnus. I'll travel in the ambulance with him. You can meet us at the station.'

At eleven o'clock they waited in the bustling crowd on the platform at Waverley station, Ian, Magnus and she. Magnus was in a wheelchair which Ian had hold of, and Ian was saying, 'In another month you'll be on your feet, Magnus. Don't rush things. You are bound to be weak when the leg muscles haven't been used.'

Magnus was not cheered. He grabbed Isobel's hand. 'Don't make a fuss. When I'm in the compartment, take the thing to the guard's van. I don't want everyone staring at me.'

The train pulled in and the crowd moved. A porter darted forward to help them, then, when Magnus was seated, he said, 'When you get to Manchester the guard will have the chair waiting for you.' He spoke to Isobel as if Magnus were incapable of speech. 'The attendant will pop along, ma'am, in case your man wants help to go to the . . .'

'Impertinence!' Magnus shouted at the retreating guard. 'Pop along, indeed! I'll send for him if I want him!' His face was scarlet.

Isobel scrambled over the bags to his side. 'He meant well. Don't get into a paddy.'

Ian, behind her, was lifting their hand bags on to the high rope luggage rack. He said, 'I've put some books up here for you. Cook has made a picnic box up, in case you are hungry between meals.' He said to Isobel, 'Got everything you need? I have to get off the train.' He shook Magnus's hand. 'Settle down. Have a sleep. You were up at five.'

Isobel went to see Ian off, stepping on to the platform behind him, her heart beating hard. Tears welled up again and she explained weakly, 'My last breath of Edinburgh air! don't mind me. I'm horribly tearful.'

He glanced down into her upturned face and love flared quickly as their eyes met and held. Then he took both of her hands in his own, pulled her close and planted a kiss on her forehead. 'Goodbye.'

She whispered, 'Will I see you? Will you come to Macclesfield at Christmas or New Year?'

'No. I won't see you again.' Quickly he let go of her hands. 'I'm not made of stone, Isobel.' He went, striding through the crowd. She watched through tear-misted eyes until she lost sight of him.

Magnus was sleeping when she went back into the compartment. She tucked the travel rug round his legs, pulled the blinds on the corridor side and closed the door. Then she sat, staring out over the undulating land of the Lothians until she closed her eyes and the magic of yesterday came back to her in all its wonder.

Yesterday when she was at Magnus's bedside in the morning, Ian had popped into the ward to say, 'I have the afternoon off. It's your last day so I'm taking you and Rowena out for lunch.'

Half an hour later she left the hospital, holding on to her hat in the high wind under a piercing blue sky. Ian was there, waiting in Lauriston Place at the wheel of his Morris Special

Coupé which had cream bodywork with black mudguards, roof and running boards. The engine was running and he sounded the horn to attract her attention, thinking that she hadn't seen him.

He came round and held open the passenger door for her, and as soon as she was in said, 'We're on our own. Rowena won't come.'

Isobel settled herself and watched him walk in front of the car to the driver's side. Admiration and love for him came tightening into her throat as he grinned at her through the windscreen. He was so handsome and assured. There was nothing of vanity or sham in him. And she loved him so.

'Comfortable?' he asked as he pulled the car away from the kerb.

'Yes,' she said. 'Why won't Rowena come with us? It's my last day. I thought she'd have wanted to . . .'

'Rowena is having a black, silent mood today. Because you're leaving.'

'Where are we going?' She tried to put from her mind the thought that today could be the last time they would ever be alone together. They were out of the main traffic, on George IV Bridge, heading for the Mound and Princes Street, and she wanted to fix all this in her memory, the buildings, the view as they crossed the Royal Mile.

'I'm taking you to the Maybury Roadhouse.' He glanced quickly at her. 'A new place. Built for motorists. Art deco and modern style. Tinted mirrors, Bakelite, everything.' He laughed and said, 'What do you want to do this afternoon?'

'I don't mind. Anything.' Being with him was sheer happiness.

'Rightio! After lunch I'll take you on a little boat trip. South Queensferry to North Queensferry in Fife. Does that appeal?'

Anything he suggested would appeal to her. She sat on the edge of her seat, watching the other motor cars and looking at the big houses on the road through Corstorphine to Glasgow. All too soon they were there at the Maybury and parking the car and being blown to bits as they ran to the entrance.

They were shown to a table by the window in a lovely big restaurant where the tables were widely spaced. Isobel was glad of that. She didn't want others listening to their talk. A young musician played at the white grand piano on a raised platform near their table.

'When do you finish your residency?' Isobel asked when the waiter had brought the menu.

'Nineteen thirty-eight. Next year. We'll have the set lunch, shall we? Can you eat five courses?'

'I'm starving.' Isobel smiled happily back at him while he ordered.

'What will you do when you're qualified?' she asked when they had been served with the cock-a-leekie soup.

His face suddenly became serious. His black brows nearly met in a frown. 'I'll go into the Royal Navy. I'm going to join the Volunteer Reserves. War is coming.'

She couldn't bear his being in danger. 'They'll need doctors here.'

'I'll be called up anyway if war comes. The RNVR will go in at the start. I'll be in the service I want.'

The pianist was playing a song that they had danced to in Southport, 'Long Ago and Far Away'. Isobel felt the colour rising into her face. She tried to ignore the piano but the words were running through her mind, ... *I dreamed a dream one day* ... She said, 'What about your dreams for your future? You said you were interested in genetics.'

'My dreams are broken.' He put his spoon down and said quietly, 'I dreamed of specialising. And I dreamed of marrying when I was twenty-four.' His steady blue eyes had no guile in them. 'I thought we shared the same dream. Marrying. Having a big family.'

Isobel felt as if she'd been punched. She had not expected this. But she didn't want to go away from him, forever, with his thinking she had broken a promise. So though her face was burning she looked straight back at him and said, in a level voice, 'You didn't tell *me*.'

His eyes were steady and true and they fastened on to hers until a trembling started in her neck and shuddered down her spine. He said, 'I didn't think you needed it spelling out. That day we spent in the hills, I fell in love and I asked you to wait for me. You said you loved me. I never considered any other girl after that.'

Her face was flaming but the waiters were back and she

could not answer. When they had gone he said, 'I was going to propose on your eighteenth birthday. And marry you a year later.'

She could not say a word in reply. How could she tell him that if only he had not waited – if only he had repeated his proposal, told her again and again that he loved her and was waiting for her – she might not now be dreading the moment she had to say goodbye. He gave her a tender look and said softly, 'You're eighteen. And here you are, expecting a baby. I should be congratulating you. Not reproaching. I'm sorry.'

She looked down, praying for him not to question her in case she was tempted to tell him the truth. The child was more important than her feelings. She couldn't bear for her child ever to have to ask itself, as she had so often done, how many others knew the truth. She fell silent for a few minutes, concentrating on the food, not looking at Ian, not listening to the piano.

Then Ian said, 'It's the ideal age for everything. Eighteen. Young men of eighteen are the first to be called up to fight.'

They were taking away the fish plates and serving lamb cutlets Milanese. The room was filling with the lively notes of 'In a Mountain Greenery' and the moment had passed. Ian said, 'We won't be able to stay out of a war in Europe. Mussolini marched into Abyssinia last year. Hitler and Mussolini are going to join forces. We can't stand back and watch that dictator and the Nazi Führer talking about the "price of peace" and slamming nations into submission.'

He was very serious. He believed every word he was saying. 'Here, we think everything has a price and the only value is competition. In a competitive world your competitor is your enemy. And having an enemy is one step from going to war.' He paused for a moment, then said, 'You don't believe me, do you?'

He might not be right but she loved to hear him talking this way. He continued, 'I've always felt disgust for people who talk about creating jobs when they mean creating profit and whose only motive is profit.' Then he relaxed and said, 'Sorry. I'm talking like a blinking preacher again. I'm one of the lucky ones. I can afford to say I wouldn't work just for money. What about you?'

'I'm the opposite,' Isobel said ruefully. 'If I hadn't been, Mam and I would have had nothing. I need the security of knowing I've a bit put by. I can't bear to spend every half-penny. If I only had two and six a week, I'd save sixpence of it for a rainy day.'

He reached over the table and touched her hand. 'You must think I'm a feckless idiot.'

'No. Oh no ...' she said quickly. 'I don't at all. I think you're ...' Then she blushed and stopped herself from saying more.

They left the roadhouse and drove on singing and whistling and humming their way through their combined repertoire of music, from Benny Goodman's clarinet jazz to singing in harmony the beautiful Schumann songs. They had discovered that they had the same tastes in music as they did in books and food and radio programmes – and humour, for they were singing Gershwin's 'Summertime' and laughing at the incongruity, because the summer wind was nearly blowing them into the hedgerows as they followed the winding road to South Queensferry.

Then they were there, and Isobel was silenced by her first close-up sight of the railway bridge that spanned the Forth – the enormous, towering network of three trusses on cantilever arms that made three shipping channels of the wide river.

She said, 'It makes me think of three giant spider's webs, stretched out from shore to shore.' Then she opened the door and felt the fierce wind that was blowing over the water. 'My God! It's cold!'

Ian brought a fringed plaid shawl from the car to wrap about her head and shoulders on top of the navy coat. 'You'll need this on deck,' he said. 'Leave your hat in the car.' He had put on a reefer coat, like fishermen wore. He pulled a knitted hat down over his ears and then, grinning, tucked a flask of whisky into his pocket. They went down to the jetty and the ferry boat, Isobel holding on to his arm to gain the shelter of his bulk from that wind that made the day seem more like March than June.

Fifteen minutes later Isobel shouted above the wind, 'I've never been so cold in my life!' They were on deck, side by side, watching the wake water curling white over inky blue.

'The cold's making my head ache.'

'Let's go inside,' he shouted back, and he had to hold her hand fast, for the wet deck was rising and falling over the swell of the river.

When they were safely inside they found a bench to themselves, for there were only a handful of people crossing over. Ian brought out the hip flask and unscrewed the silver cap. 'Take a drop of this.'

Isobel tipped the bottle up and took a great swig then, laughing and coughing, passed it back to him. 'Ugh! Takes your breath away!'

'Cures your headache, though.' He grinned, took a drink and returned the flask to his pocket.

Isobel felt the fiery spirit warming her. While the boat heaved and dropped she leaned her head back against the bench. And as she did so she was aware of his arm behind her along the seat. Her head was resting on his wrist and warm, rippling sensations were running down her spine.

It could be accidental – a coincidence. Maybe he was holding on because the boat was heaving. Maybe he hadn't noticed. Isobel dared not look. Instead she closed her eyes and let all the old familiar sensations course through her: the quick pulse, the blood rushing to her cheeks, the bated breath. She must not let him see how such a little action had affected her, so she kept as still as a statue.

Then she felt his fingers moving gently yet deliberately under her hair to touch the skin of her neck. This was no accidental touch. Isobel's eyes flew open and she turned her head. Their eyes met and held for a silent few seconds before he said, very gently, 'Why, Isobel? Why did you do it?'

Tears came springing. 'I can't tell you,' she whispered, but she could not tear her gaze away from those steady blue eyes that she felt could see right into her soul.

He said, 'You have married – *married* – a boy who has an incurable disease. You knew all about it and yet you are expecting his baby. I'm sure you'd never marry out of pity.'

Isobel fumbled in her pocket for a handkerchief, found one and put it to her face to blow her nose. She couldn't look him in the eye and lie to him. She said, 'I've always wanted marriage and children – a family round me.'

He said, 'But ... Magnus? When I'm in love with you ... And you are in love with me.' His hand tightened as he pulled her round so that she must look at him. 'I know you love me, Isobel. I won't ask you to say it. I won't ask anything except that you tell me why you turned me down – for Magnus? Have you any idea what you have done?'

Isobel did not waver. Her eyes were full of tears but she wouldn't allow anyone – even Ian – to imply that Magnus did not deserve marriage and happiness. And because she was hurt she was harsh and defensive. 'I have ninety-five per cent of what I always wanted out of life. I can't ask for more.'

She had been sharp and now he let his own hurt feelings show. He was dismissive. 'Not ninety-five per cent. I'd set it much lower. Magnus needs nursing attention, not a wife's love. No, my sweet one. In your shoes, with your capacities, I'd say I have only five per cent.'

Isobel burst into tears and ran for the ladies' cubicle, where she had another bout of the ridiculous bubbling-over of tears she tried to control. It took five minutes but when she went out on deck, into that tearing wind, she had done crying, brushed her hair and splashed water on her eyes. She must be strong, she told herself. She had to face the world.

Ian was holding on to the rail, watching the docking, because they had reached the opposite shore. Isobel stood close to him and he put an arm across her shoulder in a protective action, for the boat was heaving in the wind that was more fierce on this bank of the river. Her lips tasted salt from the spray and she drew the shawl tight about her head and shoulders. They watched the deckhand throw a rope over to the man on the dock, saw him give it a half-hitch round the capstan with a precision born of years of practice. Isobel shouted above the wind, 'Do they never miss?'

'Good, isn't it?' Ian was laughing into the wind. 'It will steady in a sec. Once the engine's held astern against the pull of the rope.'

The gap between the ferry and the dock was closing. The boat was held fast and they were dropping the gangplank for the few passengers who were leaving. Ian tightened his hand on her shoulder, put his mouth close to her ear and said, quietly, 'I'm sorry. I won't ask any more questions. All forgiven?'

She tried to ignore the warning lump that was in her throat. 'Nothing to forgive. You had a right to ask.'

'I didn't.' He squeezed her hand tighter. 'No right at all.'

They went below on the return journey and found the walkway around the engine. Ian and the engineer gave her all the facts about ships' engines – facts she'd never need. All Isobel saw were the great shiny brassworks, as clean and polished as Nanna's candlesticks. It was hot and noisy in the engine room but it was comforting, listening to men talking of pistons and flywheels and spinning governors and cranks while Isobel gathered herself together and merely watched the engine noisily clanking and pedalling away.

Magnus was asleep. The train was pulling up an incline through mountainous country. Isobel reached up to the luggage rack for the bag that held the books Ian had lent her.

The first one she opened was a slim volume. *Selected Poems* by Rupert Brooke. All she knew of his poetry was 'If I should die, think only this of me . . .' This volume was inscribed 'To Rowena. Ian. Christmas 1934'.

She read the first few poems before she came to where Ian had placed a ribbon marker. Then she read the poem, 'The Chilterns', and knew that he had chosen this one and marked it for her.

Your hands, my dear, adorable,
Your lips of tenderness
Oh, I've loved you faithfully and well,
Three years, or a bit less.
It wasn't a success.

Thank God, that's done! and I'll take the road,
Quit of my youth and you,
The Roman road to Wendover
By Tring and Lilley Hoo,
As a free man may do.

For youth goes over, the joys that fly,
The tears that follow fast;
And the dirtiest things we do must lie
Forgotten at the last;
Even Love goes past.

What's left behind I shall not find,
The splendour and the pain;
The splash of sun, the shouting wind,
And the brave sting of rain,
I may not meet again.

But the years that take the best away,
Give something in the end;
And a better friend than love have they,
For none to mar or mend,
That have themselves to friend.

I shall desire and I shall find
The best of my desires;
The autumn road, the mellow wind
That soothes the darkening shires.
And laughter, and inn-fires.

White mist about the black hedgerows,
The slumbering Midland plain,
The silence where the clover grows,
And the dead leaves in the lane,
Certainly, these remain.

And I shall find some girl perhaps,
And a better one than you,
With eyes as wise, but kindlier,
And lips as soft, but true.
And I daresay she will do.

Magnus was looking at her when Isobel turned her tearful eyes away from the window she'd been staring through for the last five minutes.

'Do you think I'll ever walk again?' he said.

She came down to earth. She had responsibilities and duties. She must be strong enough for the two of them. She had nothing to be wistful and tearful about. 'You will be on your feet in a month,' she said firmly. 'The doctors have told you so.'

Chapter Twenty-Four

Elsie was back where she belonged, in charge of her shop, everything as it was, and now, at last, she was looked up to, respected. Even Mrs Hammond, obviously thinking about her coming grandchild, was making friendly overtures – asking her and Mother over to Archerfield for Sunday lunch. And now Elsie was a member of the parish church ladies' needlework guild and had been asked to join the Mothers' Union. The older ladies of the Mothers' Union visited Howard on the days Elsie couldn't make it to the asylum. Mrs Grimshaw was very understanding. She said, 'Your husband used to be a fine figure of a man, Elsie. It must break your heart seeing him brain-damaged.'

Howard was reduced to a shambling, demented wreck. Brain-damaged was not the name Elsie would give to him. Ruined was what she would call Howard. But what status it had brought to her. She was seen as the proud, upright woman who strove to keep her husband in some comfort in an amenity bed that was costing two pounds ten shillings a week.

This morning she dressed in the sapphire-blue linen dress that so became her. She felt better than she had for years and she smiled at her reflection as she pursed her lips and applied lipstick. The diabetes was stable now she was no longer drinking. Elsie had everything under control. She ran down the stairs and popped her head in at the shop door. 'All right, Miss Duffield?'

'The hospital almoner called in to say will you drop into her office if you are visiting Mr Leigh this afternoon.' Miss Duffield's face was as long as a wet weekend. 'Mr Chancellor's in the back.'

Frank was standing, one arm casually against the mantelshelf, dressed in a dark suit as if he were on important business – his greying hair tamed, his hazel eyes alive with interest, his demeanour dynamic and energetic. He had not changed – as she had. Elsie said, 'What brings you here today?'

'I just wanted to talk to you.' He smiled at her. 'You look nice.'

She knew what he was going to ask. She must make him believe that she had meant it when she swore on Dad's grave that she would break no more commandments. She said, 'I'm going to Bollinbrook Road this morning, to make sure everything's ready for Isobel and Magnus.' They were coming home today at seven. 'And I have to see Howard this afternoon.'

'How is he?'

'Not good.' Elsie went to stand by him, in front of the empty fireplace.

'Does he want you there every day?'

She smiled. 'All Howard wants from me is what I bring him to eat. That's all. He eyes the cardboard box and says, "Any more sandwiches? Any jelly? Cake?" and when I say, "All gone, Howard," he says, "Well. Don't let me keep you, dear . . . "'

'Have you got power of attorney?'

'Yes. I sign the cheques. The insurance money paid the mortgage off. The house is safe. It's ours now. But Howard hasn't much left.'

'What about his debt to the loan company?'

'I wrote to them. I said they could sue if they wished but there was no money to be had. It would be better for them to cut their losses. My brave husband will be in an asylum for the rest of his life.'

'And where does that leave you? Where does it leave us?'

'Us?' She smiled. 'There's no "us" about it, Frank. I have a dependent husband. I'm a married woman. There's no future for us.'

Isobel collected specimens and sent them to the infirmary daily, gratified to find that there was no more bleeding. She examined urine samples and learned how to shave Magnus. She took as much care as his mother had and she basked in

Magnus's appreciation and compliments. She was overflowing with gratitude and love for Magnus. She was his wife, his mother and his nurse all in one. And he was her husband, her sometimes lover, her best friend, her very own good man.

She had hours to herself every day when Magnus rested, so she took driving lessons and passed the test and Magnus was happy for her to take the wheel. Or she would drive them both to see Mam in the mornings and leave Magnus with Mam, who was well and happy and back to her old self again. After lunch she would go out alone, for pleasure – driving miles out of her way with the hood down. She'd sing at the top of her voice when she felt carefree and she'd park and walk a mile or two across the moorland paths whenever she became frightened at what lay ahead.

She had no need for an iron will. The big life events – birth, death, being loved – she saw were all beyond the control of the will. She could only pray for strength to brazen it out – passing the baby off as Magnus's when soon it might be all too obvious.

From Magnus and everyone but God Isobel hid her biggest fear. And her biggest fear was that all was not going well with her pregnancy. Her baby had not quickened and at five months from her last period, for it was mid-August, she ought to be showing more signs. Mam and Nanna said that every pregnancy was different and she dared not ask anyone else. Magnus did not want her to tell anyone the expected date. They were going to "wait and see."

Her other worry was that Magnus had let it be known that he could not go to Sylvia's wedding unless he was on his feet. He would not be pushed out in his wheelchair and every day her poor darling struggled with exercises to strengthen his muscles. He was desperate to get back to work but seemed to dread the approach of the wedding.

'Father needs me,' he said. 'The silk industry is in the doldrums. It's never been steady. Factories are closing down, going under.'

'I can't see that happening to Hammonds, Magnus,' she said. 'Not with a business the size of yours.'

'We've had to lay a lot off. The Japanese have captured

some of our suppliers as well as stealing the markets. Our raw silk comes from the Far East. We do some rayon cloth and mixtures but we have a lot of competition from the Manchester cotton mills. Silk has always been a luxury cloth – the costliest of all fabrics. The orders aren't coming in. Father can't afford to pay wages for men who aren't working, and that includes me.'

Isobel worried. She didn't like having their money brought round by Magnus's father every week when neither of them had earned it. So she insisted on holding the fort – going to the mill to learn Magnus's job and doing it for him every Monday, Wednesday and Friday until Magnus should be fit again.

She loved her job. It took only a few days to pick up the bookkeeping side of it, filling in the Sales and Purchase ledgers and balancing the General Ledger. It took much longer to learn to work out the wages, there being so many different rates and hours and shifts. There were mechanisms on the machines, like those on bicycles, to clock up the yardage. The clocks had to be checked and the yardage counted. The increase in rates of payment over a certain yardage, the hours on the women's worksheets and time sheets, and the difference between the women's and men's rates – all had to be taken into account. Isobel needed a slide rule to work it all out. Yet if she made a mistake the mill workers were the first to march up to the office to put her right. They knew to the last halfpenny what they had earned. She joked about it to Magnus saying, 'You don't need a wages clerk. You'd save a whole wage packet if you let the workers tell you what to pay them.'

Magnus said, 'Are you happier, knowing we are earning our keep?'

He said it in fun but Isobel answered him seriously. 'I'm glad we're being paid, but the mill can't stand the huge wages bill.'

'All the workers are necessary,' he said. 'For all those processes.'

'It's the expensive silk that's unnecessary,' she said. 'The mill has to be running at a loss.'

Magnus said. 'It's always been like that. Good years and bad.'

Isobel was in no position to give the owners of the family

firm her opinion but it was foolish to be complacent and hope for an upturn. She said, 'I think the silk industry is dying on its feet. There are all these new fibres. What about the American du Pont stuff – nylon? Everyone will want nylon when it's available here.' She had seen imported nylon stockings and had bought a petticoat made from woven nylon. She said, 'It's stronger than silk. It doesn't crease in the wash. If Hammonds went over to nylon surely all you'd have to do is buy in the thread and weave it.'

He laughed. 'You don't know what you're talking about, darling. There will always be a demand for the best.'

Mrs Hammond did not approve of her working but was happy for Isobel to drive Magnus to Archerfield where he could practise walking up and down the hallways. Isobel would pip the horn at the front door to call for help in getting Magnus out of the car and then she'd drive off to Hammond Silks. Mrs Hammond only saw Isobel when she collected or delivered Magnus. Then, for Magnus's sake, his mother made a pretence of acceptance of his wife. But Isobel believed that it was a mockery.

They had all gone to Archerfield for Sunday lunch once; Magnus, Nanna, Mam and Isobel. Mrs Hammond did not speak a single word directly to Isobel. Like the Posh Girls' mothers had done when she was young, Mrs Hammond spoke through others, saying to Magnus in Isobel's presence, 'I will ask Isobel, very nicely, if I may borrow my son for half a day ...' This was said to cast her in the role of jealous, selfish wife. Or she'd say, 'I insist on your being here on your father's birthday – or for Sunday lunch – or for whatever suited her – before she'd add slyly, 'If Isobel will allow you to come and see your Mama, of course ...'

Isobel did drive Magnus to Archerfield at weekends. But she left him there and went to chapel with Nanna and Mam then spent the rest of the day at Lindow, because of the danger of bumping into Ray Chancellor. She couldn't bear to speak to him. But she often passed the Delage in the middle of the day, parked down one of the cart tracks in the lower slopes of the hills when she drove the scenic way to and from Archerfield.

*

Isobel had left Magnus at home on the day she finally settled old scores with Doreen. It was a Thursday in early September; it had rained for a week and the roads to Bollington were dangerous, so Isobel went into Macclesfield to buy the groceries and all the things she needed for Magnus. By lunchtime, with only half the shopping done, she was starving. She would go to Shandy's. Shandy would offer her something to eat. She drove the car down Jordangate and as she rounded the corner into Brock Street, the Delage, with Ray Chancellor at the wheel, came straight out towards her. She felt sick and faint and was angry with herself because it had become an involuntary reaction to seeing him. So she pretended she hadn't noticed it was he who was waiting for her to finish turning the corner. Isobel pulled on the handbrake to let him pass. Why was he at this end of town, at lunchtime?

Nobody answered her knock at Shandy's. There was no one in the bakehouse across the yard but it was unheard of for the whole family to be out, so she opened the back door, went into the kitchen, put her head around the living room door and called out, 'Yoo-hoo! Anyone at home?' as she did when Shandy was about.

There was a scuffling overhead; the sound of curtain rings scraping along the pole, a scrambling for shoes, footsteps along the landing and on the stairs; then Doreen came into the room, make up gone, hair hastily combed through. She was wearing a straight tweed skirt and a white lacy jumper, fashionable then, that had a collar and V neck and gathered sleeve heads. And she did not know that she was wearing it inside out. Ray Chancellor and Doreen were lovers still.

'It's you!' she said, and relief and spite came into her voice and her eyes. 'Miss Prim! Not so prim, eh?' She pursed her lips and said, 'I heard all about how you ran off with poor little Magnus!'

'I expect you did,' Isobel said as she put her handbag over the back of a chair and sat down. 'I thought you worked at Chancellor's, Doreen. Have you given your job up?'

'No. You're lucky to catch me. I can't give up,' Ray says, "How would I carry on without, Doreen?"' She laughed out loud. 'Normally I don't have time to come home at dinner time. I have to take sandwiches and spend the dinner hour working with Ray.'

'My word,' Isobel said. 'He's putting his back into it!'

Doreen gave the sly look. Something nasty would come next. It did. Doreen said, 'You could have knocked me down when I heard about you and Magnus Hammond. It was all over Macclesfield. Sylvia Hammond told Ray, and he told me – and I . . . .'

Isobel said, 'What did you say about me?'

The laugh exploded out. 'I said, "It's the quiet ones you have to watch. I'm all talk and no action myself. It's the prim little misses who get up to things". Mind you, poor little Magnus is not exactly Johnny Weismuller, is he?'

Isobel was glad she could summon up her self control when she needed it. She fought down the impulse to strike Doreen and said in a sweet, confidential voice, 'And what about you, Doreen? I remember you telling me how insatiable you were. Not a very attractive boast, I remember thinking. How's Cyril? Is there any improvement?' She said it without a blush.

Doreen pursed up her lips, lifted her eyebrows and said, 'Cyril's all right. He's more of a man than yours.' She waited a few moments, weighing up whether or not to say more. Then she said, 'I'm expecting a baby too.'

Isobel stood up, picked up her coat and put it on slowly, ready to leave quickly before she faced Doreen again and said, 'Congratulations, Doreen. A baby! Who's the father?'

'What do you mean?' Anger came blazing into her eyes. 'What are you talking about? Who's the father? Who do you think?'

If she had to leave Macclesfield in disgrace in three months' time – if she were to be shown up as a trollop – she would remember this moment; this moment when she opened her handbag, unfastened the button-down pocket in the silk lining and brought out the photograph. She handed it to Doreen and watched her face pale as she stared at it. 'The baby could be anybody's, I suppose,' Isobel said. 'Though it's more likely to be Ray Chancellor's. But then, I said to myself, "No! Not Doreen with a little Illy-Jitty . . . "'

Doreen's lips were white as she tore the photograph in two. 'How dare you! How dare you say that Cyril isn't the father?'

Isobel kept on smiling. 'Oh, I dare. I dare. And it doesn't matter that you've torn the photograph up. There's another one.'

'Where?'

'In my safe deposit box at the District Bank. Ray Chancellor can ask my father-in-law to get it for you if you need proof. I'm sure Sylvia's father would be happy to oblige.'

Doreen's face was red. She threw the pieces of photograph into the fire, and staring at Isobel as bold as brass said, 'It doesn't prove anything.'

'That's not the way Ray or Sylvia would see it, though, is it?' isobel said very softly. And when Doreen didn't answer, 'Unless you stop, I shall tell the Hammonds. And then we'll see how long Ray's engagement lasts. And how much longer you and Ray Chancellor can keep up your sordid little affair.'

She went to the door, turned back to face her and said, 'Let us make a pact, Doreen. Never utter my name again. And I'll never mention yours.'

A month before Ray married, Frank's mother died. She had been prescribed a laudanum tincture to help her sleep and it had eased her into a peaceful end. It was all over within a week: Ma's death, the funeral and Frank's decision to move out of Park Lane. He'd make the Swan in Jordangate his temporary home. It was his property. There was a large flat over the public bar and it would do him nicely until he found something else.

He stood at the window now, watching the men unloading the van, dumping his furniture and belongings on the pavement so that the removers wouldn't obstruct the narrow street for longer than necessary. Already, three carts were lined up waiting for some motor cars to edge past the big van.

There was a back way in from the alley so that he or anyone he invited could come in unobserved. Elsie lived next door. There was the pub below; a lively place – a working man's pub with darts and dominoes in the tap room and a piano-player most nights in the lounge. Living here he'd feel like a twenty-year-old again. Or he would if Elsie would only . . .

Oh, hell. Why couldn't he forget her? Why couldn't he find a woman he loved as much as Elsie? Why would she only offer friendship? She laughed when he told her that if Willey-Leigh died he, Frank, would marry her.

'I'll be too old, Frank,' she said. 'And I'll be a grandmother. You will want a bit of young stuff!'

But he didn't. He wanted Elsie.

Sylvia's wedding day was the last Saturday in November and Isobel's pregnancy was not very noticeable, yet there were only five weeks to go. Her waist had gone – she had a little bay window in front and a rather large bottom but all the signs were hidden under the dropped-waist sailor dress she'd made from ice blue shantung. She made a loose fitting coat to go with it and bought one of the new tilted hats that had a crown like a mortar board and a huge flat sweep of a brim, shaped like a swallow's wing. It flattened the pointed shape of her face, gave her height and distracted attention from what Magnus affectionately called her "bulge."

When Magnus and she arrived at the church there was quite a crowd in the churchyard and another at the gate in the market place. Magnus had made it. All the effort and months of hard exercising on those leg muscles had paid off though Magnus himself did not really want to be there, he said. But Isobel had insisted. He was going to return to work the following week and today he looked splendid – handsome and tall and strong as he walked down the aisle, using only a walking stick, with Isobel proudly on his other arm. Their seats were right at the front, next to Rowena and her father. Ian had sent a present and apologies.

Isobel was glad to be surrounded because she'd been afraid that the stifling, fainting feeling would come over her in Ray Chancellor's presence. She could not look him in the face or stand close to him when she was obliged to speak to him at Archerfield. She glanced at the front row where he and his best man sat as if they hadn't a care in the world. The faintness did not come over her and all Isobel felt was revulsion, tempered with fear that the baby who at that moment was turning somersaults inside her, might turn out to be large and red-headed.

She opened the wedding service programme – thick embossed vellum; the initials H and C intertwined. The doors were pulled back and Bach's beautiful Toccata and Fugue in D minor came tumbling down to the two-flats key of B minor in a superbly played diminuendo for the low slow notes of The Bridal March from Lohengrin. They all stood and watched Sylvia coming down that long aisle on her father's arm, ethereal in a dress of ivory lace with an heirloom veil worn back from her face under a circlet of stephanotis on her abundant baby-blonde hair.

Isobel glanced at Magnus when they were singing the first hymn, Love Divine, all Loves Excelling. How wonderful it would have been if she and Magnus had been able to marry in their own church in such style. Magnus looked very pale. His eyes were wet and shiny. And behind the brave exterior his heart was thundering as he told himself, 'I could not do it. I couldn't tell Father that he is the father of Ray. I could not break my sister's heart.' He nudged his darling Isobel and when she turned to smile at him, whispered, 'When it's over, don't let us hang about for photographs.'

She whispered back, 'Are your legs aching?'

'A bit.' He said, 'Would you mind awfully if I asked you to drive me home ...? You can go back. Enjoy the reception. Stay for the dancing.'

'All right,' Isobel said. 'But I'll stay home.' Then she shushed him because the service was starting; "Dearly Beloved. We are gathered here ... "

They left the church before the organist played the Mendelssohn. Isobel helped Magnus out, by the side gate into Church Street where the car was. He was feeling the strain after an hour on his feet. 'Are you really all right?' she fretted once he was settled.

'I'm sorry!' His eyes were very bright. He was going to indulge in the pessimism that so often overcame him. 'I'm no use to anyone. I want to get back to work – be like I was before – and look at me!'

Isobel was weaving between the market stalls, honking the horn until they were clear. Then she said to Magnus, 'Enough! No self-pity please. You can easily do three days a week at Hammonds Silk. I'll drive you there. You work sitting down. Stop feeling sorry for yourself. You are better than you've been for years. There's no bleeding, anywhere.'

*

Two weeks later, the bleeding into the bowel recurred and

Magnus went into hospital for another blood transfusion. It had been detected early this time the doctors said. He should be home well before Christmas and the birth of the baby. The doctors were right. Magnus came out of hospital, walking with sticks and none the worse for the set-back. Isobel helped him into the car to take him home and told him, 'Everything's going to be all right. The doctor said if they can catch it early, like this, then you've got a long, happy life ahead of you.'

She held him close. 'I want you to be strong and well. I want my child to have a good, kind Dad who loves us both.'

'You've got it,' he said. It was pouring with rain at the time but they drove up to the rain-lashed hills, singing "The Umbrella Man" and shouting "Little Sir Echo" at the tops of their voices, defying nature to do her worst. Christmas came and went – and no baby. Nanna moved in with them at Bollinbrook Road, to stay for a month to care for Magnus and help with the infant. A room was booked at the Cottage Hospital and everyone, except evidently the baby, was ready for the birth.

Isobel's ankles swelled if she'd been on her feet all day and her back ached if she lay in bed in the same position for very long but she had no predictive signs. Isobel didn't feel that the birth was imminent. But now, Nanna was in charge. When New Year's day came and went Nanna demanded, 'What did the doctor say to you? When do you see him?'

'I'd be aware of it, if anything was wrong, Nanna,' she said. 'There's no need to see a doctor until . . .'

'You've never been, have you?' Nanna gave her a knowing look, 'I'm calling doctor,' she said. 'Dial number for me.'

There was nothing for it. Isobel dialled and asked for the doctor to come and examine her.

Dr Russell came immediately. Isobel went upstairs and undressed and Nanna stood at the other side of the bed, watching him. He was thorough. He pressed his hands above and below the bulge; he frowned and pressed them round the sides of the bulge; he squeezed the poor baby until the bulge came up in a little mountain between his palms; he examined her swelling breasts. Then he searched in his bag for a rubber glove to put on his right hand before he did something more intimate.

When he had finished and he and Nanna had covered her

up, he went quiet for a few moments before finally he said, 'Well my dear. You certainly are pregnant. But this is no nine-month pregnancy. Seven months, I'd say. All is well. Cancel the hospital bed and reserve one for the end of February or the beginning of March.'

When they left the room and Nanna showed Dr Russell to the door, tears of gratitude came rolling down Isobel's face. She was expecting Magnus's baby. Her child was going to have its own father.

It was mid February; nine months and one week exactly since Magnus and she had eloped. Isobel was coming out of a fast, nail polish scented dream of stars and bright lights.

A nurse's face was swimming into her line of vision.

'It's a boy!'

They had given her a whiff of chloroform at the end of twelve hours of pain. She had only been out for a few minutes but it felt like years. She glanced at the sheet. Cottage Hospital. Then she saw the nurse's face.

'It's a boy! You have a beautiful baby boy!' The nurse had a nice face. She said, 'Ten pounds. No wonder he took so long to come.'

'Where?' Her voice was wavering. She tried to sit up.

'Lie down! You've got stitches in. Baby is in the nursery, being bathed and wrapped. Go to sleep!' She was patting the pillows, talking firmly and pushing Isobel gently down with strong hands.

Isobel knocked her hands away and sat up. 'I won't go to sleep. Bring my baby.'

The nurse spoke indulgently, pacifying. 'Mother. We let our mothers sleep for twelve hours before we bring the babies.'

'Bring him this minute!' Isobel was shouting. 'I want him now!' she said and saw with glee that the nurse went fast, almost ran from the bedside. When she'd gone Isobel plumped the pillows behind her back and edged up the bed, painfully aware of the stitching. It was seven thirty in the morning. She determined to put from her mind, as the thoughts came rushing back, all remembrance of the whole messy business.

She heard footsteps; the nurse, with Magnus dotting and clumping along behind her. Then they were in and putting into

Isobel's arms the most beautiful creature in the world. Her son had bright, light blond hair that was thick and wavy. Through the shawl she could feel the strong little body that was of her but no longer hers. She gazed and gazed. She couldn't take her eyes off him. She was feasting on the sweet smell, the solid feel, the sight and the sound of him, for he was pursing his lips and trying to suckle her arm, making little mewing sounds that were wrapping her round with love.

Magnus was seated and he leaned over the bed, one arm across her shoulder. 'Hello, son!' he said. He put his face next to hers and Isobel felt his tears running warm and wet down her cheeks, mingling with her own.

The nurse had gone. Isobel handed the baby to Magnus. 'Hold him, darling, while I undo my front,' she said.

Magnus said, 'The nurse says she's going to teach you how to do it. Later today. Are you allowed to . . .'

'Teach me? Stuff and nonsense,' she answered as she exposed one swollen breast and took her baby from Magnus. 'We'll do it by ourselves. Won't we, baby?'

The little mouth latched on to her. Strong little jaws clamped and sucked vigorously and Isobel heard him gulping down that first thick, sweet yellow milk.

She looked at Magnus. Tears were coursing down his cheeks. Her own tears had gone. She was being transformed, through joy and love, into that fiercely protective creature that was a new mother. 'Isn't he beautiful, Magnus? Which name are we going to give him? Have you decided?'

'He looks like me. He looks just like me . . .' Magnus was crying.

'He's the image of you, darling. There's no question. It's your son.'

'Robert!' said Magnus who had taken out a handkerchief and was blowing his nose. 'Bobby while he's little.'

Magnus had only been gone a couple of hours when there was a commotion in the entrance hall, just beyond the door. Then she heard Mrs Hammond's voice, loud and dictatorial. 'I insist! I can't allow you to stand between me and my grandson.'

The nurse would lose the battle if she tried to get Mrs Hammond to come back tomorrow. She was being far too polite saying, 'I think it might be better if ...'

Isobel heard her mother-in-law sweep past the nurse. 'Do you know who I am? Out of my way!' and she came sailing into the room, her face a picture of satisfaction.

'I've brought you some calf's foot jelly,' was her greeting as she swept past Isobel to sit on the chair next to the crib. 'It's quite wrong to give nursing mothers fruit or chocolate.'

'Oh,' was all Isobel could think to say while she waited to see what her mother-in-law would do next.

Mrs Hammond had not taken her eyes off the crib since she'd seated herself. She gave Isobel a quick, unwilling smile. 'Mr Hammond ... er ... Magnus's father ...' She coughed; started again. 'I have been ordered to make peace with you.'

'Oh.'

She was gazing at her grandson as she spoke. 'I said to John, "Good gracious! There's no ill-will between us. Isobel will understand what drives a mother to protect her son. Now that she has one of her own!"' She stood up and without a by-your-leave she scooped the sleeping baby out of his crib and sat down again, with him cradled in her arms.

Isobel watched closely as she peeled back the shawl. And a smile such as she had never seen on that remote, classical face before, came like lightning across it. Her eyes were filled, lit with pride. 'He's the living image of Magnus,' she said. 'I'll bring some photographs when I come tomorrow, to prove it.'

She got to her feet, holding the baby fast to her chest, and came to stand over Isobel. 'No problems with the cord?' she said. 'No bleeding?'

Isobel found her voice. 'He isn't haemophiliac, Mrs Hammond, if that's what's worrying you.'

'*Mrs Hammond*? You'd better start calling me Mama. At once.'

For eighteen months Isobel had revelled in her new life, in bringing up her baby, looking after Magnus, being part of her new family, content that her angel child had the foundation rock of his life laid for him. Bobby had what she had never known. His own true father.

Bobby, their beautiful golden-haired boy, was the apple of Magnus's and the grandparents' eyes. Magnus's parents spoke highly of Isobel too, saying that she was 'the brains of the family', 'the best thing that ever happened to Magnus' and 'the mother of our pride and joy' for Bobby was theirs – he was their Hammond grandson – and nothing was too good for him. Isobel had expected friction between Mam and the Hammonds, but to her amazement, there was none. Mam adored Bobby, and on her half-day the three of them – Isobel, Mam and the baby – went into town, Mam insisting on pushing the pram so she could enjoy the attention of acquaintances and customers and bask in their exclamations of 'My word. He's a bonny baby. And you, Mrs Leigh, look much too young to be a grandmother.'

There was nothing to indicate the coming tragedy unless one took account of Nanna's old superstition that sudden deaths never came singly. In July 1939 Sylvia's twin boys were born. They were haemophiliac and lived only two days, bleeding to death at the umbilicus. They had not got over the shock; Sylvia never would; and tragedy was coming for all of them.

It was Friday 1 September and as hot as any June day. In another two days they would know if there was going to be war. Hitler had been given an ultimatum: 'Withdraw from Poland or our country will be at war with Germany.' Nobody doubted that they would have to fight. The factories were crying out for hands. Hammonds Silks was busy again. Chancellor's was printing camouflage cloth; the other factories were making shell cases and munitions, small parts for bigger guns, bullets, shells, webbing and rope. Once the men were called up the women would have to do men's work. They would be needed in the factories, on the land, in the hospitals and the forces. Air-raid shelters were built, gas masks had been distributed and children were arriving in town, evacuated from London and Manchester and Liverpool.

Isobel drove through the Waters, where a group of evacuees were being marched up Churchwallgate to the Market Place. The older ones, excited and voluble, held little white-faced children, some as young as four, by the hand. In front of the Town Hall their families were waiting for them in the blazing sunshine.

Next to her sat Bobby in a special seat that had been made for him by a coachbuilder. Isobel said, 'You are a lucky boy.

Going to Grandma's.'

'Where Mummy go?' He stuck his thumb in his mouth.

Isobel said, 'Mummy and Daddy are going to the pictures.' They had booked seats for *Gone With The Wind* and a dinner table at the Macclesfield Arms as a belated anniversary treat. It would be their first evening alone at Bollinbrook Road since Bobby was born; the first time Bobby had been left overnight in his grandparents' care, and tonight was their last chance to see the film everyone was raving about.

Bobby understood little at eighteen months, but he liked his mother to chatter to him as she drove. He sat, blond curls falling forward over his brow, eyes drooping, as they went up Hibel Road and on towards Manchester Road and Bollington. 'Mummy is going to leave you with Grandma and Pop. You like that, don't you?' Isobel pulled his thumb out of his mouth but he stuck it straight back in, so she left it there, tenderly thinking that there was no reason to deny a baby anything. His grandparents indulged him with every comfort a child could have. Magnus was now on the sidelines of their life. They gave all their time and attention to Bobby. Magnus said it was a relief to come second, to be overlooked; not to be on the receiving end of the Chilprufe coats, the fine wool underwear, the hair shampooing with beaten eggs, the delicacies they lavished on their adored grandson.

Isobel and Magnus were in high spirits when they left Archerfield to return to Bollinbrook Road to change their clothes, Isobel into a short beige dress with padded shoulders and a crossover skirt that had buttons down the left side, Magnus into his new tweed suit. Only an hour later they were sitting at a table in the Macclesfield Arms Hotel, eating their way through a six-course dinner.

They had tomato soup, baked haddock, roast fowl, apple charlotte, savoury aigrettes and cheese and cream crackers with coffee. They drank wine with it, a claret which was Magnus's favourite. Magnus said he felt devilish because he'd had three forbidden things, the tomato soup, the apple and the red wine. Isobel wanted to stop him but he would not be ordered about since he'd put his foot down to his mama. He certainly never allowed the least criticism of himself in public, so Isobel said, 'Do you think it's wise, darling? Taking wine as well as apple and tomato?'

He was bold after two glasses of claret. 'Life's not worth living if a man is not his own master,' he said.

She agreed tactfully but stopped him from ordering more by saying, 'Come on. We'll be late for second house. We don't want to miss any.'

They left the car in the Market Place and went arm in arm down Mill Street to the Majestic. Magnus used only one stick when Isobel was with him, and especially when walking downhill.

Magnus said, 'We had a call from Ian this morning. He has passed out – finished his officer training at Greenwich. He'll be appointed to a ship soon. He's going to Edinburgh for a week's leave . . .'

'Where will they send him?'

'It could be anywhere.'

'Maybe he'll stay in this country,' she said. 'They need doctors at the naval bases, don't they?'

'Ian will want to see action. He'll volunteer for service on an aircraft carrier, or at least a battleship.' He added, 'I wish I were able to do my bit.'

'If your mill is producing parachutes, you are doing your bit, Magnus.' As Isobel said it a shiver ran through her. It was a beautiful evening, balmy after the heat of the day. The trees had not shed their leaves and the hills and farmland around Macclesfield were at their sleepy, end-of-the-season best. It was hideous to imagine that in two days' time they would be in danger from bombers and guns and gas attacks. But they were at the Majestic. The queue went round the white marble pillars outside the cinema and up the hill as far as Roe Street. They passed through the foyer and studied the photographs of the film stars. Magnus said, 'You are awfully like her, you know. Vivien Leigh. Everyone says so, even Father.'

'Oh! You flatterer,' Isobel laughed, and said, to return the compliment, 'You look rather like Leslie Howard.'

'Do you think so?' Magnus put his shoulders back in a haughty gesture.

Isobel awoke at about four in the morning, very cold. Magnus was icy. Half asleep, she tried to pull the covers higher, to warm his shoulders. Then her hand slid over his arm and it fell forward, cold and lifeless, and at once all her senses came jerking into life.

There was a stench in the room, her lower body was wet, there was silence. There was no sound at all from Magnus, and he was not responding to her touch as Isobel pulled him over on to his back.

'Magnus! Magnus!' She clicked on the switch that hung over the bed.

A glaring light came down to reveal the white, waxen face with lifeless eyes and jaw fallen open. His blood, the massive haemorrhage, had stained him and her and had soaked the bed beneath him, right up to the pillows and bolster. Magnus, her darling husband, was dead in her arms.

Chapter Twenty-Five

Magnus was buried in the little graveyard at Archerfield on a warm September afternoon. Isobel was deathly pale from shock and loss as she watched yet another coffin of yet another loved one being lowered into the earth. She had Bobby by the hand, and only his warm hand in hers gave her any comfort, any hope, any relief. She heard not a word of the service and she didn't look at a single face in the crowd of mourners.

The Mackenzies were here – Ian, Rowena and their father; the Hammonds, Sylvia and Ray. Mr Chancellor came out of respect – he was quiet this time, none of the sobbing he'd been unable to control at the funeral of Sylvia's twins. The staff of Archerfield paid their respects and a few Bollington tradespeople came, but it was the family's loss and the family members had been rendered numb.

Nobody cried. Magnus's mother and father stood silent, holding hands as their son's body was laid into the earth. The priest said, loud, so that all could hear on that golden afternoon with a soft breeze coming down from the hills above, 'Man that is born of a woman hath but a short time to live, and is full of misery. He cometh up, and is cut down, like a flower; he fleeth as it were a shadow, and never continueth in one stay. In the midst of life we are in death; of whom may we seek for succour, but for thee, O Lord, who for our sins art justly displeased.'

And fanciful though Isobel might be she lifted up her eyes to those hills and prayed for strength because, she told God, 'O Lord, Magnus was not a sinner. Magnus was a good man, who did good things. Why have you taken him from me?'

Then Bobby came closer and leaned his hot little golden head against her leg and held tighter on to her hand. 'Go home, Mummy? Bobby go home, Mummy!'

Isobel picked him up and pressed his face close to hers until the last amen was said.

After the funeral tea Mam went back to Lindow with Nanna, and the Hammonds demanded that Isobel and Bobby stay at Archerfield.

'I can't,' Isobel told Magnus's father. 'I must go home. I need to be alone for a little time. I have to cry. I have to remember Magnus, tonight.'

'Then leave Bobby here, with Grandma and me?' Pop Hammond was kind but firm. 'Mr Chancellor will drive you back to Bollinbrook Road, I am sure.'

On the drive back to Bollinbrook Road she was silent, holding back tears until she could be alone. Mr Chancellor was clearly worried. At last he said kindly. 'You've had a bad do, lass. There's nothing I can say that would comfort you, is there?'

Isobel began to cry. 'It's my fault. If it hadn't been for me . . .'

'Hey! Hey! None of that,' he said. 'We can't have you thinking like that. It's not your fault. Whatever made you think so?'

'I'm full of guilt. I'm afraid – afraid I'll go like I was before, thinking of dying and wishing I'd gone instead of Magnus. Thinking everyone's against me – whispering behind my back . . .'

'Whispering what?'

'That I'm a nobody – nothing. That nobody wants me. I bring trouble, shame, disgrace wherever I go . . .'

They reached Bollinbrook Road. Mr Chancellor had gone quiet. He helped her into the house and sat her in a chair by the fireplace. Then he stood over her where she sat, sobbing and incoherent.

Isobel saw the worried, helpless expression on that face that was always cheery and breezy. She said, 'Leave me alone. If only I had someone to share it with . . .' She put her head on to her arms and sobbed.

He put a hand on her shoulder and gave it a little squeeze. 'Can't you share it with me, lass?'

'No. No. I can't tell anyone . . . I want my husband . . . I never had a man of my own. I never knew my father ... I want my own man ... Don't you see ...? I can't take any more ...'

He was very quiet. Twice he started to say something but held himself back. Finally he said, 'You can't be left on your own like this. Don't do anything daft. I'll go back and get someone to stop with you.'

It was an hour before they arrived – Ian, Rowena and Sylvia – to comfort her and talk to her and to try to put hope and spirit back into her.

Sylvia cried, 'I know what it's like. We will comfort one another ... Ray's call-up papers came this morning. I shall be all alone ... Oh, Isobel ...'

Rowena said, 'You made Magnus very happy. You didn't think you'd have him for ever. Throw yourself into something as soon as you can. That's my advice. Don't dwell on your misfortunes.'

The girls fussed over her. They said they would stay the night, sleeping together in the spare bed. They made hot drinks for her and put her to bed. They gave her a draught of something to quieten her and at last, when they were satisfied with their ministrations and Isobel was warm and sleepy and had no tears left, Ian came upstairs and sat on her bed, holding her hands.

'You have to rise above it, Isobel,' he said. 'None of it is your fault. We'll need all our strength for the fight. Don't spend yourself on self-pity.'

'Thank you,' she whispered. 'I'll be all right. I've got Bobby.' She was very sleepy but she said, 'And you, Ian?'

'Me?'

'Have you found some girl, perhaps ...?'

He was silent for a few moments. He just sat holding her hands and looking at her puffy face. Then he leaned forward and kissed her on the forehead. 'No. I haven't found anyone. I'm joining my ship tomorrow. Write to me now and again.'

It was not until she was going through Magnus's belongings, clearing out the roll-top desk where he kept all his private papers, that she found the letter. It was tucked inside a slim volume called *Haemophilia: Clinical and Genetic Aspects*. Isobel remembered it as one of the books from the redwood bookcase that had belonged to Mrs Chancellor. The envelope was addressed to Miss Sarah Pilkington, written in Pop's distinctive hand, and just as Magnus had, she read and understood at once the significance of the words written so long ago.

Charlotte Square, Edinburgh.
5th January, 1915

My dear Sarah,
Where have you been hiding these last weeks? My letters have gone un-answered. I have missed you. I wanted to talk to you and I have not seen you since the night last November when I came, undeserving to your bed and you gave yourself so generously. Your love gave me such comfort.
I am glad there have been no repercussions ...

Magnus had kept this secret to himself because to tell would have broken so many hearts. But he had kept the letter, hoping that one day she would find it, and understand. And he had known that Sylvia, though married to her own half-brother, was a carrier of the disease that would stop her from bearing a normal son. There was nothing Magnus could have done about it. 'Oh, Magnus,' she wept. 'You were a good man who did good things. Why did you leave me?'

Brilliant moonlight lit up the countryside for miles around. Because Mam was in Macclesfield, Isobel went to Lindow to see Nanna at ten o'clock that May night. She had left Nanna only two hours before, but a little whispering voice had come to live inside her head – and it told her that she should return. That night was going to be one of the worst – and one of the last – of the blitzes. Everyone had stood on the moonlit lawn at Archerfield, watching formations of German bombers going over White Nancy – no longer white but painted green and brown and khaki in camouflage pattern – and they saw the sky burning orange and red where Manchester lay to the north.

Isobel put on her slacks – it was shocking to see a lady in trousers, Grandma said – then she went to Lindow.

Nanna was in bed. She had been tired for a few days, breathless, and unusually for her had had no appetite.

Isobel went straight upstairs to the bedroom where Nanna was lying, eyes closed, breathing fast but easily. 'Nanna!'

She opened her eyes. 'Eeh. Glad you came, Lil. I'll not see the night out.'

Isobel sat down on her bed and took hold of Nanna's little hand. 'I wish you'd have the doctor, Nanna.'

She gave a sweet little smile. 'Doctor can't do anything. It's me heart, lass. It's tired out.'

Isobel had suspected for days that Nanna was nearing her end. Mam would not face it. Mam said that Nanna had a touch of summer cold and would soon be right. But Nanna wanted to go. She had been talking a lot, these last days, about Grandpa and Magnus and how it would be when she met them again.

'Stay with me,' she said, and she was gasping for breath. 'Keep me comp'ny. Let me go easy.'

'I will.'

'Have you had another letter from Ian?' she said, knowing that Isobel wanted her to ask.

'He's in the Atlantic fleet. I'm not allowed to say which ship.'

'I shan't tell anyone, lass. Not this side.'

'He wants to marry me when the war's over,' Isobel said, and she felt the blood rush to her cheeks, remembering the words in his last letter: *You have always been the only girl for me. I have been serious and reserved in the past and I have never been able to express myself on paper. I want to tell you that I was afraid of my powerful feelings for you that first time we kissed. I was afraid of being too eager, too fast. I was a fool, Isobel, not to tell you how much I need you. I want to lay my head on your breast and tell you of the great unbounded love I have for you. Will you marry me*?

Isobel said to Nanna, 'I wrote to him and said yes.'

Nanna said, 'I'll be watching you, Lil. I'll be with you in spirit.'

Isobel bit her lip. The letter had come three months ago. They all lived on a knife edge. Nobody could guess what the next day would bring.

'When's Sylvia's baby . . .' Nanna breathed.

'July,' she said. Ray, a senior aircraftsman, was based in Kent and came home regularly on leave. Sylvia was expecting a child in July.

Nanna whispered, 'You are going to be happy when it's

over. You've had your troubles. You've fettled 'em, Lil.' Isobel tried to hush her but she wanted to say more. 'You'll have your man and your house in the hills.'

'Archerfield will go to Bobby, Nanna. He will have everything that was Magnus's.' The mill would be Bobby's when he was twenty-one. Isobel was salaried, a voting, working director of Hammond's. Magnus's father was going to work on, he said. He'd be like his own father before him and all the old mill-owners in Macclesfield. He'd die in harness.

Nanna lifted a pale little hand and patted the bed. 'Lie down, lass. Like when you were little . . .'

Isobel slipped off her slacks and climbed into bed beside Nanna. 'I used to sigh, "A-ah! A-ah!"' she said as she lay down.

'I'd say, "Is that you, our Lil?"' Nanna gave a deep sigh.

'And I'd get in and cuddle up to you, like this . . .' Isobel said, and she slipped her arm around Nanna, moved closer and said, 'I loved being with you, Nanna.'

But Nanna had gone.

One Sunday lunchtime, a month after Nanna died, Isobel cooked the Sunday dinner as she always did. They had roast pork, boiled potatoes and tinned peas with roast parsnips, there being no greens ready in June in Grandma's garden – for Grandma had taken to the soil. Isobel had made apple pie and custard – and all this because her in-laws had always eaten a roast on Sundays, and always would.

After it was over and Mam had returned to Lindow, they were all tired, Pop went for a lie-down in his room, Sylvia took Bobby up to bed with her for an afternoon rest and Grandma and Isobel collapsed into the wicker armchairs of the conservatory.

The windows were all crisscrossed with sticky tape in case bombs fell. It was cold, damp and stuffy. 'Shall I open the door so we can breathe?' Isobel asked.

Grandma said, 'Yes,' and when Isobel had done it, offered her a sherry and said, 'Your mother does very well. All that work. And a husband in the asyl . . . Sorry, the mental hospital.'

There seemed no need to reply to this and Isobel took

another sip of sherry as Grandma continued, 'War brings the best out in people.'

What did she mean? 'Why do you say that?' Isobel said. 'War has done nothing for me.'

'Class divisions go in wartime,' she said. 'Snobbery has gone.'

'You never were a snob,' Isobel said, at last daring to talk to her mother-in-law as an equal. 'You used to terrify me. You said what you meant but you never put on airs about your connections and social ambitions.'

She laughed. 'That's because I'm Scottish. We don't make the same distinctions in Scotland. We look up to people who work hard and achieve great standing. We don't admire people simply for being high-born.'

'I think you're right.' Isobel was glad that at last they were becoming companionable and settled with one another. 'I remember thinking, in Scotland, that for the first time in my life nobody probed my background – nobody asked who my father was.' She stopped abruptly. She had said too much. Grandma could have come back with, 'And who was your father?'

But Grandma laughed. 'There's an old saying in Scotland which we use if someone is getting too big for his boots.'

'A man's man, for a'that?' Isobel suggested.

'No. We say, "Aye! I kent his fayther!"' She looked at Isobel's puzzled face and translated: 'I knew his father.'

'Meaning?'

'Meaning, "I know who you are. You will never be other than your father's child."'

It was perhaps an innocent little observation; it may have been tactless. But the relaxed feeling that had come to Isobel seconds ago was gone. Her nerves were on a knife's edge. She jumped to her feet, threw the glass of sherry out through the open door on to the grass and turned an angry face on her mother-in-law. 'And what about me? What about Bobby? I never knew my father. Bobby will never know his. Where does that put us on your scale of values? Are we nobodies – because we don't have fathers?'

The telephone started to ring, but before Grandma could go to pick it up or answer, Isobel stormed out, through the garden, down the path, hurrying to get away from her and all of the self-satisfied people at Archerfield. She ran as fast as she could, heading for the hills and a breath of clean, fresh air.

She was wearing only sandals and a print frock, but she would not go back to change. The heather would scratch her bare legs and she had no cardigan in case it went chilly, but on and on she went until, out of breath, out of practice and out of temper she reached the top of Kerridge Hill.

Below, all of Bollington lay dreaming in the heat. There were no signs of war from here. Few people walked in the hills these days, with the men gone and the constant need to be near to shelter.

She had calmed down. She wished she hadn't made that outburst. Grandma hadn't meant to be hurtful. She was tactless and domineering but she had no ill-will towards Isobel. They all lived on their nerves, waiting for the next disaster to strike, waiting to hear what had happened to the men.

There had been no bombing raids for a week and everyone wondered if it could possibly be true that the tide of war was about to turn. A few days ago news had come through that Hitler had broken his pact with Stalin. He had turned on Russia. A hundred German divisions had smashed through the eighteen-hundred-mile border from the Arctic Circle to the Black Sea.

Ray was safe. He had telephoned Sylvia only last night. But Isobel had not heard from Ian, and since Nanna died she had not been to church. But she prayed, on that warm hilltop, 'Please God. Keep Ian safe ... Please God. Keep Ian safe ... Please God. Keep Ian safe ...' over and over. She didn't need to embellish it or promise anything in return. Ian's ship – a county cruiser whose name she dared not mention – had been sent from the North Atlantic, with about a hundred others, to hunt and sink the *Bismarck*.

Now, the *Bismarck* – the unsinkable – was lying at the bottom of the Atlantic and they had heard no news of home losses – which ships were damaged and returning home, how many men were dead.

It was one o'clock. Isobel had time to walk over the hills towards the pine woods and Rainow. There was a taxicab climbing the hill below her, clanking its gears, disturbing the quiet. She got to her feet and started to walk over the Saddle on her favourite route.

She had been walking for half an hour and was nearing the pine woods when she stopped to take the kirby grips out of her hair. She was warm and it would cool her to let her hair out of the confines of the roll she wore it in. She had shaken her dark hair out and put the precious kirby grips into her pocket when she heard, 'Isobel . . . ! Isobel . . . !'

For a terrible moment she thought she was dreaming, having hallucinations – hearing voices from above. She was rooted to the spot. She dared not turn. Then it came, louder and clearer, 'Isobel! Wait for me, Isobel!'

She wheeled round and saw him, running towards her, his naval uniform jacket flying open, his white cap in his hand. 'Isobel . . . !'

Then they were in each other's arms. Ian had his arms tight about her and their mouths were locked together in the kisses that made her faint with relief and love and the sweetness of his need of her.

He stopped for breath, laughed and took her by the hand. 'Marry me?' was all he said as they ran towards the pine woods.

'Yes, Oh yes,' she said. And they were running deeper into the woods, into a little sheltered hollow where their canopy was a leafy green tracery against the blue of the sky and the ground below, the flattened brown bracken, dappled in sun and shade.

They dropped to their knees and held one another close, out of sight of the world, and unseen but seeing he said again, 'Will you marry me?'

'Oh, yes. I wrote to you and . . .'

Isobel got no further, for his mouth was on hers again and he was struggling out of his jacket and putting it aside. Her hands slid from his shoulders to help him unfasten his shirt before he started to undo the button-through print dress and open it wide.

Then he stopped kissing her and held her a little way from himself and feasted his eyes on the round, bouncing breasts that were firming and sending shivers through her whole body, waiting for his touch. He gave a little groan and buried his face into the hollow space between them. Then he stopped, put his hands on her breasts and pushed her away a little way. Smiling at her he said, 'Do you want me to ...?'

'Yes.' Isobel laughed a little before she kissed him on the mouth, the eyes, the neck.

'Tomorrow ...' he said when she stopped for breath.

'What? What tomorrow ...?'

'I bought a special licence. We're catching the early train to Edinburgh. Tomorrow ...' Isobel pressed her mouth over his again and he was laughing when she came up for air. He said, 'We're getting married at four o'clock on Tuesday. Rowena and her fiancée will be there. That's all ...'

Chapter Twenty-six

Macclesfield Arms Hotel, 1948

Last night I dreamed that Ian made love to me. It is a recurrent dream and the act of love is incomplete, as I am without him. The dream began with his calling to me from a far, far distance. 'Isobel ... Isobel ... Isobel Leigh!' He came striding across the saddle of Kerridge Hill, wearing the cord trousers and Fair Isle pullover he wore when he first kissed me. I ran to him and we clung together for a moment before we sank to our knees on the grass in a passionate embrace, with his declaration of love whispering in the soft heather-scented wind that played across our swaying bodies. 'I love you ... I love you, Isobel.'

I knew from the start that I was dreaming. I always know. I tell myself with my conscious mind when I am in the half-asleep state that is the dream's precursor, 'Stop this dream. There is no need to dream. Ian is your husband. Your past is done.'

But the subconscious always triumphs and I am back in my dream to the time when I was Our Lil, the girl who had only a mam, trying to re-create myself as one of that breed of strong, unassailable north-country women who would never be bested or demeaned.

But I needed a father for that creation. I had always needed a father to complete my dream. And I believed that I had never known my father.

Such were my waking thoughts as I lay, half dreaming, in my bed at the Macclesfield Arms Hotel at the posh end of Jordangate, watching the breakfast maid pulling back the curtains.

'Mornin', Mrs Mackenzie,' she said as she crossed the room to place the breakfast trolley at my bedside. 'It's a lovely day,' and quickly she followed the observation with another, with true Macclesfield directness. 'How long are you stopping?'

'I'll be here for another day, at least.'

When she left I got out of bed and went to the window to look at the hills beyond the District Bank and, craning my neck, at our old shop. And a little voice inside my head repeated, 'You belong to Macclesfield. This old town is where your heart lives. Don't be influenced by a chance glimpse of Doreen yesterday. If you return, Doreen will have no part to play in your life.'

I had a good life; the life of a doctor's wife in Edinburgh. The voice said, 'All that can change. The choice is yours.'

I sat at the breakfast trolley and poured a cup of tea. Tomorrow Ian and Bobby would arrive at the station. Mam, who lived with us in Edinburgh, had refused to come with them, saying she was afraid to return. She said, 'I can't go back to visit. Too much of my life has been spent there. I miss it. I'm homesick. I want my old life back.' Her lovely face had been clouded.

I replied, 'I wouldn't stop you, Mam. But what is there in Macclesfield for you now? My stepfather is dead. Nanna is dead. We have nobody left.'

Mam had put an arm about Bobby and my son pressed himself against his beloved grandmother's skirt. Bobby was as devoted to Mam as I had been to my Nanna. Mam said, 'I can't leave you. But I feel as if there's a part of me that's been torn out.'

I laughed and said, 'Your heart?' then wished I hadn't, because I saw the yearning for something or someone in Mam's eyes. So I said with brisk practicality, 'I haven't ruled it out. But you can always change your mind.'

'I can't . . .' she said, as if a decision she had once made had come home to haunt her.

'Mam!' I said, 'You have nobody left in Macclesfield. Your family is here. And we want you to stay with us.' But Mam had the haunted look when she waved me off.

The Macclesfield Arms faces the District Bank, and I could see two clerks arriving for work. Magnus's father would be passing under my window soon, if he still had the same habit of working at the bank on Fridays.

I buttered a piece of toast and went back to the window. On Monday Ian would have his interview at the new hospital that once was the Institute of Guardians; the workhouse. The National Health Service was crying out for doctors all over the country. Ian was certain to be offered a post – so I had until Monday or Tuesday to decide whether our home was to be Edinburgh or Macclesfield. Four days. And the decision was mine.

When I had eaten breakfast I had a bath, brushed my curly hair as Nanna used to do until it waved and loosened so I could fasten it in a chignon at the back of my head. Then I dressed, as yesterday, in the Parisian tangerine suit. I put on sheer nylon stockings that had a thin black seam and slipped on black patent high-heeled shoes. Then I pinned a black pill-box hat on top of my head, high and tall. I liked what I saw in the long mirror when I was ready. I looked a picture of confidence and competence – so why did I have this feeling that I was still the little girl everyone in Macclesfield knew as Our Lil, the girl with no name, no father and no place in this ancient order?

I picked up my black handbag and at ten thirty left the hotel and crossed the road to the District Bank. The banking hall was busy with company clerks withdrawing wages cash, as I had done when I worked at Hammond Silks. I had not made an appointment, so I waited until the chief cashier looked up and recognised me, left his place and went through the door marked 'Mr John Hammond'.

The door opened and Pop came out, his eyes alive with welcome, the beautiful voice soothing. He took my arm and led me into the office. 'I had no idea ... When did you arrive?'

'Yesterday. I have some things to attend to in Macclesfield. Ian and Bobby are not coming until tomorrow – so we will all come up to Archerfield and stay with you and Grandma. How is she?'

His lovely face broke into a smile, though he said, 'We have missed you. We miss Bobby dreadfully. Grandma hasn't been the same since he went ...'

'Pop!' I said quickly. 'I went to the Town Hall yesterday.

They want to pull down the Bollinbrook Road house. They are going to build an estate of new houses there. We've agreed a price, though we have no choice, really. They offered five hundred. So we will sell.'

'You want the deeds?'

'Yes. I want to take everything out of my safe deposit box. The deeds to Lindow as well. There's a lot to attend to. The tenant isn't satisfactory ...' He looked sad as I added, 'We may sell Lindow.'

'Your mother? Doesn't she want to come back to us?'

'Not unless I come home.' I had said it. Home. It was not what I meant. I must keep my head, not be swayed by sentiment.

'How is Bobby?' Pop said.

Trying to be calm and practical and do what was right for us all, I smiled and said, 'Splendid. He misses you. He's been very excited knowing he'll be seeing Pop and Grandma – and his cousin Judy. How's Sylvia?' Sylvia had given birth in 1941, to a healthy daughter. I said, 'And how's the mill?'

'Sylvia is well. The mill isn't working to capacity. Nowhere near. It would be sensible to join forces with Chancellor's. Ray could take over Hammond Silks – if you were agreeable,' he said. I still had a casting vote in the future of Hammond Silks, because it would one day be Bobby's. He said, 'We will have to have a family conference. You will represent Bobby's interests, of course.'

'What are the options?'

'We have two choices. British Nylon Spinners want to buy us out. Or we join forces with Chancellor's Printworks.'

'Oh.' My mouth went tight at the corners as an obstinate frown crossed my brow. 'Magnus wouldn't have wanted that.'

'He might have changed his mind, Isobel, if he'd seen how hard Ray works. He's made a great success of Chancellor's.'

'I don't want Ray to be in charge of Bobby's inheritance.'

He looked baffled. 'You have always had a grasp of financial matters, Isobel,' he began, 'I know that you and Ray don't see eye to eye ...'

'It's not just that, Pop,' I protested.

He waved my objection aside and said gravely, 'I want you to look at it differently. Put your prejudices aside and ask yourself, "What if Bobby had been a Chancellor?"'

Heat came flooding into my face. I can still blush if I think anyone has the tiniest inkling of my past. But Pop didn't notice. He said, 'I want you to ask yourself something, my dear. Ask, "What if Sylvia had given birth to Bobby – and Magnus had fathered a daughter?"' He smiled a little sad smile and said, 'If that had been so, then the child who inherited Hammond Silks would be a Chancellor.'

I had not thought of it that way. Iron-willed, I had forced it out of my mind, and it was easy to do, being far away from Macclesfield. But here and now I had to ask myself whether it was right that Bobby would grow up knowing little about his Macclesfield inheritance. Bobby had relatives here: Pop and Grandma, Sylvia and her child. Mam and I had nobody left in Macclesfield – not a relative in the world. All I had was the old unsatisfied curiosity, the question that had plagued me for half of my life. *Is the father I never knew dead? I don't think I could bear to live here again, knowing that my real true father was alive and had no interest in me*. But I said to Pop, 'I'll talk it over with Ian.'

Pop said, 'There's no immediate hurry. Come along. I'll take you down to the vaults.' He took a great bunch of keys from the desk and led me through the offices to the back of the bank. He opened an iron grille and went ahead, down a wide flight of stone stairs, through another set of locked iron gates and into a big, barrel-vaulted cellar room that was brightly lit. Along one long wall were the steel boxes of the safe deposit customers. Mine, I saw, was marked 'Stanway/Leigh'.

I looked around while Pop tried to find the right key. On the other walls were narrow shelves with little date labels in the manner of 'January 1910 to July 1910' and so on. On the shelves were bundles of cheques and credit slips, wrapped round loosely with split-open brown envelopes that were sealed with red wax. And on each open-ended parcel was written the day's date, clearly and in sequence.

'What are these?' I asked Pop.

'Each one is a whole day's work – in alphabetical order. We seal the day's clearing, as we call it, every day, and store it down here.'

'Do you keep *everything*?' I asked. 'And how long do you

have to keep them? Some of the bundles are very small.'

He laughed. 'We keep them for ever. We never destroy them. We often have to refer to them. If a customer wants to know whether or not a cheque was cashed ...'

All at once it came to me. I could discover whether St Ursula's school did cash the cheque for my last term's fees. The school had never re-imbursed me and it had rankled, over the years.

Pop was trying key after key in my box – and having no luck. He said, 'Dash it. I've brought the wrong keys.' He was getting cross. 'Everything's changing. The new general manager wants to restrict my powers ...'

I said, 'I'll wait here. Would it be all right for me to look something up?'

'I'm afraid not. It's confidential. You see, you'd have access to information on other customers.'

'How long does it take for a cheque to return to the drawer's bank?' I asked, as if I had only an idle interest.

'Three days,' he said, and left me to wander along the shelves while he, becoming more and more exasperated, tried key after non-fitting key.

It wouldn't take a minute to slip a day's business out of those loose paper covers. The cheque had been a large one – not the little personal cheques that individuals used. I could see that there were very few large cheques inside each parcel. Pop rattled the bunch of keys. 'I think I've gone through the whole lot. I'm back to the first one again. Will you wait here? I'll go and ask one of the clerks to find the right bunch.'

'That's all right,' I said, and watched him go up the long flight of stairs. He was old now, and much slower.

As soon as he was out of sight, I pounced on the bundle I thought it might be – the one dated three days after I left St Ursula's. I slipped off the brown cover and riffled through, stopping only at the large cheques. But it was not there. There were no large cheques in the next one and I put it back. Then I took down the bundle that was dated five days after I was called home to Mam's hospital bedside.

And the very first large cheque I came to was made out to St Ursula's School – and it was signed 'Francis Chancellor.'

Blood rushed to my face. It was common practice in the old

days to give money to someone and ask them to write a cheque for you if you had no bank account. Mam used to ask Pop – Mr Hammond – to make out cheques for her on Fridays. Pop not Mr Chancellor. And when I was sent to St Ursula's Mam *had* had a bank account. She wrote cheques on her account. My face stiffened as I asked myself, Why would Frank Chancellor have paid my school fees? I must stop thinking like this. I tried to divide my mind – to resist the thought – but even as I put up objections, all the pieces were falling into place as fast as my divided mind tried to control them ... Mam and Frank Chancellor had been at daggers drawn when Mam accepted my stepfather's proposal. Of course, she would be! My face had started to burn, though my mouth was numb. There was that familiar dropping sensation in the very pit of my stomach. Could it be? Was I Frank Chancellor's daughter?

I put the cheque back quickly, and as I did, I saw that underneath the cheque to St Ursula's was another, also signed 'Francis Chancellor'. It was made out to Mrs Lily Chancellor. Mr Chancellor's mother was still alive when I was at school. Mr Chancellor's Ma. Lily. His Ma's name was Lily. And back came my earliest memory: Mam saying to one of her customers "We named her after her two grandmothers, Lily and Isobel." Then why had I never once suspected? I had taken Nanna's word, given by Mam, that the man who was my father had no children of his own. That was why I had never once suspected. Then I thought about the letter Magnus had kept – the secret that Ray was not Frank Chancellor's son. Mam had known this. And now I knew.

A dull red colour came into my face, as if I'd done something wrong, yet my pulse was beating fast and the metallic taste of adrenaline was in my mouth – the flight-or-fight secretion. Pop came slowly down the steps, a smile on his face, and with an apologetic 'I should have known there was a masterkey ...' he opened my box and handed me the large envelope containing all my deeds and private papers. They were sealed, just as I had left them.

I put them, unopened, into my handbag, went back up the steps with Pop, then impulsively and quickly I kissed him. 'Thank you, Pop. I have to fly. I want to get to the council offices ...' and I went, as fast as I decorously could, out of his door, across the tiled public area and into the fresh clean air of the Market Place.

I could hardly breathe. My heart was hammering when I reached the council offices and said to the stranger behind the reception desk, I want to speak to Mr Chancellor. Please.'

The woman lifted the telephone receiver from the little wooden switchboard, pressed down a lever and turned the handle. 'Who shall I say?'

'Give it to me.' I took the thing out of her hand and put it to my ear at the same moment he picked up his receiver and said, 'Who wants me?'

My mouth was dry and my hands shook. There was a lump in my throat. 'Your Lil,' I managed to say. 'Your Lil.'

There was silence on the line. It seemed to go on for minutes. I heard a quick catching breath, then his voice, my father's voice. 'My precious lass?'

'I'm coming up.' I thrust the receiver at the woman and went out into the hallway. He was waiting for me at the top of the grand, carved staircase as slowly I went up, my eyes fixed on his face, saying in a voice just like his – a voice strong with the Macclesfield accent – 'Your Lil! Your Lil! Your Lil, Mr Chancellor!'

He didn't speak but his eyes were bright with tears as he took my hands and led me into the council chamber room that was all oak and polished floors and shields and rolls of honour. Then we sat, because there was nowhere else to sit, facing one another across the great desk. My throat was tight and painful but I didn't want to cry and fall into his arms, though I sensed that he was waiting for me to do so. I said, 'I'm right, aren't I? You are my dad?'

He put his hand out over the table to me as tears began to roll down his cheeks. 'I wanted you to know, lass,' he said. 'Believe me. Did your mam tell you?'

'No. I saw a cheque. You paid my school fees. You had no reason on earth to do that.'

'Come on,' he said. 'Let's get out of here. I'll tell you all about it.'

And he took me, in his car, for a long ride out high into the hills above Lindow until we came to the Ship Inn at Wincle, where Magnus had planned our elopement. Now my father and

I were the only customers, and we too could sit and talk undisturbed.

He took my hand in his – my own true father – and told me about the years before I was born, when he and Mam were in love. 'We should have married when I went into the army,' he said. 'I was a fool. I had everything a man could wish for – and I let myself be enticed by Sarah, a woman who should have known better.'

I said, 'You let me be born out of wedlock – with a history of lies and no father's name on my birth certificate!' I was hot with embarrassment and cold with hurt and anger, both at the same time. And the old need for retaliation was building up inside me.

'No. It wasn't like that,' he said. 'My precious lass – I mean you – you were born when I was in Germany. That's why my name wasn't on your birth certificate.'

'You ought to have told me. But when your wife died, you could have put it right. You didn't marry Mam. And she was faithful to you all those years.'

He blew his nose and tried to blink away his tears. 'I wanted to tell you. Your mam wouldn't.'

'When she found out you'd had another child?' I said. 'Mam wouldn't forgive that.'

He gave a weak smile. 'Nellie Plant's child isn't mine, lass. I looked after them but she's married her child's real father now . . .'

The wanting to get my own back was still strong, burning inside me. I said, 'So you wanted to tell me. But you didn't want to marry my mother?'

'Listen, lass. When Sarah died, if I'd married your mam I'd have had to tell you. I'd have had to tell Ray too . . .'

I started to cry, but they were soft, held-back tears that would not spill. 'What were you afraid of, Mr Chancellor? That Ray and I might have an incestuous . . .' My voice was choking as I looked into his eyes; eyes that I now saw were very like my own. '. . . when that is exactly what did happen . . .'

He took hold of my hand and slipped an arm about my shoulder. 'Your son was fathered by Magnus, lass. I know that. So do you.'

'But don't you see ... It could have been avoided. I would never have ...'

'Never married Magnus?'

'No. Not that. I'm married now to the man I love.'

'Then think, lass ...' He held my shoulder tighter. 'It all turned out for the best. I was a proper father to Ray. I looked after your mam and you. And I'll live with my regrets for the rest of my life. I lost the only woman I ever loved. And I lost the chance to be a father to my second child.'

I shook his hand away. I opened my handbag and grabbed a handkerchief for my eyes, and the big sealed envelope. Then, with an almighty effort, I checked my tears and said, 'You lost the chance to be my father. You only have one child, Mr Chancellor.'

The tears would not be checked. I had said my piece. And I knew it was right that I had. He had to know. I had to brazen it out when I was a child without a father. My father had to know the truth of those years when I needed the love of a father of my own. I tore open the envelope and took out the letter that Magnus had found – and silently I handed it to him. He frowned, seeing the envelope addressed to Miss Sarah Pilkington. Then he took out the pages cautiously and read. And I held my breath and held back my tears as I saw first puzzlement, then shock and finally realisation come dawning in his eyes.

He put down the letter, looked at me, and now his tears were falling. He said, 'What can I do? How can I make it up to you? I'm sorry. So sorry.' Then he grabbed my hands and held them fast, and said in a pleading voice, 'I'll do anything to make it up. I need you. I've missed you. Please come back to me.'

I couldn't hold back. Tears splashed on to my hands and I fumbled with the letter, trying to stuff it back into the envelope and put it amongst the deeds and papers and all the official business of the life that had been Our Lil's. I said, 'If I come back then it's under my terms ...'

'What can I do?'

I said, 'You can put everything right. If you'll marry my mam it will be a good start. You will make up for everything.'

He took out his handkerchief and wiped his eyes before he looked at me so tenderly I wanted to weep. He said, 'She won't have me, lass. I wrote to her – proposed to her when your stepfather died. She turned me down.'

I said, 'Because she didn't want to leave me – and my son, and my happy home. But if I tell her that I want to come home ...'

'Will she come?'

'Oh, yes. And if you are waiting on the station to meet her ... And if you and I stand together, arm in arm ... She will know, as soon as she sees us, that the reason I am coming home is because now, at last, I have found my own, true father.'